AT THE
FALL LINE

AT THE FALL LINE

JEAN HUETS

gertrude m books

gertrude m books
an imprint of

CIRCLING RIVERS

PO Box 8291
Richmond, VA 23226 USA

Visit CirclingRivers.com to subscribe to news of our authors
and books, including book giveaways. We never share or sell
our list.

ISBN: 978-1-939530-30-1 (paper)

ISBN: 978-1-939530-31-8 (hardcover)

Library of Congress Control Number: 2022941979

Cover art: Moonlight on the Water, detail, by Winslow
Homer. Oil on canvas. Los Angeles County Museum of Art,
Paul Rodman Mabury Collection (39.12.10)

Quotes from *Leaves of Grass*, by Walt Whitman, U.S. editions:
1860, 1867, 1891

to Bruce, always

I SING the Body electric;
The armies of those I love engirth me, and I engirth
    them;
They will not let me off till I go with them, respond
    to them,
And discorrupt them, and charge them full with the
    charge of the Soul.

— Walt Whitman, *Leaves of Grass*, 1867 edition

February 1869

I T IS A SMALL quarry," the Federal architect said, "as quarries go."
Five massive stone benches cut into a river bluff, and the
men and women on them like dolls on a giant's porch steps.

Louis contracted his hand on the bench face, the granite
dragging rough at his fingertips. "It may be so," he said. "Yet
many tons of good stone await—Mrs. Gutman!"

He caught her, steadied her; she disentangled her heel from
the hem of her cloak. Her breath, horehound and whiskey. It
was hardly a job, to take hold of a beautiful woman, uncorseted,
but he wished she were not here. A quarry was not a place to
be tipply, even on the day of rest. Especially on this day of rest.
Louis's job depended on the Federal contract the architect might
bestow or withhold.

"And how is it extracted?" the architect's wife asked. She
had taken one look at Mrs. Gutman and said only the polite.

"Why, they blast it right out of there, my dear," Mrs. Gutman
said. She tucked a chunk of hair under her hat. It fell again, dark
gold in a glint of sun.

"That is indeed how we remove the blocks." Louis took a
deep breath and launched his set-speech. "Granite, ladies and

gentlemen, is the most enduring stone...." Mrs. Gutman took a step; he caught her, and tucked her arm tight under his. "It is the most...." The rehearsed words scattered. "That is, the stone—granite—is—it—"

"It's hard as rock," Mrs. Gutman cut in.

Louis felt a tickle under his heart. Mrs. Termey gave a little cough into her gloved hand, her eyes crinkling with what looked like merriment. She was Mrs. Gutman's sister, and the quarry owner's wife. She had a slim figure armed by corset and crinoline, a dull complexion, dark gold hair, tawny eyes, and perfectly beautiful teeth. Louis did not wish evil on her husband, but he would not mind if the man never returned from looking at granite in Italy.

"So it is," Louis said. "Good, hard, solid granite and plenty of it, right below our feet. A ledge of granite, in fact, that runs nearly the length of what will soon, God willing, be our Union again."

The architect smiled, maybe at the sentiment, unusual for a Virginian to hold, and glanced at the US belt buckle Louis wore. Every day he wore it, and to hell with anyone who did not like the side he had taken.

"We stand on the Fall Line, yes?" Dr. Stratton asked. He wore a top hat and his ears were very red. His chin bulged over his collar.

"That is what geologists call it, Doctor," Louis said. "For here the land falls from the Piedmont to the Tidewater."

Dr. Stratton answered very quietly, barely above a whisper. "Here at the Fall Line, the beloved land breaks, and begins its long slope down to the sea."

Mrs. Termey drew off one of her gloves and caressed the stone, the sparkles of quartz and freckles of jet mica. Her sparse golden eyelashes, her sallow cheeks, her lips—the bottom lip fuller—she had a way of pulling it under her teeth and letting it out again. She did it now, and Louis's breath caught.

And he was crushing Mrs. Gutman's arm. He let up. He was a fool. Just a fool.

"The wharves of Richmond and Manchester are, what, six miles downriver?" the architect asked. The group turned, as if by clockwork, riverward.

"Yes, sir," Louis said. "It is an easy journey for our blocks, by rail."

"Such a wild and romantic vista," Dr. Stratton said. "Beyond the quarry, that is."

A bright dust of snow, and a fringe of winter-bare oak, sweetgum, beech, cedar, and brambles. The railroad's stitchery along the ice-laced water's edge. Then the river, four stone-throws wide, bedded and bouldered with granite.

"Tranquil, even," the doctor added.

"Today, yes," said Louis. "On a work day, we would be near overwhelmed with industry."

Chisels and hammers on stone, carts rattling, the coarse braying of mules. Blasting. The men shouting. The train on its rounds, morning and evening: the whistle, the bell, the engine's chuff and hiss.

Now, only the river pouring icy over its silt and granite bed. Louis had come before dawn to make sure all was in order. Waiting for the light, he had laid himself down on bone-cold stone, in mineral silence covered by the dark firmament.

He craved that cold now. Despite white-puff breath, he sweated. Speaking to his men never made him shy. This was different.

They returned to the road, barely more than a bridle path, and boarded the waiting buggy, headed to the Old Quarry.

"To quarry the building blocks," Louis said as they set off, "we first drill…. The quarriers first drill holes into the face of the stone, along what is to be the base of the block. The powderman then packs the holes with explosives. That is called charging the stone."

"Charging the stone," Dr. Stratton said. "What an evocative phrase."

"The stone is charged," Louis said, "and the fuses are set into the powder. All is snugged in tight, with…. " They arrived at the Old Quarry, and the men disembarked, to hand the women down.

A cry like a river hawk swiveled their heads down the bluff.

Mrs. Gutman did not hear a river hawk. Her mouth opened, she jumped out of the buggy—Louis caught her around the waist and thrust her at Dr. Stratton.

He leaped down the sloping bluff, his heart crashing louder in his ears than his boots in the brush.

Mrs. Gutman screamed, "Eva!" and a sobbing inhale. "Eva!"

Louis tore through briar thickets of leafless, fruitless blackberry. Underbrush and vines.

A beech tree smeared with gore. Blood spatters on dirt and shrubs, on a boulder.

A pink hair ribbon.

An ice-glazed black pond.

The child lay jumbled against an oak.

Louis fell to his knees and groped for prayer. He touched the pulse, touched the dead pulse again. Sweet eau de cologne and blood's bitterness. He put his thumb and ring finger lightly to her eyelids, held them closed.

As he lifted his hand, his heart jolted into a motion so hard and fast, his body's frame shook. He thought, panting: This will go on forever.

But his breath did slow, and his heart slowed, and the shaking subsided.

The child weighed light in his arms. He stood easily and shifted her so that the battered back of her head nestled in the crook of his arm. Up on the road, Dr. Stratton and the architect restrained Mrs. Gutman. Mrs. Termey embraced her. It looked clear and yet too distant, like a brightly lit stage from the cheap seats. Mrs. Gutman sobbed, "Eva!" but not as shrill and at longer intervals, as though she felt her daughter's spirit drawing farther and farther away.

Dear Christ, he must present this dead girl-child to her mother.

He lay her down again, and broke the quarry pond's veneer of ice to wet his handkerchief and bathe her cheeks and brow and chin, and her neck and hands. The curls about her face lustrous, untouched. He drew off his necktie as softer, and cleaned the smudges of blood his fingers had left on her eyelids.

When Louis arrived to Mrs. Gutman, she kissed her daughter's little face, sobbing all her breath out to a thin whine, gasping it back in.

Louis did not give the child to Dr. Stratton's examination. He carried her in his arms to the house. Mrs. Gutman held her daughter's leg and stroked the black curls. Blood streaked her dress and her face and hair. Her sister held her.

At the top of the drive, Dr. Stratton jumped down from the buggy and strode ahead into the house. Mrs. Termey ushered Louis inside, with Mrs. Gutman, and down a corridor into a bedroom, then hurried out.

Louis laid the child on a bedspread scented lavender, a crowd of dolls and rag animals pushed aside. He put a hand over the crook of his elbow, to hide the gore from the back of her head. Mourning, her face tear-soaked, brought in a kettle of hot water, a basin, towels. Dr. Stratton nodded Louis to leave the room.

Louis found Mrs. Termey alone in the foyer. "They're going to get...." She trailed off. The undertaker, she did not say. She and Louis flinched as Mrs. Gutman's sobbing keen tore the silence. Mourning's voice rose, then fell, and the sobs quieted. Mrs. Termey touched Louis's arm, went back down the corridor to the room where he had laid the child.

Louis stood in the foyer. He just stood there.

HE HAD MET EVA AND her mother for the first time that morning, though they had come from Chicago over a month ago. The child had charged into the foyer, where he and Mrs. Termey and Dr. Stratton waited for their group to set off. Tousled black curls and chubby, rosy cheeks. At the sight of the strange men with her aunt, she stopped so suddenly, she rocked on her feet, her mouth making a little O. Louis knelt and she ran straight into his arms. Her mother following her laughed, and so did Mrs. Termey. The little girl giggled as his beard brushed her neck, then she broke loose and ran out the casement doors to the terrace.

Louis went out the way she had. All the plants in the beds bordering the terrace were clipped for winter, save some fragrant shrubs Mourning had put in a couple of years ago, lavender and rosemary lapping over the flagstones. He could hear voices: Dr. Stratton's, but it did not sound like Mrs. Termey or Mrs. Gutman with him. The sister. Eva's older sister, the poor girl. The voices subdued, the words indistinguishable.

He went out the gate of the run-down picket fence. A thin dirt path led to the bluff's edge.

The Old Quarry, disused for years, lay some seventy feet below, dark water veiled with ice. Around it, bare trees and bracken, tree duff, and heaps of old overburden. Louis could not see the foot of the ancient oak, where he had gathered Eva's body into his arms. The sun moistened and loosened the snow. The river rushed.

Here at the Fall Line, the beloved land breaks, and begins its long slope down to the sea.

Blood had issued from the little girl's nose and mouth and ears, yet the black curls stayed lustrous and clean. Her blank eyes staring at heaven.

He had closed her eyes. He had closed the eyes of the dead, until there were too many.

Fields covered with the dead. Woods and ravines stuffed with dead men, and dead horses and dead mules. Death not visited upon a person, but strewing an unclean crowd over farm yards, cobblestone streets, orchards and plantations of wrecked crops.

Dragging a man by the ankles through wheat or corn stubble.

O my Body!

Louis flinched as if struck, then broke into tears rough and loud. He pressed his hands to his face, teeth gouging the heel of his palm, but he could not quiet.

He subsided finally to gasp-broken breaths. With a fist of snow, he salved his burning cheeks and eyes. The woods, the cloud-covered sky, the deep black ice-glazed pond, stood so still, his wrenched out grief echoed in his mind loud as a shout.

He turned to go back to the house. Inside, at one of the casement doors that opened to the terrace, Eva's mother stood. Her hands lay palm-flat against the glass, her head was bowed.

May 1869

THE FUSES LIT, THE men cleared the granite. No mad scrambling, like at some quarries.

Sunlight flashed in and out of the leafing trees. Beyond the railroad tracks, the river ran tawny and high. A heron glided by. A mule brayed.

The ground shuddered. The powderman relit his cigar: safe to go back onto the stone.

The men had already drilled holes at the x's Louis had chalked on the top of the granite block that the blast had separated from its ancient bed. In each hole stood a metal wedge flanked by a pair of shims—feathers, the Scottish men called them. The holes defined the smaller blocks that would break from the larger block.

"Mr. Bonny?" One of the quarrymen held out a sledge hammer.

Louis took it, and tapped the wedges down the line. The metal on metal jarred not his arms or back or shoulders, but his maimed hip. Still, he liked to start the stone.

The wedges did not slip down. No cracks appeared in the granite. Yet the stone worked within itself. It would open clean downward. Lately, the men bragged that their foreman Mr. Bonny could see through granite, that he knew where its inner faults lay.

It was progress, the boasts. The first couple of years after the War, he had ignored murmurs: *traitor, scalawag.* He had watched his step. Now the old-timers were diluted by younger men, and blacks, and stoneworkers down from New England and Canada. Maybe he had won some loyalty, too, by being able to see through granite. Not to mention making sure they got paid on time, and no boss's garnishments taken out of their envelopes.

Louis handed the hammer back and looked upriver, toward the Old Quarry. The Termeys' house sat too far back from the bluff to see. Only a bit of the garden showed. Some yellow dabs—jonquils, and pale greenery.

Today would be the first time Louis had visited in over three months, since the ice-bound day the child Eva had fallen into the Old Quarry.

He went up to his office, as his clerk was pleased to call the little cabin at the top of the bluff, washed his face and hands and neck, put on a fresh shirt and a tie, beat the dust off his jacket, scraped the soles and wiped the uppers of his boots. Nell, saddled, waited at the roadside post. She nosed off his hat, as usual, he swatted her with it, as usual, and they headed upriver.

The Termey's house had been built of stone from the Old Quarry. A two-story veranda ran along the river-facing side of the house. Nearby stood an old slave cabin, fixed up with a plank floor and glazed windows; Wyman, the quarry carpenter, his wife Mourning who served in the house, and their son Ezra lived there.

Louis went straight in, as usual, and stood in the foyer, turning his hat in his hands. Not long before the child's death, he had come in to find the curio cabinet beside the door emptied out. Gone, the Italian glass: the circus of little animals, the lacy chalices and vases that had so oddly drawn his fancy. Mourning told him the shudder from the quarry blasts, even near a mile up river, worked things off shelves. No gimcracks littered the pier table, no mirror shone from the walls. It was as if Mrs. Termey had begun to vacate: the servants removed the outer layer of her things, then stopped. At night, alone, in bed, Louis sometimes worked out the erotic connotations of that.

Her husband Maurice Termey possessed well-cut suits and brocade vests, books clad in leather, a quarry with good hopes for a Federal contract, and a house. Hardly an elegant house, true; the shutters could have used a lick of paint and at least one of the chimneys needed rebuilding, the ceilings inside gray with smoke. But Maurice Termey had plenty for himself. He had Valentina. Yet he stayed gone, looking at granite in Italy, not returned at the death of his little niece. His wife's sister mourning her daughter three months dead now, and his wife without a baby of her own to love.

And his quarry foreman standing hat in hand in his desolated entry, dreaming of taking his place.

Even were Valentina free, he had not the means. A foreman in a little quarry, he had not a fraction of the means. He had worn a borrowed suit for Eva's funeral, his good coat ruined, carrying her in his arms up to the house that day.

Louis put his hat on the pier table and went into the library. It smelled of woodsmoke and musty paper, with pine oil and varnish from Mrs. Termey's painting studio that adjoined it. Mourning turned from dusting books.

"Oh! I am sorry, Mr. Bondurant. I did not hear you come in."

"It's all right, Mrs. Wyman," he said.

"Mrs. Termey is expecting you, sir."

She bustled from the room, leaving in her wake a plain, pleasant scent of soap. Louis continued through a curtained doorway into the studio.

Mrs. Termey stood behind an easel. Old Mrs. Hamilton sat as usual in the armchair looking out the casement doors. The terrace overlooked the Old Quarry, but from her seat Mrs. Hamilton would not be able to see it, or the river. Only treetops and sky.

"Mrs. Hamilton, how do you do. Good evening, Mrs. Termey."

Mrs. Termey murmured, "Mr. Bondurant," without turning from her work. This was usual, if he arrived while she was painting. Mrs. Hamilton said nothing. This, too, was usual. Though Mrs. Hamilton might interrupt his conference with Mrs. Termey, she ignored his greeting. Maurice Termey's great-aunt, she had raised him and Mourning, whom Termey inherited after his parents died in a cholera outbreak.

Louis's boots felt heavy and dirty, though he supposed it made no difference to the paint-spattered sail cloth that covered the floor. The wallpaper, whitewashed over, looked terribly faded and bare. The paintings leaned on the walls, their backs turned. Mrs. Termey's dress made a black block in the gap at the back of the dun painting smock.

The studio's soft brightness, the sailcloth daubed with rainbows of paint, the curious objects—a bust of an old man crowned with withered ivy, a huge empty wasp's nest, a heap of seashells, a moldy ammunition box, an empty acid bottle—seemed to dictate a new fashion: disheveled, gently faded.

Mrs. Termey stuck a paintbrush in a jar of dull-clouded liquid and stirred. She wiped the brush, laid it down. She removed her smock and let it drop to the floor, and took off her painting gloves, and she stepped to him.

Hair, bosom, hips, bend of legs, negligent falling
   hands, all diffused—mine too diffused

Unthinking, Louis reached to take her hands in his. She responded, and they stood so, hands clasped.

The roughness of his hands, the gentleness of hers.

A strand of her hair streaked a bright, deep blue. He desired to kiss her. She slipped her hands free.

He was her husband's quarry foreman, come to report square feet of stone, dollars in labor and equipment and feed.

They sat as always, he in a hard, carved Italian armchair, she on a sofa facing him, the light of the casement doors on her. Between them stood a pair of what looked like footstools straddled by a marble slab laden with books, documents, letters, unwashed teacups, and a part-played chess game.

Mourning brought in coffee and pastries. The casement doors, ajar, let in the slow panting chuff of the locomotive idling at the river's edge below.

The canvas on the easel showed the outlines of a human figure, a girl, it looked like, or a man in a robe, a religious subject, the Termeys Roman Catholic.

Mrs. Termey poured out two cups of coffee. She set the pot down. "Mr. Bondurant, your report?"

"Yes, ma'am."

But Louis had not rehearsed to himself recent quarry operations, on his way up the drive. He had been full of the memory of carrying the little girl. The flash of pain from his hip at each step. The wetness, on his face, of sweat or tears, and the metallic thick smell of blood. The icy air gripping his bare head, his hat lost. He had tried to hold the child's body together, in his arms, to hide its brokenness from her mother and aunt.

Louis made a few false starts. "I beg your pardon, Mrs. Termey."

Tears fell down her face.

Louis took a deep breath over his own urge to weep. He had wept at Eva's Requiem mass. Everyone had. O, such a river of tears for the little girl! The priest's incantations trembling.

"I'm sorry," she said. She blotted her face with a handkerchief balled in her hand.

Louis longed to comfort her, but he had not the words, his body's shelter forbidden. He breathed in the air of Valentina Termey's studio—her perfume and the oil paints and thinners, and the smoke drift from the locomotive below—pulled taut between longing and grief.

"You talk to the child, Mr. Bondurant." It was Mrs. Hamilton.

"Ma'am?" Louis turned toward the old woman.

"Jeannie is inconsolable," Mrs. Termey said. Louis turned back to her. "Maybe with you...." " She abruptly got up—Louis quickly stood—and left the studio.

Louis lingered on his feet, staring out the casement doors. From the balustrade of the terrace, the working quarry would show raw stone through the budding trees. The Old Quarry, where Eva fell, differed. Long unused, soft with loam, tree duff, tangles of blackberry and poison ivy. A deep, deep pond. If the Federal contract came through, Louis's men would drain or pump it out, clear off the overburden, the bracken, the ancient oak at whose knobbled roots Eva had expired.

The locomotive below kept at its idling chuff. A few panes of ill-glazed glass shivered in the casement doors.

Mrs. Termey entered, her niece Jeannie following. Louis drew a breath that was almost a gasp.

He had met Jeannie Gutman at the funeral but now, un-eclipsed by a mourning veil, her beauty astonished. Her skin glowed rosy, unmarred by so much as a freckle. She had abundant golden hair like her mother's, but brighter. A black frock, in the loose fashion her mother favored, draped her, in its way more dignified than corseted hoop-skirts. Robelike. The grace of burgeoning womanhood clasped her limbs. She sat beside Mrs. Termey, and they held hands. Louis sat.

"This is Mr. Bondurant," Mrs. Termey said.

The young woman's gaze, though fixed politely upon his face, held a distance both peculiar and hauntingly familiar.

"He carried Eva up to the house in his own arms. All the way up, with his war wound hurting him so." Mrs. Termey blushed, and so did Louis, but she went on, "His—his men in the War called him Major Bonny, for he is a good, kind gentleman."

Louis smiled, then looked away, so the girl would not read in his eyes the memory rising, of laying her little sister on a flowery bedspread littered with dolls, his hand cupped at the back of the shattered head. He was glad, cravenly he knew, that Mrs. Gutman had not come in with Jeannie.

He tried to think of something to say, but he could not. He felt his own presence as over-large, over-muscled. Masculine. He raised his eyes to the ornate wooden crucifix nailed above the casement doors. He never understood Jesus as a tortured man on a cross until he sat at his father's death bed and witnessed his father's anguish.

Strewn over battlefields, men stiffened, arms outflung, legs drawn up. Neither Jesus nor Father.

"Thank you for carrying my baby sister, Mr. Bonny," Jeannie whispered. Curves of golden lashes hid her downcast eyes. It was she, Louis realized, who figured on the nearly blank canvas.

The clock in the corner tick-tocked to itself. The black smoke from the departed locomotive hung over the trees.

"NO LETTERS THIS WEEK, Louie."

Mr. Beattie offered a few pieces of horehound candy, as if Louis were a little boy to be consoled. But Mrs. Beattie gave Louis a meaning look, and he lingered while Mr. Beattie shuffled along the counter to help two women bicker over kitchen linens: fancy hem or plain?

As usual, Louis contemplated the pocket watch in the glass case. His own watch was perfectly serviceable, but Beattie's was a repeater. Push a little button, and the time sang out to the quarter hour. With the watch right up to his ear, after four years of war and an earache that had made him whimper and cry like a child, Louis could barely hear the chimes. Still, it would be nice to know the time, in bed at night, without having to strike a light or lie there waiting for the church clock to say if he could fall back asleep or if he must get up.

Mrs. Beattie returned from the back and put a letter in Louis's hands. "From your brother." She glanced at her husband. "He forgets," she whispered.

"God bless him."

The old couple had been very kind to Louis, overlooking the squalor of his body and soul those first couple of years after the War, and they remembered his grandparents. He was not sure if they overlooked, too, that he had fought Union, or if they merely did not know. Four years on, people he had known his whole life still would not speak to him; a cousin spit on the ground if they happened to pass each other on the street.

He went out to sit on the bench in front of the store. Afternoon Manchester, early May, breathed a damp and overwarm fug of coal smoke, horse and hog, tannery, mill, and dust. The sweat that would stick to Louis's skin for the next five months was beginning to settle in. At least the lengthening days meant plenty of light left to read by. He opened the letter.

Jake's letter told of kinfolks Louis hardly knew, Mama's New England branch. A church picnic—if a Unitarian chapel was a church. Gratitude that Louis put fresh flowers on their parents' graves. Louis had written him about the movement to dig up the little plots scattered in Manchester, and move their tenants out of town, to keep the wells clean. Jake thought the plan sound. Louis was not sure, himself, that he liked the thought of moving their parents, but had to agree, the risk of corpsy drinking water could not be taken. As usual, Jake asked Louis to consider moving to New England.

A year after the War ended, Jake had brought Mama's remains home, to be with Papa. His first words at the depot: *Dear Lord above, Louie.* Louis had lost weight. He limped. He was poor. So was Jake, poor, but in a New England way. Not destroyed.

Louis stared at the leafy square across the street, at the dogs and a pig or two lazing here and there. The only time he had waxed wrathful at a cut on his loyalty had been on that visit, because his little brother witnessed it. *Damned scalawag*, muttered by an old schoolmate who ran a grocery. Later Jake had asked, for the first and not last time, why he stayed, why not move up to New England. Plenty of quarry work. Louis could surely land there as a foreman or better.

Jake had been just a youngster, when the War broke out and

he and Mama moved up North. He had fledged there, in New England. Louis's home was here.

Here at the Fall Line, the beloved land breaks, and begins its long slope down to the sea.

Dusty and hog-ridden though it was. And he was damned if he would be driven out. He would stand his ground, right here where he was born and raised, a Dogtown boy through and through.

He had moved up in the world, a little, since Jake's visit. He had moved from a room over Heron's Livery and Saloon to a respectable boarding house. He was supporting Jake through the Harvard Divinity School.

"Lizzie!"

The dog was nosing Ned Bass's baby girl, toddling hand in hand with her daddy. The child giggled. Ned looked dubious and Louis could not blame him. "Lizzie! Git over here." He touched his hat to Ned and his daughter. Lizzie slinked over, pouting. Left to her devices, she would have joyously bathed the baby with slobber, her doggy self all filthy from carousing in the gutter with the Beatties' pigs. She stomped on Louis's toes and flung herself on his feet.

"Good girl."

Mama's letters had been all of kinfolk and friends, and love and kind admonition. Jake's were crowded with ideas, ideals. A farm where several families lived in what sounded to Louis like bone-grinding poverty: *Learning and thinking and debate and trying out ideas Girls and women part of it like flowers in God's own Garden of Delight.* He wrote beautifully, pages filled with lofty words. He would make a fine preacher. Not all ideas, though. Was there a particular girl? *When I have a living Louie you will be free but I may be ensnared!*

Louis did not wish to be free. He, too, wished to be ensnared.

He had only to let his mind brush on Valentina Termey, and he saw her tawny eyes, her imperfect skin, her gentle hands lifting the coffee pot. Her scent: the perfume deepened by her body's exhalation, and ironed linen, and the pigments and piney solvents of her art. Her voice, high, almost childlike. From there he went to a dream of hugging her, kissing her, on the lips, on the neck under the wisps of hair that stirred there. Lately in his dreams, she wore one of her sister's loose dresses, uncorsetted, and his body embraced the softness of hers.

He was ensnared—but so was Mrs. Termey, with Mr. Termey. This certainty was like a passage of sad music, like waking from a dream of love, except the sadness took not a few moments of cold dawn but all day and all night.

Louis sighed, returned to Jake's letter. The closing: *I am so Grateful to you my dear dear Brother, for all that you do for me. I pray one day to pay you the credit and Honour you deserve.*

Jake's words filled Louis with exquisite and sentimental pride. He folded the crackly thin paper back into the envelope. The tuition at Harvard took nearly everything he had, though Jake did not know that. But things would be different, once Jake finished school, and if Louis got promoted.

Pray God and all the saints the Federal granite contract would come through. He put the letter in his jacket pocket, shook out the *Daily Dispatch*.

He had just perused the first column when a shout came from the park. Louis looked up, rose and ran across the street, leaping a hog at the curb. He shoved through the men gathered, and gripped his cousin Richard's wrist and pushed it down, along with the pistol.

"That's enough," Louis said.

Richard turned to Louis, lips parted, eyebrows raised—from wrath to utter surprise.

No one made a sound.

"The gentleman is tipsy," Louis told the blue-coated soldier, though Richard was not tipsy. Or he might be. The soldier glanced at Louis's belt buckle—US—and raised his eyebrows, but kept his weapon out. At least he had not panicked and shot.

"Put up that pistol, Richard," Louis said. "Put it away right now."

Richard obeyed, nonchalant. Among the onlookers, some disappointment. "And you hush up, madam," Louis ordered Lizzie who growled and bristled at the soldier. She did not obey, except to lower her tone. "Soldier, good day."

Louis took his cousin's arm and walked him from the quarrel, whatever it had been about. He did not bring Richard to elderly, orderly Beattie's. They went to Rob Hunt's bookstore.

Not that Richard seemed of a mind to fight anymore. He gave Louis's arm a squeeze. "Cousin Louis, it's good to see you." As if they had met by design, a pleasant rendezvous on a balmy Saturday evening. He had the kind of looks women liked, well put-together, his dark curls flecked with gray. Despite fifteen years on Louis, and taking a bullet in the stomach at Gaines Mill, his face was barely lined. He had a law practice and worked inside all day. Still, at core, he was a Dogtown boy, a tough, a rowdy. He had climbed up the ranks, same as Louis. Though Richard had enjoyed an extra step up: Papa's back.

"You could have been arrested," Louis said.

"Thank heavens you intervened."

They entered into the spicy mustiness of wisdom. Rob looked up from polishing a book of mold bloom. Louis had barely greeted his friends—Branden, lounging at the counter, smoking, and Jimmy Branch perched on a stool with the *Dispatch*—when Rob shoved a pile of books into his arms.

"Put these on the empty shelves up there," Rob said, "and you can take your pick of whatever you want. My stump's playing me up."

Louis put the books on the counter, went to test the step-ladder. It swayed, but he reckoned it would hold.

"What do you say about our country these days, gentlemen?"

Richard's hair shone expensive, pleasant smelling, but it was his frockcoat pocket Lizzie sniffed.

"*Our* country, now, is it?" Rob asked.

Jimmy lowered his paper.

It occurred to Louis, the last time he had been here together with these same men, and a crowd of others, was after the vote—the second vote, the one that severed Virginia from the Union. Everyone had been excited, shaking their heads, wagging their tongues. When Richard proposed a drink to "our new country," Louis had cursed the secession and everyone who had voted for it, then stormed out. He stopped at his lodging to pack a bag, and took the first train to Washington City, to enlist in the United States army. Near ten years ago, the memory still vivid, and Virginia not yet back in the Union.

"We'll get back in," Jimmy said.

Louis adjusted the ladder. "Can't be soon enough."

"Things do take a while."

"Lizzie, sit down."

Lizzie ignored him, especially since Richard had unwrapped a plug of beef jerky. Louis and Rob refused, Jimmy took a morsel. Branden fed a piece to Lizzie. She gulped it, put on her most winning grin, and got another titbit from Richard.

"We've been held back," Richard said.

"Everything in its time," Jimmy said. He handed some toy-books up to Louis.

Ladder of Learning, the kind of book Louis the child had disliked, as suffocatingly edifying. *The Mother Goose,* he already had. Peter Parley's *Wonders of the Earth, Sea, and Sky.* Louis flipped through it.

> *Now in most of the strata above the granite, which is nearly always in the position of the oldest formation, there are found various shells, plants, and bones of animals; and, where certain remains of different animals or vegetables are found in one stratum, it is concluded that they must have been living about the same time.*

No fossils ever surfaced at the quarry. For all Louis knew, they had been blown to rubble when the overburden was cleared. But this book would be good to have, some day, for a quarry man's children should know their father's element, the oldest formation. And here was a picture to delight a child, an amazing picture filled with ancient animals. A duck with bat's wings, and a crocodile with fins instead of legs. When Jake was a little boy, Louis had told him made-up adventures of boys fighting monsters like these.

Branden's cough pulled Louis back to the present day, and he slid *Wonders* and the rest of the toy-books on the shelf. He did not feel up to being teased by his friends. *What are you getting toy-books for, Bonny? I am getting toy-books so that I might read to the imaginary children that my imaginary wife will bear me.*

He descended a few steps, took another bunch of books—arithmetic schoolbooks, it looked like—and ascended. "True," he said. "We have been held back. The sooner we ratify the Amendments, the sooner we're back in the Union."

"God bless," Branden said, and took another breath, "our country." He had stone-workers' consumption and could not get through a sentence in one go.

"Staunch Unionists one and all," Rob said. "Who could have imagined it?"

Of them, Louis alone had stuck with the Union, from opposing secession all the way to Appomattox. Not that he had been at Appomattox, thank God. When old Lee finally gave up, he was convalescing at a hospital in Alexandria.

"You'll never sell these toy-books up here," he said to Rob. "Children can't reach them."

"I'm the bookseller. They belong where I say." Rob had become irascible; before the War his had been the gentlest temperament. He had never insulted Louis for serving on the side that had taken half his right leg, at least, though their friendship had taken a few years to revive. Jimmy Branch had helped the reconciliation along. Richard Poindexter had done quite a bit in that direction, too, and not only with Rob. Louis could not deny that his cousin's good words had opened doors that would likely have been slammed shut in his face for years to come.

"We agree in the essentials, my friends," Richard said, "but you err in the particulars."

"You err in the particulars and in the essentials," Louis said, seizing Richard's bait as eagerly as Lizzie snapped up another treat of jerky. "You think we can go backwards. We cannot." He moved the ladder, climbed to shelf the last handful of books as directed by the bookseller.

"I'm all for progress," Richard said. He had been a long-standing, ardent and outspoken Secessionist, a Fire-eater. An ocean of blood and tears later, he was beating the Union drum. Money invested up North probably had something to do with it. Papa's money.

Rob spit in the battered pail by the counter. He and Richard had been on a political committee together, before Richard quit to pursue a conviction that Germans, Irishmen, and Jews were destroying the Old Dominion. The Know Nothings come back from the dead.

"You want to rebuild the South on black backs," Louis said, "with King Industry heir to King Cotton." The ladder swayed. He grabbed a shelf and shifted his weight to steady it. His hip twinged. "But it cannot be. If you worked with men, as I do, you would know."

In part, Richard's despised immigrants made it so. Irishmen, Germans, Scots, Chinese, were rushing in to fill the Territories. Cheap labor. It could not be pumped out of the country, either, like water from a quarry pit.

"I should like to invite you to a Conservative party meeting—" Richard might have been about to name the time and place, but Louis cut in.

"I'm engaged that day." Though he would not have imagined

Richard and Jimmy Branch, political bedfellows. Richard, in on the planning of their Colored Men's Barbecue rally. Freakish as a two-headed calf.

"That's a shame." Richard lit a cigar, less pungent than Jimmy's, at least. "We could use a man like you, for you are a true Virginian who did his duty as he saw fit."

"In other words," Rob said to Louis, "the Conservative committee needs some Blue-backs to give it shine."

Jimmy mashed out his cigar on the sole of his boot, tossed the stub out the door. "The truth is, Louis was ahead of us all," he said. "We've caught up. We've seen the light."

The Conservative Party had indeed seen the light. Its members had recognized that, despite their determined contempt toward Negroes, they must court black votes. Rob had put his finger right on it: a Union man would help pull in those votes. Louis was not about to throw all that in his friend's face, however.

"I'll vote with you," Louis said to Jimmy, "but only to get Virginia back in the Union. That's as far as it goes. I'm a touch too … too Radical, I suppose, for more than that."

"I don't know about that," Branch said.

"Give the colored man a chance, and he will come up," Louis said. "Whites and coloreds working together, making our nation greater."

In him, the start of populous states and rich republics

"Could be, you're a touch Radicalish," Branch said, unperturbed.

"Women, too. I want women to have the vote. I want Virginia to be part of the United States again. I want to have a country I can love again. Dear Christ, I want the War never to have …."

Louis stopped. Not only were his words childish, they evoked such a gush of anguish, childish tears threatened.

"Amen. Amen. Amen," Branden said.

Branch, handing another group of books, met Louis's eyes.

"There's a lot in what you say. Though I don't hold with your every point." As if Louis had presented a cogent set of political paragraphs.

Branch laughed. "Imagine Martha at the polls. A fearsome prospect! You wait 'til you're married, Louis, you'll see. But friends can disagree. Certainly political friends are able to disagree."

Louis stepped down from the ladder with his reward: *The Pickwick Papers*. Somewhere in Maryland, he had obtained a copy of the book at an abandoned Confederate camp, but a few chapters in, the Rebs took it back. With interest: every one of his belongings lost at Gettysburg, saving the clothes on his body, and his wallet, canteen and weapons. From one angle, the War looked like a frenetic swap meet.

"Say, Rob, are Unitarians Christian?" Louis asked, as much to get off politics as to know.

"It depends on how you look at it," Rob said.

"How would God look at it?"

"I'll tell you how God looks at it," Richard said.

"Do, please, sir." Rob disliked Richard more than Louis had thought.

"Heaven is reserved for virtuous women, weaklings, and cowards," Richard said.

"Hmmm, yes." Rob nodded in a show of pensiveness. "And the rest of us, sir?"

"God hates us all. White, black, yellow—gray or blue, it don't matter, the color, nor what comes out of your mouth when you get on your knees."

Louis had heard enough. He held up *Pickwick Papers*.

"Good riddance," Rob said. He despised Dickens for *American Notes*. Maybe he meant Richard, too, who opened the door for Louis.

But Richard had not finished. "It's a consideration, friends, as we arrange the ruling of the Kingdom of Earth."

Branden began singing in a hoarse, wheezing tenor, "Jesus Loves Me." Anyone else, Louis would have thought was being ironic or preachy. With Branden, it was where his thoughts naturally went. *Jesus. Loves me. This I know.*

Rob said gently, "I reckon he does."

Richard raised his eyebrows. As if Branden was a "weakling"? The tight-wound grudge Louis nursed against his cousin uncoiled another tendril.

Louis headed home, his cousin walking with, though Richard's new brick house and his new wife lay west, in the sweet-smelling end of town. The sun's retreat slipped Manchester back a step toward winter, a breath of ice riffling through the spring warmth.

"I regret the breach between you and me," Richard said. "Do you know, you're one of the few men—the only man I really trust in this world."

"Lizzie," Louis said. She had begun to slink to the street. "Oh, go on, then." She bounded to her friends, a bunch of boys and other dogs playing stickball. At the corner of Twelfth, Louis stopped and faced his cousin.

"You went out of your way to smooth things for me, after the War. I'm grateful, truly. But whether you trust or distrust me? I just don't care."

Louis could have flattered himself that only he could rout his cousin. He never saw Richard astonished, no matter what other men threw at him.

"I don't care if you're full of regret or ready to dance a jig." Louis's face flushed, his gut grew hot as liquor. "And it makes no difference to me if I ruin you, or if you drag your fortune out of reach—except for the part of it that's mine. That's all I want. And I will get it. I will get what is mine and Jake's, as heirs to our father."

It was more, much more, than Louis had expected to say to his cousin this evening.

Richard, whose surprise had gone to a look of friendly interest, patted Louis's shoulder. "I don't believe that's all you want, Louis. But in any case, you won't get it."

"I shall," he said. "I certainly shall, Richard." Though certainly he could not think of how.

Maybe Richard was curious, intrigued, his eyebrows raised. "Good luck, cousin."

"And a good evening to you."

IT TOOK BRANDEN A FEW tries, and a boost from Louis, to mount his nag. They could have reached Manchester Stone faster on foot from Heron's Tavern, so slow the horses plodded, but Branden did not like walking and Louis's body hurt.

He spent part of each day working different areas of the quarry. In the trimming yard, he liked to guide the bull set—an axe-like wedged tool—along the edge of the stone, while another man wielded the striking hammer. However, his clerk, young Whittington, needed to learn trimming, so yesterday Louis had taken the hammer. Whittington did not place the bull set well and its striking surface was never quite where it should have been. Many of the blows went off; a few times, Louis nearly sprawled across the block. His back ached, and he felt a strain in his left forearm. His hip throbbed in sympathy.

"I think poor Whittington was—" nervous, he was going to say, but Branden spoke over him.

"You need to. Come over." He took a breath every couple of words. "My sister makes coffee. Good. Not your. Tavern variety."

"I bet she does," Louis said.

Branden had received the news about his wife at Fredericksburg. Louis got his letter about it months after. *My darling Rose dead.* He still lived in the house he and Rose had set up as newly weds. His sister Alice, a war widow, had moved in. Weeds gnawed the front walk, dust powdered the windows. Nobody ever visited, for all of Branden's vague invitations.

"Yes, sir," Branden said. "Alice makes a brew. Fit to set the devil. Hopping." He spit and nearly hit his own boots. He was chewing this week instead of smoking.

Louis observed to himself, as he habitually did, that Mrs. Kelly's gate posts were stone from the Netherwood quarry. He lifted his eyes to the young redbud flowering in her yard. Lieutenant Colonel Kelly had died at Camp Elmira.

"Look at. Them hogs," Branden said. A couple of Mrs. Kelly's, rooting. "Someone needs to do. Something about them."

"Let them be fruitful. We need more pork in this world."

As young people, he and she had flirted at church picnics. Now, if Louis or probably any Union man passed her on the street, she turned her face away.

Tethered mules and horses crowded the shady side of the street, especially in front of the saloons, of which Manchester had plenty, running down in respectability, the closer they got to the wharf. Manchester Stone was almost at the water, cut off by a flour mill from the river breezes and the view of Thomas Jefferson's beautiful heap, up on the hill across the river, in Richmond.

Louis sneezed as they went in the stone-dust-fogged finishing shed. Branden did not bother. A Jesus of doctors could not fix up Branden's chest, no matter how much money he might take for trying. Lungs charged with stone dust, and whiskey to wash it all down. Louis wanted to help his friend, but what could he do. Raise Rose from the dead? Branden running to her with open arms. And the saws in the sheds spewed dust and dust and dust. Nothing Rose could do for that, quick or dead.

Louis came every Saturday to inspect the rejected slabs.

Flaws in granite—patches, striping, cracks, pits, iron knots, streaks—often emerged only after the sawblocks were cut into slabs. Sometimes they remained hidden until the slabs were hammered, or even polished. Something Biblical in that, but Louis had never bothered to work it out. He looked over the flawed slabs and damned them, by signature, to an afterlife as cut-rate tombstones.

"Let's see Eva Gutman's monument." Louis had marked the block at the quarry, dead sure it was flawless.

They crossed a yard dominated by a derrick, cluttered by rough blocks. Louis paused. Branden breathed. "This is inefficient," Louis said. "You should join these buildings." He sketched a horse-shoe shape, pointing. Branden did not answer. He might have had a say about it, or he might not. He managed Manchester Stone conscientiously, but was not one for changing things.

In the carving shed, the stonecutters incised letters, carved statues. Dumb chunks of granite and marble were made beautiful, expressive, to the clink clink clink of hammers on chisels on stone. Dust floated in clouds all the way to the rafters, the only ventilation the open doors and a few cupolas with louvers mostly closed.

Branden took Louis not to where the stonecutters plied their tools, but to a standing desk with a document rack over it. He pulled a paper from one of the niches. "There you go."

The order form had Eva Gutman's name on it, and her date of death, and the slab number. Nothing else. No date of birth, no "beloved daughter of." No epitaph at all, nor instructions for dimension or shape or finish, lettering or ornamentation.

"What is this?" Louis said.

"Bianca won't talk. About it."

"I'll ask Mrs. Termey, if you like," Louis said.

"I would like."

"I'll see her on Wednesday." Louis put the form back in the niche. "You shouldn't be carousing with Bianca Gutman."

Gossip—namely Rob Hunt—named them steady patrons of Broad Rock Racecourse.

"It's just a little. Fun."

"The poor woman's in mourning." And married, though Branden claimed she had abandoned her husband in Chicago.

"She's flat down. She needs to be. Taken out." Branden looked as if he were about to cry, his eyes always red and watering, from illness and stone dust. "We just. Watch the horsies. Run."

"Well."

"You too. You need. A woman. A good woman."

"I'm in no way to go courting." Louis lifted his foot, showed the bootsole worn nearly through.

"Now the Federal contract's. Gone through."

"That does change things." Mrs. Termey had sent word of the contract's approval to the quarry along with baskets of food and cider to celebrate.

Branden dabbed his eyes with a dingy handkerchief.

Manchester Stone had been the quarry's main business. Memorials and garden statuary. It was a small concern, next to the Federal order.

"When I get the step to supervisor, " Louis said, "I'll build an old-fashioned castle. Solid granite with enough gewgaws to keep your men busy for years."

More like a castle in the sky, already built and furnished, with a few choice gewgaws. A wild run through Rob's bookstore, a new pair of boots, and new tack for Nella. Send Jake to philosophize in Germany.

"You don't need. No promotion." Branden coughed, or half-coughed. A careful heaving of his chest. "You can. Take your pick. All these. War. Widows."

Louis had evaded his landlady's hints. She would expect more than soiled sheets out of it. And Louis's pick was not a widow but a married woman. He did not want to choose parlor lamps and lace curtains, bedsteads and washstands with any other woman, maiden or widow.

He had reported to Maurice Termey, after he got promoted to foreman, then to Valentina Termey, after Maurice left to go granite-gazing in Italy. He courted her with operational reports, over coffee and pastry in her studio where the paintings were turned to the wall. They talked about books sometimes, though her library—her husband's library—was more exalted than Louis's shelf of horror, improving texts that bore no connection with his own life, travel adventures, dime novels, and whatever he could get in French. Poetry, a certain volume of which could be deemed indecent.

Yet he had seen *Leaves of Grass* at Mrs. Termey's. He dared not discuss it with her. Maybe it was her husband's. Or it could be excised. It did not have the same binding as the one Jake had sent.

The love of the Body of man or woman balks ac-
    count—the body itself balks account;
That of the male is perfect, and that of the female is
    perfect

Love, or animal attraction. Love, if romantic love was lust drawn by grace and intelligence. She knew more of the world than he did. She had married Maurice Termey in the ancient splendor of Rome, before the War.

Branden took out his repeating watch. Though he was looking right at the dial, he moved the chime switch. He listened solemnly, as if the watch were a friend who had uttered a profundity.

"You don't. Need a promotion." Branden put the piece back in his watchpocket, squinted across the shed.

Louis went still inside. "What is it, Branden?"

"Clerk at Dunaway's. Told me. They're looking at. Mt. Airy."

"The big quarry down in Carolina? But the contract's signed and sealed with the Termeys."

"I don't mean. For the granite."

"You don't…. By God."

Branden nodded.

"By God."

"It ain't. Decided." Branden put his handkerchief to his mouth, coughed, folded the cloth away from sight. "You still. Have a chance."

"Well, sure."

They left the shed, Branden heading home.

Louis walked uptown a ways, stopped at the new fountain to splash the dust from his face and gather his thoughts.

His quarry, the most productive per dollar in the area, and this was his reward. Or his punishment, for making trouble over the colored men's pay, over promoting them to more skilled positions. And his suit against Richard stillborn. Conflict of interest, claimed every lawyer he had approached. So much for granite castles.

Then a notice he had glanced over in the *Dispatch* occurred to him. Louis bought a fresh newspaper from a boy, tore out a notice about two-thirds down the right column of the second page, and threw the rest of the paper away.

LOUIS NEARLY TURNED NELLA BACK after crossing Mayo's Bridge into Richmond. No one would be at business, this hour on a Saturday—and Jews attended their services Saturday evening, did they not? But he had paid the toll, so he continued.

Arrived at the address Louis had torn from the newspaper: Moses Kohen, Attorney at Law, Louis tied Nella, tipped a boy to water and clean up after her. He looked at the building, flexed his leg, went in.

The foyer had black and white penny-tiled floor, a thinly

carpeted stairway going up, plain wallpaper, and on each side closed double pocket doors. No one was around. His assurance, already weakened, dropped lower. The law offices he had been to before were plush. Not like this, bare, almost shabby. He stood wondering if he should knock at a door when a woman in a dark dress came out the one on his right.

"Good evening, sir." She spoke in a German accent, her hands clasped together at her waist. She had on sleeve protectors. She was rather beautiful.

"Good evening, ma'am. I am here to consult with Mr. Kohen."

She slid open the other door a little, spoke in German, it sounded like, and slid the door all the way open.

A youngish man standing at a desk beckoned Louis. "Come in, please, sir."

The room was furnished with bookcases, a pair of desks with cubbies stacked atop them, a safe, a table, and several Windsor chairs. Two windows as big as doors gave light and a view of the street, and of the boy lugging a bucket of water to Nella. Everything overflowed with papers. Louis almost began to chew his mustache, a habit he had broken years ago.

"I am Louis Bondurant. Am I speaking to Mr. Moses Kohen?"

"You are, sir, indeed you are. I am Moses Kohen."

They shook hands. Kohen looked to be in his late twenties, with the same dark hair and heavy features of the woman. He gestured Louis to a chair at a tea table leveled by a thin book under one leg, and took a chair facing him.

"What business brings you to my office, Mr. Bondurant?" A melodious voice, with some scratches.

Loneliness, sir, the business of loneliness, for a man needs means to get a wife. And revenge. Richard was right. It was not only the money.

"It is about money, Mr. Kohen." Louis ran his hands along the edge of the portfolio in his lap.

"It usually is, Mr. Bondurant."

"I do not know if you will consider this undertaking to be worthy of your time, sir."

"Why, Mr. Bondurant, you may be surprised at what I consider worthy of my time."

The woman brought in coffee and cake, went back into the other parlor.

"Why don't you go ahead and tell me your story," Kohen said, "and I shall see if I might be able to put things right. You need not go into every particular. A general picture will suffice."

Louis looked at the tray of little cakes. "It concerns a matter between my father, the late Gustav Bondurant of Manchester, and Richard Poindexter, also of Manchester."

Louis waited.

"Continue, please, sir," Kohen said.

"My father Mr. Bondurant tendered Mr. Poindexter a—a large loan. He received as collateral shares in Deep Rock Granite Company. That is a defunct quarry company. I mean, the quarry itself is operating. It is where I work. But a different company leases it."

"May I ask the amount?"

"The amount … of the loan? Yes, sir. The amount was approximately eight thousand U.S. dollars. In 1850. I realize the worth is less today."

"Or one could say, the worth is more today. It depends upon which way you look at it. Not to mention interest. Pray go on."

"My father was never able to collect payment in cash. Nor did he wish to dispose of the shares, because their value dropped to below the loan amount. In 1864, Deep Rock Granite Company was declared bankrupt."

Kohen drank coffee. "What did Mr. Bondurant do?"

"He had died, sir, seven years earlier. When I tried to collect payment for the loan, on behalf of my father's estate, Mr. Poindexter insisted that the shares had paid off the loan."

"I see." Kohen nodded. "Mr. Bondurant, I commend you for

giving a tidy précis of the situation. We lawyers prize brevity, popular opinion notwithstanding. May I ask you some further questions?"

"Yes, sir, please do. Ask about whatever you need to know."

"Has this case ever come to trial?"

"No, sir. Frankly, I could not find anyone to represent me."

"Conflict of interest?"

"That is what they said, sir."

"It is a common enough situation. Many firms, and individuals, retain lawyers all around town, to pad themselves for such contingencies. I myself have never done any business with Mr. Poindexter, or with Deep Rock Granite Company."

Louis smoothed his mustache. Finally, maybe, he had outwitted Richard. He had come to a place Richard would not go. Better than a Jew would have been a Negro lawyer, but as far as Louis knew, there was none such in Richmond.

"Did the shares which your father possessed comprise a controlling stake in the company?" Kohen asked.

"I … I don't know."

"Were you or was your father ever offered a position on the company's Board of Directors?"

"No, sir. I don't think so. I certainly wasn't. Offered a position, that is."

"What had you to say about the bankruptcy?"

"I had nothing to say about it, sir. I was convalescing from wounds when it occurred."

"I take it those were war wounds?"

"They were."

"Were no papers ever put before you?"

"No, sir." Louis drank the coffee, which was very good. White sugar's pure sweetness instead of molasses' bitter dark.

"Does your portfolio carry documents pertinent to the case, Mr. Bondurant?"

"Yes, sir." Louis handed it over. This was farther than he had gotten with any lawyer so far. Still, nothing to get excited about. Kohen might see a name on the papers that he would not want to oppose. A conflict of interest.

The lawyer pointed a pair of spectacles at the tray. "Please, take some nourishment, Mr. Bondurant. Mrs. Kohen made them herself."

Little round and square cakes covered the tray, some with pecans, others iced in different colors. Louis took a piece of square flat cake covered with pecans. It was heavy and oily, not lush and buttery like Mourning's. Still, it was not a job to eat. Even if it were, he would hardly risk offending Mrs. Kohen.

The slow turn of the papers, and carriages and horses passing by the windows. The street paved with Belgian block. No dust or mud, but more noise, and the urine would pool, not to mention ice in the winter. Nella did not like block. She preferred dirt. But block certainly helped the granite business.

Kohen put the papers on the table, straightened their edges. "You fought for the Confederate States, I take it?" he asked.

"I did not. I served the United States."

"Ah."

Neck hot, Louis reached for the papers, but Kohen put his hand over them.

"Please don't take offense, Mr. Bondurant. Only allow me to put before you the prospect of a Radical Jew, such as I am, and you, a former Union—officer, yes?—pitting ourselves against various pillars of our city's old establishment. Yet we must push on. Justice must be given a chance to prevail, what though her adversaries be the most stalwart of local worthies."

Louis took in what Kohen had said. He tried to check the spreading joy, in case he had not understood.

"Are you saying you will represent me, Mr. Kohen?"

"I am. I will. "

Heavy footsteps up the front steps, Dr. Stratton through the lace curtains. What could bring him at this hour. Louis stood, raked his hair back, braced himself for bad news. Sarah showed the doctor in.

"Mr. Bondurant," Stratton said from the parlor threshold. The stained antimacassars, the threadbare velvet, the faded rug. "I hope I'm not disturbing your evening hour."

"Not at all, Doctor."

Nothing serious, thank God, if Stratton offered such limp niceties. Louis started to lay his book on the table, then put it in his pocket. Walt Whitman's verse not for his landlady to find. Or Sarah, if she could yet read. Outside, dust billowed up. Thunder brewed a storm. They would have to pump out the quarry hole tomorrow.

"Sarah, bring us some lemonade on the porch, if you please. Shall we, Doctor?"

He extinguished the lamp. They could have had the parlor to themselves, Louis the only boarder, but it felt too confining, with Stratton. The wind would probably rout the mosquitoes.

Mrs. Sully's new front porch extended across the front of the building, like a back porch, with a plank floor and a tin roof more or less held up by square columns. Louis and a neighbor had built it, and the rent saved bought Jake some books.

"Not that one," Louis said. Stratton picked another chair, a sturdier. Lizzie came around from the back yard and growled.

"Hush up." Louis patted her head. She settled on his feet.

The last time he and Stratton saw each other had been at Eva's gravesite. Hollywood Cemetery, under flowering dogwoods on an unseasonably hot day. The child's place marked with a wooden tablet. Afterwards, Louis and Branden, and Stratton tagging along, had walked to the rising monument to the Confederate Dead. A name on a marble gravestone near the site caught Louis's fancy: Little Berry Joyner. A North Carolina man. Died 1862. And a nearly identical gravestone near it. Both Little Berry Joyner, company I, 30th North Carolina, 1862. One birth was given as 1829, the other 1837. As if the same man had been buried twice, once with the wrong birth date.

Of him countless immortal lives, with countless embodiments and enjoyments

Louis shivered as a chill gust mingled with the damp wind and gray thunder rumbles. He had wondered, at the cemetery, if the gravestones were a mistake. Or maybe cousins.

"The pyramid's coming along," Louis said.

"The pyramid?"

"The Confederate monument. At Hollywood."

"Ah, yes.

Stratton solemnly launched into Innes' poem:

When once again we stand erect and free,
And we may write a truthful epitaph,
A nation, uttering its grief in stone,
Shall pile aloft a stately monument;
Not that their fame has need of sculptured urn,
For they have lived such lives and wrought such deeds
As venal history cannot lie away.
Till then shall scattered roses deck their graves,
And woman's tear shall be the epitaph.

Maybe he recited mockingly, not solemnly. He had worked in Union hospitals, piled aloft pieces of men in bloody, reeking tubs.

Sarah came out and put the lemonade on the table between them. Louis had never seen the child dejected. Her pouts were brief; she was a bright little bird. Yet she and her mother had been sold apart, according to Mrs. Sully, when she was a tiny girl of four or so.

Your mother—is she living? have you been much
with her? and has she been much with you?

The fly curtain trailed over her shoulders, let go with a soft clacking.

Who could say what she thought about a slave-holding would-be nation standing erect and free. Jake, before sending the Whitman book down from New England, had turned one page corner down:

A woman's Body at auction!
She too is not only herself—she is the teeming
mother of mothers

In the margin, the exhortation in Jake's hand: *Remember!*

Remember: the day he and Jake sneaked across Mayo's Bridge to a slave auction in Richmond, forbidden territory.

Some of the men had wrists cuffed in iron and chained together. The manacles had looked very heavy, the men's arms hanging down, hands clasped. Children wailed and clutched their mothers' skirts.

It was the first time Jake had ever seen it, the Manchester wharves no longer used for slaving. He cried and cried. Louis spent his bridge money on ice cream, to soothe his little brother, and had to beg the toll taker to let them pass for free. At home, Jake spilled it out. As the elder, Louis got the whipping. From that day, Jake was a confirmed abolitionist. Louis was, too, just as his parents had been, though preserving the Union was what sent him North in 1861.

Body, heart and soul, he had put into the Good Old Cause. He fought for Virginia, he believed, not against her. He might have killed his own kin, his friends.

Louis shook his head at Stratton's proffered flask.

The granite for the Confederate memorial had been donated, some from the Termey quarry. Blocks unpolished, and trimmed enough to heap together, unmortared, into what was to be a high, pointed pile. Louis had expected a statue. A horseman, say. When he told Branden so, his friend had laughed himself breathless. You can't have. Cavalry charging. Through a cemetery. Bonny. It ain't properly. Funereal.

"Not that their fame has need of a sculptured urn," Louis said.

And in his pocket:

Limitless limpid jets of love hot and enormous,
quivering jelly of love, white-blow and deliri-
      ous juice

Good Lord! Could two poems be more different?

Stratton cut a chunk of twist with a little pocket knife. "I came by to speak of certain matters." He gave a meaning nod toward the fly curtain.

"Honey-bug," Louis said to Sarah, "go and give Miss Lizzie Dog a bath under the pump, would you? Scrub her up good." Girl and dog skipped off, though if Lizzie had known what she was getting into she might not have been so blithe.

Stratton touched his tie. "Is there a spittoon?"

"The yard—but not Mrs. Sully's flowers, please."

Sarah's voice, raised and bossy, came from the back yard. Lizzie gave a few whining barks, but did not sound utterly miserable. By the sound of it, Sarah's little boyfriend Abe was giving a hand and the dog bath turning into a general dunking.

"Mrs. Termey mentioned you visited this week," Dr. Stratton said.

Thunder pealed long, riverward.

The doctor cleared his throat. "You must understand that the household is in a delicate state. Now's not the time to go a-courting."

Astonished, Louis could have laughed. But a darkness sprang up in him. He was glad he had turned down Stratton's whiskey, which would loosen the bonds that held it in.

"You're out of place, doctor," Louis said.

"I am the family physician." And a pompous ass. "I have charge of the welfare of the women in that house."

Louis did not answer, and Stratton did not pursue it. In the dying light of the cloud-thickened dusk, his hair glistened, lank as a laborer's, lank as Louis's, with Macassar and sweat. He poured out more whiskey. Family physician and almighty comforter. He had leased a new stone mansion not far from the Termeys' bluff.

Lizzie came up onto the porch, looking discouraged as she usually did after a bath. She started to sit on Louis's feet, but he gently booted her wet body away. Sarah was just as drenched, but jaunty, preening herself on the porch steps while Abe, somehow fallen into disgrace, pouted and kicked horse turds around the street.

"Do you know," Stratton said, "I am in the position of—"

"Sarah!"

The girl turned quickly.

Louis forced a smile. "Go put on dry clothes. You'll catch a chill." Her former master, his plantation failed, had sent her up here to his cousin Mrs. Sully. The girl had a little room of her own off the kitchen, which she had shown off to Louis. In it was a chest and a neat little bed on which sat a collection of dolls, all with something of them broken. Louis made up his mind to work her through the few toy books he had, and reward her with the book at each finish.

"Doctor, more lemonade?"

"Oh, no, thank you." He touched his lapels. "Yes, I am in a—"

"How is Mrs. Gutman?" Louis asked. Though he knew how she was. Branden had told him—after Louis rounded on him, for taking her out carousing. *She's. Flat down.*

"A physician finds himself in a dilemma," Stratton said. "Continue to treat her with laudanum, or desist?"

"Laudanum will certainly harm Mrs. Gutman." Louis surprised himself, to state such a definite opinion about a medical matter.

"I am aware of the dangers of laudanum," Stratton said. "However, I must balance them against the equal dangers of prolonged distress." He got up, spat over the railing, cast himself into a seat, and sprang up at the ominous rending, having cast his self into the wrong seat. He took the sturdy chair again. Louis stared into the darkening street, rocking silent between hilarity and rage.

He did not know why he disliked Stratton so bitterly. He had never heard ill of him, never been done ill by him. The women of Granite Bluff liked him. He had done his best, the day Eva died. He lived in a fine granite house.

Louis started as a cat jumped into his lap. Mrs. Sully's tom. Louis pushed him off before he had a chance to shed his fleas. Lizzy raised her head but was too lazy to pursue, though the cat taunted, sauntering back and forth at the edge of the porch.

"What was it you quoted?" Louis asked. "At the quarry that day. *Here the beloved land breaks...* Something like that."

"Oh. Why, that's just..." He blushed. "Just jottings."

The icy stone, the icy water rushing over the silence, the snow icing the trees and rocks. And a handful of little men and women on the immense bench of a riverside quarry, talking about getting stone for a building up in Washington City.

It came back to Louis:

Here at the Fall Line, the beloved land breaks,
and begins its long slope down to the sea.

THE WINDOW NEAR LOUIS's bed let in night air smelling of wetted dust and green and flowers. Stove and foundry smoke and all the refuse of man and beast blanketed by the rain.

"Valentina," Louis whispered.

Roses. Cedar.

Her sister said her name in a certain way: each syllable uttered, and the T softened. Not Val'ntina. Valentina. Valentina.

The cloth-covered buttons, the starched lace, the corset's tracery over her waist. Flowers cedar spice at the small of her neck, and her hair tumbling over his face and hands.

He has undressed her, and she is bare.

This is the female form;
A divine nimbus exhales from it from head to foot
I am drawn by its breath

The soft fragrant bed. They embrace. Long kisses. Deeper.

As if I were no more than a
*   helpless vapor—all falls aside but myself and it*

"Valentina."

Shocks of bliss coursed through Louis's body and soul.

Valentina.

The rain on the metal roof and on the trees and into the mud.

Canvas tents mud-stained brown gray yellow red. Campfire smoke pungent and limp.

Louis woke as Lizzie settled, damp and doggy, on his feet. Mrs. Sully would be cross.

Do you think matter has cohered together from its
diffuse float—and the soil is on the surface,
and water runs, and vegetation sprouts

With a last, soft mumble, the thunder retired, leaving the world to sigh itself into a green wet sleep.

S IR," WHITTINGTON SAID, INTO the toil of pencils and payroll and the steady hammering on the roof of the "office," as Whittington liked to call what would the cabin that sheltered their desks. "I have an innovation that may interest you."

Louis was glad of the diversion, Whittington being an inventive young man. A quarry this small hardly needed a clerk, but Whittington was kin to Maurice Termey. Once the new quarry holes opened, clerk Whittington would duly be promoted to foreman, despite his relative lack of experience. The idea was that Louis would make way by moving up to be superintendent of the quarry complex.

"What is your innovation, Mr. Whittington," Louis said. He shouted roofward, "Wyman! Take a break!"

"It is a new way to signal, sir," Whittington said, "to replace signaling by hand." He reached in his jacket pocket and extracted a whistle, held it up. "The system is already in use up North. I thought, we would not want to be too far behind the Yankees."

Louis smoothed his mustache at such clumsy and blatant manipulation. He had in fact considered whistles quite a while ago, and decided against it, not trusting his or his men's artillery-battered ears.

"Mr. Whittington, I commend your initiative. But you know, our men are very old-fashioned. And here is poor Kinny, who will never learn a new way of doing things."

Kinny, at the door, had his own way of signaling, a rotation of his head, a flap of his arms, a prancing of his feet. He frowned as a boy from Granitetown pushed past him with the dinner pail, covered with a scrap of horseblanket to keep it warm. He did not like being upstaged.

"All right, Kinny." Louis rose. "Mr. Whittington, let us try out the whistle for dinner, when there is no danger if a man or two should misinterpret it." As if any of the men would mistake a signal for dinner.

Kinny grabbed Louis's hand and led him to where a saw block was being readied to go to the trimming yard. Released, Louis surreptitiously flexed his hand. He had worked stone for years. Still, he was mere flesh and though Kinny had the mind of a child, his grip was iron-strong.

That morning, the stone had been glutted out—wedged up at the back and the bottom—to make way for the rope that now girded it. Louis inspected the block, the notches made to keep the rope girding it in place, and the socket shackle through which the rope ends had been threaded. Jopple was fairly new as a lumper, and his partner out with the measles. A mistake could crush a man's foot or hand, or worse. Louis did not expect anything to be wrong, though. Jopple had a good sense of the stone. His real name was Jean-Paul. He would have been called Frenchy, but that was already taken by a Canadian come down by way of Vermont. Louis had his eye on Frenchy, who was pleased to consider himself a spokesman for a little combination of malcontents.

Jopple said something like, *Comment c'est, eh, M'sieur Bonny.* He was a Cajun.

"*En englais,* Jopple."

Jopple grinned, showing a couple of teeth colored a solid,

tobacco-chewing brown. "How is it goes, Mr. Bonny?" His English as unraveled as his French.

"Good. Carry on."

Jopple climbed atop the block and fastened the shackle to the hook hanging from the boom. After a glance at Louis, he signaled the derrickman with an old-fashioned thumbs up. Roberts passed the signal to the hoist engineer, and his men cranked the hoist a few times.

The block rose a foot or so and paused, testing the weight, the balance, the strength of the stone for hidden cracks. Louis examined the block again, checked the shackle and the rope. "Good." Jopple gave another thumbs up, adding an upsweep of his arm.

Louis had debated whether he should order the men off the block before it was swung over to the yard or a flatbed. Before the War, a lumper had taken such a fall, he had shattered his leg and ended up losing it.

Jopple, riding the block, said something and pointed toward the river. Some of the other men looked at whatever it was: a heron gulping down a fish, a peddler in a canoe, some Granitetown boys at play, the men having hung a knotted rope swing on a tree overhanging the water.

The Federal contract had heartened them all. Cousins, brothers, friends would get jobs when the Old Quarry reopened—the Old Quarry already being called the New Old Quarry. Whittington had congratulated Louis, as if the superintendent job were a given, and took Louis's caution, about being too far ahead, merely as a warning not to jinx the prospect.

Jopple's block was landed in the trimming yard, and a trimmed block was shackled, lifted, and inspected. It began its short journey to the flatcar. Black men turned the crank in the derrick enginehouse. Maurice Termey had enthused about getting a mule-powered hoist. Then steam equipment took his fancy.

It would happen. Steam-powered drills and channelers and

derricks and everything else. Branden had visited a finishing shed up north, where they used steam machinery, and described the dust and noise as straight out of hell, which was something for Branden to say, given that he already put up with the gangsaws. Men working the same block had to use signals. It might not be so bad, in the quarries. And at least the Federal contract meant enough new work that men would not be dismissed in favor of machines. Only mules would be laid off.

The block was set tenderly on the railroad car. The empty hook came back. Jopple and Billy trusted it would stop at the right time and place, and would not have moved from its trajectory had Louis not ordained it. A shackle upside the head had knocked Kinny's wits out of him.

They worked with Kinny every day; they worked with the equipment, the stone, the heights; they knew crushed bones, wrenched limbs, falls, a drowning at Netherwood's last year. Their elders grew crippled sheerly from exhaustion, from pitting their bodies against granite every working day. And yet they remained blithe to its power. Mere laborers, most of them, in the eyes of the world, caked with sweat and dust, yet they swaggered over the stone, kings all, black and white alike.

It is in his walk, the carriage of his neck, the flex of
his waist and knees—dress does not hide him;
The strong, sweet, supple quality he has, strikes
through the cotton and flannel

During the War, Louis may well have shot at Billy, at Roberts, at his own cousin Llewellyn. Here, he would not let a hair of their heads be injured. But it was not always up to him.

A reverie came over him. He stood in the Old Quarry, his arms uplifted, for the little girl Eva was falling, and he must catch her. He willed her to himself, and she slid into his arms like a baby sliding from her mother into the hands of the midwife. He staggered a few steps as she landed against his body, slight though her weight was. She laughed, as if all was play, and he gave a shaky, tearful laugh, as terror gave way to relief.

Louis opened his eyes to Whittington, a crease between his eyebrows at the sight of his boss with watering eyes.

"Pardon me, sir." It was his way of asking if Louis was all right. He was bright, and as dense as any young man, and kind-hearted.

Louis blinked. "It is dust," he said.

The crease deepened. "Sir, the lumpers and the railroad men are at it again."

Louis signaled the derrickman to wait, and went down to the flatcars.

Railroad foreman O'Keefe was red-haired and freckled, and red in the face. He rounded on Louis.

"Your stone is not laid right. Tell your lumpers—"

"Mr. O'Keefe, if you tell me how this stone should be loaded, I shall relay the instructions to my men."

O'Keefe was not done, though. "Last week, the wheels on one of my cars overheated. Red hot they were. Thank the dear Mother of God my men saw. Do you know what happens when a railcar wheel gets too hot? We had to stop a good thirty minutes to let them cool down. And your shedman bawls me out for being late."

"You tell me how to do it."

"Why should I know?" O'Keefe exploded. "I'm no rock lumper! I'm a railroad man."

Among Louis's men, murmurs, clenched fists. Whittington struck a pose, his idea of a dangerous nonchalance. Louis's anger cooled some.

"Kinny," Louis said to the child-man watching raptly, "run up to the cabin and fetch me a measuring tape." Kinny grinned, his feet danced. Louis pointed up to the foreman's cabin and spoke slowly. "Ask Carpenter Wyman for his measuring tape. Quick as you can, son."

Kinny took off at a run. His mind was clouded, but he sprang up the ladders, bench to bench, nimbly as a squirrel. O'Keefe glared, arms crossed over his chest, jaw set. He was a Maryland man, Union navy. When he first met Louis, last month, their hands clasped in a shake, he said, "What's a froggy name doing over a Welsh mug like yours?"

Everyone watched Kinny come back down. Simpering at the attention, the child-man held out the measure.

"Good job, Kinny," Louis said. "That was right fast."

Kinny twirled in place, his face shining with joy. The railroad men laughed, made tweeting sounds.

O'Keefe turned hard. "You fuckers shut it!"

It echoed clear across the river. The ladies might even have heard, upriver at the house. The railroad men shut it, all right, tight as clams, and studied their feet. Louis's men loosened a little toward O'Keefe, Kinny their pet.

O'Keefe flipped Kinny a coin. "You're a good boy, you are." And henceforth Kinny would want a coin for every little thing.

Louis climbed up onto the car and measured from its edges to each side of the blocks. The railroad men looking on smirked. If Louis's men ruled stone, O'Keefe's ruled the rails. And Louis's cousin ruled the railroad men, Richard Poindexter owner of the spur: tracks, flatcars, locomotive and all. Louis decided Richard had not put O'Keefe up to this, tiffs with the railroad men a feature of life even before the lawsuit.

He jumped down from the flatcar and bit back a cry at the jolt to his hip. Stupid to show off. Lucky he had not fallen on his face. He kept his manner bland, though his words came more clipped.

"The stone is centered perfectly, Mr. O'Keefe. That is the way I have been told it is to be loaded. But since you are the expert on flatcars, tell me, if you please, a better way to dispose the weight of the stone. Shall we put it forward? Back?"

O'Keefe pointed under the flatcar. "The stone must be centered to the chassis. The chassis supports it." As if Louis and all his men were dimwits, not knowing the obvious. To Louis's eyes, the flatbed itself looked to be perfectly centered on the chassis. He was pretty sure it was.

"You give me the measurements of where the stone should be," Louis said. "You tell me how far from the front edge of the flatbed itself the stone must be placed."

"It's the weight that must be centered," O'Keefe said. "Do you not understand? The weight of your lubberly blocks must be at the center."

Louis stepped close to the man and said low, "Now look you, Mr. O'Keefe. Those blocks are loaded perfectly well. So don't give me any more blow about it. You tend to your almighty chassis, and your wheels and what have you, and I'll tend to the stone."

O'Keefe puffed himself up. Louis tensed. But O'Keefe wheeled away and signaled his men back to work.

Louis watched in a manner that said he was keeping an eye on the railroad men, not the quarry men. He felt his own were with him, but that was not so good either. The railroad men and the granite men must not be pitted against each other. O'Keefe should know that, too. So why had he kicked up? But there was the kindness to Kinny. And O'Keefe had given in.

Louis went over to him. "Any of your boys play base ball?"

It was the word to light up O'Keefe's eye. "We have a small little club, we do."

In the backwards patois of Irishmen, "small little" was to be taken seriously. No surprise if they had uniforms, a marching band, and enough victory cups to melt into a cannon. Louis almost regretted asking, but damned if he would cowardly back out now.

"We play at Chesterfield Park, Thursdays," Louis said.

"I've not seen you over the river."

"We're not in the league. Not yet." Nor had they planned, with their motley club.

A grin spread over O'Keefe's face. Maybe he had taken it from a shark he had met in his travels with the Navy. "We'll see if we can't give your boys some play." He roared to his crew: "Base ball with the granite boys, my lads?"

Both sides roared back. Frowns went to laughs, scorn to friendly mockery.

It would be a shame, if not downright bad, should a match against the railroad men turn out a debacle. Still, Louis could not repress gleeful anticipation. His men were muscled hard as granite. They would thrash O'Keefe's crew.

Word flew as fast as Kinny could scramble up the benches. Kinny could run all right, and hit the ball to the moon. If he did not get distracted. By anything. His mates cheering him, a child selling roasted goobers, a pigeon flying by, a thought tumbling through his battered wits. Louis followed him up with his eyes, stopped.

Bianca Gutman was sitting on the little terrace by the foreman's cabin.

The week before, the sisters Bianca and Valentina had attended the picnic celebrating the Federal order. The young bloods made sure to have on clean clothes, wives and sweethearts and sisters and mothers all come for it. And more children than Louis expected; he had chased them like a mother hen all day. Mrs. Termey gave out prizes: hams, a fresh turkey, cases of ginger beer. Dr. Stratton had run a clinic out of the cabin, and annoyed Louis when he would not divulge a thing about the men's health, except that Tristan must be put on light duty because of hernias.

Mrs. Gutman had come down to the quarry a few times more, alone, not even a stable boy squiring her. It made some of the men smile. The railroad men, too, now, following Louis's stare. Her hair was pinned up loose, and she wore one of her odd, loose-made dresses, in shades of black. Jeannie, in the portrait on the easel, was in something like it. They resembled the clothes in the Tennyson prints that Papa had hung in the parlor at home. Louis had loved those pictures: *Idylls*. Papa had read the poem aloud one winter, cozy evenings at the fireside.

Louis tipped his hat to Bianca Gutman. Unfortunately, she waved back. Nudges, glances, smirks among the men, though none dared do more. He oversaw the rest of the loading, then toiled up the ladders to the cabin. She did not wait, though. She had not before, either. By the time he arrived, she was gone.

June 1869

Mʀs. Tᴇʀᴍᴇʏ ᴀɴᴅ Lᴏᴜɪs sat out on her terrace, overlooking the old quarry. She had invited him to stay a while, after he delivered his report. A rare treat.

But the white-gray sky glared hard as granite, tightening the headache around his eyes. Damn Branden for egging him on at Heron's. *You need a good. Drunk. Bonny.* He had holed up in the foreman's cabin before riding to report to Mrs. Termey. The clanging drive up to the house was redolent with the rank, rubbery smell of privet blossom. Louis longed to lie down in a dark room. A cool cloth laid on his brow and quiet hands sponging vinegar to his temples. Mrs. Termey's quiet hands.

She poured drinks, sherry for herself, brandy for Louis. Louis knew he should not touch the brandy. He sipped, it helped, he would pay double for it later.

"How do you like Mr. Whitman's poetry?" he asked.

There the book lay, after all, on a rusty garden table with the decanter and the glasses, and a letter franked in Italy.

He's all a-fawn over Lincoln, was Rob's verdict. He could not forgive Whitman's hero for "coming to gloat over our city," freshly ruined, newly fallen Richmond. To Louis, the tragedy of the president's murder far outweighed any sin of ill-timed victory visits.

"He is new," Valentina said. She stopped, thought, began to speak again, let it go.

"Do you have a favorite?" he asked.

She straightened and took a deep breath. "The Poem of the Body." She spoke firmly, and blushed like a schoolgirl.

Though he should have been pleased, opportunistic, even, Louis was absurdly disappointed. He had hoped her favorite would be his. He flipped to the title page.

"This is dated earlier than the one my brother sent me."

Louis's book had no picture of Whitman. In this, an etching of Whitman showed the poet in shirt and trousers, like a mere laborer. Like himself, when he worked in shirtsleeves, though as foreman he did not remove his vest and tie.

Louis glanced up at Mrs. Termey, then, rather teasingly, he perused the Table of Contents. "Poem of the Body."

He found the page. A shock touched his nerves. Warmth and pleasure and confusion suffused him. His heart filled with something more than blood.

"It is the same as mine," he said, "or nearly the same."

THE bodies of men and women engirth me, and
*   I engirth them,*
They will not let me off, nor I them, till I go with
*   them, respond to them, love them*

"This is your favorite, too?" she asked, her cheeks pink.

"It is." He read. "A little different. I believe I like yours better." He looked in her eyes. "Though it is the same. The same poem, nearly."

His, more manly. He recited, though his face, too, warmed.

I SING the Body electric,
The armies of those I love engirth me, and I engirth

them;
They will not let me off till I go with them, respond
to them

"Yes," she said.

His body and heart warmed with joy. Her eyes responded. Rob had explained electricity. It was like this.

"Those I love. In your poem." Her voice was tremulous. "They will not let me off."

Louis hardly dared breathe, so tentative were her words and yet breathing immense strength beneath the overburden of what a woman might say to a man neither husband nor kin.

"Till I go with them," Louis said low, prompting maybe.

Her words, the way she sucked her lower lip, her eyes dark, holding his.

"To respond," Louis breathed. "To love."

She looked away.

On the flyleaf, an inscription: *To M, with affection, from P.* To Maurice Termey. Her husband. Her absent husband. *They will not let me off.*

"May I confide in you, Mr. Bondurant?"

"Yes."

"It's about Jeannie," she said. "Doctor Stratton has proposed to marry her."

The armies of love, already blundering, were routed. He nearly missed the table, putting down the book. "Does Miss Gutman consent?" For all of Stratton's, *this is no time to go a-courting.* Stratton had been trying to dash a possible rival.

"We haven't put it to her. She doesn't seem to dislike him."

Meanwhile, Branden and Mrs. Gutman chummed around town. Poor Jeannie left to Stratton's devices, and Valentina to cope with it all.

"I am hopelessly out of my depth, ma'am, but I have a conviction that mutual liking is essential for the happiness of a marriage."

"Were your parents happy, Mr.—may we call each other by name? Valentina and Louis?"

His heart filled his chest. "Yes. Valentina." Valentina and Louis. Louis and Valentina.

The circling rivers, the breath, and breathing it in
and out

Surely it was beautiful.

"They were…?" Valentina prompted. She looked at her skirt and fingered its folds as if sampling its fabric. Different colors of paint rimmed her nails. Was she happy in her marriage? He thought not.

"I believe so. Very much. Though they were quiet with each other. Quiet and good."

"I can see that."

What did Valentina see? She had introduced him to Jeannie as a good, kind gentleman.

"Maurice…" She must worry about her husband. She must miss him.

"Dr. Stratton is a friend of Maurice's," she said. "They were both up at Yale together."

"I see." That, Louis had not known.

"He's … pleasing, I suppose."

All that could mean was, Stratton was the best thing going for Jeannie. Her mother's reputation a mark, Jeannie Gutman's chances of happiness were slim. They should send her away, up to a school in New England or back to Chicago, to her father, if prospects there were not already ruined. Louis hated the current of his thought. Yet it was self-evident.

"And her parents consent?"

Valentina sifted the loose papers on the marble table. "This is he. Jeannie's father. Rudy Gutman."

She handed Louis a carte de visite showing a pale-haired, pale-eyed man. Union, First Corps. Gibbons' Iron Brigade. They had been awfully whittled down. After Gettysburg, the Corps had been dissolved, not enough men left to hold it together.

Bianca had met Rudy Gutman before the War, according to Branden, at a palace in Rome, where she and her younger sister Valentina and their mother were guests. The sisters' father years dead, his plantation sold to a cousin—land, house, cabins, barns and sheds, the furniture down to the dishes. The slaves, too, sold. Valentina learned to paint in Italy and like her sister she met her husband there, two Virginians at an American soiree. Maurice and Valentina married in the splendor of Rome.

Since then, they had lived mostly apart, he in Italy, she here. He had not given her a baby. He had not come home to help her through the tragedy of Eva's death. Nor had Bianca's husband come down. Eva, dark-haired, dark-eyed, had borne not the slightest resemblance to either. Yet Branden said there had not been an earlier marriage for Bianca.

Gutman should have come, for God's sake. Or at least for Bianca's sake.

The women had no one to protect them, to keep them. Louis had sifted his family tree, to see if they might be related somehow, cousins on some branch, if there might be some legitimate interest he could take in their well-being. But the sandy plantation near Bermuda Hundred, farmed now with hired labor, had produced no kin to Louis's coal-mining, clerking lineages.

"She hasn't been to any parties this spring," Valentina said, "or school." She looked so sad, Louis longed to take her in his arms. He would hold her close to his heart, and she would hold him. They would engirth each other—

"Will you speak with her again, Louis?"

Louis followed Valentina into the studio. After the bright day, the silhouette of trees and sky, reversed to bright, played on the white-washed wallpaper.

"Good day, Mrs. Hamilton," Louis said to the old woman in her armchair. As usual she did not answer.

Valentina bade Louis sit, and went out to the passage.

He wished with all his heart that he could go back and change fate. Catch Eva, as he had in the dream. She might be playing with her dolls on the terrace, or in the studio or the garden, cuddling the little cloth animals crowding the bed on which he had lain her body.

The portrait of Jeannie had a few strokes of color that matched the richly colored shawl draping a chair next to the easel. She posed in mourning, but would be painted in colors.

To make her beauty vary day by day,
In crimson and in purples and in gems.

Her features were sketched in. Yet Louis got up not to see the portrait closer but to look at a landscape propped face out on a bureau.

It was completely unlike those he had seen at the exhibitions he had attended with Papa and Mama and, later, with Branden and Rob. Those landscapes had been rendered in painstaking detail, seemingly down to every leaf on every tree. This was ... Louis did not want to think: cruder.

A white cottage, a fence, an artillery cart. Lush bright grass, a sleepy woods tipping to autumn, a brilliant blue sky. The landscape tilted slightly. Maybe Valentina had drawn it on rolling land.

As if to fill in the picture, a vision came vivid to Louis's spirit: the slaughtered. The reeking mash of grass, mud, gore, shit. The litter of personal effects, from beloved photos to bawdy cartes, to weapons and Bibles, canteens and playing cards. The spasmed, battered, flayed and fractured men.

Examine these limbs, red, black, or white—they are
*   so cunning in tendon and nerve;*
They shall be stript, that you may see them

The paint bulged and rippled thick under Louis's unsteady fingertips. The grass green, the sky blue, the building white, the artillery chest dark gray. Yet the grass was streaked colors: gold and blue, red and brown and every hue. And the blue sky, and the artillery chest. The white building was anything except white and yet it added up to white. It was more true than true. Louis pressed his fingers over the grass, the paint bumping smooth, soothing.

"Louis?" Valentina said.

He pulled his hand away. One should not touch a painting. "I beg your pardon." Valentina and Jeannie had passed right behind him, and he had not noticed.

As he sat in the Italian chair, Louis tried to hide how affected he was at Jeannie Gutman's appearance. Her pale hair straggled loose over her back and shoulders, and her feet were bare, and she clasped a rag doll.

"Miss Gutman, how do you do?" She did not look up.

Though Louis had wished, minutes ago, to be a man for the women of this house, he did not want to cope with the situation. He did not know how. Mrs. Gutman should be here; she should be taking care of Jeannie. When she was not out playing around, Branden said, she closed herself in her room. She might be there right now, sunk in the soft, bitter spell of laudanum.

Louis willed himself to enter, somehow, this unknown terrain. "Miss Gutman, will you tell me who you are, in your aunt's painting?"

"King Arthur," she whispered.

In spite of everything, Louis smiled. "And will you draw the magical sword from the stone?"

She looked up. Her eyes a dawnlike lavender blue, framed flaxen, met Louis's eyes square on.

"Yes." She hugged the doll to herself, hiding her face.

Louis drew a breath. *"And so, with brave and fearless heart,"* he recited, *"She made her bold essay."*

The fair hair tumbled over the doll.

"She grasp'd the handle in her hand, Its point leap'd sharp and free."

Louis reached across the crate and, with the back of his fingers, brushed her hair back over her shoulder, silken strands catching on the calloused roughness of his hand.

She was crying, her sobs muffled by the doll. He drew his hand back and folded it with the other in his lap and felt utterly wretched. Valentina hugged Jeannie, kissed her head, whispered something to her, stood. They went out, Valentina came back alone.

Louis stood. "I'm sorry, Valentina." He was not sure for which transgression he apologized. He had failed to comfort. He had touched the painting. He had brushed a young woman's hair back from her shoulder.

They will not let me off.

"No, Louis, you did your best." She hugged herself, and Louis reached to her, dropped his hand.

"We must have faith that time will heal." The platitude rang heartlessly empty.

Nella, waiting on the driveway, greeted Louis as usual, nipping his sleeve and knocking off his hat. He swatted her, in no mood for it, and she carried him with her head down and her ears back. Fortunately, the ride home was eastward, the sun behind. The headache crept back into his skull, his eyeballs squeezed in their sockets.

Nearly three months on from Eva's fall, Jeannie wandered a flat land, a place with neither the cheerful spontaneity of a child, nor the rich mystique of a woman. The best hope was that she would not go further and further, until too far gone to return. Louis recognized, now, the haunting distance in her eyes. He had seen it in men broken by battle, if there could be any comparison between a blood-rusted soldier and a woman-child. He had had to bring Branden back from it. He had brought himself back, in a way.

He was trying to bring himself back.

He patted Nella, wiped his face with his bandana, and closed his eyes a long moment. Nella ambled to a stop.

There lay the truth of why he had not visited Jake after the War, nor invited him here, after that first time. He did not want his brother to see him. He could not bear to hear again Jake's, *Dear Lord above, Louie.* He feared to witness, in his brother's eyes, his own flayed and fractured soul.

And wonders within there yet

Louis left the trimming yard to go up to the wooden terrace at the foreman's cabin. Mrs. Gutman stayed this time; he sat with her. She did not seem drunk or opiated, but her breath flowered with lozenges from a tin. For all her playing about town with Branden, the days must drag, and so she came down here to pass the time, to watch men cut stone. Embarrassing as her presence was, sitting there in sight of all, Louis pitied her. She had lost the robustness that had struck him, when he first met her.

He toyed with the chip of granite he carried always in his pocket. It was not the best quality. The grayer, deeper granite was harder and finer-grained, but he liked the slightly browner granite, its warmth and texture. He palmed it to pour the coffee.

"Have you seen Branden this week?" Mrs. Gutman asked. She sipped the coffee, grimaced. Louis stirred another dollop of molasses into her cup. She would be used to white sugar.

"On Sunday," he said, "we went to Saint Paul's to hear some music." And St. Paul's was near Saint Peter's where Valentina Termey went to church, so he might see her afterwards, on the sidewalk. Though he half-dreaded the chance, he had kept Branden loitering. He had not seen any of the women.

"Not to cleanse your souls," Mrs. Gutman said.

"I reckon God got a few licks in."

Mrs. Gutman exhaled something like a laugh. Her flowery breath, and her body odor, unbathed, sour, musky. Louis never noticed it, on men. He had read that in women the passions ran stronger. Having seen men in battle, he knew that to be a lie. He might smell rank, to her, in his work clothes. He had put on his suit coat over his vest and limp shirt.

The air was heavy, damp and warm. Louis liked the seasons' barter: the heat for long, soft evenings. The men working all day on hot stone might not feel that way. They had a river for bathing, that was lucky, and the quarry was mostly in shade, afternoons.

"Branden's all busted up since I told him I'm not getting divorced," Mrs. Gutman said. "He's a sensitive fellow."

"Mrs. Gutman, I know it is out of my place to say so, but a woman of your station should not be.... "

She let the euphemistic pause become a silence.

"Carrying on the way I do? Drinking with Branden at the racetrack? Is that what you mean?"

"Yes, ma'am, that is exactly what I mean."

And leaving her desolated daughter to her sister, and Valentina casting about so desperately she called out to Louis, a man who could hardly be taken as a friend of the family. Stratton angling.

"I don't want a divorce," Mrs. Gutman said. As if that was the matter. Maybe it was, too.

They will not let me off.

"Mrs. Gutman—"

"You'd rather a woman kill herself in the loneliness of her room than in a beer garden for all to see," the tears falling down her face "drinking with a man not her husband—"

"Mrs. Gutman—"

"How can you call me Mrs. Gutman after what I said?" She sobbed, her face in her hands and her hair fell down, all at once, like a glass of water turned upside down.

Louis dropped the stone. His hands hovered, helpless. "Bianca."

She wiped her face. "Louis." Looking in his face, "Don't be so stricken." She felt her hair. The loose pins fell to the planks. Louis got on his knees. Dust dulled Bianca's shoes. The hem of her dress alluring. He picked up his rock and her pins.

"I cry all the time," she said as Louis took his seat again. "This is the first time I've been able to stop, once I start. You cheer me up, Louis. I can't bear it. I can't stop wanting to hold my baby, my little baby girl."

Tears fell afresh down her face. She did not wipe them off. She twisted her hair, spiraled it atop her head. It was greasy, unwashed. The armpits of her dress were stained a darker black.

"I'm sorry, Bianca. I'm very sorry."

He held out his hand, with the pins, the granite chip among them. She took up the piece of granite. One hand holding her hair up, she turned the granite in her fingers, sniffed it.

"This smells like you."

"I have a habit of fondling it." They both laughed, heavy as things were between them.

She put the stone back on his palm, took the pins from it one by one. Her fingertips touching his palm, again and again, quickened him.

"Branden said the statue is almost done," Bianca said. She pushed in the last pin.

"He put his best carver on it." A statue of a little girl angel.

"He said you asked about the grave marker."

"I overstepped," he said. "I'm sorry."

"No, you're one of us," Bianca said. "Valentina told me. I hope the Federal contract makes you rich."

Did she mean, Valentina had told her of the Federal contract? Or did Valentina say to her sister, Louis is one of us.

"Though I don't know if I'll like it," she said. "Your hands will grow smooth and pale. You'll consider going into politics."

"No danger of that." Louis turned over the stone chip and what Valentina might have said.

"You'll join the Manchester Hunt," Bianca said.

"My days of jumping fences are over."

"You're thirty. No old man."

He shrugged, embarrassed. Yet something loosened, inside him.

"Tell me about the battle where you got wounded. You were Union. Did you ever run into Rudy?"

"No." Louis fingered the granite chip. He had a belief that one could know, by touch, the difference between stone softened by bedding itself close to air and rain, and stone compressed, deep under the ground, by its brethren.

"He got it in the chest at Fredericksburg," Bianca said.

"That was a bad one for us. For the Blue."

"The battle," she said. Where Louis got it in the hip.

He never desired to hash over battles. Most of his friends had been Rebels. Branden and he had worked the whole thing out in one short exchange: *Good thing we didn't shoot each other. Yes indeed.* If they reminisced about the War at all, it was about camp life, funny stories or gossip.

"It was out near Mechanicsville," he said. "Cold Harbor." The coffee tepid now. "Nearly on this day, now that I think of it." It was exactly on this day, June first, five years ago, and he had thought of it last night and the moment he woke up this morning.

He had been running to a new position, and then he was spinning about, his weapon flying away. He thought he had stumbled on a body, a rock, a tree stump, even as he knew he was falling all wrong for that. Right before he slammed to the ground, he sensed the violation of his body. Outrage, not fear, nor pain, was his first agony.

Bianca reached toward him, and unthinking, Louis put the granite chip in her hand.

"I was lucky, I suppose," he said. "The bullet entered too high for the surgeon to relieve me of a leg."

She sniffed the stone. "I take it this is not the reason you are unmarried, Louis."

They laughed, though Louis's face and neck grew hot. "No, it was a hip wound."

Poise on the hips, leaping, reclining, embracing, arm-curving and tightening

Men and women should always speak so frankly.

"Was it terrible?" she asked.

Outrage, at being violated, and then a bloom of pain so monstrous it blotted out creation. The sun came back in a blaze of horrible thirst. Then the agonizing jounces of someone carrying him, all battle-befouled himself.

"Was it…?" She caressed and pressed the stone.

"It was a very bloody affair all around."

"I meant, was getting wounded terrible?"

Louis looked into the quarry. He had been staring at nothing, at the past. A block suspended from the derrick boom moved toward the flatbed. It was a stately progress. The arcane signals guiding it.

"It's all right, Louis."

He looked in her eyes, and looked away.

"All of it is terrible," he said, as if nothing had gone between them. "And if—God!" He sprang up. "Get in the cabin." She was up, in the door, without a question, and obeyed when he told her to crouch in the corner, and cover her head.

He slid down the ladders, granite bench to bench. One nearly toppled with his rush. Men yelled, "Run! Run! Get away!" Railroad and quarry men scattered from the train tracks.

The boom angled wrong and a block dangling from it, over a flatcar. Louis shook his arm loose from Whittington's grip. A hush fell. Panting, Louis examined the area around the flatcar. He was careful, methodical, though his entire body shook.

"Where's Kinny?" he shouted.

The straining boom groaned. Louis crouched, ready to scuttle to the loading area to search, when someone yelled, "We got him!"

"Come away, please, sir," Whittington begged.

"Everyone stay down!" Louis shouted. "Cover your heads!"

O'Keefe echoed him, louder yet. Louis dropped and covered his head with his hands.

A wrenching cracking tear.

Silence between heaven and earth.

Twenty tons of granite crashed to earth, shaking the ground and throwing a thunderclap back and forth across the river.

Out of the dust cloud came a shrill yipping—for a moment Louis did not understand where he was. Billy's mates yelling. A slap. The battle cry stopped. Sobbing.

Louis's legs shook as he rose.

"Stay down!" he yelled. He did not hear any groans or screams of wounded. Just coughing. And Billy, his battle cry gone to whimpers. Billy had learned to live with the blasting; the crash must have undone him. Louis looked up at the derrick mast, at the broken boom and loose ropes twitching. When he was satisfied that all had finished breaking he continued to the flatcar. It was half-crushed. Not much shrapnel, thank God. The block, unbroken, was so all-consuming, it simply buried its own wreckage.

"I said stay," he said, rough, to his clerk.

"Are you all right, sir?" Whittington asked.

"Fine." Louis sounded to himself like Branden, barely able to get a sentence out whole.

"No one hurt, Louie." Lew, another flouting his orders, but it was just as well.

"Don't let anyone near the tracks until I say," Louis said.

"And for God's sake, no one is to touch the derrick. Not even Roberts. And no one leaves."

"Yes, sir." He turned to leave.

"Wait. Llewellyn. Let Mrs. Gutman know that no one is hurt and young Snyder will bring her home immediately. He can drive our rig, yes?" Though she had walked here on her own, more than once. "I'd be grateful if she will kindly tell Mrs. Termey the news and I'll deliver a full report as soon as possible." Valentina would certainly have heard the block fall. Felt it. The little glass animals nestled in straw, the paintings leaning on the studio walls.

As Louis turned back to the tracks, O'Keefe grabbed his arm. He was flushed, his teeth clenched. Whittington balled up his fists. Louis said, quick and quiet, "Together on this, O'Keefe."

O'Keefe glared, let out a gust of breath. "Yes." He let go of Louis. "Yes."

"Let us survey the damage," Louis said. "And Mr. O'Keefe, your engineer will want to come along."

The four men walked together along the tracks, pointing out to each other the hazards: the next flatcar jolted off the rails, the next with a wheel shattered, probably from being jounced. The crews stirred, curious, eager to see the disaster. On the way back along the tracks, Whittington and O'Keefe's engineer knocked together a plan for how to move the fallen block.

As they faced the men, O'Keefe went so far as to sling his arm around Louis's shoulders.

"Boys, by the mercy of our dear God, we came through this in one piece. Bow your heads now for a prayer." Louder: "Bow 'em, ya damned heathens!" The railroad men bowed them. O'Keefe nudged Louis.

"Dear Lord," Louis said—the quarry men quickly bowed their heads. "Dear Lord, we thank you for sparing our lives and limbs, on this day. Please continue to watch over us. And deliver us from evil. Amen." A murmur back; a few men crossed themselves.

Louis set Lew to overseeing removal of the fallen block. Several pairs of O'Keefe's and Louis's men combed the quarry for derrick parts. The show of camaraderie between O'Keefe and Louis went a long way toward keeping the peace between the railroad men and the quarry men, and most complied with the order against cross talk. In the cabin, Whittington took statements from the men.

Dismembering the remains of the derrick went slowly. Louis wanted to see every inch of rope, and so did O'Keefe. Roberts, the quarry derrickman and rigger, sweated by the quart and, at Louis's order, spoke only when spoken to. Louis and O'Keefe broke off a few times to check on the fallen block. A ramp made of smaller blocks and grout, a team of all six of the mules, and a sled got it safely away from the broken flatcar. Jokes about hitching Kinny; he practically put the ramp together by himself. The locomotive went back to Manchester with two empty flatcars.

By the time they got the derrick mast down, it was nearly dark. Yet even by twilight, the problem was obvious. The rooster sheave, the block assembly at the top of the mast, had come apart.

"Sir, I swear—" Roberts began.

"Quiet, Roberts." Louis said so O'Keefe could hear, "You will speak only when I say so."

He knew what Roberts would have sworn. The same as he had sworn before: that the derrick was maintained exactly as it should be. Louis believed it, though he doubted that the careful maintenance logs or anything he himself might say would save Roberts' position.

They brought the sheave up to the cabin, laid it out on the floor and stared at it. Three lanterns did not reveal more than what they'd already seen. The new ropes were sound; the mast and boom showed no sign of rot or old damage. Lew was positive the block had been hitched properly. It had risen steady and balanced. No question, the weak point had been the rooster sheave.

The investigators came the next day, one for the railroad, the other an insurance man for the quarry. Valentina joined in for a while, in a beautiful pale green dress that tinted her skin sallow. Louis had drunk an entire pot of coffee, having barely slept, and his hands were jittery, his eyes gritty. The railroad investigator had been in Richard Poindexter's cavalry company, in the War. He treated Louis with polite disdain.

The men examined the derrick parts, which Louis had ordered locked up overnight. Poor Roberts was obsequious. Whittington had told Louis, privately, there had been nothing wrong with the sheave when they rerigged the derrick a few weeks ago, and the rigging itself flawless. The young man had a sense for things. Louis directed him to take charge of rebuilding the derrick. As ill luck would have it, the quarterly reports were due. Productivity stood still, numbers marched on. Finch the head quarryman took Whittington's place, copying the last week of the logs. He had a decent hand, though he wrote with the left, the right having been shot through at Spotsylvania.

Louis's mind tossed all day between the obsession that Richard had caused the accident, and the conviction that his cousin would do no such a thing. It was by chance, very, very lucky chance, that the back flatcar—Richard's property—got it. The block could easily have crashed down anywhere between the trimming yard and the loading dock, or between the benches and the trimming yard, or even onto the benches themselves.

The interruptions of the investigators did not help Louis's attempts to concentrate on paperwork. Finally they left, ordering Louis not to discuss the incident, and to retail it to his men as an accident whose exact cause was being sought. It was dark by the time Louis put on his hat to go home.

"Good night, Nick," he called to the night watchman on his way to the stable. The man was visible by his lantern.

"Good night, sir." He was an Englishman, from a mill town that went bust during the War, the cotton supply dried up.

Louis stopped, turned back. "Nick."

"Yes, sir?"

By the lamp, the watchman's eyes were flushed, as was his nose. A few empty bottles had turned up along the tracks, in the search for derrick parts. He did not smell like drink, though.

"What happened the other night?" Louis asked.

"Which night, sir?" The tip of Nick's tongue slipped out and back in. He might be nervous, with the big boss talking to him. Most of the men were, beyond simple niceties or words passed for working together. More than one of them, giving their versions of events to several men in suits, had visibly trembled.

"The night before last," Louis said.

"Nothing, sir. Believe you me, I've thought about that." Nick shook his head. "This quarry was quiet as a tomb." He gave a forced chuckle; granite men tended to graveyard humor. "It's like that, except for 'coons and what not a-fighting."

"It must be dull."

Maybe Nick guessed where that could go, too. "Peaceful is how I see it, sir."

B RANDEN'S MASTER CARVER PALLADINO had given wings to the
statue that was to memorialize Eva. They were not spread.
They enfolded her back and arms and body, the tips crossing
over her thighs. The master had left the feathers rough, maybe
in haste. Polished were the head and chest and hands—fingers
folded over her heart—and the feet.

The other objects in the Manchester carving shed, finished
and unfinished, stood silent, no sound of chipping and chiseling.
The men carving them had stopped working to stand, hats off,
some with heads bowed, for the women visiting the statue that
would stand at their little girl's grave.

Strangely for a granite man, Louis was not much for funerary
art, but Palladino had not carved a wistful graveside cherub. Louis
only wished she were in granite, more enduring than marble,
but then someone else would have carved her. Not Branden's
dusty Michelangelo. Palladino stood near the statue in good
clothes that sagged, probably from a more robust past. He was
old, maybe sixty or so, with a consumptive hunch. Marble was a
gentler stone, not one to tear up the lungs, but granite dominated
the shed. The majority of dust ruled.

The curling hair so fresh, and the insults to the body covered with rough wings. The feet chubby, each toe nail perfect. The eyes sleepy.

Eyes, eye-fringes, iris of the eye, eye-brows, and
  the waking or sleeping of the lids

Bianca and Palladino spoke in Italian. The stonecarver contemplated Louis's face as if tracing its lines for a statue. He asked Bianca something to which she gave a startled, "No, no."

Louis stroked the statue-child's smooth hair, the cheek, the bare shoulder. He gripped the rough wing's joint.

The natural, perfect, varied attitudes—the bent head,
  the curv'd neck

The wellspring of the marble touched his spirit and stopped the breath in his chest like a sob.

He gasped and sneezed, slapping his handkerchief to his face to catch the spume. His eyes watered. He blinked, and wiped his nose and sniffed, and looked up to find them both gazing at him, the master's eyes deep-set and red-rimmed, Bianca's bemused though teary.

"It is so like," Dr. Stratton said in his poetry voice. "So very like."

It was Valentina who examined the statue in the manner the doctor might examine the living body, not for emotion or beauty, but for how the parts might add up, or not. Or maybe the way Louis sought in granite its flaws, its strength. Or like an artist, of course. When she touched the marble, it might have sprung to life, such was the feeling in her hand, resting on one of the wings.

Louis lightly put his hand upon the other wing. "How do you say very beautiful in Italian?" he asked Valentina.

"Bellissima." She gazed at the wing, at his hand. "Bellissima."

He turned to shake Palladino's hand. "Bellissima, maestro."

Palladino smiled and put his other hand over Louis's, enfolding it. The strength, the hardness of the master's hands, for all the decrepitude of his body. The sense of them. The marble girlchild, rough and polished.

Branden ushered them to the office for the tea he had laid out. The desks were pushed to the wall. A table in the center was laden with soggy pastries, tea things, and a bunch of flowers. Stone dust filmed everything, though the janitor, acting as waiter today, cleaned morning and evening. Louis forced a pastry down to help give the tea a shine of success. Branden leaned on a wall, pale and somehow both dry and sweaty. Minutes before everyone had arrived, a fit of coughing had just about shaken him to pieces. When Louis first saw him after the War, he had appeared older than his years. Now it struck Louis that his friend's face and body had something childlike about them.

"We're going to Ratley's," Bianca said suddenly in Louis's ear. "Come with us."

"Bianca, I—"

"Please, Louis." She looked around at Branden, turned back to Louis. "Don't make me go alone with poor Branden."

"It can only get worse with two of us scoundrels, ma'am," Louis said. He wanted to get Branden home, let his sister Alice take off his boots and put him to bed.

"Ma'am," Bianca mocked. "Aunt Anne is coming. She's proof against any number of scoundrels."

Louis hoped—but Valentina had taken charge of Jeannie, and Stratton would bring them home, damn him.

"Why don't we go to my house," Branden said on the way to Ratley's. His face had gained a tinge of color. "Alice can make us punch."

Ratley Tavern's neighborhood had slipped down from when Louis was a boy. The street uncurbed, Bianca and Mrs. Hamilton had to lift their skirts, the plank sidewalks half-buried in dirt. Branden stopped on the porch to smoke. Louis took the women in.

The place did its best to be respectable, with fresh sawdust, polished spittoons, curtains on the windows. A handful of clerks and merchants sat in the public room, and a roadworn family, Northerners by their dress. The private room held little more than two benches with a table between, but the cloth was clean, and so was the window, on the inside. Jeannie and Valentina could have come after all.

Branden joined them, the barkeep following with a whiskey bottle and dram glasses.

"I thought you quit smoking," Louis said.

Branden filled a dram glass and dropped it in the beer Louis had ordered him.

Mrs. Hamilton put aside her sherry. "I want that," she said.

Branden laughed and slid his boilermaker to her. Bianca added Mrs. Hamilton's sherry to her own. Louis drank ginger ale and moped that Stratton was the one squiring Valentina and Jeannie home.

"Do you understand Italian?" Bianca asked.

"If it's. Written in stone," said Branden.

"I was speaking to your friend." Bianca had fine eyes, the vivid dark bright blue of the river when the sky shone on it. She added to Branden, "You hurt Jeannie's feelings, not talking to her today."

"I said hey." Branden took out his watch, stared at it, sounded the chime.

Maybe she liked playing men against each other. Mrs. Hamilton seemed oblivious, but Louis did not count on it.

"No, I don't understand Italian." Louis said. He did not feel comfortable calling her by name in front of Branden and Mrs. Hamilton.

"Do you know what Palladino thought?" she asked.

"I'm a little deaf," Louis said. They all laughed. Then Louis looked away; Palladino must have thought he was Eva's father. He put a little whiskey in the ginger ale.

"Rudy says he believes in Free Love," Bianca said. "I doubt it. I really doubt it."

Louis did not know what Free Love was, though he could make a guess.

"Could a child's death be retribution owed to the mother?" Bianca's eyes filled with tears.

"Many children. Die." Branden's chest heaved; he shot a whiskey plain. "Before their time. Poor little. Lambs." Of stone, carved in his shed.

They all fell quiet. A pack of dogs snarled and snapped outside. Louis tried to listen for Lizzie's voice. She did not fight much, though once he had to stitch her ear, from a 'possum, he believed.

Only Branden finished his drink, and Mrs. Hamilton's.

The air outside lay hot and damp, and yellowish with coal smoke. Louis hired a hack, an expense he could ill afford. Branden half-climbed, half-fell out in front of his house. He would not let Louis walk him to the door. He never did. The curtains of the house were all drawn, the porch jumbled with broken furniture, the yard scrubby. When Rose was alive, Louis had often walked the little path, flower-lined, to eat breakfast, lunch, or dinner at a table set with rose-painted china and Irish linen. He had near forgotten he ever considered Rose plain-faced. She was lovely, and so in love with his friend, and he with her, that her parents had not kicked up too badly about her marrying down. Back then, too, Branden was on his way up. He had done well, too, very well, rising to manager of Manchester Stone finishing sheds. They would have done fine, had Rose lived.

"The depot," Louis told the driver after Alice fetched her brother inside.

"Poor Branden," Bianca said.

Tobacco smoke inside the train depot made a blue cloud. Louis seated the women and got a jug of ginger ale. A river breeze freshened the room, the smoke eddied back. The ale was flat and warm. The glum family from Ratley's occupied a bench. The ride out to Granite Station would be pretty, with the trees all greened out, even if the dogwoods were spent. Louis tried to decide if he should go with them, or merely put them on the train. Valentina would have to offer him supper. He did not want to impose. He wanted to have supper with Valentina.

"Maurice has never been any kind of husband to her," Mrs. Hamilton said.

Louis was not sure he heard right, until Bianca's mouth curved in a smile. She was clean and fresh today, in a new-looking dress, black decorated with jet fringe, and her hair washed, her breath sherry and the horehound candy she favored.

"I don't mind, really," Mrs. Hamilton said. "I suppose I should, but I don't."

Maurice not being a proper husband to Valentina? Of course Mrs. Hamilton would be partial to him. She had brought him up, after all.

"Poor Jeannie has joined the ranks of the abandoned," Bianca said.

"Nonsense," Mrs. Hamilton said.

Louis supressed a sigh, looked down the tracks. He wished the train would arrive, and he could put the ladies aboard and go home. Or he would go over to Rob's bookstore in the hopes of finding Rob there, instead of at home with his wife and children. It was not kind, to wish a friend away from his family. Rob had confessed, one night while they were shelving books, that he felt like a stranger in his own home, since coming back.

"Stratton delicately hints that he would like to take her to a ball," Bianca said.

"Better a barn dance than a ball with that lard-ridden carpet-bagger," Mrs. Hamilton said.

Louis smoothed his mustache, melancholy quivering toward merriment.

"Why don't you bring us to a barn dance, Louis?" Bianca said.

"Bring us somewhere out in the country, way out where no-one knows us. We need to have some fun. Some light-hearted fun."

"That would be splendid," Mrs. Hamilton said. She had been more talkative, this day, than ever before around Louis.

"Well, then, I shall take you ladies to a barn dance."

Even as the words jaunted out of his mouth, Louis cast desperately in his mind for how he might find a barn dance respectable enough for the ladies of Granite Bluff. He had been to guild dances, hunt and military balls, political shindigs, weddings he and his pals had crashed. Never to a barn dance at all. Drunken fiddlers and banjo players, debauched planters.

"Yes, ladies," he said without hope, "we shall go to a nice barn dance."

Waiting in Kohen's office, Louis reread Jake's latest letter. The statue for the little girl was beautiful, Jake said, and Mrs. Termey's sketch of it—which Louis had forced himself to sacrifice—itself was a fine artwork. He had met Mr. Emerson, the philosopher. *Were I your Mr. Palladino, I would sculpt his Bust, yet not even the very most Gifted of Artists could capture that manly Radiance of wisdom and kindness.* The man their father had emancipated, Anthony, not doing well, drinking, gambling and altogether dissipated in Boston town. Giving him more money did not do much good, Jake believed. Louis had sent some anyway. He did not remember Anthony, who had gone to work at Tredegar's and lived in Jackson Ward, but his sister Tessa had stayed with them, serving as a freed woman, and coddling Jake rotten. They had cried on parting, and Jake had moped for days after. She married a quarryman in Vermont, and though conditions for black workers were not much better there, they pulled along all right, one of the sons in the quarry now, and a grandchild on the way. More hints from Jake of a romantic connection, dinners with a family that hosted Harvard boys and had a daughter.

Kohen came in. "I beg your pardon for making you wait, Mr.

Bondurant." He sat at his desk. "Will you take some coffee? Or would you prefer something more spiritual, at this evening hour?"

"Coffee is just the thing, Mr. Kohen." Louis liked the man, though he could not entirely trust him, not because Kohen was an Israelite but because he was of the lawyer tribe.

Jake's letter in Louis's coat pocket crinkled against the chair. He shifted to free it. He always carried his brother's latest letters, for they made him happy.

"Do you have brothers or sisters, Mr. Kohen?"

Kohen's smile vanished, and Louis regretted his thoughtless question.

"I am the only one left," Kohen said. "One brother died for the Confederate States—Annie his widow—and the other for the United States."

"Dear Lord above. Sweet.... " Louis caught himself from saying, sweet Jesus Christ. "I'm very sorry indeed, and sorry to have caused you pain."

"Not at all. The pain is not of your making, I don't think. Even if you had fired the very bullet that killed our Danny in Gray, I could hardly put you down for it. After all, it could have been he who wounded you. Let us leave it a mystery between us, who shot whom, and where. I believe that is the usual arrangement."

So it was.

Into the dusky room Annie carried a coffee tray. The china was pretty, the gold rims worn. Kohen stirred in sugar, staring at the street outside the window. He had a handsome face, for all that a club foot marred his physique. It saved his parents one son, at least. Thank God, Jake had been too young. Thank God, thank God.

Kohen sighed and turned back to Louis. "So, to our business."

"Yes, sir."

"Let us clarify some basics. We have a quarry in which you are foreman. Granite Bluff Quarry." He waited.

"That is correct," Louis said.

"The quarry, the granite stone and the land below and above the stone, is owned by Maurice Termey of Chesterfield, Virginia."

"Let it flow, Mr. Kohen. I will stop you if you go astray."

Kohen grinned; he looked as young as a boy. "I shall let it flow in best lawyer's fashion. So. The corporation that mines the granite—I beg your pardon. Is that the correct term? Mined?"

"It will do nicely. The granite is quarried or mined. Never extracted."

"God forbid. Never extracted it shall be."

Louis smiled back, finally, at Kohen. He had been realizing lately how impaired was his sense of fun, his smiles a few beats behind. He worked the quarry each day, save the Lord's and what holidays the Directors might decree, and ate in saloons when he could bring himself to spend the coin and when Mrs. Sully's table grew too oppressive. A book, and to bed, to solitary sin. Bianca's barn dance might turn out to be a good idea. Whittington had promised to find something genteel.

"The corporation that presently quarries the granite," Kohen continued, "is a public company called Granite Bluff Quarry Company."

Louis was not sure, not quite completely sure, what a public company was, except that one had been formed, last year, to operate the quarry.

He was a fool to be so entirely in the dark. He did not know, at all, what a public company was, or how it was run, though he was employed by one. When the Company leased the quarry, nothing had changed for him, saving that a few more reports must be drawn up every month. Not yet, at least, had anything changed.

"As for the quarry itself," Kohen was saying, "the physical quarry, I understand that Mr. Termey, its owner, gets paid for the stone taken, regardless of who profits and who does not profit."

"Once separated from the bed, the blocks can sit forever in place, and Maurice Termey will be paid for them."

"Do you know if that was the case with the previous company, Deep Rock? Shares of which your father held?"

Louis shifted slightly in the chair. It was hard oak, unpadded, and his hip felt it. "Yes, Deep Rock company paid Maurice Termey for every block cut free." Louis had held that against Termey, once upon a time, believing it part of the reason Deep Rock failed. "I don't know the amounts of money involved, though."

"Was Mr. Termey's property—that is, the property occupied by the quarry and its structures and so forth—was that ever threatened with Federal seizure?"

"I wouldn't think so."

"You wouldn't think so," Kohen echoed.

"Mr. Termey was overseas during the War. He never served in the CSA, as far as I know."

"Hm." Kohen scribbled a note, put his pencil down. "May I ask if Mr. Termey is a friend of yours?"

He would take the women to a barn dance. That hardly violated friendship. It was a favor. "I report to Mr. Termey. To Mrs. Termey, while Mr. Termey is overseas. I have regard for him." He added, "I certainly would not want to damage them, with this suit."

Kohen sought something in Louis's face, Louis could not guess what. His way of speaking differed from other men Louis knew, the set of his face differed. Because he was Jewish? His eyes were almost black. An article in the newspaper had praised a Jewish minister for his eloquence, much admired by men of all faiths.

"Mr. Bondurant, the relationship between client and advocate must be completely unclouded. Clear and innocent as a summer day, if you will. An early summer day, that is. Before the heat and dust haze it over."

Kohen had been looking for a lie in his face. He would need to, in his line of work. Louis drank his coffee and watched the daylight fade from the windows.

Kohen gave up. "So, as concerns our lawsuit. There is a problem with it. Rather a large problem."

"You have discovered a conflict of interest." Louis narrowed his eyes against the sudden spur of light, as Kohen struck a match and lit the lamp on his desk. He had not realized the room was grown so dim.

"No," Kohen said. "The problem is, your father actually bought shares in Deep Rock Granite."

"And the loan?" Louis asked.

"Was not a loan," Kohen said. "It was a purchase of shares."

"It was a loan. My father referred to it as a loan. He must have purchased shares in another transaction."

"Unless you possess other papers you have not shown me…." Kohen's face softened. "Well. A man who trusted his—cousins were they? Your father and Mr. Poindexter?"

"Papa was his uncle."

Louis hardly heard his own words. He was grappling with the concept that Papa had speculated, that he had mortgaged their house to speculate. He had gambled away their family home. "He said it was a loan."

"A man who trusted his nephew could have been led to believe, by that nephew, that he was making a loan with the shares as collateral." Kohen paused, looking at Louis's face. "It won't be the first time I have seen such mistakes made. After all, stock shares are, in a very, very loose sense, a loan to the business issuing them."

"Well, then," Louis said. "That's it." Kohen's kind lie only prolonged the ignominy of it all.

Kohen put his hand on Louis's arm. "*Nihil desperandum*, Mr. Bondurant. *Nihil desperandum!*"

Louis forced himself to settle back in his seat. "A noble motto, Mr. Kohen, which I suppose you mean for its general sense, for these shares in Deep Rock would make no man less desperate, financially." His convoluted joke was flat, and Kohen's smile a polite grimace.

Louis aimed for a more dignified exit. "Had I read those papers with any degree of intelligence, I would not have wasted your time. I sincerely apologize." He began to rise again, again Kohen stopped him.

"Not at all. I am a lawyer, trained to see through chicanery. Put me in a quarry and I am nothing at all. Mere dust, as the Good Book says."

"So are we all, perhaps especially we quarry men." Louis could have winced at such a feeble rejoinder. Kohen's hands upon the papers were smooth and deft, Louis's in his lap as rough as a lumper's.

"However," Kohen said, "we have a very specific cause not to give in to despair."

"I am eager to hear it."

"We may be able to hold Mr. Poindexter and the other directors personally liable for Deep Rock's losses."

"Excuse my ignorance once again, sir. I thought the idea of a company was to shield its directors from personal liability." Rob had told him that, the other night.

Kohen lifted his index finger and his eyebrows. "You are right, sir. Yet a company is, after all, supposed to be a company. If the directors use it as a mere carapace, without regard to the welfare of itself and, by extension, its shareholders, said directors forfeit corporate protection."

"A carapace, Mr. Kohen?"

"A shell. As a turtle or insect would possess."

"I see."

"It is admittedly a tough case to bring," Kohen said.

"Let us bring it."

"Very good," Kohen said, smiling. "I shall draw up our agreement. It will take a week or so. Alas, I have only one scrivener, my sister-in-law."

Annie of the sleeve guards. "I'm sure it will be most elegant," Louis said.

"She has a good plain hand. And will a messenger bring them to your home? Or shall I send them by post?"

President Grant's spying postmistress, Miss Van Lew, against landlady Mrs. Sully. "Send them by post, if you please, in care of Beattie's Dry Goods in Manchester."

"What was the outcome of the incident with the granite block falling on the railroad car?" Kohen asked as he pinned some notes together.

Somehow, the story had gotten in the newspapers. "The investigation ruled against Granite Bluff Quarry Company," Louis said, "which was to be expected."

"Oh?"

"They could hardly hold the railroad liable. Or the Termeys. It's now between the insurance company and the quarry company."

"Confidentially, what do you think?"

Was it an odd question? After a night's sleep, Louis's hunch—that the watchman, either passed out drunk or paid, allowed someone to tamper with the derrick—had seemed overwrought. That might not be what Kohen meant. He was a lawyer. He would be interested in how the insurance company and Granite Bluff Quarry Company tried to maneuver each other into paying the damages to the railroad.

"I am very strict about maintenance, as is my clerk Mr. Whittington and our rigger. Nothing was wanting on our part."

"One more thing, if you will pardon me for what may be a personal kind of question." Kohen put the notes aside. "Have you any concern that you could be dismissed, should the directors of Granite Bluff Quarry Company take exception to our suit?"

"I don't know why they should." Though he had lost sleep trying to decide if they might. "Maybe you're thinking of Mr. Dunaway, but as far as I can see, he will be unaffected by the

suit. And I do not believe Mr. Termey would hold it against me."
So he had told himself.

Kohen tilted his head. "I was thinking of Mr. Poindexter
himself."

"Richard Poindexter is connected with the railroad, a separate
business, though we do work together of course."

"Perhaps you don't know. This month Mr. Poindexter was
brought onto the Board of Granite Bluff Quarry Company."

Louis's mouth opened, as if he would answer, then he turned
his face away, toward the window. He tried to take it in, to think
rationally about the fact that his cousin, his adversary, was now
one of his employers.

Valentina had never mentioned it. Tact? She would know of
the bad blood between the cousins—though not about the lawsuit—and perhaps had decided it would be impolite to mention.
Or she assumed he would know what his cousin was up to. The
Board had little to do with day-to-day quarry operations. It did
have much to do with who was foreman of the quarry, and who
would be named superintendent when the quarry expanded,
and who would be nothing at all. Louis could have laughed
were he not so overturned. His cousin was truly as wily as the
proverbial serpent.

"Mr. Bondurant, perhaps you would like to consider this
further. I shall do nothing more until you tell me to press on."

Outside, gas lamps lit. Louis gave the sweeper at the crossing a
coin for cleaning up after Nella, deferring a hair cut to next week.

As Nella ambled toward Mayo's Bridge, Louis fondled the
chip of granite he carried in his pocket.

If he lost his job, over this lawsuit....

If he lost his job.

He would be finished, and Jake's schooling would be finished,
too. No quarries around here would take him on. He would have
to move up North, pray he could land a position in Vermont or
Massachusetts. He would be closer to Jake.

Kin and friends would be left behind. Branden. Valentina. Bianca and Jeannie and Mrs. Hamilton, and the place where Eva fell. Home, left behind. Manchester town, and Richmond and the tawny river. His granite quarry that was not his.

The tolltaker cried cheerfully, "A very good evening to you, Mr. Bonny!"

He did not yet get his toll. Louis turned Nella back. *I'm sorry, Mr. Kohen*, he would say, *I have decided it would not be prudent to press our suit....*

The lawyer was just locking his office as Louis came in.

And his cousin Richard would keep Papa's money forever.

"Mr. Kohen."

"Mr. Bondurant." Kohen's smile uncertain.

"Mr. Kohen, let us press on."

The two men clasped hands.

"Nihil desperandum!"

"Nihil desperandum."

Y OU'LL LOSE, AND THAT's that." Daniels passed the jug to Louis.
"Nonsense," Louis said. "We have a strong club."

Their pitcher one-handed; the best batter an idiot; one of the
outfielders—himself—lame; another stumbling drunk; another
too busy haranguing his clubmates to catch the balls that came
to him; several without stockings, scratching at their ankles. A
host of complaints of body and mind. It was like the army all over
again: the Quarry Quarrelers spread out on a chigger-ridden
pasture at Frog Level.

Pants were reddish to the knees, dew and clay climbing from
the unmowed, scuffed up grass. A bunch of little boys had got up
their own game, on the side. They looked to be making a better
show of it than their fathers and elder brothers. Which was why
Louis was trying to persuade Daniels to join them, though he
was not a quarryman. He played for Snelling's Brickworks, in
the league, and as a coach he offered the only hope Louis could
conjure of knocking his men into a decent team.

"Should've made it a contest of strength," Daniels said. "You
got them Scotch boys. And your coloreds. Throw trees. That
you could win."

Louis resisted Daniels' attempt at the jug and took another

pull. Fellow Unionists, they had started the War together. Daniels got typhoid fever at First Bull Run, and by the time he recuperated, his fellows were long gone, heading to some other slaughter. He spent the rest of the War in Texas, eating 'possums that, he claimed, wore iron shells on their backs. He always was prone to exaggerate.

"Throw trees," Louis said. "I see Queen Mab hath been with you." Their school, long ago, had put on the play: Louis a bumbling Romeo to Branden's vague Mercutio and, worse, Daniels' Juliet.

Daniels laughed and got the jug. "We'll give the Quarry Quarrelers a try."

Louis wanted more than a try. He wanted a dashing victory over the Spitfire Spikers. Never mind that Daniels knew what they were up against. At least the game subsumed jealousies between blacks and whites: victory at any cost. Louis was not about to disillusion them.

Nihil desperandum!

For the rest of the evening, Daniels and he jawed and bullied the Quarrelers into staying in position, into following some of the rules, into religious vows to practice catching, throwing and batting daily. Hope sagged.

Yet the game awakened in Louis a well-being he might have thought dead, had he ever paused to miss it. The days of boyhood: swimming the foul waters around Manchester wharf or the clean granite-roiled waters upriver, running the alleys, playing stickball in the street, covered with dirt and all the kinds of mischief a pack of boys and dogs could get into. Pure, heedless joy.

To stop in company with the rest at evening is
   enough,
To be surrounded by beautiful, curious, breathing,
   laughing flesh is enough

When the sun dipped to the trees the men parted, many to

wives and children who had carried supper to the field, the good smells wafting. Not a wife or son or daughter greeted Louis. Only Dr. Stratton, with a slap on the back.

"What an entertaining game that is," the doctor said.

"Good evening to you, Dr. Stratton."

Stratton let his hand rest on Louis's shoulder as they walked to where Nella stood in the shade.

To pass among them, or touch any one, or rest my
arm ever so lightly round his or her neck for a
moment—what is this then

Louis put on necktie and vest over his sweat-soaked shirt, and draped his coat over the front of his saddle. His fingers combed through his hair came away wet. Nella nipped his sleeve, waited until he put on his hat, and knocked it off with her nose.

Stratton lunged and grabbed it, dusted it off, and handed it to Louis. "Let us call each other by name, shall we?" he said again.

"She catches me with that little trick every time."

"I'm picking up some goods from the pharmacist this evening. Ride together?"

"Why not."

Nella arched her neck; Stratton's chestnut gelding had a courtly, flattering manner. Louis and Paul talked about baseball. They stopped at Weisiger's, continued to Mrs. Sully's.

A folded paper dangled by a thread from the doorknob. Rather like a block from a derrick, Louis could not help thinking. He removed it. L. Bondurant. He put it unopened in his pants pocket.

"Set yourself down," Louis said. "I'll get us some supper, if you're not expected somewhere else."

"Delighted."

Stratton followed Louis through the house—Mrs. Sully probably at her sister's—out the kitchen to the back yard. Louis took off his vest and shirt and pumped water over his head and chest and arms.

"I could examine that old wound of yours, Louis."

Mrs. Sully's Persian rubbed Louis's legs, not minding being splashed, Lizzie and he ignoring each other. Sarah watched giggling from the kitchen door. When Louis threw a handful of water at her, she ran away. She came back with a towel and a fresh shirt for him.

"Sarah, honey, would you bring us a jug of cool beer, and tell Mrs. Archer a cold supper, for the three of us. And something for Miss Lizzie Dog, too."

She ran off, coins clutched, scotch-hopping over the holes in the alley. Lizzie disappeared after her.

"I wonder if I could steal her away," said Stratton as they went back through the house. "Such cheerful alacrity."

"Never think of it. Mrs. Sully's very fond of the girl."

"Ah, well."

The men settled on the porch. The children called in for supper, the street fell quiet, the other porches empty. Louis wished Stratton gone, so he could release his tired self into the hot, rosy dusk. His hip hurt, yet the base ball sense of well-being lingered. He felt the crinkle of the note in his pocket, wondered if it might be an invitation, his cousin Llewellyn trying to get him to join the Odd Fellows. They liked to be arcane—a note hung from a doorknob.

"Louis, I say, I'm a man of sorrows today."

"Are you?"

"I am," Stratton said. "Mrs. Gutman has not accepted my proposal for her daughter's hand."

"No?"

"You're not surprised."

"No. No, I'm not." He wondered if his own lack of enthusiasm had dampened Stratton's proposal, and if Stratton knew that.

"You discussed…?" Stratton changed tack. "I believe Mrs.

Hamilton is impinging on the matter." His chuckle sounded forced. Everything he uttered sounded forced. A man of sorrows. Was it a crown of thorns next? Except the bitterness came through true enough.

"She's a close one," Louis said.

"I had a sense that Mrs. Gutman... Well, she seemed rather indifferent. I can't imagine the father would object. A Union man, like us."

Rudy says he believes in Free Love, Bianca had said of her husband. Rob's summation of Free Love, when Louis asked him, shed little light on the matter. *Marriage is out, and every woman gets to play the whore. The Yankees get a dandy notion now and then.*

"I do have a counterattack lined up," Stratton said.

Louis's eyes drifted shut. In truth, he understood Stratton's misery well enough. He, too, longed for a woman, a family, a home. He, too, loved a woman he could not have. If he did not get dismissed from the quarry because of the lawsuit, or the friction with the railroad men, or not being the right person's nephew or son-in-law, and if he got the promotion to superintendent—or if he won the lawsuit, he would have something to offer a woman, in marriage. More than his war-battered body.

A wedding at Saint Paul's—Saint Peter's, if she wanted; he would convert. A gown with silk-covered buttons. The crisp softness of starched lace. He lifts the veil. Her perfume flows forth: flowers, exotic herbs, foreign trees and cedar. Kneeling, and plying the button hook. Her silk-stockinged foot arches in his hand.

Louis started, opened his eyes. "What? I'm sorry, Paul." He sat up, peeved, hot, taken from his warm dream.

Stratton smiled, maybe knowingly. "No, you've had a tiring day. What I said was, I shall host the base ball match between the Quarry Quarrelers and the Spitfire Spikers."

"That's very handsome of you, Paul."

Sarah set out the supper: early tomatoes, cold roast pork,

corn bread, mixed pickles and piccalilli. She stood with her hands behind her back while Louis heaped a plate for her, which she took to eat on the porch steps, to show off to anyone who might pass by, especially her swain, Mrs. Archer's son Abe, who threw a clod of dirt at her and bolted when Louis jumped up and made to run at him. Cornbread crumbs flew from Sarah's laughing mouth.

"Women are strict." Louis sat and unwrapped Lizzie's supper, a packet of scumbly chopped meat. He set it by his chair. "Really, we men don't stand a chance."

"That is a doctrine of despair to which I will not subscribe." Stratton paused taking a bite of pork. "The women will be there, won't they?"

Louis was of a teasing mind to say, he did not know, but he nodded. "Oh, yes. The ladies of Granite Bluff wouldn't dream of letting their Quarry Quarrelers down."

"And of course, everyone will bring what guests they please. Except...." Stratton put a hand on Louis's arm. "Please don't take offense, I beg. Perhaps it would be best if you did not invite your cousin Colonel Poindexter."

Louis picked up his beer, to remove the heavy, pale hand without being pointed.

"May I ask why not invite my cousin?" Not that he had planned to invite Richard.

"His son was engaged to Jeannie Gutman," Stratton said.

"Jeannie and Charles?"

Stratton—and the cat, perched on the porch rail—frowned at a pack of dogs trotting by. Lizzie put her head back down, not interested.

"Yes," Stratton said. "It's broken off."

Had Stratton warned Charles Poindexter with the same trick he'd tried on Louis the other night? *Not a time to go a-courting.* Surely Richard Poindexter's son would not be fobbed off by such a weak ploy.

Sarah looked around at their silence, and began to get up to clear away the food. Her plate was half-full. "You finish eating, honey," Louis said.

"I had nothing to do with it," Stratton said, "in the event you were wondering."

"Lizzie, for heaven's sake, don't eat the wrap."

She assumed a hangdog look, and went back to toothing the butcher paper until she licked it off the porch. She looked over the edge, gave the dog equivalent of a shrug, and flopped down on Louis's feet.

"From what I understand," Stratton said, "Miss Gutman herself precipitated the break."

Jeannie, childlike, with her ragdolly. Yet she had collected herself to jilt a boy. Was her beautiful face locked in desolate dream, when she told young Charles she would not marry him? Did he see the empty distances in her blue-violet eyes?

Louis leaned down and gave Lizzie's floppy ears a soft pull. He did not want to discuss Jeannie Gutman with Stratton. It was not just his personal dog-like dislike of the man. Louis did not care much for physicians as a kind. He had seen them too much at work with the saw. And how would they see him, too much at work with gun and knife and bayonet and bare choking, clawing, fisted hands.

"Where were you in the War, Paul?"

"I was a Union surgeon, at Campbell Hospital for most of it. In Washington." He dropped his voice. "Have you heard of the poet Walt Whitman?"

"My brother sent me a volume of his."

Stratton smiled into Louis's face. "Walt helped out in the hospitals," he said. "Tirelessly, though he's no youngster. He has a radiance, a sweetness. *You would wish long and long to be with him.*" Like a light put out, Stratton's face fell from joy into staring at the street dust.

Louis pushed down a gout of jealousy, that Stratton had met

Valentina's and his poet. He imagined Valentina and Stratton talking about "Walt."

The doctor gusted a sigh. "Yes, I did my share to maim men, in the War. May I ask where you were hospitalized?"

The question was usually, where were you wounded. "It was a house. I don't know whose. And I convalesced in Alexandria, at the Quaker Meeting."

"You were lucky. It is one of the best. Maybe the very best."

"They were good to me. I liked it when they let women visit. God bless the healing women." Mama sick that winter, her last, and Jake unable to leave her.

"God bless them," Stratton agreed. "And what battle was it?"

"Cold Harbor. Sixty-four." U.S. Grant flinging his men away and away.

Louis finished his meal. The cornbread had harbored a bitter suspicion of weevils. The pork tasted sound, fragrant with herbs.

Stratton soon left. Sarah haughtily ignored Abe's imploring offer to carry the dirty dishes, though she could not stop him trailing after her. Louis took the note from his pocket, slipped off the string and unfolded the paper.

God smiteth the man who raises against his kinsman.

Incredulous, Louis almost laughed. The unfamiliar writing was clumsy, unschooled, yet every word looked to be spelled by the book. Dictated by an educated man who wished his handwriting to be concealed?

Richard might have joined the quarry Board to discourage Louis's lawsuit. But sabotaging the derrick? Louis could not talk himself into thinking that Richard would pull such a stunt. Richard's son? A business associate of his? A friend?

Louis decided not to mention the note to Kohen. Or to anyone. Certainly not to the investigators. No point confronting Richard, either. Louis knew himself incapable of beguiling or bullying the truth out of a man, especially a specimen as tough and crafty as Richard.

He examined the string that had bound the note. He could not evade the thought that it was looped and tied much like a hitch that would carry a block.

July 1869

A LAUGH WAFTED UP FROM the trimming yard, as if to mock Whittington's frown. Beyond it all, the river moved dull through a world lidded with clouds. Pray God for rain, for this drought would break the farmers and make food costly, and the mills would stand still, too, if the river ran too low and soft.

"You need to know every job," Louis said to Whittington. "Including grouting."

"Yes, sir."

"Mr. Whittington, state your reservations." The phrase was a running joke between them, but Whittington answered without the least smile.

"Mr. Bondurant, you would not ask me to work with the grouters. The men will never respect me, after."

Louis did, in fact, have in mind that Whittington fill a grout box or two. He needed to understand what his workers did. Besides, it would be justice, to make him collect some of the wasted stone from his attempts at trimming. Even Branden, who rarely complained, had commented on the reduced size of the blocks from that day: *Tell your breakers we don't. Need no more. Lambs.*

"Mr. Whittington," Louis said, "do you want to be foreman some day?"

A slight, a very slight pause. "Yes, sir. Of course I do."

"Then let us descend to the trimming yard. We will grout, the two of us together, and let no man dare disrespect our efforts."

They descended the ladders. Whittington's hesitation had disappointed, surprisingly, acutely. Ten years difference between them, yet Louis supposed he thought of the young man as a kind of son who would take his own place, when he moved up. If he moved up.

Since Westham road was to be paved, the grouters had been busy making gravel. The labor was unprofitable, but the Board had overridden the figures on it. Likely, some of the members were invested in the road project. The grouters were also breaking stone for the extension of the railroad bed to the new quarry sites.

They did not disrespect Whittington's efforts. They were patient and kind, though they enjoyed a grin, showing the boss's clerk how to pack a grout box—a low-sided open crate reinforced with iron strapping—so that it held more than a few chips of gravel. The boy would see for himself—and feel with his hands—that grouting was not as easy as it looked. It was, actually, as easy as it looked, in principle, and Whittington had it under his hat in less than a quarter hour. He was good with the men, though, and did not let on. The physical labor demanded more, and Whittington no puny stripling. The heat told, too. Not much more than an hour of grouting raised the color in his cheeks so high, Louis laid him off.

"That's hard work, sir," Whittington said as they went back up the ladders.

Louis went behind Whittington, to catch him if he misstepped. The young man's hands could not be called soft, yet they trembled, raw.

Boss and clerk sat on the wooden terrace, a jug of spring water between them. A splash from the bottle O'Keefe had sent—Irish whiskey like burnt grass, fresh dirt, horse sweat and coal smoke—would have improved the water, but Whittington was

Temperance, so Louis abstained. The sad truth was, that while Whittington had a bright mind—his scheme for the new derrick ingenious—he did not have a feel for stone. Trimming blocks with him had been a trial of soul, not just of body.

"Tell me, Mr. Whittington: what would you do?"

"What would I...? Well, now that you ask, sir, I would build a cableway for moving the grout. First, we would need to shift the trimming yard slightly up hill, to allow gravity to do the work for us. And we would need…. That is not what you meant."

"Will you make some drawings that I can submit to the company?"

"I'd be glad to, Mr. Bondurant." Whittington gazed riverward, then looked at Louis again. "I am committed to stone, sir. I do aspire to the job of foreman. After you are promoted, naturally."

"Naturally. But truthfully, Bert."

Whittington smiled, at last. "Well, sir. I would like to be an architect or an engineer. They are building a wondrous bridge of stone and cable, up in Manhattan Town. That's my dream." He gave a laugh that touched Louis's heart: the laugh of a man relegating his heart's wishes to fantasy.

"Reality is not so shabby, I don't think," Whittington continued. Reality being, nine brothers and sisters, and a father who was a Baptist preacher. "I hope I am not out of place, sir, by saying that you seem content."

"I am content here in the quarry, it's true."

He had not always been. Had his life taken the expected course, he would be living Whittington's dream, drawing up buildings or bridges, not chopping stone. His cousin's chicanery had forced his life to take root here.

Stone, river and trees; the darting salamanders and undulating snakes, and beetles, laired in bowers of bramble, itchy vines and rock rubble; foxes sneaking away early morning; herons at their fishing holes; hawks gliding under the clouds or into the sun.

A brightness brimmed within Louis's spirit.

As I see my soul reflected in nature

Whittington was gazing at him fondly and somewhat, Louis had to admit, like the men often gazed at Kinny. He drew out his pocketwatch, tucked it back. "Mr. Whittington, I must be on my way."

"Big day tomorrow, sir." Whittington's smile became a grin. The barn dance. "Pray God I don't make a fool of myself."

"Never, sir." Whittington added, "And pray God I don't make a fool of myself." He would be running the quarry.

"I do not doubt you, Mr. Whittington."

"Thank you, sir."

Rather than going home to a book and early lights out, he met up with Branden, and the two of them, and O'Keefe's whiskey, ended up at Rob's bookstore. Louis was glad they were the only ones there; he knew what they would talk about: Jimmy Branch's demise.

It had happened at the Colored Men's Barbecue, a rally got up by Jimmy's party. The function was barely underway when disaster struck. The *Dispatch* had spared none of the details:

> There are few citizens of Richmond who were not aware that a barbecue was to have been held by the colored voters, who favored the election of Colonel Walker and the adoption of the expurgated constitution, at Vauxhall's Island on yesterday afternoon. About two hundred and fifty of the most respectable colored men in Richmond and Henrico signed the call for this demonstration, and many of our most prominent white citizens manifested a great deal of interest in the enterprise. Among these none were more active than Colonel James R. Branch, whose name headed the Conservative senatorial ticket for this district. He arrived early at the place selected for the barbecue, and was stirring about with great activity, making suggestions, and by his pleasant remarks contributing not a little to the good humor of the party.
>
> It was not intended to hold the barbecue on Vauxhall's Island, but

on the adjacent one, known as Kitchen Island. A suspension bridge, not more than fifty feet in length and about five feet in width, connected them, and to get to the barbecue, of course, this bridge had to be crossed. A policeman, stationed at the end nearest Richmond, was directed to allow none but those having tickets to pass until all the arrangements for the dinner and speaking were consummated. The fortunate possessors of tickets passed over singly or in groups, until about seventy-five colored men and at least a hundred whites were over.

This was the state of affairs, when a colored man rushed up to Colonel Branch — then on Kitchen Island — and informed him that there were a good many Walker men on the other island who couldn't come over because they did not have tickets. Colonel Branch went on the bridge, accompanied by another person, whose name we could not learn. He walked rapidly half-way across, and then beckoning to the policeman on duty, exclaimed: 'Let them come on! Dinner is nearly ready! There's plenty of room!'

The policeman thereupon gave way, and the eager crowd on the other side rushed on the bridge. There was a swaying to and fro. Somebody cried: 'The bridge is giving away,' and in an instant the heavy structure, with its human freight, fell with a crash into the rushing flood below.

The sound was heard all over both islands, and there was a simultaneous rush to the bridge. The sight that met the eye was appalling. Ten or fifteen human beings were buried beneath the heavy timbers, threatened alike with death from drowning and the crushing weight. Most of them, being only slightly wounded, soon scrambled out, and, grasping the chains and jumping from timber to timber, reached the shore.

Others, however, were not so fortunate. The first of these was Colonel Branch. He had been struck on the back of the neck by a massive iron chain. Then falling beneath the bridge, he was unable to extricate himself, and lay for several minutes, with the water dashing over his face, struggling in vain. Policeman Kirkman, who was on duty at the end of the bridge nearest Vauxhall's Island, had his head mashed between two falling beams, and was instantly killed; and others whose names were not until afterwards ascertained, were also badly injured.

There was no neglect on the part of the by-standers. A score of men, both white and colored, at once plunged into the stream, many of them not stopping to take off their clothing. Through their efforts the injured men were finally extricated and brought to land.

Rob stoked his pipe, enveloping one and all in a stinking blue haze. "Your cousin's God scored a victory—" puff, puff "—when that bridge went down."

God hates us all, Richard had said. *White, black, yellow, it don't matter, the color....*

"It was an awfully. Nice funeral," said Branden.

"It was," Louis agreed. And Jimmy's former artillery company had not kicked up about a Union man joining them walking the cortege.

"I just hope all those people—" puff, puff, puff "—who turned out for it are going to vote. Though it looked like mostly women." Puff, puff. "Figures."

"Show some respect, man," Louis said. Richmond had simmered one Christmas season with gossip that Martha Branch had discovered her husband with another man's wife seated in his lap.

Branden looked at his watch, chimed it. "And we got. Some shade," he said. "Walking to the graveyard." The businesses along the cortege had rolled their awnings down, though they had closed for the day, and put out water barrels with drinking ladles.

"If election day goes well, we're home again," Louis said. "We'll get a state constitution, and we'll be back in the Union."

"I'm not sure I would call the Union home," Rob said, "but I'll be glad when we're there."

"We're making. An obelisk. For Jimmy. Tall and fine."

"That'll be splendid," Rob said. To Louis: "How are you doing with Parkman?" He had given Louis *The Oregon Trail*.

"Don't tell Jake I've strayed." From the reading list Jake had sent—philosophy—guaranteed to cure the most intractable insomnia.

"We'll have you back in the traces as soon as the Swedenborg comes in."

"And you'll let me know what chapters are required reading and which I can skip."

Legend had it, a book never passed through Rob's hands unread. Besides deep, turgid philosophy, he read travel adventures, advice on household economies, memoirs of lusty nuns, murderous monks, downtrodden workers, slaves, soldiers, and ruined women, dime novels, and even foreign dictionaries, cover to cover: Hindoo, Chinese, Arabian. Thibetan: *As demon-ridden as the savages on our plains,* he'd said, *yet capable of sublimities that your New England preachers can only grasp at.*

"You're a dutiful brother, brother," said Rob, "but you needn't wait for heaven to reap your reward. We'll find something entertaining to salt the porridge. Dumas?"

Louis intoned: "'On the 20th of August, 1672, the city of the Hague, always so lively, so neat, and so trim that one might believe every day to be Sunday…' with its tedium, tedium, tedium."

Rob chuckled. "Not bad, Bonny. *Te Deum*, indeed. I take it your Yankee boys liked it?"

"Even on the twenty-third reading." Louis was secretly pleased with getting off the *Te Deum*, though he had not gotten it, until Rob did. "Jake and I loved it when Papa read it to us in French. *La ville si vivante, si blanche, si coquette….*" A pang of nostalgia seized Louis.

Rob dispelled it. "Your father had an atrocious accent, and so do you."

"What do you know about French accents?"

Branden cut a plug of tobacco, having quit smoking again. "Bonny read it. In school. So clear. You could see. It all." Branden sang, reedy and soft and pure:"*We are the children. Of the dawn. And the dew; We are the. Children of the air. We are the children. Of the fountain; But we are. Above all, the. Children of heaven.*"

Rob bowed his head. Louis clapped Branden's shoulder and praised him and poured out tots of whiskey.

He raised his glass. "To Jimmy Branch."

IT WAS TWO OR SO in the morning when Louis got back to his boardinghouse. He managed the porch steps and the door quietly. Crossing the entry hall, he tripped over something and stumbled, and fell with an almighty crash into an étagère crammed with gewgaws.

"Jesus Christ," he muttered. He dared not move for fear of crushing in the dark whatever trinkets might have survived. He squatted and, feeling around himself, started pushing the shards and things into a heap.

A glimmer. He looked up. A gun. He gaped.

The gun lowered, the lamp opened. It was Ellis, Mrs. Sully's beau. A die-hard Reb, he was none too friendly with Louis.

"By God," Ellis said, "you're lucky I didn't—"

"Josh?" Mrs. Sully's voice quested down the stairs.

Ellis called up, "It's all right, Cynthia. It's the boarder."

A silence. Louis, more sober than before he looked up the barrel of a pistol, guessed it was an embarrassed silence.

"Leave me the lamp," Louis said. "I'll make it right with Mrs. Sully."

"We're engaged," Ellis said.

"Congratulations, man." Louis held out his hand; Ellis hesitated, shook it.

Louis righted the étagère, got a broom and dustpan and made a pile of the wrecked gewgaws. Mrs. Sully, engaged. He would have to move out. Ellis would hardly want to share the house with a man who, in his mind, remained the enemy, begrudged handshake or no.

In the kitchen, he rinsed his face, though he did not bother to heat water. He had planned to take a bath tonight. Sarah, in her cubby, stirred to hug her doll tighter, not one of the pretty porcelains, but a rag dolly in a butternut dress. In his room, Louis hung his clothes on the headboard to air and got in bed. He began to brood over his misspent evening, let it go.

Dogs barked and howled here and there—*la voix de la Man-*

chester, Papa had called it, tongue in cheek. The cool cry of a whip-poor-will came from far away, and farther, a whistle: the coal train to Norfolk.

Valentina might be listening to the same train, if she were awake. The casement doors to her bedroom would be open to breezes from the terrace, her bed filmed with mosquito netting. Bianca could be awake, too, staring into the dark, maybe in a laudanum dream, tearful or dry-eyed. Mrs. Hamilton, for all Louis knew, sat in her armchair looking into the dark treetops, at the stars above the river. Mourning nestled with Wyman, in their family cabin. Jeannie would surely be asleep. And Eva's spirit. Would it linger at the roots of the oak, near the deep cold pond of the old quarry?

Louis's mind roved tenderly over the women and girls of Granite Bluff. The lust of his body was transfigured into a longing to live with them, to be with them, to be for them father, husband, brother, son. For once, he did not allow the futility of his longing to quench it. He let himself float on it, a river and a warm, starry sky, as tears trickled from the corners of his eyes over his temples.

L EADING OUT WITH THE prettiest girl in the place, Louis was
covered with dread. He had not danced since the War, a ball in
Maryland given by a general's wife. Frolicking at Heron's Saloon
or at a bawdy house near the race course hardly counted. He
would be shown up as clumsy, crippled, Jeannie's fresh soft hands
in his rough paws, her feet unwinged by his. Mrs. Hamilton had
remarked, on the ride here, that he looked peaked.

The barn-dance building never had housed animals. It was
a dance hall resembling a barn. People came to it from Manchester and Richmond and Charlottesville to play-act as country
folk, free of city cares. People like Louis, a town-man born and
bred, his Arcadia a riverside quarry. Out here, ripening wheat
and tasseling corn alternated with hilly pastures. The purple
blue mountains drew an undulating horizon. Evening smelled
sweet spicy, not bituminous.

The musicians struck up a reel. It was not too fast, Louis not
the only man limping. Plenty of old men, too. Down the middle,
under the bridge, swing and dosado. He glimpsed Valentina, at
their table, sketching in a portfolio, and nearly missed a step.

However poor a dancer Louis was, Jeannie's eyes sparkled
and a smile stole over her face. Louis encouraged it with a smile

of his own. Tendrils of Jeannie's pale hair sweated to her face and neck as the music wound spritely.

Louis realized he still held Jeannie's hands, the music ended. He let her go, and they joined the other women at their table. His hip did not hurt too badly. Maybe dancing was good for it; maybe, even, he had not looked a lumbering, dancing bear. He felt more gay than he would have expected. Some men cast envious or desiring looks. Jeannie's beauty shone a light in their little group.

"May I look at your drawings, Valentina?" he asked.

She handed the book over with a smile. Sketches of fields and mountains, a hawk soaring, the musicians. Bianca and Jeannie. Himself with Jeannie, her form exquisite next to his rough man-body. Another of his face in profile, oblivious that she observed. His hands, one resting on the table, the other clasping a glass. A stain on his shirt cuff he had not noticed.

Mrs. Hamilton, her face that of a woman who knew herself.

You are the gates of the body, and you are the gates
of the soul.

Masculine pride swelled Louis's chest. He wished to say something like, there is a flaw in your book, Valentina—and she would ask, what is the flaw, Louis?—and he would say, if I could draw, I would fix it by drawing you. He revised the exchange in his mind: *if only I could draw… if I could draw I would perfect your book by….*

He would never utter such sap-headed wit, if it could be considered wit at all.

"Thank heavens, Branden isn't here," Bianca said. "I need a break from him."

Louis knew he should turn the conversation. "These new dances," he began, lamely.

"I'm letting Jeannie dance with you only, Louis," she went on. "I don't want her to get ideas about getting hitched to a planter."

Jeannie kept her gaze steady toward the dance floor. She was remarkably composed, or maybe she simply did not listen to her mother's loose talk. She had danced with some other men, anyway, respectable young men connected with the Termeys. Every conversational gambit Louis tried, inwardly, struck him as inane: how tasteful the decorations, how lovely the evening, how lively the musicians, et cetera, et cetera.

Valentina looked up from her sketchbook. "Bianca, don't tease Louis," she said.

Her smile threw Louis down. Which completed his idiocy. She wore a dress in a sober dark red, with a little dun lace at the collar.

"Will you dance next with me, Valentina?" Louis asked.

He thought to add something like, I am afraid I am not very light on my feet, when the concertina player struck up "Reedy Creek Waltz." As a lover, he could not ask for more than a waltz, but he was not supposed to be a lover. Valentina hesitated, agreed. He might have seen a slight shrug of her shoulders.

Her waist under his hand flexed supple, sweat-damp, firm and corseted, willowy as a young girl's. No child had thickened it. Her hand in his, the skin soft as a rose petal, the grip more substantial than her niece's. The dance lilted. Louis's heart beat sweet and hard. He longed to crush her to himself. He had felt this way when he was young, but never so deliciously, so thoroughly. He wanted to encompass her, and he wanted her to encompass him. To engirth. He shuddered with the want of it, and their eyes met, hers questioning.

Unable and O! all unwilling to look anywhere else but in her eyes, and at her face.

Head, neck, hair, ears, drop and tympan of the ears

The music ended. He lingered; he released her.

"Now me, Louis," Bianca said.

"Give the man a rest," Mrs. Hamilton said.

Bianca sat back, pouting. The musicians took a break, so all was well.

Louis wished that Valentina was his own. He wished it so much, he dared not look at her, save out the corner of his eye. Waiters and people meeting friends crisscrossed the dance floor. Louis's hip began to throb again. It had started on the way, riding in the buggy for so long, then stopped for a while. Bianca ordered a bottle of champagne. "Rudy's paying," she said. His knee hurt, too. He flexed his leg as surreptitiously as he could under the little round table. People came by and chatted.

Louis suddenly wished he were at the house where they were staying the night. He wished for a quiet bed in the soft dark, with the song of crickets and whippoorwills and nightjars. Valentina would turn to him, and they would kiss and make love. He could hardly imagine what it would be like, with a woman he loved the way he loved her. To love completely, with all his body and all his soul. It would be the truest kind of prayer. Was that a blaspheming thought?

The marriage bond was sacred, and not his to have with Valentina Termey. Not theirs, the night, a quiet bed in the soft dark, crickets and whippoorwills and nightjars.

Valentina let Jeannie have a glass of champagne. They all clinked glasses. Bianca called it shoddy fizz, but Louis liked its sweet bubbliness. He drank a second glass, for his thirst, and to be merry. Tipsy, he got up to dance again, with Bianca.

A polka certainly made of him a dancing bear, his good leg heavy, his bad leg dragging, dragging where he should have leapt. Bianca was not much better. They nearly held each other up, laughing in spite of it all. They came back to another bottle of champagne, and Louis drank off a couple more glasses. It was time to celebrate. Virginia had voted in a state Constitution, drawing that much closer to reentering the Union. It was a night for exuberance.

Louis drank another glass to his hopeless, hopeless dream of love.

He danced again with Jeannie. He kissed her on the cheek when she and Valentina and Mrs. Hamilton said they would leave, the Termey friends having offered them a ride to the house. The carriage full, Louis said he would see Bianca back. Maybe they would walk, it was not far. She would walk, he would limp. Jeannie's cheek plumped warm with her smile. Eyes shining, her face all pink and merry and wistful, the poor girl hardly looked ready for a quiet ride to sleep. Louis impulsively, idiotically hugged her.

"Oh, Louis," Bianca said as they sat, the two of them, at the little round table. "I like you when you're drunk."

"Let me drink some lemonade, if you please," Louis said to the waiter. He added to Bianca, "No more French wine."

"I like you drunk."

"Enough." One more drink, and the room would spin. He was overheated, his head full of noise. "Bianca, will you take the night air with me?"

She grew very still.

Then she said, "All right."

The dark soothed, away from the hectic conversation, lanterns, relentless music, smoke. Louis's ears had rung for hours, after his first battle, and his hearing never went back to what it used to be. He preferred simple music, now, the concertina, or a piano maybe with a violin or flute or, better, with a woman's or a man's voice.

The ground held the sun even this long after day; the grass exhaled warmth. The moist air, clean and yet charged with life, poured into Louis. Bianca put her arm through his. They went toward a pond, a spill of moonlight. It was a place to go.

The pond lay farther away than Louis had thought. Dew soaked through his boots. His hip held up. The music from the noisy barn was subsumed by crickets. A cow lowed. Stars and moon and sky filled each other, white and velvet dark. Some believed each star courted countless worlds.

"Palladino thought you were Eva's father," Bianca said. They reached the glimmering pond.

"I know."

"He saw the true truth," Bianca said. "You carried her. You're the only man who's mourned my baby girl. No, Branden has. He has, truly."

She bowed her head. "Rudy won't divorce me." She sniffed and childlike wiped her nose with the back of her hand. "I don't want him to."

Louis supposed she should settle things with her husband one way or another, such things presumably easier in Chicago than in Virginia. Anyway, divorce, marriage—they had nothing to do with Bianca Gutman's lament.

"Why shouldn't we rearrange the scenes?" Bianca spoke so softly, Louis bent to her, to hear. "You be Eva's father. Why not?" Tears tracked her face in the starlight. "Louis, when will the grief end?"

They kissed, her mouth salty. They took off every piece of their clothing. Louis touched her breasts and belly with his lips and hands. He put his coat under her head, and she spread her dress under them.

He climaxed almost as soon as he was inside her, the hot rush of it so intense, tears stung his eyes. He was not sure how loud they had been. They rested, then bathed in the pond.

He should not have done this. She sat up, her hands over her breasts. He took her hands away and kissed her, and they lay down again. At her taste his scruples withered, as they had the moment he tasted her tears. They made love again, slower this time, and the paroxysm of her body, her panting soft cry, melted him.

They bathed and let themselves dry. Louis could have made love with her again, but his body not as eager, the moral argument raised itself. Yet he suffered no remorse. He should have. He felt clean and happy. He could have laughed were Bianca not so solemn. She helped him dress, and he helped her. They brushed each other's dew-soaked clothes, though it was hopeless to hide the red dirt and grass stains.

Hand in hand, they walked the road to the house, to their separate beds. There were many words they did not say. Louis's trance of satiation entwined with a rising sense of the sins he had just committed. His hip hurt badly, and he tried not to limp.

He stopped and turned, and put his hands on either side of her face, tear-wet again. "I'm sorry, Bianca. I have done wrong to you." He compounded the wrong by kissing her.

"No." Her voice tear-laced. "It's…. I'm married, you see."

Louis clasped her to himself. Here under the warm, pure stars, in the warmth and give of their bodies, he could not be truly sorry, even as he dreaded the sleepless guilt that surely lay ahead, for himself and especially for her. He dreaded the reckoning he would have with himself about what it meant to have made love with a married woman, the sister of the woman he loved.

WE HAD US A fun time this Saturday, didn't we, Mr. Bondurant?"

It was the first time Mrs. Hamilton had ever returned his
greeting, if her words could be considered a response to his,
"Good day, Mrs. Hamilton." She sat, as usual, in the wing chair
in the studio, looking into the sky over the quarry and the river.

"Yes, ma'am, it certainly was a fun time." Papa had taught
him a trick: if you feel yourself blushing, concentrate on your
feet. Louis concentrated on his feet. Mrs. Hamilton moved her
feet aside, and he sat on the footstool.

"I don't regret it a bit." Mrs. Hamilton's faded eyes looked
over Louis's flushed face, and her mouth twitched. "Not a bit."

*Cheeks, temples, forehead, chin, throat, back of the
neck, neck-slue*

Withered cheeks, blue-veined temples, the throat sinewed
and sagging, and the traces that long-ago bliss had left upon
her face.

He said what she seemed to expect him to say: "Nor do I,
Mrs. Hamilton."

"It made it all match, didn't it?" she said.

Louis lacked both the courage and the conviction to believe he understood her, to say, yes, coming together with the woman made it all match. Dew and rough grass, the touch and taste of her, and all the shards of this world become like pure white stars spilled into darkness by the hand of a good and loving Creator.

Mrs. Hamilton stirred her feet. Louis went to sit in the Italian chair. His eyes roamed the studio, its pale walls, its familiar curiosities: a statue of a naked man astride a horse which used to be in Maurice Termey's study and embarrassed Louis in Valentina's presence, a heap of small, bleached bones with a tiny bird skull perched atop, a bunch of rushes in a big vase decorated with fiercely grinning salamanders.

The morning's ride back to town, after the barn dance, had been subdued. Disappointed to leave their idyll behind, pensive, out of words, hung-over, sin-guilty. Bianca had redonned her mourning frock. Louis had spent the dawn scrubbing his suit, scrubbing the brick-red dirt of Albemarle deeper into his suit. That and the grass stains and creases and damp made it look as if he had been on campaign. Jeannie dozed against Bianca part of the way. And yet, no one had been out of sorts. They smiled at each other and complained about the rough road, and parted with jaunty waves.

In the three days since, Louis had lived distractedly. Distractedly he had slept and worked and eaten. Journeying, morning and evening, between Heron's stables and the quarry stables, he spun in his mind what he had done. It was completely wrong. Or it had elements of virtue. Or it was neither right nor wrong. He prodded guilt and could not wake it. He preferred to relive the sex, with variations. Raw hunger for Bianca wove into his fibers. It matched. It was not mere lust, or it was. He certainly loved Bianca Gutman dearly. He was fairly sure he was not in love with her.

Valentina came through the passage door, and Louis stood.

His eyes hurt as if at the sun, and his throat felt salty. He blushed, which made him blush all the more, and he simply did not want to concentrate on his feet. Valentina took her seat on the couch and absorbed herself in pouring the coffee, in putting a pastry on a plate. Louis sat again, belatedly. He prayed, not for the first time, that Bianca had not told her. He gathered composure to recite the quarry report. She took it in with equanimity. Bianca must not have told her.

She did not know about the lawsuit, either. Kohen had advised him not to bring it up, and he took the advice gladly, coward that he was. He had signed and returned Kohen's dense, arcane papers little understood. He could only hope his relationship with the lawyer was, indeed, unclouded as a fresh summer morning, except that he had not divulged the note he had found on his door.

He checked his pocket watch against the wall clock. "Soon." She smiled. They drank coffee. "I began a painting of Albemarle," Valentina said. "A landscape with a pond."

He veered from the subject of her painting a pond in Albemarle, pointing to a painting near the naked horseman. "The scene with the artillery carriage is striking with the white cottage in the background."

"That's the Dunker Church at Sharpsburg," Valentina sucked her lower lip in between her teeth, and pushed it out; it was a little way she had. "Not as you saw it."

"No, I didn't fight at Sharpsburg. I heard it was very terrible indeed." It was where Branden had lost his balance, Rob had told Louis, screaming and weeping in a gore-strewn cornfield, not far from where old John Brown started it all.

"Did you paint it from a description?" he asked.

"No, I used a photograph by Mr. Mathew Brady. Maurice got it somehow."

"I think I know the one. I saw it in a gallery, up in Alexandria."

"It originally … the photo … there were dead soldiers. And the church all torn with bullets." She added, "I did not mean to…."

"No, it's good, Valentina." He met her eyes. The grass flourishing where blood had soaked the dirt. "It's a better way to see things."

She had changed Brady's photograph. Louis had changed her painting back, in his mind, seeing the field as Brady had, maybe as Branden had. Was her omission wrong, or was his vision a violation of her work? When Wyman made the furniture for the terrace at the quarry, the chairs were very handsome to look at, but sitting in them was like sitting in crates. Like Valentina's Italian armchair. Louis told him he must make them more accommodating. Wyman responded, *Mr. Bondurant, you are violating my artistic vision.* It was not so much one of his men, and a colored man, too, talking back—the statement itself astonished. Louis had never again seen Wyman in the same light. Wyman changed the chairs. Louis thought the "artist" was pleased with the results, only unwilling to admit it.

The clock wound up to strike. Louis quickly moved his and Valentina's coffee cups so the rims nearly touched. "I told Llewellyn three o'clock."

She gazed at the cups together, then met his eyes. Her eyes golden, her skin lightly tanned, the cheeks rough. Winter had chapped her lips, moist warm spring had smoothed them. She looked away. Louis cleared his throat.

He sensed the charge—in his feet, in his gut, he did not know. A moment later, the actual blast, a half mile or so away, tingled the cups against one another. The clock struck. Louis and Valentina smiled at each other like children in wonder.

Within there runs blood,
The same old blood!
The same red-running blood!
There swells and jets a heart—there all passions, de-
*   sires, reachings, aspirations*

His heart surged like a hound at a hare. Without a thought

to stop himself, he leaned to her and caught her hands and held them. She followed him, drawing so near her breath touched his face—she eased herself free, smiled, went to fiddle with some paint jars. Louis sat back, wordless.

He had made love with her sister. *What a fix you got. Yourself into. Bonny*, Branden would say. But he had not told Branden. He could fall back on a gentleman's honor, not tattling on a lady, and Branden would feel betrayed, or he would not. For all of his talk and his squiring Bianca about town, he could not seriously be courting her. She could not give her whole self to Branden, for he could no longer give physical love, he had confessed. Consumption had sapped his vital energies.

Poor Branden. Poor man. That he could not have that.

Louis was lost, all a-swim in love and its physical joys, and pity for his best friend, and a salt of shame for taking Valentina's hands and trying to draw her, too, to his body. She stood looking out the casement doors, her hand on the back of Mrs. Hamilton's chair. Louis found that he had risen, reflexively.

Valentina turned back to him. "Let me tell Bianca and Jeannie you're here. They'll want to see you." She left and came back a few minutes later with her sister and niece.

Bianca looked as if she had been asleep, her hair bundled lopsided atop her head. Jeannie was fresh and neat.

"I'm indisposed," Bianca said. She and Valentina sat on the couch. "The curse."

Jeannie, who had not yet sat, flushed bright red and spun toward the casement doors.

"Oh, Bianca," Valentina laughed.

Louis, still standing, smoothed his mustache. What a lot of women he was in with! Having a shy father, he had learned about the female anatomy from his chums and from a woman he had relations with before the War. The first time he saw blood, he thought he had hurt her. He had sought her, when he came back to Manchester, to see if she needed provisions. Her brother, a roller at Tredegar, said she had moved up to Washington.

Bianca had just let him know she was not with child. Though he had not thought of it—maybe his guilt distracted—he was relieved; yet it seemed impossible: so much flow and no issue.

Valentina certainly did not know about them.

Jeannie wore one of the costumes, a robelike frock in dark purple-blue. It deepened her eyes to violet-blue; her hair rich, pale, silken against it. But she should have been in the latest fashion. She should have been attending balls, playing gentle lawn games with other young women and young men, leaving calling cards about town. Or would she? Her father, Union. At least, she should not be stealing out to barn dances in Albemarle. Louis loitered awkwardly. Finally Jeannie sat. Louis sat.

He did not know what to say, to all of the women together. If he knew something about Jeannie, at least, but he did not. Needlework, painting china, drawing. Singing. A dance master. He had no idea what any of them did, up here in the Magic Castle, as Branden called it, except that Valentina painted and Jeannie posed for her. He feared Bianca would mock him, if he ventured a comment about art. He might have tried books, but the library through which he passed each time he visited was a dead place, untouched except by Mourning's duster. The Whitman book lived outside it.

"Did you feel the explosion at the quarry?" he asked Jeannie.

She nodded. "It tickled my feet." She added, "I miss the animals."

It took Louis a moment to figure that she meant the little colorful animals of glass from Italy. Bianca sighed and leaned against Valentina, and Valentina held her hand. Beauty. He wished that Jeannie would sit with them so that he might gaze at them, all three together.

"Maybe we can make a corral for them," he said. "We'll give

it a soft floor, so they might not be broken if they tumble about."
He wished he had not said it, Eva having tumbled and broken.

Bianca sat up again, touched her hair. "She's not a child, you
know, Louis," she said.

Louis smiled, swallowed, nodded. He thought to say something gallant: *not a child but a lovely young woman.*

He stood. "I had best be getting on, ladies."

"Will you see Mr. Bondurant out, Jeannie?" Valentina said.

The entry hall, the empty curio cabinet, the bare walls.

"I had a very nice time dancing with you," Jeannie said,
handing Louis his hat from the pier table.

"And I with you, Miss Gutman."

She stepped to him. Her eyes downcast, she put a hand to
his chest, over his heart.

Louis stood still, as if her touch were a butterfly he must
not frighten off. He might have held his breath. The charge of
her light touch penetrated his shirt and undervest, his skin, his
breastbone, his heart.

She released him, and went down the passage, into a room,
and shut the door.

Curled tight to each other, slippery with sweat. Louis tasted the back of Bianca's neck. He spread his hand over her breast. She sighed and turned. He moistened his lips in her armpit. Her hair fell over his shoulder and pressed wet to the skin of his back.

"Don't fall in love with me, Louis." She said it each time they made love, these weeks since the pondside in Albemarle. At an abandoned house toward Chester. On a blanket in the woods. At a friend's house. In a barn.

Here, in her bed, in the middle of the night. He had sneaked in by the terrace. A crowd of bottles on the night table, lady's underclothes all over.

Louis took up his bandana from the floor and pressed it between her legs, so it was wet. "Now you'll be with me all day."

She took the bandana from him and smelled it. "Phew." Her laugh started brash, ended bashful.

"I love you," he said. "I love you, lady."

"No, no, Louis, don't say that." She twisted out of his embrace to face him. She put a hand to his face. "Please. Don't."

They touched each other's faces. The form of her appeared in soft gray, the world coming out of the dawn. Louis ran his index finger along her lips. He outlined them and filled them in, and pinched her lower lip between finger and thumb, and she gave a moan. He pressed her to himself, he came into her. He was learning to savor each moment of white oblivion. Each moment that drove away the reality of what they were doing.

"This is coming to an end," she said.

The window too bold, light growing. "Yes," he said, "I'd better go."

"Louis."

He kissed her mouth.

She broke away and turned her face toward the window. "I don't think Valentina knows about us."

Louis did not want Valentina to know about them. Therefore, he had decided she did not, and put it out of his mind. He lay back, his arm along his brow. "That's fine with me."

"She probably wouldn't mind." Bianca shrugged. "Well, I don't know."

"What about your daughter?" He did not want to talk about Valentina, while lying next to her sister. He did not want to talk about Jeannie, either.

"Jeannie?" Bianca said. "You mean, does she know about us two? No. Stratton wants to marry her, you know."

"You must take care of her." He was not sure if he meant, you must not let her marry Stratton. But Jeannie must marry, must she not? He could not see her on the shelf the rest of her life, living with her mother or aunt. She had time. She was seventeen. No one would count his own years against him. Men had all the time in the world. If he won his lawsuit, he would have something to offer and no-one to offer it to.

She turned her face away again. He did not like her hardening, whenever Jeannie came up. She turned back softened, her lips softened and downturned. "Would you take me to where Eva fell, Louis? Take me there."

He began to gather her, she gently pushed him away.

"Take me there now," she said. "Please. Can we go there?"

"It'll be all overrun with poison ivy and snakes."

"Please."

"Bianca."

"Please."

They stopped at the stables and Louis got a rake and a hoe and a hand scythe. Valentina's room was on the other side of the house, out of sight of the two lovers walking down her driveway in the chatter of birds.

Once upon a time, a man looked at a woman and fell in love. She painted, how well or not, the man could not say. They had the same favorite Walt Whitman poem. Alas, she was married. Her husband, absent, trusted her and the man he had hired to tend his stone quarry. She must worry about her husband being so far away, over an ocean, inconceivably far, to Louis. She had let Louis hold her hands; she had let him look into her face. They had danced the "Reedy Creek Waltz." She was full of mystery. Or she was what many women had been, what many still were: a wife awaiting her husband's return. Louis had to admit, his epic love for her waned some, in her sister's embrace.

At the edge of the quarry access road, he handed Bianca the hoe. "Use this against a snake, if you see one."

She smiled. He went on, serious, "Keep your skirts close. Don't let them brush the poison ivy." He pointed out some specimens, in case she did not know what it was.

They went off the road. He scythed. Bianca carried her skirts bundled up. Past the border of clearing and forest, deeper in, poison ivy did not grow. No snakes, only one of the little black, red-spotted salamanders that haunted the muddy, spring-fed pools. Louis and Jake had captured a salamander as a pet, near Netherwood Quarry. Papa made them carry it back to its dank habitat. *He cannot live away from his home.* That truth had recurred to Louis, and haunted him, on the train north to enlist Union.

Louis stopped at the edge of the old quarry pond. The dark

water would be warm at its surface, chill in its depths. Bianca slowly let her skirts down.

Up the cliff, the beech tree that brained the child, the jutting rock that probably broke her back. Here, the ancient oak. Louis scythed the weeds at its roots, and took the rake from Bianca and cleaned. He cut wild grape and honeysuckle with his pocketknife and twined them into a wreath he handed Bianca.

She touched him, as she had on the way to Palladino's statue, and stepped forward and laid the flowered circle on the scythe-stubbled bracken. The silence filled with songbirds and the ruffle of small creatures in the leaves, and the chatter and bickering of jays and squirrels.

It had been winter silent, the Sunday morning, back in January, when Eva fell. He had closed her eyes reflexively. He had done so, many times in his life, closed the eyes of the dead.

"Jeannie was watching her," Bianca said. "Supposed to be watching her."

That hardness, and the memory of Jeannie's hand pressed like a wound upon Louis's heart. "Do you hold that against her?"

She took Louis's hand, her head bowed. "If she had been watching better.... " Playing with his fingers.

"Bianca."

"God forgive me. It's all my fault. I'm not a fit mother."

"No, darling, it was an accident. No one to blame. And you're a good mother. Look at Jeannie. And Eva was a sweet little girl."

Bianca kissed Louis's hand. "Thank you for bringing me here."

They returned to the road. The younger house maid, carrying a slop pail, pursed her lips in a way that could have been said to be a smile.

"I can't stand that one," Bianca said, not quietly enough. "Though God knows, it's not her fault."

Not her fault? Louis almost asked, then realized: not her fault she was the offspring of Bianca's father.

And the maid had seen them—they had been seen together, at dawn. He would have to make a story. He could say he had promised to bring Bianca to the spot where Eva fell before he went to work. It would have to do, though the lie of it soiled the truth.

A N ELABORATELY WROUGHT SILVER object, about hand-tall and resembling a miniature covered chalice, sat atop the cubbies of Kohen's desk. If it held liquid, and tipped over, the papers on the desk would be ruined. A pudgy young man Kohen introduced as his nephew slouched at the usually unoccupied desk. He must be the one Kohen had mentioned, his brother's son, whom he hoped to send to the University of Virginia. Louis had wondered, to himself, would they take Jews. Louis's fees would help pay. The room had the air of a broken off quarrel.

Louis drank coffee and took a pastry, though his fatigue and the intense heat, even in late afternoon, left little appetite. Dallying with a woman all night, fighting stone all day: hard work. Though he had tried to clean up before leaving the quarry, his clothes and hair were dusty, and wilted from a light, brief rain on his way.

Kohen looked over his face as if to select a topic from it in the same way Louis had selected the pastry with pink icing.

"Is the incident with the block cleared up?" he asked.

"I don't have investigators underfoot any more," Louis said. "And I have not had to hire a new man to rig the derrick."

The office had its dust—motes of paper, not stone, floating in the light of the tall windows.

"To avoid an appearance of culpability, I take it."

Louis shrugged. He agreed, but he was not sure how much he wanted to get into it, with Kohen.

God smiteth the man who raises against his kinsman.

Kohen shuffled through the papers on his desk. Louis drank the rest of his coffee, poured another cup. He had wanted to hop the quarry train to Manchester and walk the rest of the way here, leaving Nella at the quarry overnight, but the engineer had come up with a new rule: only railroad employees could ride the flatcars. God smiteth, indeed. The long plodding ride in the heat had flattened both him and Nella, and fostered a good long brood as to whether the new rule was his cousin's set up against him, or Engineer West's own fancy.

Kohen pulled out a folder, and was about to speak when the nephew got up. "I'll go fetch the mail." He took a piece of cake and left.

"*Ab incunabulis,*" Kohen said. After Louis worked out the Latin—*from the cradle*—he took it to refer to either the boy's bulk or his lack of industry.

"*Luventus ventus,*" Louis ventured. *Youth is like the wind,* so he hoped. The *vent*'s could be dangerous, the sober proverbs easily supplanted by schoolboy scatology.

Kohen's face gentled into an unexpectedly warm smile. "Very true, very true." He patted the folder. "So, to your case. Let us lay out what we know, and together we'll see what picture we can make."

The silver vessel, if it was that, struck Louis as both fanciful and purposeful, its use a mystery.

"Before the War," Kohen said, "the now-defunct Deep Rock Granite Company, shares of which your father bought, bid on a large Federal project, a building in Washington, D.C."

"That's correct. And it looked like a sure thing. It is what made the loan collateral—as my father saw it—acceptable. He was no fool. He was gentle and honest, not foolish. Or maybe he was foolish, if foolish is to trust one's own nephew."

Kohen gave a shrug both philosophical and deeply cynical. "Why did Deep Rock not win the contract, do you think?"

Louis had pondered it many a time. "It could be for any number of reasons. Cost is obvious enough."

"It was not cost," Kohen said. "A colleague of mine in Washington examined the bids. What other reasons?"

"The kind of granite required. Yet Mede's stone—the quarry that got the contract—is much the same as ours. I've always thought that someone at Mede may have had influence in Washington."

"With the architect, do you mean?" Kohen wrote *Meade* on a piece of paper.

"Mede, m-e-d-e."

"M-e-d-e it shall be." The a was crossed out. "Thank you."

"It is the architect, generally, who chooses the stone for a building. The engineer and the client—in this case, a Federal department—have a say, too."

Architect? Engineer? joined *Mede* on the paper.

The sun came out again, evening slanting, strong enough to make steam of what little rain had fallen. Nella, hitched outside, shifted her feet, stuck her nose in the trough and blew water everywhere. Poor girl. The ride home would be just as miserable as the ride here.

"By the way," Kohen said, "may I ask, what was your father's occupation?"

"Papa? He was a customs clerk for the Commonwealth. And when he went bankrupt, they turned him out, saying he was unreliable. Of course, they never completely trusted him. He emancipated two slaves, his own inheritance from his father." It was far more than the question needed.

"I'm very sorry."

"We got by, sir. We did all right in the end."

Louis's eyes went to the object again, not to dwell on his father's ruin. A little lion, rearing up, stood upon the peak of the cover, which resembled a bell tower.

"Mr. Bondurant, I'm determined to win this case for you. Please pardon me if my probing is painful."

Louis looked back at Kohen. "Don't worry, please, Mr. Kohen. I have been probed far more painfully with lancet and what have you. The surgeon deemed it necessary, and here I am today, alive and more or less useful." Coming out of the ether, he had never been so sick in his life, nor felt such pain. His stomach lurched at the mere memory.

"I have thought sometimes.... " Kohen broke off with an embarrassed smile. It was the first time Louis had seen him discomfited. He might have been about to refer to his club foot, if it could be remedied by surgery. He cleared his throat.

"So, to continue with lancet and what have you," he said. "Would you tell me the names of any Federal agent whom you have met in connection with the quarry? The present quarry company and the old."

"I don't know any from the old company. Felix Anderson is the architect for the new project." He watched as Kohen added *Felix Anderson* to the list. "You understand, I do not negotiate with the quarry's customers."

"And Dr. Stratton?"

"Dr. Stratton?"

"He was in the quarry on the day of the tragedy," Kohen said, "the day of the unfortunate child's death. Mr. and Mrs. Anderson, you, poor Mrs. Gutman, of Chicago, Mrs. Termey, and Dr. Stratton."

Ice fringing the river, and the benches death-cold. Eva fell, yet the earth continued to make its circuit around the sun; this morning, in this office and all the others this side of the street, people would have closed the blinds against the heat, and opened them again this afternoon.

"That's correct."

Kohen must have searched, after Louis's visit to him, through old newspapers and reread the story. Or he had an impressive memory.

"Is Dr. Stratton connected in some way with the quarry company?" Kohen asked.

"The doctor was there as a friend of the Termeys," Louis said. "He and Maurice Termey were classmates at Yale College."

"Pardon me for reminding you that this information, including what questions I ask, must be kept strictly between the two of us. As we know, the adversary can be very wily. We hardly would like to give him—or them—a chance to outwit us."

"Of course not," Louis said.

"I take it your cousin has not communicated with you about our suit."

"Not a word." True enough, unless the note counted. If the note was from him.

"You'll let me know if he does, won't you?"

"Of course."

Louis ran his eyes again over the object: a hexagonal filigree container, with the lion on top, the vessel held up by three curving legs—one with an arabesque broken, he saw now.

"Now. Mr. Poindexter and Dr. Stratton. Have they ever done business together, do you know?"

Uneasiness settled on Louis's neck and shoulders and head. "You must realize that I'm quite ignorant about... well, about everything except stone."

"Rest assured that to most citizens, the ways of business and the law are as obscure as the ways of the Lord. I would not have work, otherwise."

"Am I to believe that Dr. Stratton is involved in all this?"

"He has a proximity to the events. And he is from Washington, DC."

"He was a Union surgeon up there, during the War."

"Was he?" Kohen said. "Was he now. Who knows but that he laid his hands upon my poor brother."

As I see through a mist, one with inexpressible completeness and beauty

"God bless the hands that comfort," Louis said.

Kohen replied in an exotic tongue, Hebrew, probably. He looked weary, too. "We will consider Doctor Stratton merely interesting, for the time being, if that is all right with you."

"It is all right with me."

Kohen smiled. "Which leaves us free to examine the object that has arrested your attention."

Louis laughed. "I am curious about it."

Kohen picked it up and held it balanced on his palm. "This is a besamim, a spice container, not for the kitchen but for Jewish ritual. I'm sending it to a silversmith for repair. We have not been very observant in my family, for years. Lately we're thinking of going back to the old ways, our old Jewish traditions."

Kohen spoke of the Jewish religion, yet Louis had a curious sense of knowing more than he did, or understanding more. Or Kohen was confused, between the old traditions and the less defined habits he had slipped into. He might not know the impossibility of going back to the old ways. But that sad news, a man could deliver only to himself.

"Not Orthodox, you understand," Kohen said.

"Orthodox?"

"The Orthodox Jews hew more exactly to the ancient laws. We Reformed allow modern life quite a bit more sway in our lives."

"And the spice container, if I may ask?" Louis asked. "The— the bessmen...."

"The besamim. It's the one thing left, that my parents brought over from Germany." Kohen tilted his head, as if the object were as exotic to him as it was to Louis. "The Fire took everything…. "

The outside door opened. Louis's back was turned; he guessed it was the nephew. Kohen spoke sharply in what sounded like German. The young man clumped up the stairs without answering. A door opening; children's voices, the young man; onions and fish cooking; the door shut. Kohen sighed and turned the silver object in his hands.

"We use the besamim at the end of our Sabbath," he said, "when we leave the sacred to enter once again into the mundane. The aroma comforts the soul, for she is sad as she departs from … from her home, you could say."

The evening around them was no Sabbath, but softly blue and quiet. Outside, the curls of vapor on the cobbles glowed in the lowering sun. Kohen chanted in what must have been Hebrew. He opened the vessel, lifted it to his face, and inhaled. He proffered it. Louis took the besamim, looked inside, glanced at Kohen, who nodded. Louis brought the empty vessel close to himself and closed his eyes. He breathed in.

A faded, far aroma of dried lemon peel, and cloves, and bitterness.

The two men walked together into the entry hall. It was beautiful for all that it was a black and white tiled floor, mahogany doors, plain-papered walls, and a thin-carpeted stairway.

Iｎ ｔｈｅ ｆｏｙｅｒ ｏｆ the Termey's house, on the day of the base
ball game, Mourning put a hand to Louis's arm—her other
hand holding his hat—shook her head and pursed her lips; her
fingers tightened. He hardly had time to take in her warning—of
what?—and piano music—when she opened the parlor door.

The music stopped. Louis's hands iced and his heart hammered hard and slow, his breath stolen. A flaxen-haired man
rose from the piano and stepped, smiling, toward him. Louis
responded to the introduction. He had never seen Rudy Gutman
in life, but plainly this was Jeannie Gutman's father: the fine
blond head, the blue eyes. Gutman spoke in a Western twang
with a Germanish touch.

No one seemed to notice anything except, maybe—of course,
Mrs. Hamilton. And Mourning. It might not be obvious to
everyone else, then, that Romeo had not been braced for this.
Louis did not give a damn, they could all go to hell. Though for
Valentina and Jeannie, he made an effort to be normal.

Gutman lit a cigar and scrutinized Louis with the friendliest
expression

Don't love me, Louis, while taking his love, and her husband on the way. She had taught him the word in Italian. *Amore.* To make love. *Fare all'amore.*

They bundled into a barouche. Wyman's son Ezra secured the awning, climbed up to the driver's seat. Louis had offered to squire the ladies to the baseball game. Why did Bianca not send a message that Gutman was there to do the job? Mrs. Hamilton insisted on sitting between Gutman and Louis; the other women sat across from them. Bianca kept her face to the passing scene. Jeannie smiled shyly.

Mrs. Hamilton took Louis's hand and held it tight.

The curious sympathy one feels, when feeling with the
hand the naked meat of the body

Louis put his other hand over hers, grateful for her love, for the strength of her elderly hand. Long ago, her husband and their two little children died, all at once, of scarlet fever.

Stratton's house, off Westham Road, was new, of rusticated granite taken from the property's own little quarry.

"It looks like a castle!" Jeannie said. "Remember, Daddy, the castles in Germany?"

A beautiful girl whose debut was a barn dance, whose social round was a baseball game of working men at a carpetbagger's mansion. No beaux for her, unless Stratton counted. Louis had hardly improved her situation, dallying with her mother.

"Good job, Ezra," Louis said to the driver before climbing down. "I'll be sure and tell your daddy." Wyman had mentioned it would be his son's first "big time" driving, and would Mr. Bonny kindly keep a watch on him.

"Thank you, sir."

Louis helped Mrs. Hamilton and Jeannie disembark, Gutman handing down the sisters. He and Gutman would have to settle things at some point. Rage and gloom shook his heart. He tried to keep it from his face. More likely, he would not have the chance to settle anything. Gutman would simply resume his marriage where he had left off. Free Love, and Eva under the earth. Louis had nothing to say about it. An adulterer could hardly take up a point of honor.

"If you'll excuse me, ladies and gentlemen," Louis said, "I shall join my ball club."

The game was laid out on a mowed and raked field not far from the house. A diamond, Daniels called the four bases and the paths between them, grass shaved down to the ground. The dirt here was yellowish and hard-packed, and studded with smooth rocks that the geological survey called river cobbles. The spectators, most of them women and children, occupied several islands of quilts, past center outfield.

"Will they be all right?" Louis said to Daniels. "What if someone hits the ball out there?"

"They'll be safe from the Quarry Quarrelers," Daniels said. "You can count on that."

O'Keefe had his Spikers limbering up beside the field, winding their arms and shaking their legs like fly-bitten horses. Daniels had tried to talk the Quarrelers into the Knickerbocker-style pants, and been scoffed down. The pants looked different, though, on the Spitfire Spikers strutting around the field, and with ridiculous red stockings, and brogans. The Quarrelers ranged from Sunday best to work clothes, from moccasins, to brogans, to boots, to bare feet. The thing with the uniforms, though, the main thing, was that the Spikers could go half-clad—no ties, vests, coats—and the ladies looking on. Louis began to shed his coat, glimpsed Valentina dandling a baby, shrugged his coat back up. He would die of heat, that was all.

O'Keefe came up, looking cool. "Ready to be thrashed, Mr. Bondurant? Or do I say, Mr. Bonny?"

"It's a shame we'll mess up those pretty uniforms of yours," was Louis's feeble rejoinder. The Quarrelers were limbering up, too: Kinny clubbing a tree with the bat; Jopple and Llewellyn throwing and missing a ball; Southeby and Wyman emptying a jug by turns.

O'Keefe followed his gaze with a comfortable laugh. "Aw, don't you worry about our uniforms."

Jopple threw the ball straight, and Llewellyn caught it, dropped it.

Gutman jogged up smiling, his coat off, his sleeves rolled up to his elbows. "I'll play for the Quarrelers, if I may."

O'Keefe's eyes flicked him up and down. "No, sir," he said. "Sorry, it's quarry men against railroad—"

"No, we're a man short," Louis cut in. Roberts the derrick rigger had quit last week, an uncle having gotten him a job at Tredegar's. *It is but a few steps down, sir, and I know how the wind is blowing.* And so, a good, conscientious man left his employ with no more than a handshake and well-wishes. The Quarrelers had planned to fill in with Tristan, a hernia-riddled grouter who was the only other quarry man who had attended practice, but O'Keefe must have seen something good in Gutman.

"Mr. Gutman is brother-in-law to the owner of the quarry," Louis said. "That makes him a quarry man." Daniels chimed in arcane rules. O'Keefe was forced to give in, with the threat that he would "look it up" later.

"I'll go last," Gutman said. "I'm just an interloper, after all." He smiled at Louis, showing a wealth of teeth.

Louis nodded with a forced smile back. An urge to pound the man with, say, the baseball bat, came and mostly went. Daniels put Gutman last—in the white part of the lineup. Wyman and the two grouters had to go after, which was a shame because certainly Llewellyn and Jopple should have been kept off the plate as long as possible. Louis, too, for that matter.

Daniels did not want Louis up first. *We need a man who can actually run.* The men had insisted: *Mr. Bonny goes first.* Finch followed; he was a surprisingly strong and consistent hitter and a decent runner. It was maybe telling that Finch, their best all around player save Whittington and Wyman, had a maimed right hand.

The Quarrelers had won—or lost—the coin toss and got the top of the inning. Louis was the very first man to face the diamond, and the spectators. He had been a stickball star and was not too bad with a proper bat. It was running he dreaded. And missing the ball altogether, out of nerves. There was that. He gripped the bat then loosened up, remembering Daniels' sound advice not to choke it. A nightmare image flitted through his mind: forgetting to drop the bat and running to first base clutching it, the women giggling and Gutman grinning with his teeth. Of course, Louis had to hit the ball for that to happen. He glared at the pitcher.

The first throw looked good, looked perfect, went inside—*strike!* Louis licked his lips, took a breath and squared off again with the weedy looking youth who did not look fit to throw a bone to a dog. And instead of throwing a straight honest pitch, he coiled and twisted like a snake—*strike!* A groan from the Quarrelers, and Llewellyn scolding to give the boss a chance. A loyal kinsman. Louis held up his hand for a halt. The pitcher uncoiled himself, smacking his palm with the ball while Louis threw his coat to Whittington. There. They assumed positions: snake versus over-heated, half-crippled man.

Louis could hardly believe the crack of the bat, as he chugged along toward first. He made it, pouring more sweat than he thought he had in him. He became aware of Llewellyn screaming for him to keep running, and the ladies cheering. He took a few steps out, jumped back, the shortstop's throw smacking into the first baseman's hand, a lucky moment too late. Louis wobbled between humiliation and pride. Hard and bouncy to left field, his hit could have been a double. He could have been on second base right now. He needed to concentrate on the game, not on how the ladies were taking it. He wished Llewellyn would shut it. One of Stratton's servants handed Louis a dipper.

His hurry drinking it down was wasted. Finch hit a lovely fly—*out!* Whittington got Louis to second. Jopple at bat: one strike, a foul that sent the Spikers' bench scrambling for cover, strike three—*out!* Billie managed to drive one inside the foul line. Louis got tagged out at third. Gutman never made it to bat.

At the bottom of the first, Quarrelers: 0.

The Quarrelers' defense, like the offense, was hobbled by social considerations. Wyman should have been pitcher, but the pitcher must be white, so it was Finch. The black men must play outfield. Kinny was put in right field—the least likely place for a ball to go—with Wyman center, to watch over him, and Southeby left field. That meant putting Llewellyn on second base and Jopple on third. Whittington was shortstop to make it up. Louis was catcher because, as Daniels bluntly put it, he would fall over his own feet in any other position. Gutman, who claimed to play in a Chicago league, was at first.

The Spikers' lead-off was their engineer, West, a sour-faced youth with pomaded hair, the same who had tagged Louis out and told him he could not ride the train anymore. The engineer got a walk out of Finch. Next up was O'Keefe, who struck out, violently. The Spikers' pitcher Horace popped a fly to right. Kinny gazed in wonder as it arced up and fell, slow and easy, to the grass at his bare feet. The Quarrelers screamed, Horace jogged to first, and West headed toward third. Wyman managed to get the ball from Kinny and threw it to third. Jopple missed. By the time the ball was back in play, West and Horace were home.

Gutman tagged the next batter out. On the fifth at-bat, the waterboy was forbidden the field after a collision with Llewellyn that left them both bloodied. At least Southeby caught the fly, and the Spikers were out.

First inning, Quarrelers: 0. Spikers, on the other hand: 2.

And so it went. *Nihil desperandum* was all very well to say in the cozy confines of a lawyer's office. Not at sixth inning, with Quarrelers 1 and Spikers 6. The best Louis could come up with was, it could be worse. Gutman was useful, no denying that, and in the fourth inning the Quarrelers' defense finally sat down hard on the Spikers. Whittington somehow worked it so that Wyman and Southeby, nominally outfielders, more or less covered second and third, though if they took a catch from Lew or Jopple it had to be a hurried, *let me get that for you, sir.* Whittington came through on offense, too: the Quarrelers had scored their one run when he hit a double that put Southeby home. Finch, their one-handed pitcher, struck out a few batters, too, and sidelined O'Keefe's engineer with a knot on his shin that looked like a pigeon's egg had slipped under his torn red stocking.

Louis hit a double right off the bat in the seventh. Unfortunately, when he tried to steal third, which he was sure he could have done, his idiot cousin gave it away with a whoop, and Horace picked him off. Back on the sidelines, he broke up a near fisticuffs between Llewellyn and Jopple. Llewellyn: "He never would have made it!" Jopple: "He could if you don't opened your big, fat, Wale trap!" His English had a ways to go, and likely he did not realize the boss, too, had "Wale" blood. Daniels settled it in Lew's favor by savaging Louis: "A three-legged ox can run faster than you, so don't think of trying that again!"

Working some sleight-of-hand with the rules, Daniels changed the batting order at the eighth inning. Louis remained first, and Whittington third, but Gutman went second, Wyman fourth, Finch fifth, and Kinny sixth. None of the white men grumbled, not even Llewellyn and Jopple, bumped to seventh and eighth.

Daniels' wisdom became clear almost immediately. Louis made it to first, Gutman pushed him to second. Whittington at the plate tested his swing. He batted, surprisingly, backwards—left-handed, though he wrote with his right. He could do it upside down, as far as Louis was concerned. As steady on the diamond as on the granite, he pushed them all around again with a hard, right-field grounder that bounced at all the right places to confound the defense. Wyman popped a fly—an out. Finch struck out.

Two outs, and bases loaded. Louis, on third, took a deep breath and tried to be calm. He stood to make his first run of the day. If he stumbled.... And there was the problem of Kinny at bat. He had struck out—one, two, three—every time, so far. His brow was lowered in a look of intense concentration. Louis prayed *dear Jesus* that Kinny was concentrating on the ball—no, on hitting the ball. Make that, hitting the ball with the bat. Hitting the ball with the bat into outfield, way out—

"Throw it!" Kinny yelled to the sky.

The pitcher threw it. Kinny hit it. The women scattered and tea things shattered. Louis ran. The moment he crossed home plate, he snapped around to see if Jesus really had answered his prayer. Gutman nearly ran over him coming home; Whittington next. The Quarrelers pounded each other's backs when Valentina held up the ball, triumphant. Gutman blew Valentina a kiss. Louis trembled between elation and a lust to knock the man flat. The Quarrelers' hero wandered the field.

"Kinny!" Louis called. "Go to first, son! First base!"

Valentina would not give up the ball. The Spikers' outfielder did not seem to mind, grinning and wheedling and cajoling. Bianca linked arms with Valentina, the baseball between them. The damned fool went down on one knee, hands clasped.

"Don't worry," Gutman said. "If I know those women, we'll get this run if it takes all day."

Louis kept himself from turning and staring at Gutman, took a deep breath and called, "Kinny!" It came out as a croak. He cleared his throat. "First base, sonny!"

"Kinny boy, over here!" the Spikers first baseman yelled. A chorus erupted: "First base, Kinny! First! Over there! Kinny!"

Eventually, the two teams coaxed Kinny to touch all the bases. One of the Spikers took Kinny's hand to bring him back to second, after Kinny crossed to third from first. They allowed the run. Maybe the Spikers were ashamed of their trick in the fifth: calling Kinny to throw the ball, from inside the foul line, to their first baseman, which Kinny had kindly done.

The Quarrelers scored once more, in the ninth, when Whittington hit a triple that put Wyman home. The game ended with Spikers: 8, Quarrelers: 5.

They had lost, but it was not a debacle, not a completely bitter pill, and the Spikers' generosity to Kinny went a long way toward making it up.

Llewellyn, who had dropped nearly every ball that came to third, swaggered. "Not too bad a show, Louie." Out of the quarry, he took a cousin's prerogative, calling the boss by first name. To O'Keefe: "Next time, sir, with respect, you'd better mind—"

"God almighty," Louis broke in.

Kinny had not taken the loss well, once it got through to him. He was upset. He had a bat in hand, and he was upset. The quarry men circled him. The railroad men milled, uncertain.

"Kinny! Kinny, child, it's all right," Louis called as he jogged up. "It's all fair and square."

One of the railroad men broke through the ring and dared to go right up to Kinny, a cup in hand. "Kinny boy, you did well. Now drink up like a man."

He stood his ground when Kinny hefted the bat, though his friends stirred, poised to take Kinny down or pull their friend away. The railroad man held out the cup. "Come on now, have a swig, boy."

Kinny lowered the bat, took the cup. The men all cheered. The bat was tactfully removed. Kinny grinned and downed the drink, coughed and spluttered, gave a triumphant yell. "I got whiskey!"

The railroad men cheered; the quarry men knew better. The next cup was plain lemonade, the railroad men grumbling about how Kinny was being deprived, hard enough he was simple, and hadn't he played like a hero.

Louis caroused a while with the men, then he and Whittington followed a servant inside the house, where they sponge bathed in their drawers.

"Good work, Bert," Louis said as he put on a fresh shirt. Luckily he'd thought to bring an extra. "Reliable quality, as always."

Quilts and bottles and plates and hampers and toys spread under a huge oak. Valentina was absent. Mrs. Hamilton sat with a few elderly people in wicker chairs. Whittington settled down with a plump young woman with a lovely, plump-lipped mouth, and brown hair worn in two braids pinned around her head. Gutman seemed to be dozing, his hat over his face. Louis was surprised and pleased to find his cousin, Alicia Stowell.

"Take off your boots, Louie."

Louis did, glad he had on fairly new stockings. He was still standing when Valentina came back. She wore a dark, silvery dress. He put a hand under her elbow, to help her balance while she slipped off her shoes, dance slippers.

"By golly, Valentina," he said, head swimming from it all, "you're taller than I."

A gale of feminine laughter punished his idiocy. Laughing himself, he sat next to Alicia and they kissed. She was Richard's younger sister. They had spent a lot of time with each other, during a period of reconciliation between their families. Louis's crush on her had been swamped by awe. She was powerfully intelligent and, unlike many girls, not afraid to show it.

"It's awfully nice to see you here," Louis said.

"Wouldn't have missed it for anything."

She had moved to Saint Louis on marrying, and was rather fat and sun-tanned. She pointed out her children. A little baby girl slept, thumb in mouth, on her stomach in the middle of their circle. Her son toddled this way and that under the smiles of a crone in apron and cap. The eldest, a boy, was on the diamond being coached by Daniels on how to bat. Louis heard Whittington say to his girl, "Reliable quality as always, he said...."

Alicia told Louis she was in Richmond while her husband conducted business in Baltimore.

"You must stay," Louis said. "Tell Rainier he must carry you home."

"Never, my dear. We shall never move back East. In fact, Rainier and I are considering San Francisco."

"What? Why, that's a city of speculators. A mere gaming hell."

Jeannie, smiling, took the extinguished cigar stub from her father's hand, and fanned him with her hat.

"It's a growing town," Alicia said. "And we can take a train all the way out there. You should come, too. A man of your parts could get a job in a minute."

"Well, I suppose that might be worth considering someday," Louis said. *But I am stuck here, like the little spotted salamander who must stay in his home.* Not to mention being in love with a married woman or two.

Louis told Alicia of Jake's doings, his job, some mutual friends. Her brother might have told her about the lawsuit, or not. Richard and Alicia were not close.

Jeannie joined in with some questions about granite, the geology of it. For years, Louis had rattled off geology lessons to his men—until last week, when Rob and he debated about geology versus the Scriptures. Louis had read Hitchcock's *Elementary Geology*, but the Reverend's reasoning, which rang so true and sound in his book, had thinned in Louis's mouth under Rob's atheistic pounding.

Louis began, "When—when God made the earth.... That is, when He—"

"She's not asking for a sermon," Bianca cut in.

Louis had to laugh. He forgot for a moment his grudge. "No." As they all looked at him, expectant, he grew tongue-tied. Alicia kindly rescued him.

"Some men believe that granite came about from a great cataclysm," she said. "When the continent of Africa collided with the continent of North America. The pressure compressed the stone into hardness."

Gutman took his hat off his face and sat up. He was flushed and sweaty, heat-addled. Beer, too, Louis guessed. Give him a handful of years, and he would be bald and gone to fat.

"Daddy, you're all red," Jeannie said. Daughter and father smiled at each other with tender delight. So why had Gutman waited so long, whoever was Eva's father, when he so evidently adored his elder daughter.

"The collision of Africa and America was brought about by man, I think," Bianca said.

"Quite true," Alicia said, "and it has certainly generated a good deal of hardness." Her smile said she did not hold any of that against Louis.

Louis found his tongue again. "Granite was formed of molten stone, deep in the earth, and pressed hard as it cooled. And thrown up to the surface by the mighty collision of the continents alluded to by Mrs. Stowell."

He got a chip of granite from his coat pocket and handed it to Jeannie. "That is from your uncle Maurice's quarry. It is a type of granite called biotite. The stone is excellent for building blocks and pavement." Too coarse-grained to be the best grade for statuary, though he did not say so. "The sparkles are black and white mica, and other minerals."

The chip went around the circle. Bianca sniffed it, glanced up at Louis. He looked away, and took from a colored man a glass of something called Poney Punch. It was sweet and cooling. He drank it cautiously.

"No, don't get up," Alicia said, rising. She and the nursemaid went into the house, the nursemaid carrying Alicia's whimpering daughter.

Louis picked up Valentina's sketchbook. Kinny at bat.

Llewellyn chasing a grounder. Himself, edging out from second. The sketches were far better than any in *Harper's* magazine, they really caught the spirit of things. Louis smiled at the sketched ring of railroad and quarry men, with Kinny in the center reaching for the dented cup of whiskey, the men's expressions ranging from fear, to leering hope of a good knock-about, to concern, while Finch sneaked the bat from Kinney's other hand.

"I hope you were not frightened," he said, looking up from the pad.

"Terrified." Valentina's eyes narrowed, twinkling. If he might see her laugh every day—imagine waking up to know he might see her laugh like that, over breakfast, or when he returned from work and their children running to the door.

Jeannie began playing a banjo. It was an instrument for cabins and camps, for minstrel shows, not a beautiful young woman, but in her hands, the instrument was plaintive. Stratton, who flung himself near her, heaped compliments. Jeannie smiled. Gutman looked on, amused, judging by his face. Did he understand, at all, the sorrow that burdened the girl? The sodden idiot, the lack-wit, the cheese-brained cad. Gutman rose and wandered to the diamond, where Daniels, O'Keefe and a bunch of little boys were playing ball.

Louis took his eyes from the man, who was ignoring or oblivious, and caught Valentina glancing between himself and Gutman. She turned to Stratton, "Will you show us your rose garden, Doctor?"

Louis helped Jeannie to her feet. A strand of hair strayed onto her face. It stuck there, damp. Louis began to raise his hand, to brush it away, stopped himself. Jeannie smoothed back the lock, releasing as she raised her arm the scent of freshly washed linen and a rank whiff of woman's sweat. She wore a conventional dress like Valentina's, linen in shades of blue. Her upper lip was wet. The clothes would be a mix of softness and starch, and many buttons to undo, and the wilted underclothes.

The lustful vision sent a hot embarrassment over Louis. Stratton's eye, lighting on him, reproached and pleaded. It was not up to Louis to relieve Stratton of his misery. Not his fault, if Jeannie put her hand on his arm, and smiled into his face. And Stratton had his revenge, even if he did not know it: he took Valentina's arm.

They rearranged themselves in Stratton's pretty layout of flagstone and flower beds, though not quite to Stratton's satisfaction: Bianca and Valentina took up Jeannie. Louis was glad to find himself with Alicia, who had come back out, the baby in her arms, the nursemaid hovering behind.

"Let me," Louis said. Alicia handed him the baby, with instructions on how she liked to be held.

He would never forget the first time he held Jake. Himself a little boy, Mama helped nestle the baby in his arms.

This is the nucleus—after the child is born of
woman, the man is born of woman

Looking from his parents' smiling faces to the questing eyes of the infant, little as he had known of how his brother came about, he had been wonderstruck at what they four were to each other. Cradling a baby was more contenting than anything Louis knew, when the baby was contented.

This one was not, quite. Maybe the mustache frightened her. Maybe she sensed his lingering wrath toward Gutman. Her face wadded up, her mouth limbered itself for a wail. Louis turned her over to the nursemaid. He and Alicia wandered away from the others, Alicia guiding their steps.

"Louie, may I ask you a question?"

"Of course you may." Here it was, about the lawsuit.

"Are you the reason Jeannie Gutman broke off with my nephew Charles?"

"Jeannie…. Me?"

"I guess not." She laughed. "Or at least, not to your knowledge."

"I'm merely a friend of the family. The foreman at their quarry."

They turned at the herb bed, and Alicia's skirt brushed the rosemary, scenting the heavy air. Bees buzzed. "Charles is heartbroken," she said. "So is my brother, in his way. Richard approved of Jeannie despite, I have to say, her parents."

Louis covered his embarrassment and vexation by stooping to pick up a rock from the edge of the path. It was smooth and brown as an egg. On the inside, he knew, it was crystalline.

"But that's not what I wanted to tell you," Alicia said.

Louis looked at her again.

"Watch out for Richard," Alicia said quietly.

He drew a breath to answer; she put a hand on his arm, to stop him. "He loves you dearly. You know that, don't you? Still, be careful. He's very clever. And he does not like to lose."

The locomotive panted, idle, from around the bend in the track, though the flat cars were loaded, ready to be coupled with the locomotive and hauled to the finishing shed. Louis glanced up at the sky; the clouds spit a few drops in his eye. Everyone had been praying the drought would break. It would hardly do to ask the rain to wait until they got to the bottom of whatever O'Keefe was on about this time.

"Put your men to something useful," he told Llewellyn. "Don't let them come up the tracks." One of the waterboys was already carrying a message to Mrs. Termey, that Louis would be late with his report today.

As he and Whittington walked up the bridle path along the tracks, the drops abruptly became a downpour—"I shall dash back for an umbrella, sir," said Whittington. However fast he sprinted, the rain was already soaking through Louis's coat and trousers, his vest and shirt and undershirt and drawers, to mix with his sweat. All day hacking away at the monthly accounts, the tickling trickles stirred hopeless cravings to be with Bianca. He could not get it off his mind.

Near Gettysburg, with a woman in a hayloft, rain hammering the roof. Absent without leave.

Lost in the cleave of the clasping and sweet-flesh'd
day

The train, motionless, chuffed and sighed. A half dozen men milled around the tracks. The train engineer squatted to examine the base of the switch.

"Good day, Mr. West," Louis said.

West stood up and brushed his hands on his pants. He favored his left leg. The right leg, Finch had hit with a baseball, hard. "The switch has been tampered with, sir," West said. "Luckily, we were taking this bend slow. Imagine, sir, if we had missed the siding."

They would have plowed into the loaded flatcars. Slow as the locomotive would be going, the rest would have been bad. Very, very bad. Locomotive and flatcars derailed, granite blocks tumbling, maybe fire, maybe an explosion with granite and iron shrapnel.

"Thank God for your vigilance, Mr. West," Louis said.

"Engineer West, if you please, Mr. Bondurant." He was young, with a brisk, honking New England voice. Pray God, Jake would never sound like that.

"Good work indeed, Engineer West. You've saved lives this day, I'm sure. Now, show me what you mean, about the switch being tampered with." He saw O'Keefe jumping down from one of the flatcars.

"Right here, if you would, sir."

They went to the switch stand. The switch lever was an iron rod that rose from a metal plate set in the railroad bed alongside the tracks.

"As you see, sir, the switch is presently in position to allow the locomotive to continue on the main line." The lever slanted toward the tracks.

"Yes, I see that," Louis said. The sun out again, the rails steamed.

"Yet after the locomotive left the flatcars at your quarry this morning, sir, our operator set the switch to the siding."

The siding forked away from the main track. In the afternoon, the locomotive took it to bypass the loaded flatcars. It turned on a loop of track, passed the flatcars again by the siding, rejoined the main track where it was attached to the flatcars, to haul granite blocks to the wharves or the finishing sheds at Manchester.

"You set the switch as you leave each morning," Louis asked, "rather than setting the switch in the afternoon as you come back?"

The engineer bristled. O'Keefe pursed his lips at Louis. Not all well, there.

"Yes, sir, we do," West said. "It is more efficient that way. You see, given that your quarry is the sole destination of this spur, it is best for the switch operator to go behind the train to set the switch, rather than to go ahead. Do you follow, sir?"

"To prevent him being run over?"

"It is to spare the locomotive from having to stop, sir, should the switch be uncooperative. Furthermore, setting the switch ahead of time allows us to reach the quarry that much sooner, sir, so as to adhere to our mutual schedule."

"That is most considerate."

"Yes, sir. This morning, my operator set the switch, in order that the train might be shunted onto the siding on our return this afternoon. I saw him, myself, set the switch."

Whittington huffed up, umbrella in hand, a useless effort, the rain having stopped. Louis looked to where the locomotive sat. The bend in the track made it impossible, even if the engineer were leaning out the window, to watch the operator set the switch. West followed his line. His face tightened.

"I checked, Mr. Bondurant," he said.

"You checked. You got out of the locomotive and checked."

O'Keefe cleared his throat.

"Go on, if you please, Engineer West," Louis said. "And I'll ask you not to light that cigar."

West's lips thinned, he shook out the match. "This afternoon, the switch was set back. It was re-set, so that we would have stayed on the main track, rather than diverting to the siding."

"Would you show me how to set the switch?" Louis asked. "We can set the switch properly, and finish our load. Does that suit?"

"Yes, sir." The engineer eyed him. "I would not ask a weakling, but you appear to be a hardy.... " The young man took a step back, at the look Louis bent on him.

"Show me how to operate the switch, if you please, Engineer." Louis tightened his voice, to prevent it shaking with anger.

Not meeting Louis's eyes West touched the lever. "To switch the train to the siding, you pull the lever all the way over, toward yourself, as you face the rails."

Louis wiped his hands on his pants, though the fabric was soaked and the handle was wet enough, too. As he wrapped his hands around the lever handle, which was about as high as his chest, he was startled to see grayish spots, like bruises, on his hands and wrists. On his shirt cuffs, too. The cloudburst, barely enough to wet the parched ground, had set his new suit's black color running. Blackish spots on his skin, gray spots on the black suit. Like cheap mourning clothes. He took a sharp deep breath to quell an urge to laugh. The tailor must have cut the suit from re-dyed Confederate wool-and-cotton.

Pulling the switch was easier than he had feared. He had not wanted to fail, to be a weakling before this little Boston bean who had had the sauce to assess his physique. Louis tested the switch. It did not move and would not fall out of place by accident. He wiped his hands again.

"I must confess," West said, "we do not lock it down, as

we would in more populated areas, such as Manchester and Richmond, for who is there, in this place, to change a switch? Nevertheless, and very fortunately, I keep a sharp eye out as we approach."

"May I speak to your switch operator?"

The man was sure he had thrown the switch correctly, and the engineer backed him, as did the railroad lumpers. Everyone backed him, as if they all hung out the back of the train to watch the switch operator do his job. Except O'Keefe, who said nothing.

"This is a very serious situation, Mr. West," Louis said.

"I could not agree more, sir."

"Do you have any thoughts on it?"

The engineer looked down the tracks. "I recall, sir, some ill feeling between the quarry men and the railroad men."

Louis kept his tone cool. "The quarry men would certainly be most grievously injured, if the locomotive rammed the flatcars. So you think, do you, it might be railroad men who tampered with the switch?"

West's face darkened. O'Keefe stalked away, barked his crew back onto the flatcars. "I did not imply that, sir," West said. "We would not do that. Harm our own train."

Louis examined the ground around the switch. No one had conveniently left a calling card to say he had stopped by to sabotage the train. And to ruin the derrick, maybe.

"I must insist you lock the switch from now on," Louis said.

"I have already decided so." West's jaw jutted. "It will take getting a smith out here."

"I have a smith among my men."

"It is a particular job, Mr. Bondurant, and we shall use a railroad smith."

"Have it your way, Engineer. For now, shall we finish our day?"

"Let us proceed, sir."

On the way back down the tracks, Whittington said, "You

got some good ones in, sir, if I may say so. About the cigar, and them tampering with the switch."

For Whittington, that was an expression of rage. He was a good, steady young man.

The seeping dye probably splotched all the way to Louis's drawers. False colors, running, and another quarrel with the tailor. He would have excused himself to Valentina. He could have sent a written report, with an addendum, I beg your pardon, Mrs. Termey, I am too dappled to visit. But he could not resist seeing her.

One day too soon, he would surely find her husband with her. His prayers answered; even after he began to love Valentina, he had continued to pray, Sundays, for his boss Maurice Termey's safe return. He could only aim at sincerity.

The sultry thick air dried his clothes enough to stop outright dripping. He would not dare to sit on any of the furniture, for fear of staining it. He was a clown in motley, a poor, stinking wet dog.

Halfway up the driveway, he turned off, and followed the path he had made with Bianca.

The green was creeping back toward the place where the little girl had fallen, the wreath of honeysuckle and wild grape withered. When they reopened the old quarry, this green, this oak, the wild grape and honeysuckle, the salamanders, the snakes, the wilted wreath would be blasted away. Louis knelt and tried to turn his mind to prayer.

He had prayed, or tried to pray, or pretended to pray, in countless places soaked in blood, not from a child's pure body, but from the bodies of men opened by bullets, bayonet, by gun stocks, by his own hands and the hands of their brethren, by the hands of surgeons.

Where else does he strike soundings, except here

He had done it for the Good Old Cause, the striped banner,

and so the black body of carpenter Wyman, and those of his wife Mourning and their son Ezra, would never be assessed in the markets of Richmond more coldly than Engineer West had assessed the white body of quarry foreman Louis. He had fought against his home; he might have killed friends. He had certainly raised against his kinsmen.

The girlchild's blood, running hot through his clothes onto his skin, had run clean against the darkness of himself, his man's body, his own body enslaved by turns to wrath, to war, to adultery, to soul-deep apathy.

The soggy bracken stirred. Louis, on his knees, turned. It was Jeannie, creeping up on him.

"Oh," she whispered, daunted, maybe, by his tear-bleared eyes. "I saw you go in." Not daunted. Pitying.

Louis stood and brushed his knees' mud and crumbled leaves. "You shouldn't have followed me." A young woman alone with a man here.

She stepped to what Louis thought of as Eva's grave, though the little girl lay at rest in the cemetery across the river. Jeannie crossed herself, then put her hands over her face and burst into tears.

Louis did not touch her. Benighted as his spirit was, he saw the danger lurking in that. When her sobs let up, he proffered his handkerchief, soggy and blotted indigo. She looked up at him. Her mouth was truly like a rose bud, and her eyes a blue-lavender.

She smiled, though tears gleamed. "Your face is smutty."

"Dear me." He smiled back.

They went back along the trail. She knew to keep her skirts close about her.

O my body!

In the studio, female fuss, to the accompaniment of Bianca's husband playing piano in the parlor. Schubert, Louis recognized, from his mother having played it.

Mr. Bondurant must let them draw a hot bath. No, he must; Mourning was already heating the water. He must change out of those damp clothes; he would borrow a suit of Maurice's. He must stay to dinner. He must stay the night.

That, Louis refused, absolutely.

Wyman valeted for him. Having a man shave his face while he sat in a tub of warm water in a private room, and hand him a soft towel to dry with, was a luxury Louis never before had in his life. It was a little embarrassing: one of his quarry men, attending him so intimately. Wyman seemed at ease.

"Sir, if you allow me, I can limber up that old wound."

Louis hesitated, lay on the bed—Eva's innocent bed, part covered with a towel. Wyman pressed and kneaded the mess of scar. Louis bit his lip. He wondered if Valentina or Bianca knew that Jeannie had gone alone into the woods, to follow a man. Snakes lurking. She might have come out by the terrace, as had Louis slinking in and out of her mother's room.

"Is that better, sir?" Wyman asked.

Louis sat up. "By God, Wyman." He flexed his leg. "It hurts worse than ever."

They both laughed.

"I know a barber, sir, in Granite, does it better. He has a secret ointment, and the healing touch."

Louis put on one of Maurice Termey's topshirts. It was fresh-starched. Maurice was a willowy fellow, and never in life would Louis select a plaid vest. It was good enough for borrowed. He decided not to make anything of being in Maurice Termey's shirt and drawers. The pants and coat were probably Wyman's; they were more his size. His Sunday best, or what he wore when serving in the house for an occasion.

Wyman, wiping the shaving things, cleared his throat.

"Mr. Bondurant, I have something to tell you. If I may." Wyman arranged the shaving kit on the basin stand, rearranged it. His chest rose and fell fast.

"Of course." Louis prayed, *Dear Jesus, please. Do not shatter me.*
Wyman sucked his lips into his mouth, released them. He
took a breath, then looked Louis in the eye. "Mourning and
Ezra and me, we are going out West, sir, to Texas."

"To Texas." Not shattering, but nearly. And who would keep
the Magic Castle safe? He could hardly ask Wyman that. "But
that is a very risky journey."

Wyman did not answer. He was so nervous, Louis realized,
it was difficult for him to speak. He might even take his boss's
words as a threat.

"No, it's all right, Wyman." Whatever miracles Wyman performed in carpentry at the quarry, he would get hardly more
than a grouter's pay. The damned Board — now not the time to
raise that anger. "We'll miss you very, very much, but you must
do what you think best for your family."

Wyman literally sighed with relief. "Thank you, sir." He had
probably rehearsed and lost to nerves a more elaborate speech.
But he had looked straight at his boss, his white boss, and told
him — not asked for permission — that he was leaving. It was
nothing like what he'd been raised to do, even as a free man.

"You've been one of my best men, Wyman, and I will surely
miss you, but I know you will succeed wherever you go. And of
course, I shall write a letter of recommendation for you."

He went to the writing desk. Maurice Termey would not
mind him using a sheet of paper, a finely made blue stationary,
and a pen. Luckily, the ink bottle had not dried out. He tore off
the embossed name using the desk edge, carefully, to more or
less match the deckled edges of the paper, wrote out the letter.

"And for Ezra?" he asked. He tore another sheet. "We can
say he was a carpenter's assistant, or a lumper or a grouter." He
considered an office boy, but that would be too far-fetched.

"Carpenter's assistant, please, sir," Wyman said.

Louis dipped the pen. "Carpenter's assistant young Ezra
shall be."

He blew lightly on the ink. "And who will watch over Granite Bluff, with you gone?"

"Shaw is a very good man, sir, very reliable. I brung him along myself."

Louis added some money to a separate envelope. Luckily he had taken some from his savings wallet in the safe, to send Jake.

"Do you read, Wyman?"

"I am learning on the sly, sir."

"You don't need to do that. On the sly, I mean. No more of that."

"I don't want my son to know, sir."

"I see. Well, here are your letters. It says you are a hard-working and reliable man of a good, sound character. Same for Ezra. Except that he is also bright." Both men laughed. "And if you need a pass or what have you, I shall prevail upon Governor Walker himself." And perhaps beg a job for himself, should he be in the petitioners' line.

"Thank you very much, sir."

"As for this small gift from me, use it as you must, Mr. Wyman, for I would not have you or yours go hungry or unsheltered. But I had rather you use it as help to school young Ezra and any other children that might come along, in whatever place you make your home."

They shook hands, then clinched each other in an embrace.

As they left the room, a popular air wafted from the piano. Gutman played well; he would do fine in a saloon. Jeannie began singing.

Louis paused in the passage to listen. Her voice rang surprisingly rich: "Write me over the water Write me over the sea Whether 'tis sad or joyous...." The piano fumbled to a stop. "Why, Daddy...."

Louis continued on to the studio. Sitting in the awkward Italian chair, he presented the switch incident to Valentina as a mishap, though he knew the deception would come back to him, once West's report reached the directors of Granite Bluff Quarry Company. He assured Valentina he would have one of the men check the switch each day. They spoke a little of Wyman and Mourning, both too downcast about it, he guessed, to go into it much. He escorted her in to dinner. Mourning was a good cook, but Rudy Gutman's moody blond presence at the other end of the table blunted appetite. Bianca said little to Louis, which did not matter at all, as far as he was concerned. Jeannie talked about Tennyson, Valentina joining in. Gutman conceded that Chicago ham could not rival Virginia's, and he put his hand over Bianca's.

Bianca had taken an Italian lover over the sea, her black-haired, dark-eyed daughter Eva the result.

Whether 'tis sad or joyous,
Write very soon to me;
But oh, do not close the fond pages,
And this little thing forget,
For all my waiting and longing:
Write that you love me yet.

Mrs. Hamilton observed.

Louis left as soon as he politely could. Jeannie was disappointed he would not stay for a game of chess, and he was sorry for her. He simply could not endure more. Nor to be shown up as a bad chess player.

Riding home, Louis brooded over the day—the quarry part of the day, rather than Wyman's notice or sitting at table with Gutman.

The switch could have been thrown by a personal enemy of his cousin Richard. Or it could be against the granite company, or one or the other of the quarry men, against the black lumpers. Or the Termeys, though Maurice Termey had served the Confederacy. Or himself, a Union man. It could just be a prank, though even little boys knew not to do such a thing. Or it could be God smiting a man who was raising against his kinsman.

Very likely, though, God had not been the one to throw the switch.

O N THE DAY THE newspapers gave for the solar eclipse, the quarry stopped work early. By midafternoon, the most comfortable rocks—big, worn-smooth pillows of granite—in the drought-low river were dotted with quarry men and their wives and children, dogs, picnic hampers, dinner pails, crates of drink soft and hard, blankets, and toys. Gloomy prophets and harbingers of better times were in their element.

Louis rinsed the shaving soap from his face in the age-spotted mirror hung in the foreman's cabin, combed his hair, buttoned his fresh shirt, put on his tie, vest, and coat, and released a gallon or so of sweat. He put on his hat. He was half out the door when he almost collided with Bianca. He made to go around her. She blocked the way.

"I warned you, didn't I?" she said. "I did warn you."

"Excuse me, if you please, ma'am." He did not look at her. He had not looked at her since the ball game, except when he had to, for appearances. He took another step, so did she.

"Get away," he said.

"No."

"Get away from me."

"No. I won't."

He faced her. "You shot me down."

"It's not war, Louis. It's love."

"Love. What's love? I don't love you, damn it. I only liked—" He stopped himself, but he might as well have said it. She took a step back, her eyes filled with tears.

"Liar."

Louis stepped close to her and put his hands to her head and pulled his fingers through her hair. "Yes." He pushed her away. Not hard. Her hair snagged on the rough skin of his palms and fingers.

They left in silence, to meet the rest of the party at the road down to the railroad tracks. Louis was half-suffocated with mortification. He went to the stables to check in on Nella and the other animals, then to the river. He joined the women at the rock—Rudy Gutman not with them—and spoke as if nothing had happened, as if he might not have strands of golden hair caught on his hands.

Wyman's son may have seen seen the quarrel, he had been scuttling off the porch when they left the cabin. The maid, and Mourning. Any of the quarry men, too, and their wives and children. Not to forget the dogs. The rocks. The sun and the moon. Maybe they would forget it in the excitement of the eclipse. Maybe it looked like a brotherly sisterly spat. How could Bianca do this to him. Valentina knew nothing. Jeannie knew nothing. Mrs. Hamilton saw it all. Bianca sat at the old woman's feet, leaning against the wicker chair.

How could he have been such a damned fool. Kinny had more wits, leaping and dunking with the boys and dogs.

Hot inside and out, he put on the best face he could muster, poured iced tea, ate cake. He wished he were on the wharves with Branden, watching the eclipse. When he attempted to explain the impending cosmic phenomena, Valentina put aside her sketchbook and, with tactful questions, made sense of it. Wyman had filed and softened the edges of bottle bottoms, and Louis

171 AT THE FALL LINE

passed them out, taking brown so that the ladies might all have pretty blue viewing glasses. The moon moved over the sun with agonizing slowness.

"It is God showing his might," Llewellyn said, a rock over. Were it not for the women, Louis would have told him to shut it. The darkness pressed his heart; the cries of exaltation and wonder came like wails.

At the exact moment a cloud ran over the sun at Gettysburg, a soldier next to Louis got shot in the throat, and spraying blood had filled Louis's ear.

"It's cool, isn't it, with less sun," Jeannie said. She had seen his shudder. Louis sensed that, oddly, she understood what he felt.

"There is Venus," Valentina said, pointing.

The goddess of love gleamed in the moon-wrought twilight, Louis's spirits too ruffled to take her cue for fantasy and wit: embarrassed, angry, chagrined, oppressed. He admired the orb with words. Dogs howled but he heard no panicked bellows or brays from the stables. He had tied Nella, in case.

Finally, it was over. Louis brought the ladies back up to the house. No, he would not stay for supper, thank you; so sorry to miss Mr. Gutman, who had an engagement in town.

The sun shone wan, as if exhausted from its struggle with the moon. After all, it was evening. In the quarry stables, Nella's nip nearly broke through Louis's coat and her move to throw his hat down nearly punched him in the face.

"Calm down, would you," he told her, listless as the sun. She might be unnerved or maybe she had a tiff with her boyfriend, such as he was. A mule, Jimbo, his pouts all in vain. Louis gave him a molasses cake, to make up for it.

Branches slapped Nella's and Louis's faces on the bridle path along the railroad tracks that edged the river. Louis would have to send one of his grouters to trim it, his own man, since neither the railroad men nor the property owners along here would stir themselves. He tried not to relive the quarrel with Bianca, nor to speculate on who did or did not see their theatrics. He tried not to guess whether Valentina would hear about it, or Jeannie. If the maid would tell. If Ezra would tell. If Mourning would tell. If Gutman would find out, and they would have to salvage their honor by shooting at each other. Louis carried his Remington revolver, freshly loaded. He tried to relax into the evening ride, ambling along the river.

Crack!

Louis jumped free of Nella moments before she dropped. He rolled into the brush for cover. Nella cried and thrashed on the bridle path.

"Shh," Louis breathed. "Shh, girl. Hush, girl." He panted through his mouth as silently as he could, and tried, through his heart's thunder, to figure out where the shooter was.

Between fear for his life and anguish for Nella, he worked out that the shot had come from the empty tracks ahead. The shooter might have taken cover on the river bank, or, like himself, in the bushes on the off-river side of the tracks.

Louis crept up the embankment by the bridle path, deeper into cover, and stole downriver, crouched, each step careful, silent as an Indian. He stopped.

Below him, evidently oblivious, a man squatted, couching a rifle. His hat covered his face, his hands were black. But Louis had known it was not Gutman. A man who was in the right did not lurk like an assassin. And Gutman had been a sharpshooter in the Western Iron Brigade. If he wanted to kill his wife's lover, he would just do it.

Louis, motionless, debated with himself. Should he draw and shoot? Yell a warning? Give a warning shot? If he killed the man, he could be up for murder. He would be exonerated, but he would have to go through it. If he did not shoot, he might be killed. Whatever he did had to be decisive, for once things got started, the bushes offered paltry cover, and the man below had a longarm. It looked old enough to be a smooth-bore. Pray

God, it was unrifled. A longarm, against a pistol. Louis put away from his mind the fact that Nella was not on her feet.

He drew his gun slowly, silently. He had an excellent line, and he was close, and he had the element of surprise. He breathed in, and out. The man below him rose, crouching, and peered down the tracks. He might have thought Louis was behind Nella.

Do it now.

The man jumped back as the bullet hit the ground near his feet, then duck-scrambled toward the river bank. Louis shot again. The man turned toward him, raising his weapon. Louis shot. The man yelped and his gun clattered onto the tracks. He began to reach for the gun. Another bullet at his feet, and the man abandoned his weapon and leapt down the river bank.

Louis jumped from the embankment, stumbled on the tracks and went sprawling. By the time he recovered his pistol and reached the river bank, the man was casting off in a canoe. Louis shot. The canoe wobbled or his aim was off. The canoe's course was swift though sloppy, blood pouring down the paddle. Last bullet, and Louis aimed as carefully as he could, missed again. He sprinted up to the tracks, grabbed the shoulder gun, and scrambled back down the bank. Foolishly. The man had not reloaded. He escaped.

At least the gun was not a rifle. Thank God. Nella had not been hit with a Minie ball. She had managed to get up but she held her front right hoof off the ground and breathed rough and high. The wound was to her right shoulder. It was a flesh wound, Louis convinced himself. She would not let him examine it. He managed to remove all her tack, leaving the bridle and blanket, and forced himself to take the time to conceal it in some bushes and to site a landmark to find it again. With saddlebags slung over his shoulder, reins in hand, he asked Nella to walk.

The journey was long and painful. Louis held as many branches as he could from Nella's face and several times filled his hat with water and gave her to drink. He encouraged her.

When she began to drag her hoof, he begged her to keep on, for his sake. He did not let himself weep, for it might worry her more. He hoped the man who wounded her would lose his hand; he prayed to God that a butcher like Stratton would regretfully saw it off. He wished he had shot him dead. He considered trying for the Taliaferro farm, but that would mean hauling Nella up a steep embankment and through rough brush and maybe swamp.

The white servant who answered Richard's door nearly closed it on the filthy, woebegone man at the threshold before he recognized his master's cousin. Richard himself was up in Philadelphia. Louis did not care. He had come to his cousin's house because it was on the west edge of town, the closest place he knew to get help. He followed Brickey around to the stables—Richard had his own. A boy ran for hot water and rags.

Brickey, as he told Louis, was a Frenchman who got tangled up in Mexico in sixty-two, deserted, walked to Louisiana and fought for the CSA. He claimed a bullet lodged in his gut, and he hated Louis Napoleon. The tale was a kindness to distract. Louis could hardly follow it, Brickey switching back and forth between French and English, and his own wits scattered. He drank brandy to ease the ferocious pain in his hip.

The horse doctor arrived after what seemed like hours. Twenty-three minutes by Louis's pocketwatch. He examined the wound, shook his head. "Best to put her—"

"*Non, non,*" Louis broke in, before the doctor could say, she will have to be put down. "*Extractez… Arrachez…* Take it out. Extract the ball. Extract it, sir, and sew her up."

The doctor raised his eyebrows at Brickey. The servant said, haughtily, "Proceed, sir, if you please."

The three men bound Nella so that she might be supported. Louis forced upon himself a military calm and maybe he was of some use. The doctor applied ether and cut and dug, cut and dug. The ball had worked in deep. The doctor rolled it in his fingers to make sure it was intact, and cleaned and dressed the wound.

"Don't expect much," he said. He declined Brickey's offer of refreshment, as did Louis.

Louis was so exhausted he almost got lost on the way home, though it was barely dark.

In his night prayers, he asked God's forgiveness for his malice toward the shooter. After all, the man bore no malice toward Louis, no more than a soldier shooting a rifle in battle. It did not matter, even, who he was. The question that begged an answer was: who had hired him?

T HE BOARD OF GRANITE Bluff Quarry Company assembled
in a private room at the bank run by Dunaway, president of
the Board. Mahogany paneling, a big polished table, paintings
of dour men in old-fashioned clothes, a thick Turkey carpet.
Venetian blinds covered tall windows closed against dust and
street noise.

Valentina must have found out about him and Bianca, her
"Good morning, Mr. Bondurant," an icicle, though her cheeks
flushed in the stuffy, hot room.

Louis wished he were not sweating so much, and that his
hands and feet were not so clammy. And that the drawstring
on his drawers had not broken at the left knee, so that the leg
bunched up in his pants. And that the scent of his hair oil was
not so cloying.

In the presence of mine enemies—and whatever Valentina was—
Thou anointest my head with cheap macassar.

Having dispensed of the niceties, Dunaway rounded on
Louis—or rather, strictly speaking, on Louis's men, one of
whom was presumed guilty of the ambush. His voice shrilled
sharp and steady as a gang saw. He had been shrill, too, calling
for Secession, calling for younger men to fight, calling for his

oysters and his French wine, in Richmond, while the boys in butternut and gray griped on green apples and weevily corn pone. His bank had repossessed Louis's family home, the little house on Porter Street. Louis listened, trying to breath through his nose, rather than panting through his mouth. A pause: he was expected to speak.

"With respect, Mr. Dunaway," Louis said, "it was not a quarry man who shot at me. I am quite certain of that." Maybe his voice sounded calm enough.

"As you said, Mr. Bondurant, it was dusk and the Negro was wearing a hat."

"If you have ever faced an individual pointing a gun at you," Louis said in the most level tone he could manage, "you would understand how very clear his facial features are." *But you let other men face the fire*, he might have said.

"Could it have been a hunter?" Edwards asked. He was from Baltimore.

"No, sir," Louis said. "There was enough light to tell the difference between a deer and a man on a horse."

"That would depend on his eyesight," Edwards said.

"Or it could have been a bandit," said Collins, a New Yorker.

Louis studied the grain of the polished table and prayed to Jesus.

Richard rapped on the table and let a silence fall. "No need to waste our time in idle speculation. I have hired a detective to investigate the attack on my cousin Major Bondurant. A detective of tenacity and sound method."

"Excellent," said Edwards. Something uneasy in Edwards' voice made Louis look up again. Richard had fixed on Dunaway. The clerk, taking minutes, glanced between the men.

"You will let us know the findings, I hope?" Collins said. Sarcastically?

Richard did not deign to answer.

"Mrs. Termey and gentlemen," Dunaway said, "I have reviewed the reports on the switch and the investigation concerning the derrick, to see if there might be some connection between the events. I am wondering if in fact Mr. Bondurant might have—"

"We have established that no fault can be found with the quarry concerning either of those incidents," Collins said. He had a particularly nasal accent.

"I did not mean—" Dunaway began.

"The proper maintenance of the derrick is beyond reproach," Collins broke in.

It took a few beats for Louis to figure they were not defending him, or Roberts. They were concerned that Dunaway would blather something that could open the quarry company to liability.

"The likelihood is that the rooster sheave—" Collins pronounced it as if it were a foreign word "—was defective. Defective in a manner undetectable by normal inspection. Therefore the culpability must be laid to the manufacturer." The others, naturally, agreed.

Though it was morning, the heat bored through the blinds. Louis wished the windows were open, that the room had more air. He was trying to follow several currents—Dunaway, Richard, the other directors, the person who sent the note *God smiteth*, the man who shot at him, the man who hired a man to murder him. He could not discern how those currents converged.

"It could have been any darky, after all," Collins said. "From what I understand, they live nearly atop the tracks, not far from the switch."

"Was there not a Negro quarry worker under suspicion in another incident?" Dunaway said. "I beg your forgiveness, Mrs. Termey, for raising a painful memory. I am referring to the tragedy—"

Louis jumped to his feet. "Mr. Dunaway!"

A stir all around—except Valentina, blank and dignified as a statue. Richard raised his fingertips: *Easy, cousin.*

Forcing his voice to courtesy, Louis said, "I beg your pardon, Mrs. Termey and gentlemen. I assert that no quarry man white or black, no man at all, fell under suspicion in that tragic accident, and there is no call to raise it here or anywhere." He sat, tried to stop trembling.

Dunaway cleared his throat. "Again, I beg your pardon, Mrs. Termey," he said. "Mr. Bondurant, it is true, is it not, that you have misgivings as to the loyalty of your colored workers?" Louis's weekly report, in mid-July, advised that if Granite Bluff Quarry did not promote his best colored men, they might leave for better situations.

Louis drew a sharp breath. "Does honest ambition have no place in my quarry? You suppose a colored quarry man tampered with the switch and the derrick and shot at me for not being promoted? Really, sir, you are…. " Louis clamped his tongue between his teeth. Dunaway raised his brows and, with a tight little smile, gave Louis a chance to finish sinking himself.

Richard's eyes crinkled at the corners and the ends of his mouth turned up. To think he was amused would be a mistake. Louis knew the expression: Richard was seriously vexed. Collins and Edwards frowned and shuffled. Maybe it was not only the quarry foreman's forwardness. They might not like the line Dunaway was taking. To them, it would seem to be against the quarry. They were wrong, though. It was against the quarry foreman. Dunaway wanted Louis fired.

Dunaway continued with a hint, an oblique hint, at improper behavior, at setting an example. A worker who "cracked up" —referring to poor Billy, who still, a month after the block fell, according to his wife's note, *cannot hardly talk any nor rise up out of his Bed*. Dunaway claimed slipshod accounting, some irregularities with the payroll.

That worked. "Irregularities with the payroll?" Collins brayed.

Valentina said nothing. If Dunaway said, *You are dismissed, sir*, she might nod, *yes*, smooth and silky as a cat.

The fear of it stole over Louis. His shirt and necktie wilted, and the scents of his hair oil, cigar smoke, and camphor from Branden's suit he'd borrowed congealed in his belly. He felt so craven within, he wanted to slouch down in his chair. He kept himself sitting up straight.

Richard broke in. "Gentlemen, I did not interrupt an important business trip to listen the minutiae of daily operations at Granite Bluff Quarry, which is known to be one of the most productive and efficient in our area."

"It is small relative to—"

"I called this meeting in regard to possible acts of sabotage to my property, the railroad, and an ambush on Major Bondurant." In a roomful of Northerners, only Richard addressed him by his Union rank.

"As Mr. Edwards pointed out," Collins said, "we have not established—"

"Quite right," Dunaway broke in. "I apologize for keeping you, Colonel Poindexter. Perhaps we can reconvene when your investigator furnishes his report."

He stacked his papers to a general bustle of adjournment. But when Richard rose to his feet, whoever else had stood, sat again and stilled. Richard's gaze fixed on each man in turn—passing over Valentina with a slight bow of his head—and stopped on Dunaway.

"I will not tolerate any further damages inflicted upon my railroad or the Termeys' property. And keeping in mind that any man might be taken by a cowardly ambush, I want to make clear that should a ruffian again attack and injure my cousin Major Bondurant or his chattel, I vow on my sacred honor, I will respond with heartfelt conviction."

Silence.

"Mrs. Termey. Gentlemen." Richard left.

The Northerners looked incredulous, maybe amused: the Rebel asserting his sacred honor. Dunaway scowled at his papers, his wattles flushed, his jaw jutted. When he looked up, at Louis, his pale eyes were chill as hailstones.

Valentina stood; the men stood. "Mr. Bondurant, if you will kindly…?"

Louis wanted to go to Richard's stable and look in on Nella, but he climbed into Valentina's buggy. "Straight home, Shaw, please," she directed.

Not much progress had been made on paving Westham Road; the gravel gave out not long after Gumtree Tavern. The dust multiplied. Valentina was silent, her face covered with a veil. Louis tried to think through the implications of Richard's vow. He was too unstrung to get further than the assumption he had already made: it was not Richard who planned the attack.

Not an assumption. A certainty. Richard would not harm him, his kinsman, his cousin. Not bodily, at least.

Taliaferro and Archer had at least smoothed and oiled the road through their properties, so that stretch would not be so bad.

When Papa went bust, and the plans for Louis attending Princeton put away without a word spoken, Jake had been about Eva's age. He did not fall into a quarry, as his brother did. He had moved on. He was at Harvard, studying to be a minister.

Louis did not care what happened, as long as he got Jake through. He would break his own back. He would serve up his colored workers, he would sell them at the price dictated by his superiors. He would let Dunaway take potshots at him. He had fought on his honor, he had helped shatter his homeland, only to find himself coiled in the Devil's arms.

Soon it would be over, God willing. Virginia would be a state in the Union again. Louis closed his eyes—

"Why did you not tell me?" Valentina demanded. "But you must wonder, which? Which thing is she talking about? Which of all that you have kept from me!" Through the dusty tulle, her tawny eyes squinted; her lips pressed thin and hard over her beautiful teeth. Shaw's shoulders scrunched up.

"I don't find we're confidential with each other, Mrs. Termey, and so—"

"Mr. Dunaway has informed me that you are bringing a lawsuit against the quarry."

"Mr. Dunaway can go to hell!" Louis heard himself. "I beg your pardon, ma'am. Please pardon me." He governed his breath. "My lawsuit has nothing to do.... It is not against the quarry. Still, if you wish to have me dismissed, ma'am, it is your choice."

"I thought you were a friend. You betrayed us all!" Her eyes sparked with tears, her cheeks dark. "Me, Maurice, Rudy—Shaw! Stop this carriage. Stop it now!"

Shaw stopped the carriage. Valentina took a step down—her skirt caught and she went sprawling, her hat and veil flying. Louis and Shaw leaped down. Shaw did not dare touch her. She staggered to her feet, palms and chin bleeding, and thrust Louis away.

"Valentina!" Louis grabbed her hand, pulled her to him. He gripped the back of her head, her hair, licked his bandana and dabbed her chin, as if she were Jake as a little boy. She bridled and swatted his arms. He ignored that. Part of her hair came loose and fell over his hand, the softness, and his heart beat hard.

Trying not to pant, Louis let her go. Her scalp's sweat wet his fingers. "Mrs. Termey and I will take a stroll up the road," he said to Shaw. "You will follow, if you please."

He entwined Valentina's fingers with his own, clamped her arm under his, and walked her. She sniffled and fumed and pulled. Her blood, and sand and dirt, ground into his hand. He stopped on the little bridge over Reedy Creek and turned her to face him, and her perfume surged through his senses.

"I did not tell you," he breathed. "How could I? How could I, Valentina? Was I to say, I am having a love affair with your sister? Was I to tell you, I am an adulterer? Is that what you think?"

She tried to pull her hand away and he tightened on it. They crossed the bridge, and he took her resisting through the mud down to the trickle of water. No poison ivy. Her dress snagged on blackberries, juicy and ripe. He dipped his bandana in the water and cleaned her face and hands properly.

"There."

Mosquitoes whined in the green shade. Valentina, subdued, stared at the creek. The wet mud seeped up her skirt. Her boots, her little white boots all stained with mud. Women's shoes so thin, though they must travel the same smut and roughness as a man's. He would carry her over the muck. Why, if he was to be a sinner, had he sinned with Bianca rather than her? Bianca's frank willingness. A woman unfaithful, and true.

Valentina climbed slipping up the bank. Purple blotches and brown streaks on her dress and shoes. She glared down at him, using her skirt to wipe her hands, dirty again from grappling her way up.

"We were free with each other," he said looking up at her. The wild brambles around him fluttered with little birds, at the berries. "Her husband, yes, I wronged him. About Bianca, about her, God forgive me, I am not.... "

Valentina's heels clattered angry over the planks of the bridge.

"I am not sorry," he finished, alone. Not about Bianca's husband, either.

He arrived back up to the road. The buggy was rolling on ahead, in a cloud of dust. He limped on. About a quarter of a mile further, in the shade of a hickory, he handed Valentina's hat up to her and got back in the buggy.

Valentina kept her face turned away from Louis. If he took her hand, as he longed to do, she would think, first one sister, now the next. So he could not touch her.

At the foot of the driveway: "Good day to you, ma'am."

She nodded. He was starting to get down when she grabbed his arm. He froze. He turned to her very slowly. Her fingers

relaxed on his arm. She did not look at him, and he did not
stir. He nearly held his breath. Shaw faced straight ahead. Her
profile: the pouting lower lip, the pock marks on her cheek, her
brows drawn down. The sun poured hot through the awning.

Damp laundry starch, a slight odor of stale blood—female
blood?—her sweat and his, their flesh, cedar flowers musk.

The womb, the teats, nipples, breast-milk, tears, laugh-
ter, weeping, love-looks, love-perturbations and
risings

"Thank God you were not hurt," she said in her high little
voice. She sat straight and stiff and wet-cheeked.

"Valentina—"

"Good day, Mr. Bondurant."

T HE DRONE OF FLIES within the shed penetrated through the closed door, as did the stench of rotting flesh. Richard's detective put his hand on the latch. The planter, who had ridden alongside them across his property, loitered on the dirt road.

"Are you steady, Major Bondurant?" Detective Brown asked. Trained by Pinkerton himself.

Louis nodded. Though it had been a while since he had viewed decomposing bodies, he was, he believed, steady.

Brown threw the shed door open. The fug that billowed out made Louis gag rapidly several times, like a cat hawking up a hairball. He managed himself, wadded his bandana over his nose and mouth, and walked with watering eyes to where the dead man lay, on the straw-littered dirt floor. Brown swiped at the clustered flies with a gunny sack and moved out of the dust-loaded light.

It was the man who had shot at Louis. His features were bloated or absent. The hat was new, but the plaid flannel shirt was the same, and the dungarees, torn at the knee. Louis, half-holding his breath, leaned to look more closely. The burst-open shirt exposed a crosshatch of scars on his chest. A bloody bandage trailed from the right hand, which puffed more or less into a ball.

Pity stroked Louis. It felt all the more odd, in that he had stopped pitying the unknown dead soon into the War. He had seen plenty of them, and right around here—maybe right here, Fair Oaks Station a mile or so away.

"That's him," Louis said, his voice muffled by the bandana.

The wounded and dead strewing the ground, the heat-rippled miasma of blood and gore and pain. After the thunder of artillery, Louis's hearing had come back clanging. His wits numbed, he had stumbled over a body, fallen upon another, rose to his feet filthy. A church bell clanging, away over the field.

On the road, while Brown secured the shed door, Louis patted the horse's nose and mopped his face and neck with his bandana. The two men declined dinner with the planter, who said a few words of farewell and headed back toward his house. He looked ill and low-spirited, though not because of the dead colored man in his shed, Louis reckoned, nor the bones under his drought-ruined corn.

"You're sure," Brown said.

They had marked the graves with sticks. A church bell rang the Sabbath, and cicadas rasped under the shimmering hot sky. Louis closed his eyes. The church bell clanging. He shuddered violently, then quickly leaned over and vomited. He spat, straightened. His heart pounded. He panted and spat again.

"I'm sure." Louis blotted his face. Though he hardly wanted to linger, he dreaded the ride back. A buckboard, especially the way Brown drove it, would not have been his choice of transport right now.

"That's too bad," Brown said, unperturbed. "I doubt we'll ever know why he took a shot at you, sir."

"And who do you think shot him?" Louis stuffed the bandana in his pocket. "In the back of the head, that is."

Brown squinted over the field. The corn dead on the ear, the stalks dried pale brown. The church bell stopped, the cicadas kept on.

"Can't say," Brown said finally. "We don't know the boy's name, or who's he was."

Gentlemen, look on this wonder!
Whatever the bids of the bidders, they cannot be high enough for it

The scars, lash marks.

The laborer who found the body in a drainage ditch had not recognized the dead man; the planter claimed not to know him either. Whoever did him in had known him, though, and made fast work of it. Barely more than a week had passed since the ambush. They might have arranged a meeting, the payment, maybe.

"He could be from anywhere," Brown said.

The church bell, cicadas, and a hundred, hundred acres of dead corn.

"WELL. BONNY. WELL, WELL." Branden took out his watch, listened to it, pocketed it with a shake of his head, and poured himself another whiskey. "I thought you. Were. My friend."

"I'm sorry, Branden. Truly, I am."

They sat on Heron's back veranda, as usual, Branden's feet up on the rail, Louis's legs stretched out, Lizzy snoozing on the floorboards between them. Louis had seen Gutman, at the beer garden off Decatur. It was not Bianca who was with him.

"You are not. Sorry. Confound you." Branden laughed. "Least. You shouldn't. Be."

So, Branden was not heartbroken, on hearing his best friend confess to a liaison with Bianca.

Branden's heart was long-broke, and falling apart in his chest. His eyes were sunken, his lips pale. A fitful wind snagged in his clotted lungs.

"Good for. You."

"Are you seeing a doctor, Branden?"

It was the same old question, and Branden answered the same old way, with a nod. Louis did not believe him. How the man got to work every day.

"Too bad. She's not. Divorced."

The pianist crooned "Beautiful Dreamer." It would be "Dixieland" next.

"Her husband's come back to get her," Louis said. "Rudy Gutman. He's with a trollop at Schwartz's right now, celebrating the joyous reunion."

Branden laughed again. He had adopted a way that did not make him cough. It was like a leaky bellows pumped softly.

"No wonder. Bianca ain't. Been. Around."

"All for love."

Branden wheezed. "Now you. Got yourself. Some trouble."

"I don't think so."

Branden coughed, gripped his chest, waved Louis off. He wiped his face with a handkerchief gray with stone dust. "Free Love. Or not."

"They're going back to Chicago next week."

Bianca's note to Louis: *I would of run in battle Louis I am such a cowrd I cannt tell you to yor face.*

"Statue of Eva. She said. Put it in. Hollywood. Cemetery."

One stayed a little when the rest were gone
Beside a grave. Quite motionless she stood
Until the paths grew dim, then turned away;
And twilight gathers—

"Shoulda. Seen it coming. Boy." Branden rubbed his chest, over his heart.

"You need to go to a doctor," Louis said.

"Shoulda seen it. Bonny."

Louis's anger—about the Board, being shot at, the women, Valentina if he had ever really been angry at her at all—had died some time after the third beer. Too, whenever he was with Branden, whatever else was going on had to make way for worries about his friend's mortality.

"Shoulda." Branden ruined Louis's beer by pouring whiskey in it.

"It's not as if I ever got any warning from a friend." As if Branden should have told him: *She is going. To run. Bonny.*

"Well." Branden's eyes sank closed. He looked battered as a half-done sculpture.

Dust. Clay. Mere flesh. A leaf of grass.

And in man or woman a clean, strong, firm-fibred
body, is beautiful as the most beautiful face

And what of the sour, weak, unraveling body, Walt? The falling apart body. The consumption-riddled lung-sponges, the liquor-raddled stomach sac, the bowels loose and stinking. Branden must have given up on the nitrate papers he used to burn for his lungs, and the lozenges. He smelled only of stone dust, tobacco, and ill-washed clothes.

Louis took his hand. "Never mind, man."

Branden smiled without opening his eyes. His hand was cold. "Remember. Back when. We was. Jumping fences."

"Those were the days," Louis said. "You took good care of Jake and me." Branden the strongest boy in Dogtown.

"Little. Jake. Tell him. Come. Back home."

"One of these days he'll be back." He would not, though. He had made his home up north, in chill, white New England.

Branden let his feet fall to the porch. His hands braced on the chair arms, he succeeded in pushing himself to his feet. He even managed to mount his old gelding, who was himself fit only to plod the round of Heron's, Branden's house, and Manchester Stone. Better off than Nelly, laid up at Richard's stable. And Lizzy who was so fat, Louis had to carry her down the steps. Mrs. Sully was feeding her too many....

No, by God. Louis felt her nipples. How had he missed that?

"For the love of God, Lizzy." He should have kept her in the shed longer, or maybe he had missed her first days in season. No wonder she had shredded Mrs. Sully's old horse blankets. Making a den for a new batch of fine, upstanding Dogtown citizens.

Louis stopped at Gorman's after he and Branden went their separate ways.

"Another finger tip?" Louis asked, the butcher's thumb swathed in linen. "How much this time? *Wie viele?*" Last year, it was half Gorman's pinky.

Gorman looked at his bandaged finger, as if just seeing it. "No worry. I save it for the hound." He shook the packet of scraps and laughed so loud, it raised the flies.

Louis let Lizzy eat half the scraps outside the shop, and took her home and locked her in the shed, though it was a little late for that. He headed back to Heron's to get Jimbo and rode in starlight to the quarry, where he stabled the mule. He sneaked, the usual way, to the terrace casement door of her room.

"What are you doing here, Louis!" She smelled of sleep, of herself, her hair loose and tangled. "He's in town tonight."

"I know. I saw him."

She lit a candle and sat on the bed. Louis sat at the foot of the chaise.

"I don't know when he's coming back," she said.

"Why are you leaving us, Bianca?"

She heaved a sigh. "We're going to Chicago. Rudy's pianos are there. His business."

"Your home—"

"Jeannie will be better off without me."

"What? What? You're leaving your daughter?"

"Shh!"

"You can't do such a thing. You can't—"

"Stop, Louis. Just…. Don't. I've made up my mind."

"You're her mother. She needs you."

Her wrapper slipped open; she pulled it mostly shut. "She's a woman now. She needs a husband."

"Who? Stratton? You'll leave her to him?"

Bianca raked her fingers through her hair; the wrapper opened again. "She'll have other suitors. The moment she steps out of the magic castle. That's what Branden calls this place. The magic castle."

"What about our family?" Louis said. "You and me and Valentina and Jeannie and Aunt Anne. And Maurice Termey, whenever he gets back. And Branden. Branden is dying, Bianca. You're breaking up our family." Grief flowed cold over him like a cloud shadow, and he covered his face with his hands.

"Oh, God, Louis, don't cry. For God's sake, please don't cry."

Louis did not. He breathed down a sob and sat up again. A steamer trunk was open, beside the wardrobe. He got up, silently, and went to the painting propped there. One of Valentina's: Bianca, nude, candlelit, the painting dim in the room's candlelight.

"I've tried to get poor Branden to a doctor," Bianca said. "He says he's been. He said it's too late."

Branden told his best friend: *I'm. All right. Bonny.*

Bianca got up and rummaged in the wardrobe and took a flask out of some pocket. "Have a nip, friend."

Louis had a nip.

"May I point out, my dear," Bianca said, "you didn't mention Rudy, as part of our family?"

Carousing in a beer garden. "All right. Rudy."

"I know he's out with another woman tonight. Even if your face hadn't given it away. You've got such an honest face."

"In that case, I might as well get into bed with you," Louis said. "Rudy has looked at my face. He will not be surprised to find us in *flagrante delicto*."

Bianca laughed, and so did Louis.

"You don't want me anymore, sweet," he said. "I shall live with that, though I might have been lying when I said I don't love you. But how can you abandon us? Jeannie. And Valentina."

"I'll follow Rudy to Chicago, like a fool, and we will try to be…respectable. And your life, my dear Louis, your life will flow on."

"And they all lived happily ever after."

"Each in his own way."

The terrace door open, Louis listened. He was only human, to listen for the husband's footstep.

"Valentina is spitting mad at me," he said.

"No puff pastries this week?"

He laughed. "It's not funny." He moved next to her on the bed and took her hand. "Us."

"She wants you to marry Jeannie," Bianca said. "So do I."

He dropped her hand. "What are you saying?"

"So does Jeannie. That's why Valentina's so upset about us. Partly why. Jeannie needn't know. Please, Louis, don't ever, ever tell her about us."

Louis had to laugh. "What is happening to me? How was I ever caught up in this weaving?" He turned to Bianca, serious again. "I will not marry—"

"Don't say it, Louis." She got up and passed him. The perfume of her. She stepped barefoot onto the terrace. Jeannie's room, at least, was on the other side of the house. And Valentina's. Amazing, he had never worried much about being discovered. So eager for his mistress's bed. She had her head cocked. Listening for her husband's step. Or her sister's step. Or her daughter's step. Louis laughed again, very quietly.

She came back. He embraced her. She pushed against him, gave in. They did not make love. They did not go that far, in the room where her husband's clothes draped the edge of an open steamer trunk. Too, her need for him was quenched. Though they parted breathing hard.

"You'd better go." She gathered her hair up, let it drop. "Did you walk?"

"No, I've got Jimbo to use."

"How's poor Nella?"

"She's getting fat."

They tried a laugh, it was exhausted.

Louis wished he had not come at all. The dregs of what they had once shared were heavy and jagged as a sack of gravel.

"Louis."

"Bianca."

"Goodbye, Louis."

LOUIS AND JIMBO PLODDED SIDE by side on Westham Road under a gibbous moon, Jimbo having thrown a shoe. At approaching hoofbeats, a slow trot dull on the packed dusty dirt, Louis reflexively checked for his gun—which he had left in the quarry safe. This stretch of road was wild, wooded. Not a good place for any man to travel, without a weapon. Bianca never let him carry, around her. She despised guns and swords and daggers….

It was Rudy Gutman. Louis's apprehension and his lingering wistful lust flashed into the white-hot wish to blow Gutman clean out of his saddle. He let go of Jimbo's reins, just dropped them, and walked toward Gutman.

"Who is it?" Gutman said, slowing to a walk. "Louis!" As if he were pleased to see his wife's lover, coming from her direction.

Louis knew how to do it, and he had the element of surprise. He waited until Gutman put his gun back in his belt, then he leaped forward and pulled Gutman right off his horse. Gutman managed to kick out of the stirrups and land more or less on his feet, hanging on to Louis's shirt, almost bringing him down. The two men stumbled, clinging. Louis clawed the gun from Gutman's midriff and threw it somewhere. He doubled back to avoid Gutman's knee, clenched his fist to demolish Gutman's face. The back of Gutman's hand on his cheek sent him staggering back. A fist followed, to Louis's gut, not full on, hard enough. Coughing, Louis dove, threw his arms around Gutman's body and hurled him to the ground.

His nostrils filled with exhalations of tobacco and beer and a woman's smells and violet shaving cologne and hair oil, and they were clinched tight as cats rolling, bodies mashed together, hands filled with wool and linen and flesh, too close for kicking, punching, choking, gouging, head-butting—

A catch in Gutman's breath, a tiny wheeze like a moan, loosened Louis's hold.

It was all Rudy Gutman needed. Still grasping Louis's coat and shirt and skin, Gutman hauled him to his feet, all the way up on his toes, and flung him hard away.

Louis spun stumbling over the rough road margin. His feet crossed each other; he flailed to catch himself; he fell on his hip, barked shrilly, tumbled into a ditch. His vision spangled. Rising to all fours, he shook his head to clear it and grappled his way back onto the road.

Crack—boom! Louis hit the dirt.

Gutman had shot in the air, the after-image of the discharge like a jumping candle flame, up and down. Louis stood slowly. Through the shim of shifting bright blobs, he saw the gun aimed at his chest now.

Blobs of light repeated, faded. Powder smoke dissipated into dew, dust, and moonlight. His own heaving breath, and Gutman's breath.

The night recovered itself. Crickets and frogs. The mule and the horse companionable, unfazed, munching away at the roadside grass. Click-click: the revolver's hammer eased back down.

"You've got a hell of a nerve," Gutman said.

Louis got no satisfaction from whatever caused Gutman to mumble—a split lip, a broken tooth, a bit tongue. He did not taste blood in his own mouth. A couple of his fingers felt sprained. The side of his head hurt where he had hit it on a rock, crashing into the ditch.

Gutman stuck the gun in his belt—though he kept his hands on his hips, his coat tail back, the gun clear. For all Louis cared,

Gutman could shoot him through the skull. He just wanted to finish going home and put the man behind forever and ever.

"Go back to Chicago," he said.

"I should leave my wife here for you?" Gutman touched his lip, looked at his fingers.

"You're a low blackguard."

"I'm the one who's supposed to say that."

"You have not," Louis said.

"So that's it. You're outraged that I'm *not* outraged that you've been conducting a liaison with Bianca."

"I'll get my gun, and you can say that again."

Gutman did not move his hands. "You southern gentlemen are so touchy. Well, I'm not. Though maybe, I don't know, if I'd come home an hour or so earlier?"

Louis lightly fingered his cheek, tender and swelling. "You'd have been touchy? Or not touchy?"

Gutman did not rise to it. "No honest man can say what he'd do in the heat of the moment, though I doubt I would shoot you in Valentina's house."

"I suppose that's a code of some kind."

"No, Bonny, I don't see the world and other men—and women—on those terms. Sure, I don't like what Bianca's been doing, any more than she likes me stepping out. But that's not what's important between me and her."

Louis hunted for a rejoinder and could not find one. This argument belonged to husband and wife. Gutman was right, on those terms.

"You are wrong." The words welled up from the depths of his soul, and his voice trembled with the force of them. "It is important. It is the most important thing."

Gutman stared at him. He had been a sharpshooter and would not miss if he shot. No one would miss, anyway. They stood close enough for Louis to smell again the violet water, and beer and tobacco. And Louis, exhaling the scent of Bianca Gutman.

Rudy Gutman eased his coat back in place. "May I continue on my way, Louis?"

The song of crickets and frogs filled the shadows.

Louis went back to Jimbo and fooled around with the tack until Gutman passed by and the road was lonely again. He tested the first and second fingers of his left hand and decided again they were sprained, not broken. He touched his cheek—the skin torn; Gutman must wear a ring. He thought of how he would look to his men tomorrow, to Valentina, next time he saw her.

The moon lay dewy white over road, trees, shrubs, and grass.

The careful reasonings he had used to balance his love for Valentina against his affair with her sister ghosted away. His makeshift morality; his married and not married; his reckoning of what Free Love allowed; his loneliness, her willingness: it was as if the naked luminosity of the moon showed them up as the vaporous lies they were.

He had wanted to abide among the women at Granite Bluff. He had wept with longing, to be part of their lives. It seemed a lifetime ago. The wish had been borne to him on lust and drunkenness, and grief, too, and love, and its heart was pure innocence. He had thrown that away. He had betrayed them all, just as Valentina said. He had looked right into her face, on the bank of Reedy Creek, and capped his inane self-justification—*we were free with each other* —with the words, *I am not sorry.* By his own terms, by the terms of his very soul, he had betrayed Valentina. He had betrayed his beloved woman's body with his own.

Jimbo sighed and shifted. Louis entwined his fingers in the mule's rough, stubby mane and sobbed with sorrow and shame.

Louis walked with Whittington and Theo Yarborough, the railroad superintendent, to the end of the narrow dirt ribbon the railroad had cleared between the river and the New Old Quarry with the help of two of his grouters—his former grouters, his own men the railroad stole from him, making the other grouters jealous. He looked at the stakes driven into the ground to show where the rails would be laid. He looked upriver and down along the imaginary track.

"It will flood," he said.

Yarborough tightened his lips, probably to hold in a curse. He wore a linen suit, rumpled and nearly as dusty as Louis's cotton-wool. Yarborough's father, a cotton factor, had sent him to the University of Virginia. He quit to enlist in Richard Poindexter's cavalry company. His body listed in a slight curve: ribs shattered in a fall from a horse. He was not a bad fellow, really, but Louis was in no mood to humor anyone connected with the railroad.

"Mr. Bondurant," Yarborough said, "the tracks here will be at exactly the same elevation as the tracks at the Old Quarry."

"There is a natural berm between the Old Quarry tracks and the river," Louis said, "and riprap at the water's edge. Yet the tracks have flooded, in springs past. Some of our—the quarry's—equipment was damaged as well."

"Are you suggesting we raise the entire line?"

"I am not suggesting anything. I am passing on an observation. These tracks will be flooded when the river rises. It is not for me to decide what to do about that. You are the expert at railroad building, not I."

Yarborough stared along the tracks and over the river's edge. His face lightened. He made a sketch. A mere diagram, nothing like Valentina's art. Louis thought he might ask her to draw the New Old Quarry as it was now, before it all changed. It might be a way for them to make up with each other. She could draw Eva's place, and send it to Bianca. No. Bianca would not want a reminder. It would be cruel, in fact. She had left it behind.

An oak for a tombstone, and a shabby wreath of honeysuckle and wild grape for decoration. But Eva's body lay at Hollywood Cemetery. The statue would soon be erected there. Bianca had left that behind, too.

Louis lifted his eyes from the ground. The tip of Yarborough's tongue stuck from the corner of his mouth as he refined his sketch. He had probably done that since he was a child and did not know it. Or maybe his schoolmates had teased. He was the kind of man Louis might have been, in a way, had he gone to college.

Yarborough made arrows and scribbles around the drawing. "I think we can improve this area, and the old tracks, too, in order to prevent flooding." He looked up. He blinked, then smiled at the change on Louis's face. "Of course, my employers must permit."

"Of course," Louis said.

"If I may consult you when I have some drawings."

"Mr. Whittington and I will be happy to assist you in any way I can."

Whittington stayed with Yarborough, and they began

pointing at the river, up and down the road. As Louis passed his former grouters they chopped studiously at some bracken, so they would not have to face their old boss whom they had left without notice. Louis climbed the ladders, stopping on the way to his cabin to tell Tristan, "Get me a rag and a bucket of cool spring water, would you?"

"Sir."

Tristan had been discontented ever since Stratton decreed that he be given a less strenuous job. The ease of his present position was envied by his former mates in the engine house, yet he resented being, essentially, a servant. That irritated Louis. The man was lucky to have any kind of job. Even if he were white, he would not do any better, what with his wife having to wrap his belly up in a bandage every day, to keep his herniated guts in. Or maybe he would, were he white. But he was not. And he would not do better here, at this quarry, in this city, in this state, and in this nation, north or south.

Louis wrung out the rag and put it to his swollen cheek. Rumor had somehow grasped the gist of his battered face and bruised fingers: a fight over a woman. He was beginning on the Manchester Stone reports when Whittington came in.

"Sir, Mrs. Termey requests that you call on her at your earliest convenience." He handed a folded note to Louis with a gloating air. The young man had wanted to recopy the weekly report this morning, nearly illegible and all full of blots, Louis's hand swollen. *Send it now, Mr. Whittington,* Louis had directed, vinegar-sour.

Louis stared at him a few beats. "Mr. Whittington, what is it with you reading a personal note from Mrs. Termey to myself?"

The mindless jab changed Whittington's smirk to hangdog. "Excuse me, sir. I did not guess it was personal." A smirky hangdog.

She had been out yesterday afternoon, when Louis went up to report, if Rebecca was to be believed. Which she was not. She was a very bad liar. Or maybe Valentina told her to be obvious about it, to let Louis to know that the lady of the house was not willing to interrupt her daubing and dabbing to see the man she had left at the side of the road the week before. Nearly left.

"You will complete the reports for Manchester Stone, Mr. Whittington." *Touche.* Whittington hated having to read Branden's handwriting.

Louis took Jimbo up the side of the drive, rather than make him walk on the burning hot cobbles. He took a little longer than usual, tying Jimbo to the post in the shade, patting the mule's neck, asking the stable boy to bring a bucket of water. He wanted badly to see Valentina, for all his battered face and hand, and he was not sure if he could endure whatever mood she might be in.

In the studio, Mrs. Hamilton sat in her chair like a cat in the sun. Valentina, on the sofa, wore a yellowish brown dress that played up her amber eyes and golden hair. If only her mouth were not set so hard against him.

And he against her, yes, and everyone. Bianca and Rudy Gutman were gone. Jeannie moped on the terrace with her banjo. First her father, then her sister, now her mother. Pity softened Louis's heart.

He sat in the Italian chair. Rebecca set the tray on the tea table. Wyman and Mourning and Ezra gone, too.

Valentina did not pour. Louis did not pick up a pastry. He and she, set against each other.

The continual changes of the flex of the mouth, and
around the eyes

He never could just look at her; he had to take her in, thoroughly: the eyes, the eyelashes golden and sparse, her bottom lip he could imagine sucking in between his teeth, her ear lobes, ornamented with pearls, her throat moving as she swallowed, the hands paint-stained.

He did not know how he would ever make things up with her. He had nowhere to stand: he was only her employee, after all.

Maurice Termey's employee, and she Maurice Termey's wife. An envelope with foreign franks lay on the tea table. It would have come on a series of packets: Rome, Louis saw with a covert glance. Rome, to New York or Baltimore, or maybe straight to Norfolk, and up the James River. By hand to end up here, between himself and Valentina.

"I am sorry we lost Wyman." Louis tried to keep his voice flat, and did not succeed. "Yet who could begrudge him the wish to do better by his wife and their son and whatever other children they may have. May God prosper them."

She nodded, her eyes downcast. Her throat moved as she swallowed. The notes of the banjo came from the terrace, stopping and starting a tune Louis could not quite recognize.

"I have told the rest of the colored men they will receive no promotion this season," he said. "I lied, not admitting they will never ever be promoted. It's a very hard thing for a man to toil on without hope, as if he is a slave. So. Is there anything else I need do? Shall I lay out tea for the railroad men, when they come each day? Will my colored men polish their boots? While I am made to lick Dunaway's and yours, ma'am?" His voice shook. He could hardly believe what he was saying, his neck and face hot, his chest stiff, too full of air.

Valentina did not answer, though she made a sound. It was like a little whimper. Louis took a deep breath and pressed his sweaty hands on the arms of the chair.

"I—"

"For heaven's sake, Valentina," Mrs. Hamilton said, "tell him."

Louis's stomach dropped; the heat in his skin went to ice. She was going to dismiss him. He picked up a coffee cup, for something to do, put it down again. His hands shook. Hers were knotted in her lap.

"What is it, please." He could call her neither Valentina nor Mrs. Termey.

"*Tell him*, Valentina," Mrs. Hamilton insisted.

"Aunt Anne!" She stood so suddenly, her face flushed dark, Louis barely kept himself from flinching. She stalked to the terrace doors and stood facing out, drawn up tight.

Aunt Anne broke the silence, quietly. "He should know, darling."

Valentina drew a deep breath, let it out and her shoulders slackened, though she spoke without turning toward them.

"We had to mortgage the quarry. To pay the taxes. But the money...." She fell silent again, for a long time. "The thing is.... He.... The Italian government. They will not let it go." She turned to face him. "Yes, that's the problem." "Maurice has it in a Roman bank, you see."

Mrs. Hamilton gave a sharp, exasperated sigh.

Louis drank coffee to wet his mouth, and to give himself time to take all this in. It was more the kind of business disclosed to a finanical advisor, not an employee. Or to a family friend, but surely she would not consider him such. He really did not know what to say. He tried to put her revelations in order, in his mind.

Valentina returned to her seat, finally. "With the Federal contract, we should be able to pay our way."

"Well, then it's just a matter of time, I suppose, before—"

"But this lawsuit, Louis. Your lawsuit. It worries me."

"The lawsuit....?" He nearly asked, stupidly, the lawsuit against Richard Poindexter? As if he were Jimmy Branch, with several actions coming and going. "There's nothing to be concerned about, Valentina. Nothing at all. The lawsuit is to recover a debt owed to my father's estate. It doesn't touch Granite Bluff Quarry." It was true, yet in a sense he deceived her. Already, again.

The river's drought-starved music, and the banjo, could be heard through the open terrace doors. Maurice Termey had a modest house, for a wealthy man, and peaceful, at least when the quarry lay at rest, the stone drowsing, in its way, when men were not drilling and hammering and blasting at it. The banjo stopped.

Jeannie came in from the terrace, the instrument in hand. The sight bemused, a well-washed young lady in a pink sprigged dress, carrying a banjo. Then Bianca's words about Jeannie and him marrying came to him. He prayed Bianca had kept that idea to herself. But Valentina's disclosures about the quarry. As if he were a suitor. Surely not. Himself, for Jeannie. No.

In his eyes, she was little more than a child. But her skirts hid her feet, and her hair was pinned up. She was a woman. Orange blossom wafted lightly from her, as she sat on the sofa next to her aunt. The scent had been favored by a lively young lady Louis courted one winter, a cargo of erotic associations. Yet, looking back, it was nothing. The nice young ladies and the fancy women: fond memories. It was Bianca who had opened to him the world of passion. And what was he to her? The dust on her shoes.

"How do you do, Mr. Bondurant?" Jeannie asked.

The flush impending crept into his neck and face. He was so sunblown, it might not show. "And you, Miss Gutman?"

"I'm quite well, thank you."

"Will you play us a tune, Miss Gutman?"

Pink spread over her face. "Do you like Bach?"

"Why, yes, I do."

If that was what she had been playing, no wonder he did not recognize it. Mama had played Bach on the piano, not a banjo. He brushed his mustache with his fingers. He could not help seeing the way the girl looked at him, through her lashes. It could be she liked him, as Bianca claimed. She might be out and out flirting. Good Lord. Valentina got up smilingly, signaling him not to stand, and smilingly went to her easel, leaving Louis alone, as it were, with the banjo-playing girl.

She played an elaborate tune, presumably by Bach.

Could they possibly want a man like him, worth so little in the world, to pick this flower?

"That's a very nice air," Louis said, "and well played."

"Do you enjoy music often?"

She would not mean, the saloon tunes at Heron's.

"My Mama played the piano at home. Corelli, Bach, Schumann. And Schubert, with Papa singing." Nostalgia pierced Louis, nearly took his breath away.

It must have shown on his face. The space between her eyebrows creased in sympathy. She would be beautiful to the end of her days, however many they might be.

"And opera?" she asked. "Do you enjoy opera?" And she could flog along a conversation. Young ladies trained to it.

"I have enjoyed a few. How about you, Miss Gutman? Have you ever attended an opera?"

"Yes, I have. They were beautiful."

"Of course you have." In Italy, Chicago, New York, likely. Vienna, Rome, Paris. He thought of her as a child, but she had seen far more of the world than he likely ever would.

A painting caught his eye. It looked like rock. That was all: rock that filled the whole canvas.

"It is a study," Jeannie said, following. "A study of granite."

"Aha. I see."

"You come with us to the opera, Louis," Mrs. Hamilton said. "I need an arm to lean on, and yours will do splendidly."

Valentina stepped from behind the easel. Grayish-brown paint smudged her chin.

"What will they be performing?" Jeannie asked.

"As long as it's not *Cosi fan tutte* we'll be fine," the old woman said.

Valentina tittered and blushed deeply. Louis and Jeannie looked at each other, equally at a loss.

"Why not *Cosi fan tutte*, Aunt Anne?" Jeannie asked.

"It's a comedy called *La Fille du Regiment*," Valentina said quickly. She rolled the r, more Italian than French.

"*The Daughter of the Regiment*," Louis said. "A French work."

Jeannie clapped her hands. "You can translate for us! How perfect." She added, "If they sing in French."

Louis smiled. Valentina and Jeannie looked at him, pleased, in much the way Branden looked at his repeater watch when he made it chime. Mrs. Hamilton gave an unladylike snort of laughter.

THE SALOON NEAR KOHEN'S offices was hardly better than Heron's, blue with tobacco smoke and dense with the odor of beer and men. And sour food: sauerkraut, soused beef, sliced potatoes dressed in vinegar. The bread tasted sour, too, and so did the dark wine. It brought to mind army rations, except the beef was wondrously tender. Louis ordered a plate of oysters that never came. During their meal, during Louis's recitation of his latest trials and tribulations, he and Moses Kohen slipped into calling each other by first name.

The waiter collected the plates. "My oysters?" Louis said. The waiter glanced at Kohen, left.

Moses stuffed and lit a pipe. "My wife doesn't allow me to smoke in the house, or the office or even on the porch or in the garden."

"My landlady is the same. Her fiancé has switched to chewing, in preparation for wedded bliss." Louis could not blame the women, really. Papa had extracted from his sons the promise never to partake, believing tobacco to the wellspring of slavery and a breaker of manly health and character.

They were at a table in a corner missed by what little light remained in the windows and nearly the lantern light, too. Moses refilled their glasses. Louis would have preferred beer to the vinegary wine, the better to rinse down the grit of the day.

"How did you know the would-be assassin was shot?" Moses said. "In the back of the head, you say. I take it that the wound was concealed."

"With a clean hat."

"Ah."

"If I hadn't said anything, Richard's detective would have come up with some story of drunkenness and drowning or exposure. Or fever from the wound in the hand."

"Yet you don't believe Mr. Poindexter is responsible for the attack on you."

"No, I don't."

"You believe his pledge."

"I know what you're thinking. That my father trusted him, too. Sure, he'd cheat me down to my last dime, but he would not cause me bodily harm." Richard's sister Alicia: *He loves you dearly.* And: *Watch out for him.*

"And Mr. Poindexter's threat at the Board meeting was directed against Mr. Dunaway?"

"Dunaway resents my lawsuit. Though I don't know why he should."

"Mrs. Termey and Mr. Dunaway are acquaintances?"

"Mrs. Termey?"

"And Mr. Dunaway."

"They're both on the quarry company Board. I mean, Mr. Termey is on the Board, and she his proxy." Louis took a swallow of the wine and suppressed a grimace. It was very bad. And Moses's line of questioning made him uneasy, though it yielded no more than common knowledge. It was Moses's choice of questions, and his way of arranging the answers.

"Given that the lawsuit is against Mr. Poindexter," Moses said, "Mr. Dunaway should have no reason to fear it."

"I would think not."

Or to fear Louis himself. Painful as the foreclosure on the house had been to the family, Louis had considered it an impersonal evil, inflicted by a banker, when Papa could not meet his debts. He had never threatened Dunaway. The Board meeting, in fact, had been the first time they ever spoke with each other beyond *Good day, sir*, if they happened to pass each other here or there. Quarry business, Louis conducted through Maurice Termey, then Valentina. He banked at Branch's.

"What about one of the other directors of the old company, Deep Rock?" Louis asked.

"I don't think so. Of the three, including Mr. Poindexter, one died in the War, the other of natural causes. Both were wealthy men for whom Deep Rock was a small concern." Moses picked up his glass, swirled the wine in it, put it down without drinking. "Apropos to Mr. Dunaway, I did learn something interesting lately. You may know already, of course."

"It could be." The foreclosure, Moses would say.

"Baxter Dunaway was a partner in Mede Quarry Company."

Louis's stomach jumped into a fist. Mede, the rival quarry that had won the Federal contract from Deep Rock, rendering its stock worthless and his father bankrupt. "That's…. I had no idea."

He should have had an idea. He should know each actor, their interests. How would he? How was he to know all these twists and turns? He was a quarry man. He spent his days with laborers and stone, not gadding from bank to office, sitting in tufted chairs at their drinking clubs. He was not a member of the Manchester Hunt.

"Mr. Poindexter had no connection with Mede," Moses said. "At least, none that I have been able to find." He looked into Louis's face. "I think there is history here."

"Dunaway…. He—his bank held the mortgage on our home. The mortgage that Papa used… That is, the collateral for—for what he believed to be a loan."

Unavoidable, the thought: how unwise, how downright rash Papa had been, to speculate against the house, no matter Richard's blandishments. "When Papa couldn't make the note, Dunaway possessed our house. His bank did, that is."

Moses made a sign to the waiter. If he thought Papa a fool, he did not show it.

A dinner crowd was in, noisy, and the waiter had to twist and turn through it to reach their table. A pianist struck up a tune Louis did not know, a melancholy tune in a merry measure.

Papa had told the family that he had lost their house in jagged fits and starts. Trying not to break into tears. A breath gulped, every few words. Mama had held his hands. She never said a word of regret about the house. Never said she saw it coming. Not a reprimand passed her lips, no silences hung about her. Never a reproachful look. Louis had not complained either. That did not mean he was not bitter, later, when he understood what his father had done. Yet he had not understood it fully, until this lawsuit of his. Had not understood that Papa had lied to them, that it was pure speculation, not Richard defaulting on a loan, that lost their home.

"Coffee, if you please," Louis said to the waiter. No more wine.

At the barn dance, he made love with Bianca, in the grass by the pond. He had not been drunk, when they did it. Only drunk enough to get there. He wanted to be there right now. There, with Bianca.

Gutman had her now. This adulterous lust right on the heels of speaking about his father. Louis stared at the table.

"Richmond is a small town, isn't it?" Moses said.

Dunaway surely knew why Papa had mortgaged the house. A banker had to know that. He might have known, too, the quarry would fail, as Papa signed over his house. Or he might not have. Or he might have. He got a house to resell and he turned a tidy profit on Mede Quarry, both in one stroke.

Moses said, "I have never been to Manchester town, I admit."

If property values were high that year, Dunaway would have done quite well on the house, the cozy house that Grandpapa helped Papa build.

"Louis?"

Louis affected a jovial air that no doubt rang utterly false. "It is a mere dogtown. That is what we call it. Dogtown." He began to invite Moses over, bumbled away on remembering something about Jews and dogs, and he was not sure Moses could eat outside a Jewish establishment. He could hardly invite someone who could not take an ale to rinse down Dogtown's dust and hoggish aroma. Hogs, for God's sake. He did not know if Moses, trying to find again the old ways, would break his race's commandments.

Unlike his murderous, adulterous, blaspheming, self-abusing self.

And if the body were not the Soul, what is the Soul

"Plenty of industry," Moses said.

Louis said, "He is building a mansion on Franklin Street."

Moses looked in Louis's face with his dark intelligent eyes. "It's what bankers do, Louis."

"And Stratton?" Louis said. "You mentioned him. Shall I add him to my band of enemies?"

"It's possible Dr. Stratton helped to negotiate the Federal contract recently made with Granite Bluff Quarry Company. He has friends in Washington city."

"Well, then he's a friend, isn't he."

Moses did not answer.

Louis's stomach clenched again. "Did Stratton help scotch the Deep Rock contract, do you think?" His antipathy toward the doctor an intimation of truth.

"I've not seen his name connected with Deep Rock itself,"

Moses said. "Yet he has connections with nearly every individual who was involved in Deep Rock."

As if on cue, the pianist crooned, *"I dream of Jeannie.... "*

Louis half-turned in his chair. "I swear to God, if I never hear that song again.... " He turned back to Moses, embarrassed. "I beg your pardon, Moses."

"I'm not fond of Foster's ditties myself. Except, of course, when my wife sings them."

The two men laughed, and Louis remembered Mrs. Hamilton's, *as long as it's not....*

"Do you know opera?"

"Yes, I do," Moses said.

"What is the piece, cozy ... cozy.... "

"Cosi fan tutte?"

"That's it," Louis said.

"By Mozart. A comedy."

"What's it about?"

"The fidelity of two sisters is tested by their fiancés," Moses said. "The men disguise as each other and woo thus."

"And the sisters pass?"

"They do not."

Louis digested that as he shepherded a cockroach over the edge of the table. He defended the sisters: "So the women fall in love with the correct men, strictly speaking. The women's hearts see through the disguise."

"No. I'm afraid the men switch sisters."

Louis laughed. At least Valentina had seen the humor in it. And Mrs. Hamilton.

It was almost completely dark when Louis came out onto the street, hot and stinking as the saloon. Worse. Brimstone, excrement of all kinds, rotting vegetables.

After crossing Mayo's Bridge, Louis lingered on the Manchester wharf. A few ships were being loaded by torch light, mostly by black men and O'Keefe's brethren. Some families, off shift, still dun-dusted from working the flour mill, came down to the wharf. Maybe they sought fresh air, though it was hardly fresh, more like a dog's breath, extra-laden with the effluvium of tanneries and paper mills.

This is what Jake wanted him to leave. It could not be worse than any city, and New England ill-famed for its manufactories. Up there, though, as Jake put it, he would be honored as a man who courageously stood up against his kin and friends to fight for a noble cause. Here, that courage was equated with rankest betrayal. Four years and an army of carpetbaggers later, together with Jimmy Branch's—and admittedly Richard's—good words on his behalf, he was no longer quite so reviled as he had been on his return.

At the boarding house, he went straight up to his room. He knelt at his bedside like a little boy and recited the Lord's Prayer. It made him feel better.

To make it stick, he went to church the next day, his own church in Manchester, the service held at the Mason's Lodge, the new Chapel not yet complete. Louis put more in the collection plate than he had planned, his week's beer money a sponge to wipe his befuddled conscience.

Outside on the plank sidewalk, his face turned up to the hazy hot blue sky, he looked at his day.

"Will you take Sunday dinner with my family, Louis?"

Louis turned to face his enemy, his cousin Richard.

RICHARD'S CONVEYANCE WAS A covered buggy, the kind Papa had called a Brougham. The driver climbed up onto the box carefully, so his boots did not thump.

Mrs. Poindexter and a maid sat on the freshly tufted gold satin bench, the maid white, like all of Richard's servants. Richard and Louis sat on bare jump seats. Despite the dust veil over Mrs. Poindexter's face, Louis could make out that gossip had it right: she was very young and very beautiful, a belle. She had a refined, haughty way about her. Her maid, too, kept her nose in the air. The party spoke little on the ride.

Richard lived in a new part of town, west, in a new house of brick. An ironwork fence bordered the front of the property, a brick wall protected the rest. When the ladies disembarked out front, both Richard and the driver steadied Mrs. Poindexter, for she was pregnant. Louis swallowed down a shot of 100-proof jealousy.

After letting the ladies off, Louis and Richard rode around to the carriage house, so Louis could look in on Nella.

Nella loyally nipped Louis's sleeve and knocked his hat to the ground. The stable boy chased it, picked the straw from it and brushed off the dust. He hugged Nella's face. "Silly girl," he whispered.

"Richard, I'm deeply grateful to you for taking care of my old girl. And you, too, Nicky. " Louis tousled the stable boy's hair. "I shall have trouble separating you two, I think." The boy hid his face in Nella's mane. Louis regretted his words.

"Nicky walks her up and down the alley three times a day. Doctor's orders." Richard added, reading that Louis was about to speak of payment, "She was hurt at my railroad. Let us leave it there."

Louis had never been in the house before. It was spare and gracious. Jake would like it. When he still lived at home, he used to complain of being like "a bull in a china shop amongst Mama's gewgaws." A photograph of Louis, presumably part of said clutter, the one from when he was brevetted to Major. She would not have risked displaying her Union-uniformed son, had she and Jake not gone up to New England after Papa died. Or maybe she would have. She had complained to the Manchester postmaster, when her copies of *The Liberator* stopped arriving.

The dinner, in a cool, high-ceilinged room, was delicious. Not a heavy beef roast, as Mama used to make for the sacramental Sunday dinner, winter and summer alike, when they prospered. Boiled chicken in a pale sauce, pickles, oysters, a brothy soup, smoked fish, New Orleans rice. Mrs. Poindexter did not eat much, despite her husband's impatient prompts. Conversation was as untaxing as the food: weather, architecture, the growth of the city, streetcars, gas lines. Richard's son Charles had been graduated from his medical studies, and was staying with friends in Charlottesville. He might set up practice there. The corners Richard's mouth tightened for a moment.

They retired after dinner to the garden behind the house, to sit in wrought-iron chairs on a circle of brick-pavement shaded by a scuppernong arbor. A hedge of boxwood, with its odd, not unpleasant, fragrance of horse urine, stood between the garden and the stable yard. The shrubs, Richard said, came from the old Martin plantation.

Burgeoning grapes dangled. Brickey, formal in front of his master, served tiny glasses of red liquor. It was very bitter and yet flowery. After one sip, Louis put it down forever, though it sat strangely well in his stomach. Birdsong covered the silence. It was restful, or it would have been, were the company more congenial.

Whatever physicians had to say about pregnant women and delicacy, Mrs. Poindexter and most of the other pregnant women Louis had ever seen looked exceptionally hearty. Mrs. Poindexter's beauty, in any case, was not delicate. She was of the marble kind, scarlet and white to Jeannie Gutman's peachy pink and gold. She had a college degree.

Louis resisted feeling shabby. He tried to fend off a thick, melancholic jealousy. A breeze stirred a flag he had not noticed. Richard's regimental flag.

Brickey brought out dishes of ice cream covered with shavings of chocolate. A perfect paradise. The jealous melancholy built toward despair. Puffy clouds built into thunderheads, riverward.

Mrs. Poindexter excused herself. Brickey poured what Louis thought was brandy but turned out to be another kind of liquor, much better than the first: nutty and sweet. The discreetly placed battle flag was tattered and stained.

Louis nodded at it. "How did you manage to keep your colors?" Yet he really did not want to rehash any part of the War, beginning, middle or end, with his cousin.

"We had the fortune never to be part of any formal surrender. We were merely informed that the Confederate States of America had been vanquished."

"And freedom reigns."

Richard lit a cigar. "You know, when your daddy emancipated his slaves, we were all put about, in my family. A man careless discarding his property."

Louis could have assured his cousin, had he been in a mood to defend, that emancipating Anthony and Tessa, giving them a start up North, had hardly been a careless gesture. It had cost the family dearly, and not only in coin.

Richard's father would have seen it differently, of course. After his losses in the Panic of '37, he had turned bitter, proud. Eventually, his fortunes rose. When each man reached about even, the families grew close once more. They split again after the quarry business went sour. The two men died within months of each other. But Poindexter senior had lived to be elderly. Papa died barely in his forties. Richard started to say more that Louis cut over.

"What do you know about these railroad pranks? And someone trying to kill me."

"I know I would not allow any harm to you."

"That's not what I was asking," Louis said.

"Owning the spur don't make me a know-all, but I'm fairly sure—and so are you, I believe—that Dunaway has been at mischief. Has anything happened since I told him off?"

"No."

"Good." Richard added more liquor to Louis's little glass. "Now, this lawsuit of yours, Louis. I'm sure that Mr. Moses Kohen has enjoined your discretion. However, I would like to confide in you some matters that, while they are peripheral to your case, are of great importance to your friends." For all of Richard's lapses in and out of his old way of speaking, he could be long-winded. More the traditional lawyer than Mr. Moses Kohen.

"Your confidence is safe," Louis said, "except where it will help my case. I am determined to win."

"Of course you are. I don't fear for your discretion in this, Louis. I am certain I can rely on it."

"You may confide or not, as you see fit."

"Your lawyer, Moses Kohen, is a Ferret."

Louis had to smile. Ferrets had made it their business to expose men with stubborn Confederate sentiments, to keep them out of public office. And Moses, a Ferret? If that was all Richard had.

"You don't need to worry," Louis said. "President Johnson has put the Ferrets out of business."

"I'm not concerned for myself. I have the president's pardon framed upon my parlor wall, in a manner of speaking, and it don't take a Ferret to know me. It is Maurice and Valentina Termey that concern me, and might concern you as well. You know he was quite busy in Italy during the War."

Louis was about to say, yes, busy looking for stone. His naïveté crashed upon him.

Maurice Termey must have been in Italy as an agent of the Confederacy. Whether his mission for the Confederacy had been financial, military or political—more likely all three, Maurice Termey was not likely ever to display a Federal pardon anywhere. *Quite busy in Italy.* Implying he had been not merely a military officer, or a Confederate government functionary. He was guilty of high treason: he had conspired with a foreign power against the United States of America. Others like him lingered, too, overseas. A Ferret could take hold of that. Maybe the Federal government would, too.

Valentina: *Your lawsuit ... It worries me.* Mrs. Hamilton: *Tell him, Valentina.*

Richard had gone down a brick path to clip the spent blossoms from a white rose. He might or might not know that Louis was privy to the quarry's true ownership. But there was the house, the things in the house, and any of Valentina's possessions, which belonged, legally in Virginia, to Maurice Termey.

White petals fluttered to Richard's feet and the brick path. He put the defunct flowers in a basket looped over his arm. He came back, sat, then caught Louis off guard by leaning to him and pushing a white rose, partly open, into the button hole of his lapel.

"Though red would suit you better. A blood red rose for Bonny."

The wildest largest passions, bliss that is utmost, sor-
row that is utmost, become him well—pride is
for him

Louis fingered the creamy bud. He did not tear it out and throw it on the ground. Why should a flower be savaged by his grudge? Why should Valentina?

"You are a fine gentleman," Richard said. "But you ain't the gentle man your daddy was. Deep down, I believe, you're just like me. Heart hard as granite, and a soul propped up by hate."

Louis hardly needed Richard's opinions on himself, and certainly not on his father. He removed the rose from his lapel, gently, and laid it on the table between them. What he knew now was no more than anyone knew, though it had taken him an age to arrive at it.

He stood, and the two men went through the house, to the front entry.

"I believe you will not carry through with your law suit," Richard said. The entry hall was cool, its floor marble-tiled.

But the quarry had not been confiscated. Not yet.

"I will carry on with it, Richard, and I will win. For, to be sure, I want that money badly."

And with it I shall buy a quarry. And then I can get me a wife. And though she will not be Valentina, I shall cherish her unto death do us part.

And I shall never, ever fail her and our children.

Lizzy growled at a mutt venturing toward Heron's porch steps.

"Hush up, Lizzy." She grinned up at Louis as if he had praised her, thumped her tail, put her head on her paws.

"Why I ever took you along when I got that horse," Louis said. "As if you know anything about horses."

Branden laughed, wheezed into a wet cough, his mouth covered with a bandana that he folded against his friend's eyes.

Louis had bought the graying gelding now hitched to Heron's street rail on Branden's advice, after the horse doctor said Nella would never be up to the daily ride to and from the quarry. Spotty was sweet and elderly, more elderly than his seller had let on, his teeth, apparently, filed.

Branden pushed himself up to standing, then sat, or rather fell back into his chair. "Lord." He bent over and pressed both hands over his heart.

A long-brewed fear rose in Louis. "Let's get you home."

Branden nodded. His eyes were closed, the lids fluttering, his skin pale nearly to transparency. Louis helped him stand, and they went down the porch steps. Branden abruptly sat on the bottom step. Louis pushed down a burst of panic and whistled down a cab. His friend's weight, insubstantial, shocked him, as he and the cabman carried him to his door. Curious children clustered at the rusted gate.

The house was dim, foul-smelling. Rags and bottles and newspapers littered the entry hall. Louis carried Branden up the stairs.

"Who's there?" A frightened voice from the foot of the stairs. Branden's sister Alice.

"It's me. Bonny. I've got Branden. Which room is his?"

The stairs, with their stained carpeting, groaned under Alice's every step. She squeezed past Louis, and he followed her to the front room. It was as squalid as the entry hall, as the stairs, as the passage. How could he have let his friend go down so far?

He lay Branden down on dirty bed linens. There was no blanket. What happened to all the pretty things Rose had, the colorful quilts, the lacy testers, the smell of lemon-infused beeswax.

"Get a doctor," Louis ordered Alice. It came out gruffer than he intended, his throat tight. After all, squalor was the way they had lived, growing up. He removed Branden's shoes.

Alice pushed past him and looked down at Branden. "Oh, dear Lord."

"Stay with him," Louis said. "Sit him up if he starts coughing. Don't let him choke, for God's sake." He wished Stratton did not live so far away.

She did not take her swimming eyes from Branden. "I ain't never seen him this bad off."

When Louis came back with the doctor—his landlady's—Alice had Branden propped up against the headboard. A little color was in his face, a fever's grace. "Bonny. I'm. Oh. Rose. Rose." He clutched Alice's arm.

The doctor went to work. Alice was an able helper. Louis sat on the porch and went up and down the stairs. Branden was stripped. An enema, a purge. Louis wanted to go in and say,

Stop, stop it, and did not dare. The doctor came onto the porch. Louis had never met him before; he was from somewhere south.

"I am sorry to say, it is a hopeless case," the doctor said. "Lieutenant Hix cannot withstand any compounds that would ameliorate his condition."

The doctor's degrading ministrations had probably robbed that much more of Branden's strength. He was no better than a battlefield butcher, after all. The blue pill or the black or the red.

"Send your bill to me at Mrs. Sully's, if you please," Louis said.

"No. No, I will not charge a veteran of ours."

Louis shook his hand and went back up to Branden's room.

They had found a quilt, immaculate, flowered, smelling of camphor. Branden lay peaceful, asleep, dosed probably. Alice was gone. Louis wound the clock on the wall and set it going. Boys shouted on the street as they went in to supper. He turned from the window and Alice was there.

"You be sure and fetch me at Mrs. Sully's if anything happens," he said.

Louis went to his lodgings. He took the parlor lamp up to his room, and diverted himself with Parkman's adventures with Indians and illness. He woke from a dead sleep. It was dark. He must have put out the lamp, at some point.

"Mr. Bondurant." Mrs. Sully. Notes of terror. He sat up. The door cracked open.

"What is it, Mrs. Sully?"

"Someone's in the parlor."

He got out of bed and pulled on his pants.

In the passageway, "An intruder," Mrs. Sully whispered.

"Stay here, ma'am." He felt no fear, only a sense of the absurdity of it. His trousers wanted to slip down. He had removed the suspenders with the idea that he would switch them to his clean trousers.

"Mr. Bonny." Alice's voice came from downstairs, from the entry hall. "Come quick."

He strode back in his room and collided with Mrs. Sully. "It's all right," he said. "It's Lieutenant Hix's sister."

The lethargy of sleep sloughing off, he began to realize the import of Alice appearing here in the middle of the night. He wished he had stayed there. He never should have left his friend.

"Mrs. Sully, would you call your doctor? Have him come to the same house as this afternoon?"

"Mr. Bondurant, it's night time."

A respectable woman would hardly dare go out at night.

"Mrs. Sully, if I may attire myself please."

"Oh!"

Louis struck a light and finished dressing. He carried the lamp downstairs and left it on the entry hall table—Alice had a lantern. It was needed. Clouds covered stars and moon. Louis took Branden's stairs two at a time.

Branden was half-sitting, half-lying down, the quilt blood-spattered. "Stay by. Bonny."

"I'll just go for the doc—"

"No. No more. Stay here. Please."

Louis situated his friend more comfortably and put a chair next to the bed. He had heard somewhere that fresh air was good for the health, though surely not at night, what with falling damps. Branden's eyes were closed. Louis could not tell if he was asleep or not. Every breath short, staggering. The lamp burned low.

Louis watched the clock hands move toward the hour of four. The suffering hour. At four o'clock in the morning, men died, or they lay awake, praying to make it to dawn. In hospital, the muffled stroke of four had seized Louis with terror, if he awoke untimely. More acute than in battle, the fear. He would lie inert as a block of ice, praying for the light as if it were his life.

"The girl," Branden said. "Bianca's."

Louis looked at his friend's waxen visage. "The little one? Eva?"

The clock ticked. It went slowly. "What, Branden."

"Not." Branden sobbed, coughed, gulped. He moaned.

"What happened?"

The clock ticked. Branden's breath labored.

Louis touched him. "Say what you fetched me to hear, my brother."

"I wanted. Love. Bonny. Can't know."

Louis paused. "Miss Gutman? Jeannie?"

"Jeannie. Beauty."

"Yes?"

"A kiss. Touch. Soft. Oh."

"You kissed Jeannie and—and caressed her?"

Branden nodded, gave a sob.

"It's not such a very bad thing to do, Branden." Though he was not sure.

"It was. That day."

"The day… the day Eva died."

Branden nodded again. "Poor. Girl. Oh my soul."

There was no water in the room. Louis got a flask of whiskey from the highboy. He put it to Branden's mouth, and Branden drank a little, and some trickled down the side of his face. Louis wiped it with his sleeve.

"Alice," Louis called.

She was in the hall, on a chair swamped by her bulk.

"Alice, ma'am, would you bring us some ale."

"We don't have no ale, Mr. Bonny." Her voice was teary.

"Go and get some. Go to Heron's. They'll be up." He gave her money. He should be sending her for the doctor or the minister. "Go the alley way, to the back." So she would not have to cross the tavern room. "Tell Saul I sent you. The big black chap."

Her footsteps went down, slower than the clock. Heavy, heavy, heavy.

Louis wiped Branden's face. It was dry now. "Alice will bring some nice cold ale from Heron's."

The clock ticked.

"I just. Want. To die. Bonny."

Louis put a hand on his friend's shoulder. He wept as silently as he could. He swallowed to steady his voice. "You were my true friend when I came back. After the War."

"Brothers."

The armies of those I love engirth me, and I engirth
them;
They will not let me off until I go with them, respond
to them,
And discorrupt them, and charge them full with the
charge of the soul

"Yes," Louis said. "Brothers."

Branden whispered something back. Louis kissed his friend's dry brow.

Alice brought the ale. When they tilted it to his lips, Branden choked. They tried again and he choked, and again and he choked, so they desisted. They wet his lips, he did not lick it up. Even whiskey. Alice could not find a Bible. Louis recited the bits of it that he knew were beautiful and calm. When he ran out, he said the Lord's Prayer several times. He opened the window and stood there, breathing.

He turned back to the bed. Watery blood pulsed weakly from Branden's mouth and nose. Alice sat at the head of the bed, the mattress giving under her weight, and propped Branden up as he groaned and choked out blood and phlegm and decades of stone dust. Louis held a towel and then the foot of the quilt to staunch the blood. Branden quieted. Alice cleaned his face and neck and chest.

Branden Hix sank down and down and down.

At 4:58, Louis put his hand to the clock.

O my Body! I dare not desert the likes of you in
other men and women, nor the likes of the
parts of you;
I believe the likes of you are to stand or fall with the
likes of the Soul, (and that they are the Soul)

September 1869

Louis had drunk a precise amount of beer and whiskey to get himself through the speech he must make, the speech that Jimmy Branch's widow had persuaded him to make, at the Patriotic Virginia picnic. The day had risen unexpectedly warm, though, and he had not been able to get down the requisite padding of food, only a slice of sponge cake he regretted. Tipsy and queasy, he sweated on the platform, on a bench with the other speakers. Trestle tables stretched endless before him. Beyond the tent, a shamble of plantation outbuildings, fallow fields, the dilapidated big house. The tables were shaded; the platform was not. It did not help to spot the arrival of Mrs. Hamilton, Valentina, and Jeannie. He hoped they would see him before he had to get up and give his speech. He did not want to do both at once: make contact and begin a speech.

A few days after Branden's funeral, Louis had been in the midst of a report to Valentina when he broke down. Mrs. Hamilton had cuddled him as he sobbed, loudly, into her lap, his fists twined in her skirts. It occurred to him, after he was as over his embarrassment as he would ever be, that Valentina and Mrs. Hamilton had seen him in tears, as a man, more times than his own mother.

The three women wended their way among the tables. People spoke to them. It was Jeannie who saw Louis. Her face uncertain. He smiled and touched his hat.

He could not mistake the radiance of her smile, the color flooding into her face. She put a hand over her heart. Lord, Lord. Louis found his own smile widening. Jeannie took Valentina's arm and spoke, nodding toward Louis. Valentina looked to the stage, where Louis sat in splendor with a state senator, the governor-elect, and other men more worthy than himself, and she smiled and gave a ladylike wave. Mrs. Hamilton touched her hat brim, like a man.

Louis accepted a glass of punch to discover it heavy with rum. Still, his throat was dry. He just needed to introduce a few ideas. That was all he needed to do. He went through the points of his speech again, or tried, and dredged up senseless fragments. Incredibly, he had left his notes at home. The papers in his pocket—he looked again, as if they had rewritten themselves since the last time he looked—were tailor's bills with his own angry pencil marks through them. That was a big problem. A big, big problem. Surely it would all come to him. Jimmy Branch had made plenty of speeches in his time, and never used notes. Louis longed for a cold lemonade. He took another gulp of punch. His stomach yawed on it and whatever else he had already drunk, and on the greasy, heavy cake.

The women sat at a table nearly center, close to the platform. Louis smiled at them. They were not looking. He raised his eyes over the crowd. Waiters bustled with beer, cold tea, lemon soda. Before the War, the waiters would have been dark against pastel and pale linen, cotton, fustian. People dressed more soberly now. The waiters' aprons glowed white. Some were grouters and lumpers from the quarry. After the speeches, they would pour a round of champagne and the meal would be served.

First, they must get through the speeches.

Louis closed his eyes. His heart beat unpleasant hard; his

hands were icy, even as sweat cascaded over his temples and ribs and back. Valentina was occupied with the ribbons on Jeannie's hat. Louis nervously feasted his eyes, and looked away the moment she began to lower her hands. An alderman got up and spoke.

The alderman returned to his seat. Louis stood. He hoped his shaking legs did not show. He went to the center of the platform. He smiled. Such a racket raised from the children, no one would hear him, though he never had trouble making himself heard to his men.

He got through greeting the list of honorees, surreptitiously counting on his fingers, ending with, "friends of unity."

A daunting hush fell, or it was already quiet. He must not say union. Unity.

"Friends of unity."

Not a tag or phrase, not a word more came to him from the speech he had so laboriously composed. His eyes fell on the women. Jeannie's hands were knotted on the table; her eyes shone, her throat strained.

"We are here today as such. As friends of unity. That is the idea I have been asked to express. The words I rehearsed have flown away and I am left speaking from my heart." Scattered smiles, some sympathetic.

Black men in white aprons stood with arms folded. The ladies and gentlemen sat beneath the awning. The lesser folk squinted and sweated in the sun, the men rough-handed, the women in old-fashioned bonnets. Boys played stickball in the meadow adjoining. Girls sat under a spreading oak, nursing their dolls, rag or porcelain-faced.

The tiniest girl rocked a baby doll in her arms, a strong oaken root her bench.

This is the bath of birth—this is the merge of small
and large, and the outlet again.

"Sweet is unity," Louis said. "It is like a meeting of friends and yet it is not, for it is a meeting of opposites. Like a meeting of man and woman."

Children's yells and laughter, from the field.

"We come together as a way to become more than our mere selves. We come together with that which is not the same as ourselves. A different person, and yet beloved."

A murmur. Skeptical? They would think him indecent. He would make a fool of himself, and of his cause. This cause. Union. He was staring at Jeannie. He raised his eyes. He told himself that the upturned faces were merely waiting for supper. They used to sing at church suppers: *Here we sit like birds in the wilderness….*

"Beloved."

Jeannie's face was open, rapt, as if his bumbling words and helpless pauses were pouring into her. His set speech tumbled into his mind. It was as inept as his improvisation.

"It is time for Virginia to take her rightful place in this reforged nation, from the gold-dusted lands of the West, to the icy forests of the North, to the rice fields of the deep South."

There was more, much more. Louis dropped it. He simply could not get himself to say the words. He introduced the senator—who was annoyed? bemused?—shook the man's hand, and returned to his seat. The alderman next to him patted his arm. Louis spent the next few hours of speeches in an exquisite stupor of embarrassment and relief.

After the conclusion, cheers, and more handshakes, Louis went to the women, who were with another family, cousins of Maurice. Louis knew the father from boyhood, when they attended the same academy. Valentina moved, making a place next to Jeannie.

"That was a nice little speech, Louis," Woods said across the table, eyes twinkling, "though you might have been distracted."

"I'm afraid I dried up," Louis said. "I left my notes at home, fool that I am."

"Well, you hardly need notes if you speak from the heart."
His eyebrows raised.

Louis held out his glass of lemonade. Woods nourished it
from a flask. A waiter put down plates of ham and rolls and
sweet potato pie and boiled greens. Bianca had scoffed at Louis's
fondness for sweet potato pie. Sticky muck, she called it. Louis
ate all of a bowl of corn and salt cod chowder, and drank more
lemonade. He put a hand over his tumbler when Woods made
to pour again from the flask.

"On second thought." He let Woods top it up.

He and Valentina exchanged pleasantries. He wished she
had her sketchbook, so that he might have some topic of conversation, though the price might be to see a picture of himself
blathering on the platform.

He wished Maurice Termey would return to wake him from
this idiot dream of love.

When Branden died, Louis had taken a vow of chastity, as if
to push his erring friend into Heaven with his fortitude. Yet he
would not attend church. Maybe he was angry at God. He had
had enough. No Job, he, though he dared not curse God, either.
He just would not talk to Him. He sent money, after consulting
O'Keefe, for a mass, though neither he nor Branden had ever
been to St. Peter's except for Eva's funeral. As if he would sidestep
his own, affliction-dealing Deity by going to a Catholic One.
Branden would have laughed at him. Louis missed his friend
laughing at him. He had never loved Valentina more than when
they wept together over their friend.

One day, he would go to the house on Granite Bluff, and
Valentina's husband would be there.

Thank God.

He chatted with Jeannie. It was not too difficult. She was
bookish and musical, so they talked of books and music. Valentina
looked satisfied to see things proceeding. A slight breeze fanned
Louis's face. She was a sweet young lady.

"Will you walk to the riverside with me, Miss Gutman? Mrs. Termey, may I—may we?"

He could not read the first look on her face—regret? It was covered too quickly with a smile. And he was a fool. "Of course," Valentina said.

The plantation, once populated by dozens of slaves and a few handfuls of whites, was barely a farm, acre after acre stripped away by Federal taxes. The master and the missus were likely more realist than Unionist, realistic enough to bear with the irony of leasing their lawn for such a cause. Louis and Jeannie passed the unkempt box garden, the old slave cabins, derelict now. He should not be taking her this far. He should not be taking her for a walk at all. He had taken her mother for a walk—this was not at all the same. They went along an old wagon road that might have carried workers to the fields. In the shade of a big old oak they stopped and gazed at a dried up branch of Reedy Creek. Like a swain with his sweetheart, Louis put his arm around Jeannie's waist and hugged her to himself. She stiffened; he released her.

"I shall not offend you, Miss Gutman." They faced each other, and he took her hands. He stayed close to her. Better to breathe moonshine all over her than chance her seeing how aroused he was.

"Your aunt—and—and your mama would like us to marry." Her eyes searched his.

"Would you like that?" he asked. "Would you like to be my wife?" His amazement at the joy that dawned on her face was nearly as great as his amazement at the words fresh-fallen from his own mouth.

"Yes," she whispered. "Yes, Mr. Bondurant."

"Louis. I am Louis." He put his hand on her neck, ran his thumb over her lips. She froze; fear entered her eyes.

"Sh-sh. I will not offend you, Jeannie." Confound Bianca, for leaving her daughter with not an inkling of what men and women do. And confound himself, while he was at it, for being so taut.

"It is proper for a man to kiss his fiancée," he said. That was true, and unwise at the moment. She tilted her face up to him, her eyes wide. He lightly clasped her temples and gently closed her eyes with his thumbs and put his lips to hers.

Lust shook Louis's frame. Her eyelids fluttered under his thumbs. Their lips barely touching, he drew back and swallowed the moan, part desire, part chagrin, that wanted to creep from his throat. Something between awe and horror bloomed within himself.

He had just asked Jeannie Gutman to be his wife, as coolly as he ever shot down any graycoat. Not that he had been particularly cool in battle, any more than he was now.

He tucked her arm under his, turning her to walk beside him. He was so hard, the prospect of facing her, anyone—a picnic full of people—was sheer despair. They could sit beneath a tree, on knobbly roots, and he would take Jeannie into his lap, and they would kiss and kiss and kiss. He took a deep breath, let it out.

"I will spread my coat on the ground for you, and let us sit and enjoy the breeze."

They sat beneath the tree. Louis did not take Jeannie into his lap. He feared even to touch her again. He repeatedly put various erotic fantasies out of his mind. He contemplated the stupefying fact that he and Jeannie might be married, before the year was out. She was silent, pensive. He prayed she would say, *I'm sorry, Louis, I have changed my mind.* He prayed she would not. Her parents might.... They would permit it. Unless that providential bolt of lightning struck, he was to be Jeannie's husband.

Louis and Jeannie did not have the music of Louis and Valentina.

Well, that was too bad.

Back at the picnic, Louis told Valentina and Mrs. Hamilton the news, putting it in proper form as a petition. Valentina smiled and kissed them both. Flowers, spice, and cedar. She said she was sure Bianca and Rudy would be overjoyed. She did not quite meet anyone's eye. Mrs. Hamilton did meet Louis's eyes, frowning, and shook her head.

The small gesture plunged Louis down. He had not said to Jeannie any words of love at all.

Louis handed Valentina up into the train, at the Manchester depot. Mrs. Hamilton he impulsively lifted up the steps by her waist. She giggled like a little girl tickled. Their dresses and hats seemed to fill up the whole train compartment. Louis sat across, his knees buried in crinoline braced cotton, silk, and linen. He liked it.

"Jeannie is not with you?" he asked much too belatedly.

"She stayed with friends in town last night," Valentina said, "so she'll meet us near the Confederate monument." She added, "She knows not to mention the engagement until we hear from Bianca and Rudy."

"I suppose I shall have to face them, eventually," Louis said. "Her friends, I mean." Making a bad joke worse.

"It is inevitable, if things continue on their present course," Mrs. Hamilton said. As if it were a collision.

The bench was soft, with clean new upholstery matching the curtains at the windows. The city looked picturesque, framed like so. Louis cast about for some—for any conversational gambit.

"Doesn't the city—"

"May I count on your confidence, Louis?" Valentina asked.

"Of course."

"You must not mention what I am about to say to anyone—especially your lawyer. Please." She glanced around, as if lawyers lurked.

"You have my word." Here it came. Maybe she would say the whole thing was coming to a head, that Maurice was returning to fight for his property.

The train approached the bridge. Valentina stared out the window, as if to gauge how far they had to go, how long she had to talk. She turned back to him and spoke so low, Louis had to lean forward. "During the War, Maurice was on a secret mission in Italy. He purchased armaments for us… I mean, for—for the Southern side."

"I figured as much." As if it had not taken Richard's heavy hints.

She gave a pained smile. He might as well have said her secret was common knowledge. Which it was; Rob had confirmed it. Still, he should have kept quiet. He really was a dolt. She looked out the window, and so did he.

They were crossing the river. Not far from here, Jimmy Branch and a policeman and a score or so of black men had spilled into the rocky water from a broken chainbridge. Did Jimmy have time for regret, before the debris pressed him under? Or to suffer being sundered from his wife and children whom he loved dearly, for all his philandering. Or maybe he had prayed.

Louis dreamt it, the other night. Except it was he on the bridge, alone. No one at all around. The bridge gave. He grabbed the rope rail. And instead of praying, or sliding onto the rocks, he dangled in midair, clinging to the rope with all his might, for in the dream the river was not a droughty meander, as it had been that day. It was a flood torrent, and if he let go, he would be dashed away.

The train rumbled to the Richmond end of the bridge. "They can't touch the quarry, though. The Federals." She gave another smile, as forced as the last. "You'll be fine."

"Well, that's best all around," Louis said, though he doubted the quarry, or his job, was safe, given the business with the taxes. "And very kind of you to let me know."

Mrs. Hamilton stared at him. "I don't believe she's told him, Valentina."

"But surely Rudy would have…." Valentina blushed, looked out the window again, toyed with the brim of her hat. She turned back to Louis. "When the War turned against us, Jimmy Branch helped us secure the property. It belongs to Jeannie. We hold it as her trustees. I'm sorry…no one told you."

"Please, Valentina, it's nothing… I mean, it's nothing to apologize for," he managed to say. He wished he could loosen his necktie; he wished he were not here.

"Open the window, would you, dear?" Mrs. Hamilton said. "It's stuffy in here."

Valentina lowered her veil over her face. Louis opened the window.

"I think Maurice will be home for the wedding," Valentina said.

Louis smiled, as if glad to hear the news.

"That's queer," Mrs. Hamilton said. "I was sure he'd stay in Rome."

"Oh, Aunt Anne." Valentina spoke as if it were an untoward joke. She frowned out the window.

Mrs. Hamilton stared at Louis. The old woman might as well have said aloud, *you are a fool*, and so he was. Louis forced another smile. Mrs. Hamilton grimaced and looked away.

"He can come back," Valentina said. "All that is over."

So, Maurice Termey would return for the wedding. A few weeks crossing to New York, or Baltimore. A steamer down the coast, another up the James to City Point or Rockett's Landing. The ladies would meet him. The lucky fiancé, himself, would be enlisted to come along. And Maurice Termey would take his place as man of the house. Not to mention, of course, paying the mortgage on the quarry.

Louis would be nephew, as it were, to Valentina and Maurice Termey. He would be son-in-law to Bianca and Rudy Gutman. They would gather all together for family occasions. A mordant flash of humor lit the abyss.

Happily ever after.

God surely hated him. Surely, this affliction was for all his sins, too numerous to count. His just deserts, for putting his body into the Devil's hands.

"Oh, dear," Valentina said, "I left my sketchbook in our buggy."

The train reached their stop. Louis could not find small talk as they disembarked, got in a hired cab, rode through the black squalor of Gambles Hill, the white squalor of Oregon Hill. It was as if his tongue were granite—along with his heart, if Richard were to be believed. But whatever composed his heart, should he not be glad? Richard's cheap deception had fallen through. And more, much more, on his marriage, the quarry would be his.

"I hope it doesn't rain," Valentina said as the ill-sprung hack jounced through the cemetery gates. The road dipped to cross a rocky little stream, then ascended.

The driver glanced around. "Ma'am, I will put the canopy up when we stop, if you would like," he said.

"Yes, do that," Louis said. The man, masterfully taking control.

The cemetery made a lovely place to moulder, with many large old trees, and the winding little roads. Branden had devoted himself to fixing up the soldiers' section, he and Rob and others installing neat iron fences, flower beds, replacing the improvised planks with a clutter of granite and marble. Hit or miss, he had said, matching bodies to names. Remains dug up from around the improvised hospitals—churches, mansions, schoolhouses— reinterred. Many of Louis's men were buried up in Gettysburg, in the graveyard he thought of as Lincoln's. Nearly six years now, since the battle.

The Confederate Memorial towered over the cemetery, two-thirds complete. Somewhere in its granite were blocks from the Termey's—Jeannie's, rather—quarry, the drill marks left on them, the stone rough-trimmed. Should he not turn it back over to Valentina and her husband? Jimmy Branch dead now, not able to advise.

Jeannie, seated with a few other boys and girls on a blanket not far from the monument, saw them, waved. As usual, her beauty caught Louis's breath, but his heart was not in it. The brightness of love, for him, shone not in the tilt of Jeannie's head nor in her violet-blue eyes.

Yet he scented a rival right away. Young Charles Poindexter, well-turned-out, stood near her. He took after his father, the dark curls, the deep-set eyes, the physique well-proportioned. He had finished his medical studies; he would soon enter a practice. He followed Jeannie as if tethered to her. She could have had a physician—she could have chosen between two physicians. Instead, she landed a quarry man. And he could have had a quarry. Did Richard know? His warning a low sham.

At least Jeannie did not seem ashamed of her fiancé. Not that her friends knew who he was; she introduced him as a family friend. They guessed something, though, their faces brimming with curiosity and gossip. Louis was struck at how much Jeannie differed from them. If she had seemed childish at her aunt's house, now it was her friends who seemed childish, and she the woman. The engagement seemed to have thrown off the spell under which her maturity had languished. That much, Louis could claim. If he wished to rob time of its all-healing due. To jilt her would be inhuman.

By most reckonings, he was young enough for Jeannie. Only thirty. Yet he felt old amongst the boys and girls. He was old, compared to them, compared to Jeannie's former beau. Jaded. It hardly mattered. Louis had her. And the quarry.

Was that what had made Jeannie's parents acceptable as in-laws to Richard? Had Charles known about the quarry? His father put him up to the engagement with Jeannie? Louis offered Jeannie his arm.

They visited Jimmy Branch's grave, the monument, an obelisk, newly set in place. The granite, from Netherwood, was of the mellow brownish kind he favored. One side was lettered for James R. Branch, the other three left blank for, some day, his wife and children.

Jeannie clung to Louis's arm. Charles Poindexter glowered. Louis could nearly concede that the youth looked to be in love with Jeannie, not her granite. Louis disengaged from her to touch the Branch monument, handsomely carved. He dragged his palm over its roughness, its strength. He traced the chiseled furrow of the death date, and stepped away.

A deep rumbling, and a tremble, like standing near a block being shot. Louis's feet moved under him, slipping on old gumballs. He tried to grip the stone. Cries, like birds—the women. His head struck an edge. It was not that glancing blow, but rather a white hot flash of pain at his shoulder that severed his consciousness. He came to on his feet, held up by Jeannie and Charles.

"Are you all right, sir?" Charles asked.

"My shoulder," he panted. "Dislocated."

The driver tried to calm the horse—"whoa, whoa, there"—dancing and nickering in her harness.

"If you allow me, sir, I shall reduce it."

Louis nodded. The pain was so intense, he swallowed down bile.

"We will sit down, sir," Charles said.

A whole rookery of crows cawed and cawed.

"Aunt Anne?" Louis said.

"We're all right, darling."

Charles knelt at Louis's side. Pinning the upper arm to the ribs, he took Louis's wrist, bent the arm, and rotated it outward, and back, slowly. The pain receded.

Louis let out his breath and blinked his watering eyes. "Good." He carefully flexed his arm. "That is very good. Thank you, Doctor. No, I'm fine now." He was confused about what had happened. He tried not to let it show as he began to get up.

"Don't use that arm, sir."

Louis used the other arm to help himself up.

"It's Judgement Day," Mrs. Hamilton said.

Bianca had taught him games with a set of Italian playing cards, the two of them on a blanket near an abandoned mill. One of labels on the cards was the Italian word for judgment, Bianca said. A grave cracking open, and out of it a man and two women, naked, arising.

"I want to see Eva," Jeannie said, suddenly tearful.

Louis tried a smile at her, she tried a smile back. They all got in the carriage, including Charles, uninvited. He might have known Eva, after all, and wanted to pay his respects. She lay buried in the Termey plot, up and up, at the crest of the cemetery.

"It was an earthquake, I think," Louis said. He had felt, more than heard, the low, deep grinding of rock. He wondered how the quarry had fared. Deep within the earth, far below the reach of man, it might split itself. He hoped the mules were all right.

"You're bleeding, Louis!" Jeannie dabbed at his head.

He gently pushed her hand away, took out his bandana and tested it. "A little scrape, Miss Gutman." It was. Just a trickle from his hairline. He would have used spit to clean it up, but for the ladies. "Not worth spoiling your pretty hanky."

She pouted, for some reason. He put the bandana away, and though her sulkiness made him want to laugh, he wished he were gone. He did not want to be here. He would rather visit Jimmy's and Eva's graves alone, some other time. The company of these women tortured him. Louis could savor neither his beautiful fiancée, nor the prospect of a small kingdom of granite. It could have been August, so torrid was the day. They chattered about the 'quake: a minor rumble, and no damage done or the bells would be ringing. The carriage rolled to a stop. A little iron gate. The women's skirts dragged clumps of dried scythed grass.

Palladino's child-angel, wrapped in her wings, gazed sleepy toward the river, itself sleepy with drought, far below, through the trees. Louis touched the neck, and the rough wings, the smooth curls, the cheek. Marble was a softer stone than granite. It had life, a true life that granite lacked. It was a more human stone. If stone could be human.

Jeannie was at Valentina's side, her aunt's arm around her. Charles stood near them, with Mrs. Hamilton. They stared at Eva's grave, as if waiting for it to open and Eva to come dancing out, arms upraised. The stone bore Eva's name, her dates, *Beloved Daughter.* Missing, the names of her mother and her... And Rudy. At the end, would Rudy and Bianca lie here, or out West, in Chicago?

Branden slept under a slab in a little graveyard off Decatur Street, with his parents and a few brothers and sisters. *He wanted it plain,* his sister had said. Grandmama and Grandpapa were out at Manakin. Papa and Mama lay in the new cemetery out on Maury.

And when his body met its end, and the gritty, rock-cobbled clay cleft by the river finally enfolded his own flesh, its final resting place could well be right here, with Jeannie eventually at his side.

The conviction that nothing would ever be right pierced Louis's soul. The Union had been saved, but his own country, his home, his part of the Union—misbegotten, wounded and warped since its beginning—had been destroyed. His little girl, never his to start with, lay dead at his feet. His best friend drowned in stone dust and blood. And he had tethered himself, body and spirit, to a young woman for whom he felt only affection and pity.

Jeannie should have a loving man, a man who could give her his whole heart. But Louis had not a whole heart to give. His country had split his heart in two, and the women and girls of Granite Bluff had all innocently broken it into mere grout.

He touched the statue again and said something about its beauty. An ancient holly stooped over it, so dense that rain, if it should fall, would not moisten its roots. Yet it bore fruit, unripe clusters on every branch.

In the green darkness, the pure lines of the winged girlchild glowed.

WHITTINGTON, BRINGING A CUP of coffee into the foreman's cabin, almost dropped it at Louis's expression. The coffee tilted and sloshed into the saucer.

"No, Bert, it's not you." Louis took the cup. He leaned to sip, so as not to stain his shirtfront.

"What is it, sir, if I might ask?"

It is letting go a dozen or so men.

"Mr. Whittington, send word up to Mrs. Termey, if you please: with kindest regards, I beg to visit at her earliest convenience."

Valentina sent word back: any time. Louis rode Spotty to the house. The Board's message was in his pocket, as if Valentina did not know. She had never said a word about it, yesterday when he had reported. Maybe not to diminish what she showed him, Bianca and Rudy Gutman's telegraph, with their felicitations. They would all go to the opera tonight and Jeannie would wear Grandmama's garnet ring Jake had sent on getting the news. Jeannie had worn it at the little quarry party Whittington had got up, cake and punch, and the quarry men moonstruck, incredulous, gazing upon the fair nymph their rough-handed boss had caught.

The maid who took Louis's hat was the one Bianca had disliked, the one who was, maybe, her half-sister. Louis had nothing against her, except that she was not Mourning. Same with the new carpenter at the quarry: he was competent enough, but he was not Wyman.

Valentina sat on the sofa in the studio. Louis sat in the knobby Italian chair. The maid—Rebecca—brought in coffee and slices of cake.

"What is it, Louis?" Valentina must have read the storm in his face as Whittington had, surely she knew its cause.

"The latest decision of Granite Bluff Quarry Company means I shall have to…. I'm sorry, Valentina. It is hardly your doing, after all."

"Louis, please tell me what," she said.

"I am talking about…. Valentina, are you not privy to the business of Granite Bluff Quarry Company?"

"I have not yet read the minutes of the last meeting."

"They have…. " Louis forced himself to a more gentlemanly tone. "The Federal architect, Mr. Anderson, has stipulated that the stones for his building will not be trimmed in our yard. They will be trimmed on the building site in Washington. I suppose that was his decision, not the Board's. Some particular interest, a contractor who—"

Louis jumped up and laid Valentina out on the sofa. "Rebecca!" he called. The woman came in. "Run quick and fetch a vinegar sop."

Mrs. Hamilton looked around, but did not get up or say anything. Louis's fingers hovered at the buttons at Valentina's neck. He gave in. Kneeling by the sofa, he undid the top button, the next, and the next. Her eyes fluttered open, and he felt, even through his calloused fingertips, the softness of the skin at her collar bones. He wished he could loosen her corset, to ease her breath. He saw the strong beat of her pulse.

She blinked and met his eyes, and blushed and pushed his

hands away. He made way for Rebecca, who cooed and dabbed at Valentina's temples with a damp cloth. She had tawny eyes. Like Valentina's. Louis had not noticed before. She could nearly pass. The two women ignored Louis. In a way, they ignored each other, no great store of affection demonstrated between them, for all of Rebecca's soft soothing.

Louis went to Mrs. Hamilton. She moved her feet to make way for him to sit on her footstool.

"Mrs. Hamilton. Aunt Anne, please tell me what's going on."

"I wondered if you would ever ask," she said. "Before I tell you, you must make a vow."

"Yes, ma'am."

She was silent until, at a murmur from Valentina, Rebecca left the room, closing the door after herself.

"I swear on my honor…. " Mrs. Hamilton paused. Louis realized he was to repeat after her.

"I swear on my honor."

"That I will never duel…. "

"That…. That I will never duel."

"With Richard Poindexter."

"Mrs. Hamilton."

"You must take the vow, Louis, or you will get nothing from me."

Louis looked toward the couch to catch Valentina rebuttoning her dress.

"Louis," Mrs. Hamilton said.

Louis looked back at her.

"Now, say the whole thing," Mrs. Hamilton said.

"I swear on my honor that I will never duel Richard Poindexter." Louis added, "Not that I would. I'm no duelist."

"Good."

"What has he to do with this? This will make things more difficult for his railroad."

"I suppose that's true, in a literal sense," Mrs. Hamilton said.

Louis glanced at Valentina again. Buttoned and sitting up, she stared into space.

Mrs. Hamilton said, "How many blocks will fit on each boxcar, Louis, when they are not trimmed?"

Louis opened his mouth to answer, nothing came out. She did not need an answer, the question merely rhetorical. What it taught him was perfectly obvious: more flatcars would be needed to transport untrimmed blocks. Therefore, Richard would profit.

Mrs. Hamilton continued the lesson in the same fashion. "Now, given that the price of the building stone has already been agreed upon...."

"The Granite Bluff Quarry Company must absorb the increased cost of transportation," Louis finished, "not to mention the loss of the incidental advantages of doing our own trimming."

"That is correct."

"But the quarry—the Termeys—will receive the rents. That cannot change."

Valentina stood, swayed. Louis jumped up and hurried to her. She let him ease her down. He sat next to her. He wished with all his heart, she were his own. They would comfort each other, and lend each other strength.

What thoughts. Jeannie must be at school, or somewhere with her friends.

"I thought to pay off the mortgage with our Granite Bluff Quarry company shares," Valentina said. She added, "The lease won't cover the taxes ongoing."

"Mr. Poindexter could have had the courtesy to warn us," Mrs. Hamilton said, tartly. "So we could sell our shares, as I'm sure he did his own."

Richard: *So you do mean to go on with your suit, regardless?* Louis: *I do.* Like a bridegroom.

Louis went to sit again at Mrs. Hamilton's feet. "How did Richard make this happen? Or did he? Or is it ill fate? Why would the contract not stipulate ... something. To prevent this."

"In a nutshell," said Mrs. Hamilton, "Richard Poindexter had a large hand in writing the contract. From that, we can deduce he has a confederate—so to speak—with Federal connections."

Louis said quietly, just to her, "You did not make me promise not to kill…." He stopped himself from saying it: Stratton, a Washington man who had, as Moses had pointed out, connections with nearly everyone involved in Deep Rock, which meant also Granite Bluff.

Mrs. Hamilton waved her hand. "I'm not worried about that, darling."

"At least the mortgage was made with Jimmy," Valentina said. Meaning, with the James Branch bank. In the hands of a friend. Except Jimmy was dead. His successor would be more likely to call in the note.

Louis summoned all the jauntiness he could. "As my lawyer says—and believe me, he's very clever and able—as he says, nihil desperandum! The settlement I receive from Richard will put an end to our troubles."

Valentina sighed. "Oh, Louis, I'm so sorry." That Jeannie's dowry of a granite quarry might end up on the auction block, or forfeit to taxes.

"You know that's not why I agreed… Why I proposed to marry Jeannie. I'm no fortune hunter."

"Noone would suspect you of that," Mrs. Hamilton said.

In the entry, as Rebecca handed Louis his hat, Jeannie's bedroom door closed quietly, down the passage.

THIS EVENING LOUIS AND Jeannie would have been on display at the front of an opera box as a couple newly betrothed. Instead, the lingering decorum of mourning little Eva had them seated back from the edge. Jeannie wore a dark purple gown that deepened her eyes, her hair tumbling curls. Grandmama's garnet ring decorated one of her gloved fingers. They got hardly more than a few bites of the dinner delivered to the box, what with people stopping in to offer congratulations. Moses sent a bottle of cold champagne. The place seemed made of red velvet and gilded wood, chandeliers sparkling with hundreds of candles. Silk in every color peeped out here and there, brilliant against the black of the gentlemen's clothes and the elder women's somber dress.

Louis bitterly regretted breaking the news about the Federal stipulations this morning. How lamentably gauche he was. Tomorrow would have been soon enough, or Monday. They were supposed to be merry tonight. He wished he could stop searching Valentina's face, when he could do so without being noticed. She looked sad. She had no one to help her, really, her husband in far away Italy. When Louis married Jeannie, he would be family…. And he would be married. And Maurice would be back.

Jeannie and he could get a house in Manchester. Not the granite castle he had promised Branden, given that his settlement—and he *would* get it—was to pay off the mortgage, but something that would please Jeannie, a cozy nest in which to raise their children. In time, with other parents, they would organize an academy. They would have a parlor with many books and a piano. One of Rudy Gutman's, no doubt. Jeannie would choose carpets and drapes. Out of reach of the quarry's blasting, she could set out whatever ornaments she liked. Her aunt's paintings would hang on the walls. A study of stone, her mother nude, a battlefield stripped of its dead.

Assuming the quarry survived and his own job along with it.

And assuming Jeannie would not come to her senses and realize she could do better than a man wearing hand-me-down clothes, Branden's legacy. The clothes, some regimental effects, an old Navy Colt that would not stay cocked, and the repeating watch, which Louis could not bear to use, so familiar it was. His sister got the house and its trinkets. That was about all; Branden had made the mistake of investing heavily in the James River and Kanawha Canal Company. Debts took up what little was left: doctors' bills—a surprising heap of those—pharmacies, shops, Heron's, debts of honor.

The suits fit well, Branden beefier back when he and Rose went out on the town. The tailor had updated the evening suit, so he claimed, lapels narrowed, tails shortened. Thankfully, no moth holes or rust, and the camphor mostly aired out. Good enough for a working man who might soon be out of work.

A man who could not make himself say "I love you" to his fiancée, but bristled when a gentleman smiled and bowed and ran his eyes along her bare neck. For all the bawdy talk at camp, he did not know if all men, attending an opera, would look at a woman's neck and long to touch and taste, to breathe in that perfume at her nape. Maybe they were able to put away their lust, in refined surroundings. Louis was as miserably ruttish as he had ever been in his life. Yet Christmastide—wedding time—loomed too close.

Jeannie sensed his awkwardness. She must have. She must have known something was wrong, her lovely eyes uncertain, her smiles brave. She sensed he did not love her. Of course, he had no idea, either, whether she loved him or not. He could begin to love her once they were married. When it was done. She was a fine girl, better than a man like him deserved. She would grow on him. Moses would win his money from Richard. Maurice would come back. Valentina would be a wife again.

And everyone would live happily ever after.

Or at least tonight they would be merry.

He spotted the arrival of his erstwhile rival—Stratton. A petty triumph. He was with some women, relatives, maybe, older and younger than himself. Manners and maybe the same force that made a man probe an aching tooth brought the doctor to their box to convey felicitations.

"Poor Dr. Stratton," Valentina murmured in Louis's ear after he left. Her breath nearly made Louis shudder.

"He'll live another day," Louis said. Poor Charles Poindexter was more like it, but Charles was not here to be dashed. Louis took Jeannie's hand and looked at her and smiled.

The opera was being sung in French. Rob had given Louis a libretto, so he was able to relay the gist of it to his companions. It was a fine show with a renowned soprano in the lead, and the waiter brought another bottle of champagne. Louis began to relax. He thought, maybe there's hope. He could be a good husband to the girl next to him. He listened to the singers, described the story to his companions. The sense of being in a dream deepened. Jeannie wore a heavy scent, maybe a French perfume. Rob said the skin's own heat caused perfume to dissipate. Louis found his attention wrapping around it: sweet flowers and, lurking, the gamey crassness of musk.

"Marie has agreed to marry Scipion," Louis said of the regiment's daughter, "now that she knows the Marquise is truly her mother. She does not want to go against her. Though—though she does not love him. She does not love Scipion." Maybe *Cosi fan tutte* would have been better, after all. Better the faithless sisters than the abandoned daughter doomed to a loveless marriage set up by her mother. Louis translated all the way to the end, when Mama la Marquise declared that her daughter would marry the man she truly loved.

And everyone lived happily ever after.

Back at the Spotswood Hotel, they sat in the parlor room of the suite Valentina had rented for the night. More champagne, and Jeannie's cheeks were bright. She removed her gloves. The little garnet ring was a poor trinket, really, against the room's velvet settees and gilded mirrors, its fashionably garish wallpaper, and gas-light. Valentina and Mrs. Hamilton retired, leaving Louis and Jeannie alone on a couch. Their talk tapered off. Instead of kissing his fiancée, Louis struggled against a champagne-sodden doze.

It was Jeannie's stillness that brought him clear awake. When he turned to her, she took a few breaths to speak. She wanted to say something she had not the courage to say.

"What is it, Jeannie?" Louis touched her back, at the top where the dress did not cover. Her skin was like the petals of a flower, that richly soft. "Don't be afraid of me. You may talk freely. I would like for us to know each other more."

She burst into tears. He embraced her; he drew her to himself. Her shudders like the paroxysms of sex, her fragrant body strained within the dress, the petticoat, the corset. He knew that neither Mrs. Hamilton nor Valentina would come in here. He kissed Jeannie's hair. Her neck. He kissed her shoulder. She was compliant, awkward. He raised her chin to kiss her mouth, and she put a hand to his breast.

Timid as her touch was, it took the breath right out of him. He removed her hand from his body and kissed it, and took her other hand, and tried not to pant like a dog in a race while his heart tried to crash out of his chest.

"Excuse me, Jeannie dear."

He kissed her hands, and went in the water closet to break his latest vow of chastity. He had no choice. He climaxed quickly, as quietly as he could. He told himself she knew nothing. Or if she did, she did.

He must be the first man in history to shun a beautiful young woman. He came back when his heart and respiration had subsided to a respectable calm. Inwardly, he was mortified, but he could speak with her now, on a couch in a dim room where they would not be disturbed.

"Now, Jeannie, would you tell me what is wrong?" A blush crept over him. In the low light she might not see.

She must have gathered some courage while he was in the water closet rendering himself capable of at least acting like a gentleman. She looked in his face.

"Why are you marrying me, Louis?"

The lie ready to trip from his lips—she put her fingers to his mouth. Her gaze, at this moment, was like her mother's. "Why did you *agree* to marry me, Louis?"

Louis took a long breath, let it out. She must have heard his slip, to Valentina, that he had not "agreed" to their marriage on account of whatever fortune she might have. As if it were a contract, as if he had been coerced. True, he had been managed.

"We will do all right together, Jeannie. I will do my best for you. I will do everything I can to make you and our children happy."

"I know." She looked down. "I know. Except…. " She did not say, *except you do not love me.* As if to kindly spare his feelings.

She had something else to say. Her mouth trembled with it. Louis guessed. He could have assured her that he did not care if no blood spotted their honeymoon bedsheets, but what if that were not what she meant to say? She would be outraged. Though he was pretty sure he was right. Some young cad, among her Richmond friends, or Charles Poindexter, low-down as it would be, to break off at a condition he himself had violated.

"Dr. Stratton said…. He said I am no longer … intact."

Louis touched her cheek. "My dear, I do not mind. Do you understand? I do not care if you are a virgin or not." She blushed so hot, tears sprang to her eyes. Louis pushed on. He would say this. "Your body is complete. Just as it is. You are…. It is whole."

The tears overflowed. "Mr. Hix…. "

"Branden?" Louis drew a breath, held it, let it out. "You had relations with Mr. Hix?" Surely Branden had not lied on his deathbed, surely not. And lied about being impotent? That, no man would confess falsely. "What about it, my dear?"

Jeannie bowed her head and breathed in and out, shakily. When she spoke, it was barely more than a whisper. "I was chasing Eva. We were playing. I had almost caught her when—when she ran over the cliff. We were playing." Her voice dissolved. "I killed her."

"Dear God." Louis enfolded her in his arms. "My poor girl. Sh-sh. It was not your fault, my love. Do not say so."

She spoke, sobbing, so softly Louis had to keep her close to himself. "When she was a baby, I… I wanted her dead. I…. "

Louis kissed her hair. "Now, now," he murmured.

"But I didn't! Not really. She was so sweet. I tried to be a good sister. I loved her. I couldn't help it."

"My poor, poor child. Listen." He tilted her chin so that she would look at him. "It was a terrible accident. A terrible, terrible accident."

She wept quietly, then worked free from his embrace, and took another deep breath.

"I tried to scream. Nothing came out. I ran and fell. And—and I couldn't…. I just lay there. That was when Mr. Hix found me."

Hix, who was supposed to have taken Bianca and the girls on an outing that day, and showed up late. Too late.

"He helped me up, and kissed and hugged me and—and petted my neck and arms. And he put my clothes to rights. My … stockings."

Her breath choked. Louis poured a glass of the champagne, warm and flat. She shook her head and pushed his hand away. She let him tuck a shawl around her shoulders.

"I ran back inside and lay in bed. I didn't know what to do. I was so afraid."

She dabbed at her nose with a little hankie mostly of lace.

"After Doctor Stratton questioned me… I shouldn't have… The doctor promised not to tell. Because Mr. Hix… he didn't mean to ruin me. I know he didn't. He was trying to—to comfort me. He was gentle and kind. He was always so kind to us. I miss him."

Louis tried to sort it out. He could not.

"Jeannie, please forgive me for asking what I am about to ask. But we are speaking face to face. We are speaking as a man and a woman tonight. I hope we are true friends."

She nodded.

"Jeannie, have you ever…. Have you…. "

Had intercourse with a man. Did she even know what intercourse was? It seemed that Bianca had taught her nothing at all, nor Valentina, nor Stratton. This could be construed as preserving her innocence. For that matter, he had learned the exact, proper term from Rob Hunt. Papa had explained the whole thing awkwardly, mechanically, and Louis could not bring himself to say to Jeannie things like, "a man's organ" and "a woman's parts," let alone bawdy terms.

All attitudes, all the shapeliness, all the belongings of

my or your body, or of any one's body, male or
female

"This is difficult for me, my dear," Louis said. "Men and women are not used to talking to each other about these things. And when men talk amongst themselves, love is all too often cast into the dirt." He wished he had not added that last.

She nodded, her face solemn. "Please speak frankly, Louis." Ignorant and innocent she was, yet she was no child. She was all woman at this moment, and that released a great deal of tension in Louis.

"Thank you, honey. Now, remember what I said to you, that I shall cherish you as you are."

She nodded.

"Jeannie, has a man ever been more familiar, more…. That is, has a man ever done more than kiss you and—and touch you? Touch you with his hand, that is. Do you understand what I mean, my dear?"

"Yes. Charles hugged me and kissed me, but he did not put his tongue into my mouth as Mr. Hix did." She dropped her voice to a whisper. "Or as you have done. Nor touch my knee with my stocking down."

Something inside Louis unraveled. He almost laughed. "Jeannie, that is not a breach of your purity. That is a kind of kissing. And an impropriety. The knee."

"Dr. Stratton said—"

"He was wrong. Mistaken. You are a pure maiden, Jeannie. You are undefiled." No Whitman, he.

She looked down at her hands knotted in her lap.

"I want you to tell all of this to your aunt Valentina," Louis said. "Ask her to tell you what you need to know, as a woman. It is not proper for me to go into such—such mysteries with you."

She took a deep breath—and burst into giggles. Louis found himself laughing, too. Rays of hope fell on his heart. If they could be like this, they would be fine. They would have a good marriage, and once they grew used to each other's bodies, they would surely love each other. He would make sure of that. She would cleave unto him, and he unto her.

Louis's laughter caught in his chest, choked by a nearly physical pain, for his soul feared that at this moment he was losing Valentina forever, and he could not bear it, he could not bear it.

He paced to the window, to hide his face from his fiancée with whom he was discussing physical love. His hand clutched the curtain, bunching it up. He released it and took a deep breath, let it out carefully.

"I am just a dog from Dogtown, Jeannie." He faced her and added, more seriously. "Not a fine person, like your aunt, nor a poet, to explain the—the marriage state as it deserves to be explained."

Inexplicably, her eyes filled again with tears. Maybe he had not succeeded in hiding his sorrow.

He sat again, and kissed her cheek, kissed her mouth. His soul might be veiled in mourning, but his body's guiding spirit swayed toward staying here on the couch and kissing and caressing her to the end.

She pushed him away, gently, decidedly.

Just a dog indeed.

"Well. Good night, darling." Louis's voice strained with the effort of not panting. He left her with a final kiss, his body half-swooning, half-springing toward lust.

The moment he stepped out of the suite, as if a spell fell from him, he saw through Stratton's talk with Jeannie. His tenderness soured to wrath.

It was not a mere misunderstanding that Stratton had laid on the young girl. It was a calculated deception of a most vicious, heartless kind.

Louis checked out of his room. He was going to ride almost

ten miles, in the middle of the night, to pay the doctor a call. After all, Mrs. Hamilton was not worried about Stratton.

LOUIS STOPPED AT THE house—Branden's sister's house. Alice had moved in with a cousin, saying she could not bear being in the house where her brother died, and Louis was living there until he might sell it for her. He changed into his everyday sack suit and got his revolver from a box of jumble. As if he would shoot Stratton down, then coolly go on to the quarry, all in a day's work. He took the revolver to the kitchen with a lamp and a box of cartridges he could only hope were not defunct. He had not used the gun or checked it for a year or more. The house was dead quiet.

Louis had enlisted with a Virginia-made flintlock pistol and graduated to a Colt .36, taken off a dead man at First Bull Run. His Remington, locked in the safe at the quarry—not to spoil the lines of his evening coat—he had won in a poker game in Richmond city. His one lucky streak. Branden had named that night their gala spree, to celebrate the revival of Pink Alley after the Fire.

Louis grabbed a stained tea towel. It must have been one of Rose's: embroidered at each end with strawberries. He hung it back on the hook, fetched one of his bandanas. He opened the chamber.

He started awake from a doze, near falling out of his chair. He straightened, rubbed his eyes, and looked at the gun on the table before him.

"What am I doing?" he asked the lamplit dark.

It was utterly futile, what he was doing. The powder was old, the gun was dried up. He would have to completely disassemble it, to make it right. He had gun oil and some tools jumbled in with the stuff he had brought over from Mrs. Sully's, but his best tools were at the quarry. He used cleaning the Remington there to help him think things through. He smiled at the memory of Whittington's eyes widening, the first time he came in and found his boss cleaning a gun at his desk, after a tiff with Wyman. So stop at the quarry and get the Remington. Why did he not think of that in the first place?

"God damn it." He brought the Colt back upstairs, threw it back in the box at the bottom of the wardrobe, and clumped downstairs. He was about to open the front door when a scratching came from the back door. "God damn."

Lizzie would not come in. She spun and whined, *Come on, come on, come on. Now, now, now.*

"What is it, girl?" He knew, though. He followed her to the shed, lamp in hand, his heart lifting despite his temper.

In the circle of lamplight, five puppies, five squirming little doggies. Lizzie grinned up at him and plopped down in her nest of shredded horse blankets. Her sons and daughters latched onto her teats.

Louis squatted and patted and inspected them all, and Lizzie, too. "Ain't you a good girl, ain't you the queen of Dogtown." She licked his hand. He thought she looked tired. He went back in and chopped up some beef that had begun to turn and boiled it on the spirit stove, blew on it until it stopped steaming. Lizzie dumped her pups and gulped it all down, then lay on her side again to pass the nourishment via her milk to her offspring. Louis rubbed her head.

"What a fine hearty bunch of girls and boys you've got there."

He could not see a runt. Either there was not one or it had already been dispatched. A litter of puppies was worth less than nothing, here in Dogtown, but they were his puppies, and he felt absurdly proud of them. Maybe he would bring one to Valentina—to Jeannie. Would she want a mongrel dog. They were outstanding little creatures. One white, like Lizzie, and one mostly white with a black eye-patch, two spotted brown and white, and one all brown with black tips. Rob claimed that one litter of pups could have several fathers. Louis caressed them all again, enjoying the greed and vigor of their lives. They soothed his spirit. It would not hurt to be calmer when he confronted Stratton.

"Good boys. Good girls." He scratched Lizzie's head, pulled her ears out gently as she liked. "You're a good old gal, Missus Lizzie. You're a good old thing."

He stood up with a sigh. Time to go kill Stratton. Such a shame to start his day that way. It would be about dawn when he got to the granite mansion.

He went to Heron's by the alley, to the kitchen house where Saul was pulling loaves of bread out of the giant oven.

Louis pinched up some flour, rubbed it in his fingers. "Oak or hickory?"

"A little chaff is good for the soul, Major Bonny. Thus sayeth Meemaw H." The mythical founder of Heron's. "It balances things out, you see, sir."

Louis dusted his fingers against his other hand. "Saul, would you send a boy or girl around to Branden's house this afternoon to give Lizzie dinner?" For I might be in leg irons and unable. "She's back in the shed. Tell them to be careful. She has new puppies and might be a little tetchy."

Saul grinned. "I'll do that, Major Bonny. And may I extend, sir, my most hearty congratulations."

Louis paused in the alley to adjust Spotty's saddle and leathers.

He wished he had not traded Nella's saddle away, rundown though it had been. The new was jauntier, but what Louis had thought was comfort turned out to be a lack of support, or something. Whatever it was, his back was tired, and his hip ached. The horseseller had claimed that Nella's saddle would not fit Spotty, though to Louis's eyes they were of a size. Maybe he would get used to it.

What in the world was he doing, going off to murder a man.

A hint of dawn gave light to go by. Frogs managed to make their racket, not every pond drought-parched.

Louis was glad he had never fought a battle out this way. He would not have to think: this is the earthworks where we got shelled and I saw a friend's leg hanging over his shoulder. He did it anyway, did he not. He was tired of it. Tired of the War. Tired of his current problems, too. If he could get to the quick of it—but he was not sure where the quick of it was.

If Eva had not died, and if Stratton had not misled Jeannie, and if Branden had not fumbled, and if Bianca were a more attentive mother, and if Mrs. Hamilton were more forthcoming. And if Maurice Termey were not Valentina's husband.

And if Major Bonny were granite, rather than a dumb dog whose half-baked fleeting convictions melted to every woman—every blessed female—dog, horse, or mankind—who touched him.

Things would be different.

But Stratton had deceived and dishonored Jeannie. That was a certainty.

When Louis reached the quarry, he resisted going down and lying on a stone bench. He went straight to his cabin, stuck the Remington in his belt, and rode on. He glanced down the road toward the Termeys' house: no lights. Of course. They were all still at the hotel.

Stratton's granite mansion was dark under the pinkening sky. The air balanced a perfect sweetness, before the sun burned it into day. Louis noticed a bell pull and pulled it. Then he walked in. Footsteps came from somewhere, upstairs it sounded like. Louis went to the right parlor, a morning room. Heavy, carved furniture was rendered insignificant by a huge painting of a nearly naked man being flayed.

A few minutes later, Stratton came in. He still wore evening clothes, his tie undone, his hair rumpled, as if he had passed out dressed, or been carousing all night. He did not appear to have a weapon. His eyes went straight to the Remington stuck in Louis's belt, then to Louis's face. Something like resignation touched him. It raised Louis's respect, though he had egged his wrath back on, between the quarry and here.

"You are trespassing," Stratton said. He sat in an armchair, gestured to another nearby at a conversational angle.

Louis had a temptation to make it all simple and shoot Stratton down. He was rescued from the impulse knowing it would be low, to gun down an unarmed man in his home. He sat.

"Let us talk about Jeannie Termey," Louis said.

They both turned to the door.

"Sir?" A black man in trousers and a linen shirt untucked around suspenders. Judging from the sag of his pocket, he was armed.

"It's all right, Kelly." Stratton's mouth curled up. "Mr. Bondurant is a friend."

Kelly hovered.

"Bring us some, I don't know, port," Stratton said. "Or brandy. No, coffee. Right. Coffee, Louis?"

Kelly left behind a long, tense silence and two men staring at the horrible painting—the naked, blond man, blue eyes rolled upwards, a strip of his rib-flesh being peeled away by the hands of an otherwise unseen person or deity—and came back and unloaded a tray onto a little marble-topped table between the armchairs. Cups and pots of this and that, some cold cakes, biscuits, slices of ham, a butter bell. He closed the doors after himself. Louis and Stratton drained a cup of coffee each.

"Yes," Stratton said finally. "Let us talk about Jeannie. The woman I was courting. The woman you—"

"Stop and compose yourself, sir." Louis did not want Stratton to utter an insult. He did not want that.

Stratton did stop. He smoothed his plump hands over his lapels and huffed himself down to size. He changed tack, or something like that. He put a hand on Louis's arm and leaned close to him. Louis found Stratton's physical proximity remarkably unpleasant. He endured it for a moment, then leaned away. Cool, dewy air wafted in a window.

"How could you, Louis? How could you steal her away? You knew I was courting her."

"Your idea of courtship being to lead a girl to believe herself despoiled? Is that it, Stratton?"

Stratton's pallid face colored up. "How dare you."

"Don't lie now, Stratton. Don't try it."

Stratton drew a breath, huffed it out. "I never had a chance to do more than question Miss Gutman. I would not discuss it with you at all, but I suppose since you—"

"Stop that. I have spoken with Jeannie. She is an innocent, pure maiden beyond a shadow of a doubt. Why did you not tell her what it all means, kissing and…? God! To talk this way about that young woman!" Anger rushed over Louis—yet it did not touch him, deeply.

Stratton's face went tomato red; he might have seemed genuinely indignant, had his gaze not evaded. "Do you think, in the eyes of the world, it would matter to what exact degree she was molested? For she was, I do assure you. Her clothes were…. You don't wish me to discuss it. Happily, sir, I bow to your delicacy. It is your position as her fiancé, your undeserved position, that has forced this much out of me."

"That is not why you lied, damn you."

Stratton frowned, pouted, tried on a few other expressions. Then something went out of him. He said, flat, "It was the only way I could take her from Charles Poindexter."

Now was the time to issue the challenge, but now Louis understood what Mrs. Hamilton meant, about him dueling Stratton: *I'm not worried about that.* He had thought that it was all right by her if he did. The reality was, she knew he would never challenge Stratton. It would be ludicrous.

"You never stood a chance," Louis said. "You never had a chance against young Poindexter or me or anybody at all. To put it plainly, the family don't like you."

A clock on the mantel of the cold fireplace ticked, whirred, chimed a half hour.

"She was my chance," Stratton said finally. "Jeannie Gutman was my only chance."

"That's nonsense, Paul. You have more chances than most. Certainly more than I do. You know, if you hadn't lied, if Jeannie had not broken off with Poindexter, I would not have—Jeannie's family would not have considered me, either. If that makes you feel any better."

"You underrate yourself."

"A working man? Foreman of a little hillside quarry? They would never have considered me as a match for that girl."

"You don't understand." A crooked smile moved Stratton's lips. "I'm not referring to your position, though that's more than respectable. You are handsome. You have a masculine charisma that attracts. In case you've never noticed."

"I do not attract any more admiration than the next man. Though it may seem so, with Jeannie Gutman on my arm."

Stratton shook his head. "Jeannie is the only woman I have loved, Louis."

"Find another, Paul. I'm not trying to be unkind. On the contrary. You need to find another woman to court. With or without me in the picture, your situation would be the same."

Stratton got up and paced to the big painting, and looked up at the man whose flesh was being torn off, a martyr whose name escaped Louis or was it a mythical man. "Do you know," he said, without turning from the painting, "the worst wound I ever treated was not inflicted by minié ball, or artillery, nor by the enemy."

"No?" What that had to do with it, Louis surely couldn't say. The painting was of a myth, Louis recalled. Apollo was the tormentor. His victim in the painting was hardly more than a boy, hairless, vulnerable.

"It was inflicted by our own." Stratton spoke as if to the painting. "A young man, a boy really, was assaulted by his mess-mates. Brutally. Mercilessly." Stratton swallowed audibly. "With the barrel of a musket."

Louis thought, a beating, then he breathed in something like a gasp.

"I could not save him," Stratton said. "Then again, as he told me, he didn't want me to. He wanted to die."

Louis closed his eyes and a memory sprang up unbidden. A soldier in his regiment, a soldier who had been beat up repeatedly. Brutally. Mercilessly. He would never tell who did it or why, and Louis could not figure it out, nor make it stop. In the end, he got the soldier discharged for some minor crime, for the boy's own sake if not for general morale.

Now, Stratton's ugly story unveiled the inner workings of the beatings. Stratton had revealed, as if peeling flesh from the body, that it did not do, for a man to go with another man from fellow comfort to what lay beyond.

Stratton turned from the painting and came back and sat. In case Louis had not drawn the proper inference, he said, "I tell you, Jeannie is the only *woman* I have ever loved." He took a breath broken by something, a sob. "*She* was my chance."

Rising birdsong filled the silence. The lawn was brown with drought, though the hydrangeas clustered along the walls had endured, their blossoms faded to pale tea. Louis breathed, he looked back at Stratton, in his eyes.

Stratton said quietly, "Thank you, Louis."

For not reviling him, presumably.

Louis sighed. "Let's talk about the quarry. That is, about Deep Rock Granite Company."

Stratton's face shut tight as an oyster. "I know nothing about that."

"Come on. You do."

"Your cousin, Colonel Poindexter, is the one to question." Stratton gave a laugh. "Although I beg you to go cautiously, for my sake, at least. And for yours. The colonel has a lively store of information."

"Are you implying that Richard is a blackmailer? He is not. And I have nothing to be blackmailed about."

Except the affair with Bianca, which would surely crush Jeannie, were she to learn of it. It would kick over the trust they had reached, last night; it would show him up as the hypocrite he was. How would Richard know of it?

"You think your cousin is all made of honor, do you, Louis?"

Louis did not answer. Richard might know, somehow. The Board had hinted about setting an example.

"Richard Poindexter—if you'll excuse me for speaking of your cousin this way—has no more scruples than a water moccasin."

"A ... moccasin?"

"The water moccasin, Louis, is a poisonous viper. And so is Poindexter. He cheated your father, did he not? And all the other shareholders of Deep Rock Granite Company. But there. I've said too much." He added, "A cottonmouth, you call them."

"Do you go back that far with him? Or was Dunaway your friend? Did he put you up to scotching the contract, back when?" Louis was amazed that he was not in a fury. A Bible quote came to his mind, something turneth away wrath. He could not remember what the something was.

"Neither Dunaway nor Poindexter are friends of mine," Stratton answered gently. "I doubt they're friends with each other, either, these days. To your point, I have no relationship with Dunaway. Poindexter, though, is what you could call my deadliest enemy."

"He is blackmailing you."

"What nimble wits you have, Louis."

"Please."

"I'm sorry." Stratton touched his arm, drew his hand away almost immediately. Paradoxically, Louis did not mind the contact anymore.

"You knew my father was ruined by my cousin's and your scheme."

"I guessed as much, not long ago. At the time, to me, it was not a scheme. It was a way to extricate myself from Richard Poindexter's coils. Of course, it didn't work that way. It never does."

"Again, lately with Granite Bluff Quarry, with the blocks being trimmed up in Washington?"

"Yes."

Louis did not know where his anger had gone. He did not know, either, if he felt pity or indifference or a sort of fellowship toward Stratton. He was not close to challenging him.

"What does he…. " Louis began. He realized he already knew *what* Richard had on Stratton. "How could Richard have anything on you?"

Stratton stared at the empty fireplace. "A domestic in his pay purloined certain letters by my hand, letters that would ruin me and the recipient—and anyone close to us."

A wave of weariness struck Louis. He could not nap in the cabin, with the men arriving for work. Whittington might already be there.

Kelly came back in, cleared the dishes. He was dressed properly now. "Would the gentlemen like anything else?"

Stratton looked at Louis, who shook his head. "No, thank you, Kelly."

Kelly bowed and left, the tray so steady in his gloved hands, the stacks of china and silverware made not a sound.

Stratton gazed after him. "I envy them," he said. "I wish I had an Abraham Lincoln to set me free."

THE BOARD OF DIRECTORS, seated around the mahogany table, wore an air of contrived conviviality. Louis forced a smile as Dunaway introduced him to a Mr. Dickinson, who had been named the new quarry superintendent—the position Louis had earmarked for himself. Valentina, with exquisite tact, looked neither happy nor sad nor angry. She looked ladylike. Richard was absent.

Valentina had told him what was coming, before the meeting, and he was grateful to her, very grateful. It was hard enough, as it was, to keep countenance. The Boardroom at least was less sultry this time, the windows closed against street dust and noise. And Louis had instructed the barber to put a less pungent oil upon his head.

Dunaway continued, gesturing to a young man at the other end of the table, "Our new manager for quarry operations will be Mr. Smithman."

Thus, the Board disposed of the job earmarked for Whittington.

Louis had spent the last couple of days trying to settle into his role of a man passed over for promotion. Yet here in the reality of it, his chagrin waxed again to a rage so intense, his ears burned inside. He kept his mouth firm. Every breath he took, he let out carefully. He feared he trembled visibly. He tried to force his mind to the business at hand, to discussing quarry operations with the man who would be his superior, the new superintendent of the quarry complex, though Dickinson looked too deferential to make a peep. He had been head quarryman at Mount Airy. Louis tried to think: He is more qualified, Mount Airy after all a much larger quarry. Such reasoning, damp powder.

They would be procuring modern machinery, steam-powered. Steam-powered drills, a steam-powered channeler. Louis had been chaffed by other granite men about how old-fashioned his quarry was. Not his, anymore. Dickinson remarked, almost too quietly to be heard, that he was not convinced of the efficacy of steam-powered channelers, after seeing them in use up north. Smithman had plenty of other ideas.

"I have examined the payroll, Mr. Bondurant." The payroll over which Louis and Whittington labored each Thursday. "A very neat job you have made of it."

"Thank you, Mr. Smithman. I will relay your compliments to my clerk, Mr. Whittington."

"Now, I am considering introducing a piece-rate system. What do you think?"

"You will meet resistance from the skilled workers."

"Well, it is the skilled workers who would be affected," Smithman said. "We can hardly pay the grouters by piece."

Dunaway's clerk hurried in, flushed, late, wreathed in tobacco smoke. He sat down small at the empty place at the table. Louis recognized him as a chum of Whittington.

"The point is," Louis said, after the clerk dipped his pen, "the skilled workers will resist. A piece-rate system, that is," he added for the benefit of the young man. "They may leave. Skilled granite workers are mobile. If they don't like conditions in one place, they move to another. They are well-organized, all up and down the Atlantic states." He had said too much; he was barely not ranting.

Dunaway said, "We will not allow unionism to dictate our wage system, Mr. Bondurant."

The answer Louis wished to give—*why not? The workers are the ones winning your profit!*—would hardly win the argument, nor gratify his superiors. "With respect, sir, we will not gain in productivity if we lose skilled workers." It would be even more fun to say, *well, you cannot use the quarry at all, gentlemen, come Christmastide, when I am a married man.* But that contract was signed and sealed. He might not own the quarry at all, come his wedding day. The Federal government might have it, and their untrimmed stone for free.

"That is true," Smithman said. "And to that point, I do not plan to put in place an odious system. Rather, the intent is to motivate the workers toward higher productivity. In fact, it is the skilled workers who will benefit. Your best workers will earn more money."

More money, perhaps, than their fellows, more than the men with whom they worked side by side, not more money than they were presently earning. The young men would have the advantage, too, for being less battered and worn by years on the stone: experience punished.

It was pointless to point it out. After all, that was the idea, was it not? To cut wages without seeming to do so. Smithman continued, illustrating with figures from quarries in Vermont, Pennsylvania.

The foreman and workers in the new quarry might earn more. Not only would they have new equipment, their sections would be easier to quarry, once the over-burden was cleared and the first blocks removed. Theirs would be the more productive quarries. They were hillside, whereas Louis—named supervisor of the Old Quarry—and his men would be in the hole, cutting deeper and deeper, and would have to pump out every time it rained. Overall, the quarry might gain, though. Dickinson would gain. He was a small, gentle looking fellow; at Louis's look he gave a small, gentle smile. His hands told a different story. They were a true quarry man's hands: rough, burly. They might know stone, its inner life.

Louis looked at his own hands, folded not clenched, on the table before him. What ideas he had. He lowered his eyes and removed from his heart all hope of advancement, of success. He went further, deeper into his gut, to extract the burning jealousy seething there, the rage of ambition dashed.

He stopped.

He was not sure how far he dared quarry into himself, if he would be able to hold himself together if he went too deep. How amazingly well his cousin had read him: a heart as hard as granite rock, and a soul bolstered with hate. Though the heart was more gravel than block, at the moment.

Dunaway, whose gaze he caught when he raised his eyes, looked away immediately. Smithman who had asked Louis what he thought, remained polite, attentive. Dickinson smiled gently. Valentina met his eyes.

—she is in her place, and moves with perfect
balance

Louis found his spirit settling.

"I advise against the piece-work wage system," he said. "The possible gains will be outweighed by damage to morale and by turnover of skilled workers. Good management of the workforce, not a punitive wage system, is the key to productivity. Yes, I say that the piece-work system is punitive. It will certainly be perceived as such by the workers. Mr. Dickinson, was that your experience at Mount Airy?"

Dickinson glanced around the table. He had come up the ranks, in the quarry, Louis guessed, and this position was a big promotion for him. That made him cautious. Louis foresaw that

Dickinson would lean on him, that the new superintendent was the type who knew more about stone than about leading men.

"I must admit, that is true," Dickinson said. "Maybe…. That is, conditions vary, from region to region. Piece-work wages have been adopted in places, without disaster."

"That is exactly the point," Dunaway said. "We must—"

"There is no exactness about it, Mr. Dunaway," Louis cut in. "Productivity is not an exact science, and it never will be, however much we might wish it. Now, you have my plain, unadorned opinion. Nevertheless, I have always done my best for Granite Bluff Quarry, and I will continue to do so, whatever wage system my superiors choose to adopt."

"I appreciate that, Mr. Bondurant," Smithman said. "I appreciate both your expertise and your forthrightness." And Smithman would step upon anyone's back, Louis's, Dickinson's, Dunaway's, to go higher. "I see you are a man on whom we can rely."

Valentina excused herself; the men rose. Louis, at an angle to the window, saw her buggy outside. Shaw handed her in.

As if Valentina's departure had taken the life out of the meeting, it trailed to a close. Smithman would be at the quarry tomorrow. *I look forward to that, sir.* Dickinson was heading back to North Carolina tonight to fetch his family; he would begin next week. Louis duly looked forward to that, too.

LOUIS STARTED TO GO TO Rob's bookstore, to recover from the meeting. Instead, he crossed over into Richmond, on foot, to visit Moses's office.

"Thank you for seeing me, Moses." Louis sat on the chair near the desk. Though the cubbies overflowed with papers, Moses never seemed to be working when Louis called. His business would suffer if people thought he was a scalawag. Or a Ferret. He was, inarguably, a Jew whose brother had died for the Blue. Never mind the one who died for the Gray.

"Any time, Louis." Moses shifted his leg, touched it, maybe

to try and rub away a spot of pain. The coffee was delivered, and the heavy cakes. A breeze touched the starched lace curtains.

"The besamim—"

"I'm all done in, Moses, unless you can get money from Mr. Poindexter. I have been passed over for the superintendent position." Pause. "The besamim."

"Is repaired and filled with fragrance," Moses said. "I'm sorry to hear that."

Louis did not get into how the quarry belonged to Jeannie, that it was mortgaged, that they would probably lose it. He should release Jeannie, though their imaginary children romped already in their imaginary home. Moses Kohen could do nothing about any of that, or about his job, for that matter. Louis did tell him that the Federal blocks were to be trimmed off-site, which would consume most if not all of the quarry's profit. He left out Stratton's possible role in prompting the Federal decision, though he was not sure why.

"How unfortunate for Granite Bluff Quarry Company," Moses said. "However." He steepled his fingers under his chin.

Louis stared out at the street. If Jeannie did not marry a man with money, the Termeys—Jeannie—would lose the quarry. That was all there was to it.

Moses woke Louis from his gloomy reverie, saying, "How I hate this city."

"You hate…Richmond?"

"Yes. I hate Richmond. It is a city of ghosts. A ruin. A coffin. My brothers were killed by the evil Secessionist spirit coddled by evil men all over the South. My father and my mother perished in the fire set by our dear, noble protectors as they turned tail and ran. My neighborhood, this place where I grew up, suffers the label, the Jew's nest. Even the poor Blacks were taught to hate us. How did Jesus Christ die? He was nailed to a cross of wood, by the wicked Jews. That was the catechism for the instruction of slaves."

Louis's own preceptor had said so, too, though at least he had distinguished the wicked from the virtuous Jews.

"It is my birthplace, Richmond, Virginia," Moses said. "My home: a Jew-hating city. Such is the fate of my race. We Jews are outcast everywhere in all the world now and forever and ever, and I am a crippled…. Dear me. I'm sorry, Louis. I apologize for this display, this…. Please forgive me."

A thick silence filled the room. Louis poured out a cup of coffee, pushed it to Moses. His own spirits were so heavy, he could hardly lift the pot, but apparently not so heavy as Moses's. He wondered, if he had never started this suit, would he be in Heron's right now, standing drinks to celebrate his promotion to superintendent. Or would it have ended the same way. Branden, were he alive, would be wheezing out, *Should've seen. It coming. Bonny. Should've.*

Outside, a man rode by on a pretty chestnut horse. Louis had entertained the fantasy of a fine new outfit for Nella. Childish.

"But." Moses put his cup down. "*Nihil desperandum.* I did not want to tell you the latest development, until I had more information, but we need cheer. Here it is: I have found another way to take care of Mr. Poindexter."

"No ferreting, please, Moses. It will do no good for either of us."

"What if I told you that Mr. Poindexter, in collusion with Mr. Dunaway, deliberately defrauded the shareholders of Deep Rock Granite Company in order to funnel money to the Secessionist cause."

"All the way back in '51?"

"All the way back in '51. The equipment purchased with proceeds of Deep Rock Granite stock was substandard, down to the last mangy mule. Not to mention the geological studies, and the imminent Federal contract. In short, Mr. Poindexter and Mr. Dunaway sold shares, used the money not for the quarry but to promote secessionism, then deliberately let the company go bankrupt, so the shares were worthless."

Richard—and Dunaway—would be ruined in more ways than one if such a scheme were exposed. That their shareholders were defrauded for the Southern cause would not help them a bit, North or South.

"Surely to say so would take a very big load of proof," Louis said.

Moses patted the string-bound folio that held Louis's case. "A few more pieces—which I am optimistic of procuring—will be enough to force Mr. Poindexter to pay a goodly sum to keep this out of court. We could go after Dunaway, too, for that matter."

Moses raised a hand at Louis's imminent protest. "It is called a legal settlement."

"Whatever you call it, it smacks of blackmail." Louis thought of Stratton. "Yet there is some justice to it."

"There is much justice to it." Moses chuckled. "To be honest, Louis, I could hardly shake the impression that you were painfully naive in your certainty that your cousin would not injure you, physically. Yet when I followed the line that shunted the blame to Dunaway, everything fell into place! Paradoxically, and cleverly, your cousin warned Mr. Dunaway *not* to harm you, then defended Dunaway, and of course himself, from exposure by having the man who shot at you murdered."

"There's no indication whatsoever that my cousin was involved in the murder."

Moses raised his eyebrows, looked as if he were about to make a case for it, then shrugged. "True. The scenario is but a train of speculation that yet brings us toward what is of interest to us. Which is, why did Mr. Dunaway want so desperately to wreck our case? Consider. First, he tried discrediting you: the block falling, the problems with the railroad men. You had an ally in Mrs. Termey, if not the other Board members, and so he tried a more desperate tactic: the attack on a lonely stretch.…"

Moses's sister who clerked for him came out of the room opposite. She glanced in at the two men, went upstairs.

"We suspected all along, didn't we," Moses continued, "that the defunct company in which your father held shares was a carapace. Yet I could not find the money from the shares sold, before or after the War. There was no evidence that any of the Deep Rock directors benefitted. That alone would have made it child's play for Mr. Poindexter to overturn our entire case. The same goes for Mr. Dunaway. He certainly did not need to take such risks concerning you. Their recent tactics, in fact, achieved the opposite of their aims and led me, finally, to where the money went."

To Italy, maybe, where Maurice Termey had purchased armaments for the CSA. *Your father's misfortune issued from my granite*, Maurice Termey had said, on helping Louis to his position as foreman. As for Poindexter—if Moses was correct—he had cleared himself of suspicion with the warning to Dunaway, then hired another assasin to silence the would-be assassin, to keep Dunaway above suspicion.

The upstairs door opened and closed. The office grew quiet. The man on the chestnut horse passed by again. A ragwoman strained at pushing her barrow.

"Louis?"

"I will settle privately with Richard Poindexter. And of course pay your fee."

"No, don't do that." Moses put his hands on the folio. "If you're worried about your position, I assure you, once we have sprung our trap, Mr. Dunaway will be *persona non grata* at Granite Bluff Quarry—"

"I will settle with Mr. Poindexter." Louis held out his hand.

"You will ruin everything," Moses said. "If you must talk with him, wait until we are a little further. I'm telling you, this is not to be entered lightly."

"I will settle with Mr. Poindexter."

"Take the Sabbath dinner with my family, Louis, I invite you. You need only—"

"Mr. Kohen, if you please, give me all of the documents related to my lawsuit."

As Moses stared at Louis, his young face, with its race-deep stamp of suffering, darkened and hardened with anger. He shoved the portfolio into Louis's hands.

"I quit."

Brickey invited Louis to peruse the bookshelves of Richard's library, as the Colonel was presently occupied. He unbent to chat about Nella, how well she was doing, though she would probably limp forever. The boy Nicky doted on her. Brickey offered Louis a drink. Louis asked for sweet coffee.

The lacy curtains were parted, the dusky garden at the window overlaid with the room's reflection. An aroma of cigars and paper. Worn tufted chairs. A writing table littered with books, some open and carelessly facedown, a whale-oil lamp, an hourglass, pens, paper, decanters, stubs of sealing wax—the accoutrements of masculine intellectual exertion. By the window, a desk very much like Papa's. Richard did not seem to use it much, the desk chair at the writing table.

Not the books, but a display of war mementos on the mantel drew Louis. Cavalry spurs, a silver flask engraved with Richard's regimental arms, a dagger, a Rebel officer's sash. A saber lay naked and shining beside its scabbard and belt. Louis picked it up. Southern-made, New Orleans, maybe. The door opened. Saber in hand, Louis turned. It was Richard's son Charles. The young man hesitated on seeing Louis, then came in and closed the door after himself.

Louis had a moment of thinking Charles would challenge him, that he would see the saber as a challenge. Such an impulse, the sort of thing Richard's ilk would do, as Mrs. Hamilton well knew. Despite the agitation of his spirit, Louis felt cold about it. He lay the saber back on the mantle.

"Major Bondurant."

"Dr. Poindexter, good evening."

Louis waited to see if young Charles had anything to say. He did not, at least for the moment.

"Your daddy has a very fine library," Louis said.

"With all the pages cut." Louis could not tell if young Charles mocked his father or his father's guest.

"Are you fond of any one subject?" Louis asked.

"You don't love her at all, do you?"

The sound of birds settling in the evening.

"Do you?" Charles pressed.

"That is not a question to ask another man about his fiancée," Louis said.

"And that is an evasion. Yet to the point, I believe."

Louis knew he should feel angry, outraged. He should say something like, how dare you, sir. He did not feel it, and he did not say it.

"Did she throw me over for you?" Charles asked.

The note of incredulity at last stirred up Louis's ire, but Charles' grief impressed him more. He had a lot of dignity, for a young man, especially for a young man foiled in love.

"No," Louis said, "she did not."

Richard Poindexter came in. "Pardon me, Louis, for keeping you waiting. Son."

The young man left without another word to either his father or his father's guest.

"I will get directly to business, Richard," Louis said. "I have come to collect the debt you owe me. I shall not be fobbed off with the fantasy of Deep Rock Granite Company. I know how it worked. I had rather settle it with you here than in a court of law, though that will cheat the other shareholders."

Richard gestured to the chairs and, after Louis's abrupt, gauche, downright Yankee-like start, the two men sat in what might have seemed a companionable silence. The cousins had some resemblance to each other, the Huguenot lineaments in their dark hair, the compact body, the skin fair where it was not tanned—Richard very fair-complexioned. Brickey brought in Louis's coffee and poured a brandy for Richard.

The garden niche where hung the battle flag was overlaid with Louis's own reflection in the window glass.

"How did you manage to keep your colors?" Yet he really did not want to rehash any part of the War, beginning, middle or end, with his cousin.

"We had the fortune never to be part of any formal surrender. We were merely informed that the Confederate States of America had been conquered."

Though the Fire had not touched Manchester, like many another after the War, Louis had wandered the ruined streets of Richmond in a daze. Watched by blue-coated soldiers as if he, who had served the Union, were a dangerous animal. The old men, the women all covered in mourning, were as stunned as any battle survivors. And the colored people all free. That, at least, went easy with Louis.

"Your cause," Louis said. "It should never have been. It was rotten."

Richard shrugged. "It's lost. Now, to get directly to business, as you say, I will pay you half what your father paid for shares in Deep Rock."

"You must pay the full amount, plus ten percent of that. In U.S. currency, and at today's value."

"How about ninety percent, plus ten percent of that for your lawyer."

Louis pretended to consider it. His heart pounded. "All right."

Richard went to the desk and took out a bankbook. "The ten percent in a note to Moses Kohen?"

Louis did not trust Richard to make it right with Moses. "Put it all in one note to me." He wished the banks were open. Monday seemed an eternity away.

Richard laughed. "Very well." He sat at the table to write out the note.

The desk was exactly like the one Papa had. As a little boy, Louis had delighted in playing with its various drawers and compartments, crawling around Papa's legs. As always, when recollecting his father, Louis's heart contracted with nostalgia.

Richard handed over the note; Louis read it over, and read the receipts, and signed them, too. He had looked at every paper in the portfolio and could not see much to prove Moses's case. That could not be why Richard was settling the debt between them. Or it could be, after all. Richard would know that Moses could add up pieces of paper; they were both lawyers.

"Richard, would you keep Nella? You would be doing me and her a favor."

"Why, Louis, that would be grand. I will need a gentle dame like her, when my child is old enough to sit atop a horse. And my stable boy will be overjoyed."

Louis squinted out the window, cleared his throat. "I know he'll take good care of her."

"You come by any time to see for yourself," Richard said. "Now I'll get Brickey to bring us supper. A bachelor supper, I'm afraid. Mrs. Poindexter is indisposed."

The nick in the desk's leg, the streak of wallpaper glue on the side from when Papa repapered the parlor.

Louis strode to the desk that had been his father's and opened the center cabinet.

"Really, cousin," Richard said.

Louis reached behind the inkwell, sprang the latch, and groped within the secret compartment. He pulled out a packet of Confederate paper money, tossed it on the floor. He reached deeper, pulled out a bunch of letters between Richard and his first wife. These he put on the writing surface. He reached in again, half an arm's length, fished out a small bundle of blue-tinted letters tied with string. He turned it over. A paper labeled "Stratton" was pasted over the knot. Louis stuck the bundle in his pocket. He glanced at Richard, who had that very young look on his face: astonished and bemused, once again, by cousin Louis.

Nothing else was in the compartment, except a sack of coins. Louis put the coins and other letters back in, closed up the desk, and left.

A T Gumtree Tavern near Frog Level, Louis stopped to rest Spotty and give him a drink from the trough out front. A hedgerow obscured the front of the building and, by day, gave it respectability. By night, piano music and laughter, and men hollering would rollick through, and there would be a youth out front to take the gentlemen's horses.

A temptation came upon Louis to go in the house and climb the stairs. He set Spotty in motion again. He catalogued birds as they plodded past Frog Level. He thought about the Revolutionary War. He thought about the War, his War, its violence-spattered tedium.

He hoped Saul at Heron's remembered about feeding Lizzie. The children would take care of her. They had been bringing her scraps, waiting on the puppies for weeks, pestering Louis every time he stepped out: *When they here, Mister Bonny? When they coming?* How they got into calling him Bonny, he had no idea. Branden, or maybe Saul.

Lines of candle light leaked from Stratton's closed parlor shutters. Louis knocked on the door and went in, as he had before, barged into the parlor—and backed out as fast as he could.

"Good Lord," he whispered. He stood in the entry hall, by

the light escaping under the parlor door, his stomach flipped halfway up his throat, his mind reeling with what he had just seen: the Spitfire Spikers' star pitcher straddling Stratton's lap, clad in his drawers, the two men joined at the mouth.

Louis clumped down the entry steps and paced the lawn, crumpling his hat in his hand. He wanted to flee. He knew that men did that, of course he did, but he had not really let himself know it. He had never pictured two men….

It was why he was here, was it not? He could leave the letters with the butler. He could not leave the letters with the butler. And he did not want to come back later. He simply could not carry these letters back home.

The coats and caps thrown down, the embrace of love and
*   resistance,*
The upper-hold and under-hold, the hair rumpled over
*   and blinding the eyes*

They had been giving it everything they had, by Jove, not much resistance in that embrace.

Louis sat on the steps and waited. A few minutes later, Stratton came out, in shirt and trousers and bearing a candle. His hair was rumpled. Louis stood up again.

"I apologize," Stratton said. He did not seem particularly sorry, though, or embarrassed. He gave a gusting sigh. "I would ask you in, but under the circumstances…. " He laughed. Still, a spark of fear.

"It's…. It's cooler out here." All over again, embarrassment washed Louis. At least they were in the dark, the cool dark. He held out the letters. "I came by to give you this."

Stratton took the packet, stared at it, held it as if it were about to burst into flames. "My God," he whispered. He counted the corners, recounted. He tore off the label and tried to undo the string, his hands trembling violently. Louis cut it with his pocketknife. Stratton opened each envelope, each one inscribed, "to my darling M," looked inside, took out the letters, mostly one-page, looked at them front and back.

"My God." He let out a long, shaking sigh. "It's all of them. All of them. My God." He crumpled the letters to his heart, sat down hard on the porch steps, and put his face on his knees. He wept hard, with barely a sound.

Louis wandered onto the lawn. A whip-poor-will called in the woods, another answered. It was a beautiful music, with the crickets and frogs going, too.

To my darling M.

Louis closed his eyes and wondered if he would laugh or cry. He did neither. He returned to the steps and sat next to the doctor.

"Paul, may I ask you...."

Stratton sat up, wiped his face. "Anything."

"Does Valentina know?"

Stratton sucked in a deep breath, let it out in a gust. "It's obvious enough she doesn't know about me. My suit to her niece wasn't turned down *that* unceremoniously. I am pretty sure she is aware of Maurice's predilections, though. At least to the extent of knowing her marriage isn't what it should...." Stratton raised the candle. Disconcerted in its light, Louis stared back at him. "You're in love with her, aren't you, Louis? Do you know, if you—"

"If I can have a little snack for my horse, and some water, I'll be on my way."

"A snack for your horse. I owe you my life."

"Just do one thing. Burn those letters right now."

"I will. Watch me."

He burned the letters, one by one, there on the porch with the candle. They both watched like children in wonder. When all was ash, they stood.

"May I embrace you?" Stratton asked. "In a brotherly way, that is."

The two men embraced. Stratton led Louis and Spotty to the stables, broke open a bale of fodder. It smelled sweet and fresh. Spotty put his nose into it with gusto.

"You'll spoil him," Louis said.

"For heaven's sake. Look, why don't you take one of mine. I'd say, have one of mine, if you would accept."

"No."

"At least borrow my mare. See, she likes you. Why shouldn't she? Let your old boy rest here. You can bring my Sassy back any time. Ride her in on Monday."

Louis accepted. He had some getting around to do. This weekend he would spend with his cousin in Midlothian, then, on Monday morning, all the way into Richmond town, to Branch's bank, and back out here. He wished he could ride Nella to Valentina's. She had carried him through many a time of up and down. White nights, gloomy nights. She should at least have carried him on his victory march.

Monday morning did not feel like a victory march, though. Louis did not know why he was not exuberant. He should be feeling like a king rather than a cold dog.

The problem surely was that he had been down so long, he was scared by up. The cussed bank had not helped, the clerks reluctant to release the lien. It was not anything with Richard's cheque; no hitch with that. They wanted a meeting with Mrs. Termey, as trustee of Miss Gutman's property. Jimmy Branch's brother prevailed on the clerks to complete the papers, though he grumbled it was an irregular kind of transaction, very irregular, betrothal or no betrothal. Louis sent a bank note to Moses, with his cover: he trusted young Isaac would do his uncle credit at the University. After it was gone, he worried whether he got the nephew's name right. He would ask Jeannie to have a portion of the quarry rents sent up to Jake. He had no qualms in asking, nor doubts that she would agree. When they married, at any rate, it would be his.

He should have been king of the world.

Louis checked the portfolio with the letter of deed in his saddlebag. His heart began to thump. Rather, continued. It had thumped through the whole morning. Like before battle, that was all. Merely the enervation of impending action. It rose to near pain, as he began up the driveway at Granite Bluff.

If Rebecca told him the ladies were not in, he did not know what he would do.

Daydreaming of the house he and Jeannie would dwell in, and the children they would have, calmed and cheered him.

When Rebecca opened the door and said, "Mr. Bondurant," she did not look at his face. She took his hat and hurried into the library, closing the door after her, leaving him in the entry hall. That was odd. She came out again, eyes downcast. "If Mr. Bondurant will join Mrs. Termey and Mrs. Hamilton."

If Louis had an urge to smile—to say, it is all over; our troubles are over—as he came in the studio, Valentina's face would have taken it right away. The tender skin around her eyes was smudged grey, her eyes red-rimmed, her complexion dull as clay.

"Valentina, what is wrong?"

She waited until he sat in the Italian chair, then handed him a letter with his name on it, in Jeannie's hand. He felt it, looked at Valentina, looked down at the letter. He drew a breath and opened it. The garnet ring fell out, the poor little garnet ring. *My dear Louis....*

"I sent messages to your house.... " Valentina's voice was tear-riven.

Louis could not speak to say anything, to ask anything. *She eloped to Chicago? When did they go?*

How could she do this?

How could she, how could she.

His tongue might have been a slab of granite within his mouth. A witty remark, even, passed through his mind: *Well, I have here the perfect wedding present for them.* He could not think, not really.

He had been tossed up in the air, and fallen down hard onto the ground, at Gettysburg, by the percussion of a shell, and though he got to his feet right away and went on acting the officer, he had been stunned for hours. It was like that.

And must everything go back to the cursed war? Must everything be measured by the War for the Lost Cause, the War for Slavery, the War of State Against State and Brother Against Brother, of Northern Aggression and Southern Rebellion—the War and his part in it?

Would it never end.

He put the bank papers on the table and went and waited in the entry hall. Rebecca did not bring his hat. Maybe she was afraid to face him. She might know that he had guessed, all at once, that it was she who had told Richard Poindexter whatever he needed to know to set all this up, she who kept Dunaway informed as to who came and went, and when, from Granite Bluff.

A woman's Body at auction!

Not hers, for she had been born into it, here, but her mother's, maybe, or her grandmother's.

In the library, Valentina sobbed. He prayed she did not think he was angry at her. He certainly was not.

He had his eyes closed, his head bowed. He was so absorbed, it was almost like sleep. He opened his eyes to find Mrs. Hamilton before him. She took his hands in hers. He looked into the bright blue eyes folded into her wrinkled cheeks, then leaned to gather her to himself. Louis felt strength come to him from the old woman's frail body. Her dearness sank into his fibers, while his soul quaked with something like an intimation of a violent storm. He let her go and fled, without his hat, down to the quarry that would soon belong to Charles and Jeannie Poindexter.

Whittington was kind and quiet. In some mysterious way, word must have come down. At least about Jeannie. Presumably not about the quarry, not yet. Louis tried to wear his usual expression and found he could not remember what it was. He settled for a bovine nonchalance. Whittington had probably known before he did. And Llewellyn. And Tristan. And Kinny, too, in some dim sympathy.

When he emerged from the cabin and went to the benches, he could not doubt that every man who saw him knew he had been jilted by his beautiful fiancée. They were aggrieved for him, baffled, angry. Though even Llewellyn was too tactful to outright commiserate, Billy muttered to one of his pals, in Louis's hearing, "You can't trust women, at all. They'll let you down every time."

Louis worked long hours, through the week. In addition to regular business, he had to help prepare for the extension of the quarry complex. The new superintendent Dickinson, for all his shyness around his superiors, turned out to be good with the men. He knew granite, too, and did not mind learning more.

They went to Heron's together Friday evening. Louis drank coffee, for he had made a vow, some time during the long, numb week, to keep away from spirits, and even wine and beer. Dickinson told Louis he had wanted to be a sculptor, but his father made him go into the quarry. Papa had inflicted a similar blow, more accidentally. Louis had come to believe such reversals were like stripes in granite. Inevitable flaws. He vowed to get Whittington into the building trade somehow. He did not want a stripe in Whittington's life, though God was apt to stripe every man's life, in some way.

Louis also vowed to keep away from Richard. But Richard did not keep away from him.

WHEN LOUIS CAME HOME from work Saturday, his cousin was waiting on the stoop of Branden's house—not long to be Louis's to live in, its sale pending.

Louis did not greet his cousin. He walked into the house—Richard following as far as the parlor—through to the back, and rinsed his face and hands at the kitchen pump. With Richard's bank note, he had considered trying to buy Branden's house, and decided it was more sensible to pay off Jeannie's quarry. The lease, he'd figured, would provide income, whether the blocks were trimmed at the yard, or in Washington, or in Timbuktu. If he'd let the quarry go, he could have had his friend's house. He would have added a covered front porch, like Mrs. Sully's.

He called out the back door. Abe ran up and suffered his face and hands to be cleaned at the pump.

"Have you fed Missus Lizzie Dog?" Louis asked.

"Yes, sir." Abe's grin told that his other front tooth had come out. "She likes me now."

"Why, she always has, Abe. It's only that new mamas can be contrary."

Abe nodded sagely. He had gained a baby sister this winter,

though his mother was so amiable, surely nothing would crank her up.

"How is your pitching arm doing?"

Abe's grin grew sheepish. "We lost the ball in Mr. Cage's window."

"Jes … Gee. Was the window open?"

The grin beamed again. "Yes, sir. Oh was he mad! He ran us all over! We threw him off at Beattie's alley."

"Did your mama give you a good whipping?"

Abe giggled through an assumed contrition. "Yes, sir, she sure did."

Louis rummaged in a chest, pulled out a ball whose cover was half off. "Get one of Heron's stable boys to stitch it up. You must practice catching and pitching every night, or our club will never win."

"Yes, sir."

Not even a gold-plated ball would give them a win, with Louis as their coach, but they could at least give it their best.

"Now go and fetch us a jug of lemonade, would you? And some biscuits and whatever cold meat your mama has on hand. Tell her it is a little supper for my cousin and me."

Louis stood in the kitchen for a few minutes to gather his wits. He had thought many thoughts over the last week about what had happened to him. He had not answered the happy, grateful, congratulatory note from Moses, or the one a few days later, re a possible suit for breach of promise, nor had he gone to see him. He could not face him.

It was like a precise clockwork, each cog and gear moving the others. Not "it." Louis himself was the clockwork machine Richard had wound up and set going, as he had Papa. Rob claimed that the colonel had not been known for his strategic sense during the War—the damned War. No one could deny that in civilian life, he certainly knew his way around best-laid plans. Or it was luck: the pieces falling his way. Louis had played cat's cradle with every bit of it—trying to figure out which thread was chance, which deliberate—and ended up with a tangle.

Louis considered going upstairs for the Colt; he had reconditioned it. Now Mrs. Hamilton's promise came home. She had not known the full of it, he figured, but had grasped the gist, the essence.

He headed back to the parlor. The window showed street dust billowing golden in the late day sun; Little Walt's buggy rounding the corner, too fast as usual.

The parlor was a comfortless room. Even cleaned up, it smelled stale.

"Have a seat, Richard," Louis said. "I have sent for supper." And if Richard did not like taking his refreshment from little black hands, he could go without.

He hardly seemed to hear Louis, nor did he sit. He twisted his hat in his hands and paced to the window. Dread stole over Louis. Something had happened to Jeannie and Charles: a wreck, fever, train robbers. He wished them no ill; that much, at least, he knew. Maybe he was happy for them, in a maimed, limping way.

"I thought Charles and Jeannie were up in Washington," Richard said to the window, "at the Willard. They never checked in there at all. Or anywhere I could find."

As much as Richard deserved whatever he got, Louis could not bring himself to laugh. "Have you not communicated with Mrs. Termey? Or Mrs. Gutman? Has neither of them sent you any word?"

Richard turned quickly. He did not read disaster in Louis's face, though, and his own face relaxed a little. "I telegraphed Mrs. Termey. I must've left before her answer. I just come off the train from Washington."

"Take a seat, Richard, will you? We'll eat in here. It's cooler than the dining room."

Richard looked around, as if to make sure the armchair had not moved from its place, before he sat.

Soon, anything in bloom would release its scent. Flowers, and dust, food, horse, coal and wood smoke, refuse, and a man's or woman's own sweat would coalesce into a perfume as unpoetic as whatever its name might rightly be. *Eau de Manchester Town*, Papa had called it. It put peace in Louis's heart—or it usually did. When Richard was not with him.

The kitchen door banged open and shut, cutlery and plates rattled. Abe carried in the sweating jug and glasses and plates and cold ham biscuits with a sweet pepper relish, ginger snaps, chopped tomatoes and crumbled bacon sprinkled with buttermilk. The food was arranged prettily on a blue and white platter with a chip off the edge. Abe set everything out on the whiskey table and stood at attention in a ludicrous imitation of a butler, or maybe a soldier. Soon, God willing, Virginia would re-enter the Union, and there would be no more soldiers in the streets.

"Thank you, Abe," Louis said. "Tell your mama it all looks very delicious."

Abe raced down the passage with his coins, banged out the kitchen door. He would have been born a slave, born before anyone ever heard of Abraham Lincoln, his name drawn straight from the Bible.

This is not only one man—this is the father of those
    who shall be fathers in their turns;
In him the start of populous states and rich republics;
Of him countless immortal lives, with countless em-
    bodiments and enjoyments.

Richard picked up a ham biscuit and took a bite, the prohibition against black hands presumably relaxed outside his home. Louis drank some lemonade and said, "They are in Chicago, Richard. The two of them eloped to Chicago."

Richard lowered his hand, biscuit in it, to the armrest. He had gone up to Washington to toast his son and his beautiful new daughter, and perhaps their quarry. It took him a long time to finish chewing, to swallow, to say, "Chicago."

"Chicago."

Richard, very quietly: "Well, I confess that is a disappointment."

He stared somewhere across the street, and startled Louis by giving a gasp, or a sob. He rallied himself, turning it into a deep breath, and put the biscuit on his plate and brushed a crumb from his coat.

Louis got up and went back through the house, across the yard to the shed. He picked a few puppies from the warm little jumble snoozing by their mother. "I'll bring 'em right back, Lizzie." Her tail thumped: *all right*. In the parlor, Louis dumped the pups on his cousin's lap. Richard must have been dozing. He started, blinked up at Louis.

"Cheer up, cuz," Louis said. "They'll do fine out West."

"You and your mutts." Richard sat up and rubbed the little dogs and allowed them a chew on his fingers. "I wish you were on my side, Louis. You're the only man I trust anymore."

Louis would never, ever trust his cousin. He could understand Richard trusting him, though.

The thing he had worked out for himself was, he was in the same position as he had been in this spring. Better, in one sense: the prospect of prosperity having been dashed, its corresponding ghostly lack no longer haunted him.

His true losses had nothing to do with money or with Richard. He would give away all that money again and again, a million times, to have Eva back. Or Branden. Or Bianca. And Jeannie, yes, her, too. He could have loved her. He had made a start, that night after the opera, even as he unknowingly set her free.

He had lived four years in a world of blood and mud; he had fought for the Good Old Cause, for country, for Union. He had helped destroy the land that had been his home.

"Still, I will keep on," Richard said.

"You'll never succeed," Louis said. "Nor will Richmond. Not your Richmond, that is."

"I have found plenty of like spirits."

"Oh, sure. Yes. Plenty of other..."

Defunct Rebels. Ghosts.

"Your Richmond," Richard said. "Carpetbaggers, scalawags, ruined planters, working belles, freedmen, radicals, and hard-up widows. Not to mention some mighty sharp Jews." He poured himself another tot, raised his glass. "It's all yours, Bonny."

A terrible sadness ripped away the vestiges of Louis's anger.

"I'll take a dab of that whiskey after all."

Richard poured. The two men raised their glasses.

"All mine," Louis said. "Every hair of their heads."

Or maybe it was love, touching his spirit.

October 1869

M R. Bonny."
"Quiet!" someone ordered.

Louis walked along the top of the bench, his eyes downcast. At a few points he squatted, put his hands to the granite. The quarry man who had spoken to him was new, or he never would have made a sound when Louis was getting ready to chalk out the holes for the powderman to shoot a block.

"All right," Louis said, to himself. The quarry man made to talk again; he was hushed again.

Louis marked the block. He left it to Llewellyn to fill in the line. He turned to the quarry man. "What is it, Hazelton?"

"Now remember," Jopple warned. He had been promoted to Dickinson's crew.

"Sir," said Hazelton, "we found something new. In the New Old Quarry."

"Kinnyboy, he found it," Jopple said with an air of correcting.

Louis guessed what it was, though he did not let on. They had been hoping to make another spring house so the water boys would not have to carry their jugs and pails so far. He followed Jopple and Hazelton. A mushroomy scent rose in places. It wafted in the woods along the river, every autumn.

He had not gone up to the house, since that day the garnet ring had been returned to him. It was simply too painful. He had sent a letter to Valentina, assuring her he bore no one ill will. At times he was sure he should write to Jeannie, but he certainly did not feel like writing to his former fiancée, all is forgiven; may you and Charles be happy. Though he did, truly, want her to be happy. He tried not to wonder when he would enter Valentina's studio—once he had the fortitude to do so—and the sight of Maurice Termey would fell him like a punch to the gut.

Louis had been deeply untrue to Valentina. Now, like retribution, his love for her was punishing, acute, so painful and real, it wracked every part of his body, and every part of his soul. Unsoftened by hopes and dreams: straight-backed and unpadded.

The lumbermen were nearly finished clearing the trees. Soon the quarrymen would begin blasting the overburden loose. Torn limbs strewed the edges, their leaves not yet withered off: bronze, dark yellow, and dark red, the beeches' bright gold, the sober brown of the old oak. He thought of asking the men to save him something from the ancient oak, but he did not know what he would do with it. He did not carve wood, like Branden with his broken-winged angel.

"You've made a lot of progress, sir," Louis said to Dickinson.

"It's coming along all right." Dickinson never played his authority over Louis, which helped.

The place was unlovely, all torn apart. It would be worse, when the blasting started. Valentina and Mrs. Hamilton were moving to town in the next week or so. The little glass animals would never again be set out in the house on the bluff.

They climbed the ladderlike stairway knocked together up the side of the bluff. Llewellyn, tagging along, got so winded halfway up, they had to stop and rest. Louis had not realized he was so bad off. He had switched from cigars to cigarettes, claiming they helped his lungs. Louis had his doubts, watching him pant and hack his way through a smoke. Jopple looked on with the genial contempt of youth and robust health. Neither he nor Hazelton dared smoke or chew in Louis's or Dickinson's presence. They continued up.

They arrived below the edge of the Termeys' yard. The stone house and the autumn roses glowing in the sun within the whitewashed picket fence were closer than he had expected. It was dreamlike.

He was about to say, "Lead on," when Kinny's chuckle from a thicket of blackberry guided him. One day, Kinny had suddenly decided he would no longer be a grouter, nor a dog's body. He wanted to be a water boy, and refused to be anything else. Still, Louis doubted he had been the one to find the spring. He did not have the wits to figure out the significance of a patch of ground that stayed muddy, rain or shine—yet it could be true, in a way. The childman came upon water issuing from the ground in a drought, and wonder illuminated the darkness of his mind.

He had dug out quite a little pond. When he caught sight of Louis, he made to dig some more. One of the other waterboys stopped him. "Let Mr. Bonny have a clean drink, Kinny."

Louis dipped his hand in the water. "No, let us wait. May we? I shall fetch Mrs. Termey to take the first drink."

They liked that. They liked that he asked, and it was a good luck idea, too, to have the mistress of the land, as they thought, baptize the spring.

Louis labored up the bluff. At the top, he took the dirt path Jeannie and Eva had taken. He passed through the gate into the garden. Already neglected, untrimmed, late roses dropped their petals and lavender shrubs brushed and perfumed his trousers. At the back door, he raised his hand to knock, lowered it. He stood in the scented shade, his head bowed. He entered.

The passage was dim. Silently, almost creeping, Louis looked in the room that had been Jeannie's.

It was neatly made up. In the wardrobe, he might find her mourning dress, though the blue dress she wore to the picnic, and the opera gown, and her gloves and slippers would have been sent on by now.

The next room, Eva's. The flowered bedspread, the dolls and rag animals, all cleaned. Quiet and still, as if spellbound.

He knew the next room well, though his habit had been to enter by the side terrace. It was more orderly than he had ever seen it. No crowd of bottles. The bed made. Ladies' underclothes did not strew the rug. He smiled and shut the door. His hand lingered on the knob.

He was not sure if he was merely gathering up his courage. He drew a deep breath, blinked.

Mrs. Hamilton stood at the other end of the passage. "You kept your vow." She moved to him, and spoke very quietly yet did not whisper. "Now I will break a promise I made to Valentina, who is more a daughter to me than my nephew is a son to me."

Tell him, Valentina.

The dim passage was close. Louis felt as if his feet were not quite touching the carpet runner.

The female contains all qualities, and tempers them
*   —she is in her place, and moves with perfect*
*   balance;*
She is all things duly veil'd—she is both passive and
*   active*

He took her old hands and kissed them.

"You know they mortgaged the quarry to pay the taxes," Mrs. Hamilton said. "But it didn't go to taxes. He took the money to Rome and had their marriage annulled." She added, "They were married by the Church, not the State. One could do that, back then, in Italy."

She patted his hands, turned away.

Louis stood alone, breathing, working to take it in.

It must have been what that letter said—the one on the table between them, with the foreign frank, the day she nearly fainted on hearing that the stone must be trimmed up in Washington city. The mortgage money misspent, the quarry doomed, and there he had sat, trapped in an engagement that represented the last hope of keeping the quarry in the family. Louis understood why Valentina had withheld what Mrs. Hamilton wanted her to tell: that she was free to marry whom she pleased. She might only have wanted to hold on to the quarry, but surely she had also feared that he, too, would abandon Jeannie and she could not risk that. Her wrongs against him weighed as a feather, compared to his own sins against her.

He found he had walked into the studio.

The portrait of Jeannie had been put aside, hardly more complete than the first time Louis had seen it. In its place was a painting of a quarry bench. Stone not merely gray and brown but in the multitude of hues that made it part of the living world, more colors than he had ever seen until her paintings revealed them to him. The paint showed the men as a wealth of color, too. Himself, pointing up the cliff, hat in hand, coffee-dark hair and faded black suit. The lopsided stance to favor his hip.

Valentina stood not at the easel but looking out the casement doors, in her painting smock. He had come in so quietly, maybe she did not hear him, or she thought it was the new maid.

"Valentina."

She turned, her mouth opening with surprise. He gave her time to say, *you must leave, sir, it's not right.* She did not. He crossed to her, and her perfume imbued him, and he put his hands to her dark gold hair. He kissed her on the mouth, their faces even, he in boots, she in slippers. It was so sweet, his eyes filled with tears.

She laid her hands on either side his waist, careful, maybe shy. Her hands tensed and pulled; they drew together and embraced, tight. They kissed like that, deeply, eased apart. They smiled at the paint daubs on his clothes.

He was going to say, his life pulsing within him and through him and through her, and her life through him and within him: *Come and take the first drink from the new spring.* He found it easier to kiss her again, and take her hand and lead her out, through the garden, along the path where Jeannie and Eva had frolicked, down to the muddy spring.

Epilogue

LOUIS TRIED A DEEP breath, gasped at the pain, realized he was on the ground, that he must have collapsed. A shout *Give him air!*

Another surge of pain smothered the world.

When he came to, the crushing sensation had receded to a numb echo. It was quiet, quieter. The machines shut off one by one: the channelers, the drills, the derrick motor winding down. He read, in the quiet and in his men's faces clustered over him, that his body was in a very bad way. The doctor had warned: *Your heart is too large, Louis. You have used it too hard.*

The rest of his life reckoned in hours, maybe minutes, he would not see his daughter's baby, coming along any day now, and he was sorry that the family's joy would be stained with grief. He longed to see his grandchild, to know if it was a boy or a girl, to cradle the baby in his arms. To kiss his daughter's birth-sweated brow, to embrace his trembling and awed son-in-law. To enfold Valentina in his arms as she held their grandchild. And he could say to Jake: *There, now, I'm starting to catch up with you.* The summer house on the Maine shore would be more crowded than ever.

All the machines silent now. The river's flow, the trees stirring. It was as it used to be.

"Whittington. No.... " Whittington in New York. He had tried to persuade Louis to stay up there, the quarry having shrunk back to as it was when Whittington clerked, half the pits filling with rain and silt and green.

He wanted to say goodbye to Branden. But Branden no longer carried the burden of this life. Gone five and twenty years or so. Louis choked, his mouth filled with tears. Blood.

Within there runs blood,
The same old blood! the same red-running blood!
There swells and jets a heart, there all passions, desires, reachings,
*   aspirations,*

Someone carefully turned his head, and the blood ran onto the granite beneath him, the good solid stone. A waterboy sobbed and sobbed, and one of the men tried to hush him. The boy broke loose and knelt by Louis and wiped his face. He took off his shirt and put it under Louis's head.

The pillow gifted Louis with a dream of Valentina: turning to take her in his arms, making love with her in their bed warmed and softened by their bodies over the years.

Cold crept into Louis's body—into his upper body. He could not feel the rest.

Broad breast-front, curling hair of the breast, breast-bone, breast-
*   side,*
Ribs, belly, backbone, joints of the backbone,
Hips, hip-sockets, hip-strength, inward and outward round, man-
*   balls, man-root*

The cloth under his head soaked red. A man could bleed to death very quickly, though he had hung on long enough, lying wounded on the battlefield. He had been young. He had thought that to be the center of his life, the War, the Good Old Cause won. His home lost. He had thought the War like the Fall Line, from which everything must slope down, broken.

"Papa!" A face pushed through the other faces. His cousin's son and then his and Valentina's, by Richard Poindexter's last will and testament, the mother dead birthing him. He smelled of whiskey; he had been sent down from Princeton.

Louis closed his eyes, not against his son's beautiful young manly tear-drenched face, but to lend strength to his voice. "I've been happy. In life."

"Yes, Papa." Louie's voice cracked.

A woman in old-fashioned clothes tilted a canteen to his lips. A dream, a memory. Mrs. Hamilton, years dead, too. She sat at the casement doors overlooking the quarry and saw all of this.

Louis dreamt that Valentina arrived to him. He dreamt his beloved woman was nigh. He and she lay entwined, damp and sated, telling each other the lines of their favorite poem.

O my body!

He opened his eyes. A bird flew through the sky.

"Papa?"

The sun slipped between the men and caught Louis in the face.

He looked full into it.

Now these are....

O I say these are not the parts and poems of the body only, but
*   of the soul,*
O I say now these are the soul!

Acknowledgments

Many thanks to:

Writing teachers Jamie Feuglein and Fred Leebron;

Tuesday Night Writers Group: Ron Andre, Ben Cleary, Helen Montague Foster, and Lenore Gay;

Marta Bliese and Catherine Patterson for their insightful reads of the manuscript.

Many people helped in researching this book. In particular, I'd like to thank:

Paul Wood, author of the invaluable "Tools and Machinery of the Granite Industry," who answered my many questions in a cheerful correspondence.

Staff members and supporters of:
Beth Ahabah Museum & Archives in Richmond, Virginia
Chesterfield Public Library
Library of Virginia
United States Library of Congress

United States National Park Service
Virginia Museum of History and Culture
—not to mention the many independent historians who share
online their passion for American history.

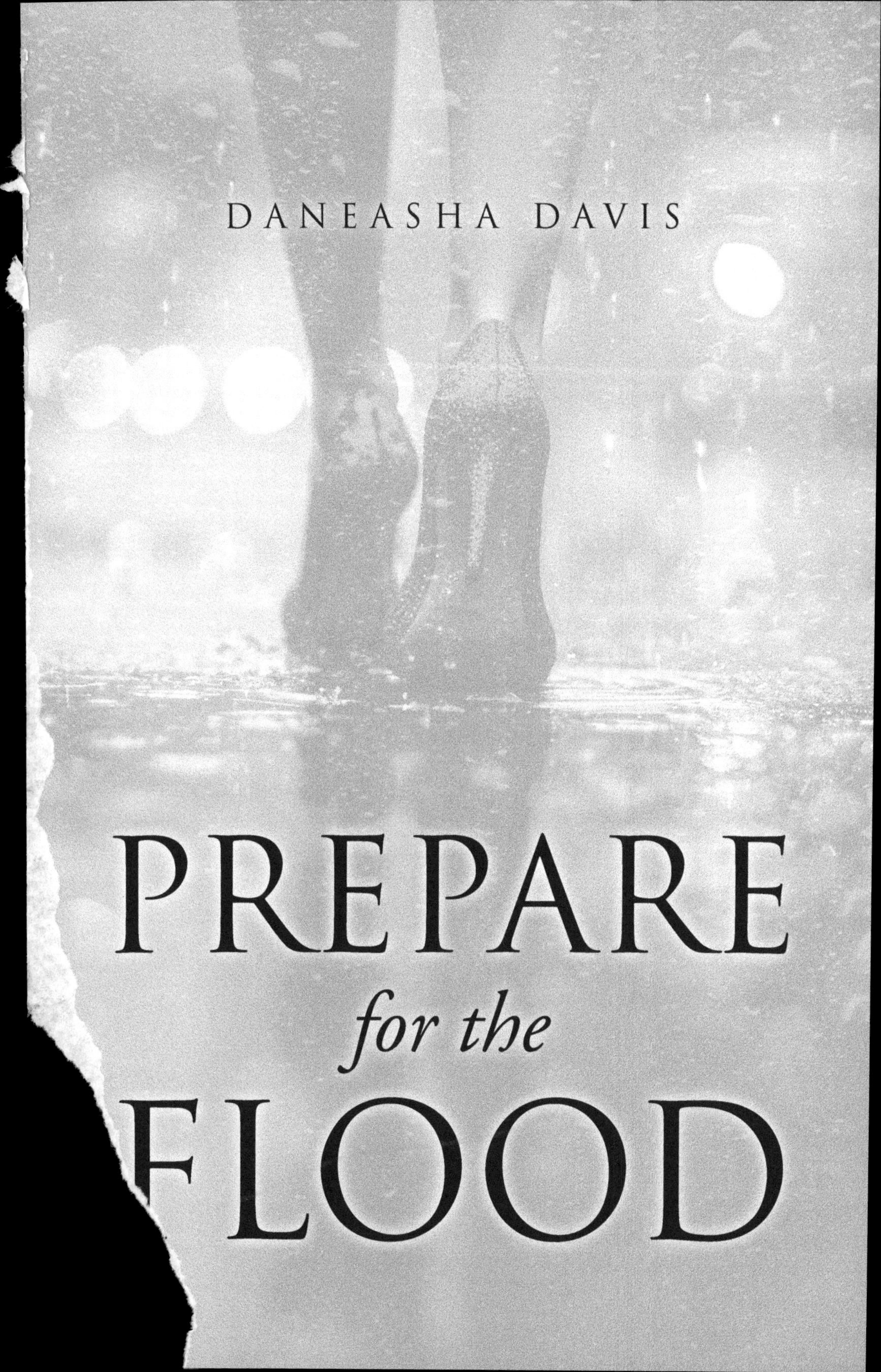
DANEASHA DAVIS
PREPARE
for the
FLOOD

Ordering Information:

Books to Life Marketing Ltd
128 City Road, London, EC1V 2NX, UK

Printed in the United States of America

In Loving Memory Of
Barbara Jean Cannon/Heggie
Earl Heggie Sr.
&
Maxine Vera Wright/Conner
George Conner Sr.

I AM WRITING this book in dedication to my Grandparents which are all a huge inspiration for me especially Barbara whom taught me the power of prayer, grace and mercy. I didn't get a chance to meet my grandmother Maxine although, I know she would have been a very special lady as well. I salute Barbara because she was a huge blessing in my life and to be able to share her Holy Embrace made a huge difference for me on my day to day life occasions. Barbara was a Beautiful woman of Color and she is the thread that kept our family together so once that "Thread" was broken things started to fall apart. I love to think of my Grandma Barbara in the sense of "Big Momma". Have you ever watched the movie "Soul Food"? Barbara is and will forever be My "Big Momma", my Rock. Barbara taught me how to get down on my knees and Pray, to be thankful to God for EVERYTHING. Barbara taught me to never give up, she taught me how to respect, how to love and her passing and leaving me so soon taught me the harsh reality of life. Barbara left me when I was 5 years old but in just that amount of time that BRILLIANT woman left with me some self morals and knowledge that I will not ever forget or let go. God has his ways of doing things and I know now that God took my wonderful Grandmother because he loved her that much, God didn't want grandma to hurt anymore he loved her and wanted her presence right beside him in PEACE. I know that my Lord, My God is sitting with my grandparents watching over me. I am writing this book in dedication to my wonderful grandparents who once lived in this world where BLACKS were degraded and humiliated as if we don't as well serve a purpose in life as if WE BLACKS are not equal and one with ALL. I'm writing this book so that my Grandchildren and Great Great Grandchildren will know who I am and where they came from and to know that LOVE overcomes ALL things and that THE CREATOR of this Earth is looking and watching down upon ALL of us and it's NOT OKAY to live your lives full of hatred. It's time to REPENT of ALL your sins and turn from your sinful ways because this world we live in was CREATED BY SOMEONE CALLED GOD/LORD not men so don't be so quick to judge because of the color of the skin LOVE LOVE ONE ANOTHER take your children close and LOVE show them how to LOVE EVERYONE as a whole. I've saw so many things in life and I'm here to tell you "My Story" and why it is so important to LOVE one another as a whole, I support ALL LIVES MATTER because with Change comes Change of thinking and living. I honor All my Grandparents because they were married under a Covenant of God, they knew how to EMBRACE one another even through bad times which people these days know nothing about. Don't get me misunderstood I have changed a lot of things around in my story because of the LOVE that I have for my family knowing and understanding that NO ONE is perfect WE ALL make mistakes. We live and we learn how to be better and do better. LOVE OVERCOMES all things and I have a BEAUTIFUL family there is a STAR in a lot of US, I watch US STRIVE to take care OUR FAMILIES so SALUTE to my FAMILY in PHILLY, North Carolina, Texas, Florida, Baltimore, Virginia, New York and ACROSS the WORLD wherever someone SOME CHILD is struggling this ones for you KNOW that your NOT BY YOURSELF and YOU can Make A Difference.

PROLOGUE

GROWING INTO THE woman I am today has been hard—silver spoon, plastic spoon. I am in the middle of the Jungle "Krazy Killer Kansas" as some would say "The Wild Mid West". "When It Rains It Pours—Be Prepared For The Flood". I didn't ask to be born into this world filled with evil. God created me for his own special purpose and God's purpose I want to fulfill. As a child I would always ask the Lord "Lord, why me"? God does everything for a reason (his special reasons). If God brings you to it, God can and will bring you through it. I ask the Lord, "Lord guide me please, Lord protect me". Sometimes we (as people) feel like the pains we face in life are unbearable and we ask "Lord, why me"? WE CAN'T QUESTION GOD WHEN HE DOES THINGS FOR HIS REASONS—there are reasons for different seasons. I've found out that, the trials and tribulations I faced in my life are WHAT MADE ME. My situations didn't break me and if they did BY HIS STRIPES I AM HEALED. Without the pain there would be no lessons, without no lessons there would not be "My Story". Now this is my season. I will speak to you the truth and only the truth because its FACTS and I can always back up the FACTS. I will always "Tell The Truth—Shame The Devil". I am far from perfect and I am not defined by my past, I am defined by my present and future. I will strive for the best and I will strive for the Truth to be told. Some families like to sweep things under the rug "My Story" is coming from under that rug, that has been swept up for many many years. I have a mission to accomplish, lives to save, and hearts to heal. I want to open an eye to you the harsh reality of life because with an open eye you (the people) will be able to see clearly. I will save many children from this day forward from traveling down that dark dark road. I will open eyes to the pedophiles that lurk in our families thinking that they are getting away with taking the innocence of our children and getting away free. I will put a stop to the wicked mind a pedophile tries so hard to hide behind KNOW THAT PEOPLE LIKE ME SEE YOU!! Mothers I will show you how to comfort your children and cherish their very presence because the enemy is always lurking and it's going to take ALL mothers from every single nationality to stand together as ONE and teach our children how to SPEAK UP, teach our children how to LOVE, teach our children how to be better men and women of today so that the world becomes a better place because WOMEN teaching starts at home first. I am currently going through a healing process from within and it's not easy so I need ALL of you to uplift me on my journey. Ladies we need to just have simple talks with our children in the morning, noon or night just find time to talk and communticate with your childern building relationships of trust so that we can defeat the enemy. A pedophile usually strikes when her/him feels comfortable like they won't get caught WE NEED TO MAKE THE ENEMY VERY UNCOMFORTABLE. I'm writing this book because I feel that there are too many children in suffering because their not comfortable enough to talk with an adult about their sitaution, NOW'S THE TIME TO OPEN UP all it takes is someone to find it in thier hearts to communicate and protect the innocent which is our children. I guarantee you that theres a child somewhere right now whom is suffering in silence while thier most valuable gift is being taken away from them without any control, that this being their "Self-Worth" their "Verginity". A pedophile has a sickness and as I like to call it "Sick In The Head". They invade, they pretend, they manipulate, and then they strike. If (us) as a people dont stick together we can easily put our children at risk and fall victim because men aren't the only ones that prey "molest". I think that it's sad how the laws are set up basically giving pedophiles a slap on the wrist and then sending the back into society only to feed their sicknesses not realizing how bad it scars and hurts people like myself. Do you know my struggles? I will let you in on my life so take the bitter with the sweet and strap on your seat belts and prepare for the ride (for me it's back down terror lane). There's a dark dark cloud hovering over Kansas City so don't be fooled by Dorthy and Toto because this definitely isn't the Wizard Of Oz were dealing with but more like "The Wild Midwest"-" Coming From The K" Killer City indeed.

Feb. 4 2014

Last night I had a dream that I killed my cousin's Filthy Husband. All I ever asked for was an apology. Sometimes I feel like if I could just hurt the people who hurt me in life then I would be just fine. I was told that vengence is the Lords not mine. You tell me, how do I control my feelings when people have inflicted so much pain on me then laughed right in my face like nothing ever happened while stabbing me in the back the whole time and saying that they love me? Tell me what is love? Especially when the ones who say that they love you are the ones who seem to hurt you the most. How do you take the most precious gift from a child then continue on with your life like nothing ever happened? I can honestly say that I WILL KILL when it comes to my children!! How dare you walk around here like nothing ever happened and calling me a liar!! Today the truth will be told and you will be exposed!! You are a pedophile and you should be registered. I was scared, I was young and innocent and you took that from me. I tried to tell someone what was going on and you also took that from me and called me a liar right to my face HOW DARE YOU!!!!!!! Being that the system does not protect children to the max I WILL BE THE ONE WHO PROTECTS MY CHILDREN along with my warrior angels. Truthful, my life hasn't been the same ever since my grandmother passed away. My grandma is probably one of my guardian angles watching over me and my children, I know for facts that God sends his angles to watch over me and my family even through bad times I refused to lose my faith. It's been a very bumpy road for me. I have seen things with my own two eyes that would have driven any normal person insane. Listen to "My Story" as I take you through my life step by step. Beware, some of the things you read will be unbearable and you might break down and cry (I've cried so many times before). Some parts will make you grab a hold of your children and cherish their very existence and that right there alone is my main goal because children are so precious and vulnerable. Now listen as we take a trip back down memory (Terror) lane. Like the movie Jasons Lyric "Things that happened in the past always got some kind of way to make you remember". Difference is "My Story" is truth, real life events and my past always comes back to haunt me NO MATTER WHAT these events will be stuck in my head for a lifetime…. Don't forget this is my story from the beginning in my eyes. I also did my own editing so if you run into some misspelled words keep in mind the message behind "My Story" and that message is to save souls, "God's Precious Souls" and to protect our children our innocent youth from those that prey. There's too much social media, not enough books. Predators Prey Online! Stop the school shootings, stop hurting innocent children, let's work together to keep our children safe by putting love and God first.

When It Rains It Pours
But Be Prepared For The Flood
I'm In The K-All day
Got It Straight Out The Mud
Lioness They Call Me Lady Juice
When In The Real
I Speak Nothing But The Truth
Shaped Like A Two Liter Bottle
Black Genie Live And *Full Throttle-ugh"
I'm 100 Proof
Won't Tell No Lies To You
You Don't Wanna See My Life Through My Eyes
From Day One I've Been Goin Threw
When I Pop
I'm Aiming Full And Direct
Spit You Out Like Sunflower Seeds
Squirt Like I'm
Bustin A Tech
Mia X Said
"How I Love The Rainy Days"
She Got Me Threw My Stuggle
Not Even Knowing
That I could Feel Her Pain
SALUTE
I'm Bout That Life
Cause I Came From That Cloth

This Game Came All So Real To Me
Don't Get Cha Head Knocked Off
I Keeps It Kosher
Cause I'm A Loyal 100 Lady
I Keep My Nose Turnt Up
Cause I Know You Niggas Shady
I Don't Do 16
But I Do Write Poetry
I Can Make Your Ass Laugh
Or I Can Sing Like I'm Floetry
I Can Be A Freakin Artist
Or I Can Be Your Next Designer
Praise God, Put No One First
Now Take This HUGE PILL AND SWALLOW
"My Story Is Like A Movie"
So Sit Back And Read Along
Chief Helped Me Lace My Boots
While We Were Wilding Alone
Came From the Heart Of This Earth
Ya'll Tried To Play Us Like Oz
But I Hit You With Some Knowledge
Like A Real Nigah Nas
Again I'm Not A Freestyler
I Like To Right Poetry
But I Can Hit You With Some Bars
And Sing Like I'm Floetry

CHAPTER

1

. . . .

1986

"NOW I LAY, me down to sleep. I pray the Lord, my soul to keep. If I should die, before I wake. I pray the Lord, my soul to take. Lord can you bless my momma, my grandma, my grandpa, my brother and my sister Amen". Goodnight grandma, I love you so much (hugging and kiss granny). My grandma was sick and I was just to young to realize it. I was only a child but my grandmother meant the world to me in my tiny world. I spent alot of nights with my grandparents. My grandma and grandpa were married before I was ever born and they remained married. My grandma would not let me lay down at night until I got on my knees and prayed (no praying in the bed laying down you had to get down on your knees). Grandma was the most kind and loving woman that you would ever meet. I heard stories about her being very overprotective of her husband and her family (I picked up alot of my grandmothers ways). My grandma was a dark skin woman of color, standing about 5'6"-5'8". I didn't realize it at the time but my grandma wore a wig and had only one of her breast. I was told that grandma had one of her breast removed to prevent the spread of Cancer, grandma was sick with Cancer. Grandpa was a bit shorter than grandma, he stood anywhere from 5'5"-5'7". Grandpa was literally half Indian, his mother was a full blood Indian, so grandpa has this Indian skin complexion with grey eyes and grandpa was a handsome man. Grandpa worked at Sunshine biscuits where he retired from so he would always bring us (his grandchildren) snacks, cookies and doughnuts. Grandpa would bring us Krispy Creme doughnuts every Saturday not missing a beat. Me, my brother (Rico) and my youngest baby sister (Poody) were always at our grandma and grandpa's house being that my mother was the only girl out of 5. My grandpa was born in North Carolina so we have lots of family there and I'm not quite sure where my grandma came from or how her and grandpa met but I'm sure that it's an interesting story.

One warm and sunny day over my grandparents house I remember alot of family being over at the house for some aparent reason. It was like a gathering except that people didn't look so happy to see one another. I knew that something was wrong because my mom would not let me enter my grandmothers room but I observed others going in and out of grandma's room with sad looks on thier face. I remember this day like it was yesterday. Rico was running around playing like everything was okay but, Rico was only four years old and didn't know any better. I got mad at Rico and rolled my eyes at him in a mean way. I felt something going on this day and it was terrible. Poody was a baby and I remember her being in a high chair. I felt a sadness come over me and I couldn't explain it but it made me begin to cry. I wanted to be in that room with my grandma but no one would let me. No one wanted to tell me anything so I waited with an agonizing sadness and pain. There's nothing that anyone can do to help so next thing I heard was an ambulance. Less than a day later, the sad news flooded my ears. My grandma had passed away, God called his angel home and left me here with only a memory that I am truly blessed to have. I can't remember going to the wake and momma wouldn't let me go to the burial. It seems like I had nightmares The same reoccuring nightmare almost every night for the next 4 or 5 years later. This was only the beginning of the chain of events that have taken place that day after.

CHAPTER

2

....

1987

"POLICE AND AMBULANCE sirens sounding loud and close."

Me, "Rico, do you hear that? I wonder what's going on."

Rico, "I'll be back. I'm thirsty and I got to pee, Im going to get something to drink".

We lived in some Townhomes (In another project complex) and in the backyard was a small park. me and Rico were out back in the Park and I was on the swing swinging, Rico was playing in the sand when we heard those Sirens. Rico went in the house and as I look up I see the ambulance and Police all in the front of our Complex where we live so I immedialty stop swinging and go up front to see what's going on.

One year earlier after my grandpa passed, my mother started to change. My father wasen't ever around and I remember the last day seeing him. I remember being at home in our Townhouse and momma and daddy were arguing loudly. All of a sudden, I saw daddy storm out of him and momma's room in a full rage, he punched the wall so hard he left a huge hole in the wall before he left. I didn't see my dad for almost the next 5–10 years. So, momma was single to mingle and she meets this new guy named Toni. Toni came around alot and while Toni was around dad was definitly not in the picture. I can't remember much about Toni's appearance except him being kind of tall and brown skinned and he had this bad boy kind of way about himself. My mom met Tony after my grandma passed because I'm sure that my grandma wouldn't have approved of this new relationship mom had with Toni. One particular day, thier were alot of children over my grandparents home. The adults were all upstairs and the children were all in the basement being kids. I remember that the adults would smoke weed and have drinks because one night me and Rico had gotten into the liquor, got drunk and passed out (I was about 3 when that happened so I can't remember but momma told me what had happened). With grandma now deceased and grandpa always at work trying to maintain all the bills momma had more than enough time to party and get wild. The grown-ups almost always left us kids unsupervised while they did thier thang. So, us kids got bored and started playing house, we were humping and being bad unsupervised kids. Toni walked in and caught us. Out of all the kids in that room he gave me a whooping. I cried and forced myself to throw up. My mother was furious, she cussed Toni out and told him these exact words "Dont you ever put your hands on my daughter again and if she's doing something wrong, you come and let me know." After momma cussed his ass out, I felt better just knowing that he couldn't put his hands on me ever again and if he did!! During that year Toni and my mother stayed together and as a kid I didnt notice any relationship problems that I can recall although I dont think Toni to much liked me after that incident of him whooping me. One night at home it was me, my mom, Rico, Poody, when all of a sudden me and my mom started smelling smoke. I remember thinking "oh my God the house on fire." Smoke detectors started going off and my mother ran all around the house trying to find the cause of the smoke and burning. Finally, she found it. My little brother had went underneath his bed and using a lighter, he set his mattress on fire from underneath the bed. Thank God momma caught the fire before it spread throughout the house. She was furious and she gave Rico a beating that he won't forget. The next day momma and Toni set the burnt mattress on the curve for the trash. Frequently Toni would leave to walk to the store and I would ask, "can I go" he would say no and he would take my brother with him every single time. Toni never took me anywhere with him and at the time it hurt my feelings because I was the oldest child and I felt like it wasn't fair. I was a child and I didn't understand then but now its perfectly understandable. Me and Rico would be outside playing with the neighborhood kids and there was a saying that the killer clown would be in the woods behind our house. The kids in the neighborhood would say things like "Dont come out the house at night or the killer clown is going to take you, or if you see a clown around here you better run because it's the killer clown and he kills kids. Look back up there in the woods, that's where he lives." I was beyond scared of those woods. One of the other neighborhood girls named T.T used to come and sit on the porch with me and she liked to play in my hair. My hair was real long when I was young it was long and pretty so people liked playing in it but, my momma would get mad and tell me to quit letting T.T play in my hair or I'm going to get in trouble. One sunny day me and Rico were outside in the back playing at the park when we heard the police and ambulance sirens. Rico went in the house to get water so I thought and continued to swing that is until those Police ambulance ended up in front of our complex. As I ran around to the front of our building I noticed Rico standing by the door with a shocked expression on his face and as I tried to run in the house the police grabbed me and told me I could not enter our home. A few minutes went by me and Rico stood outside by the front door I heard a woman crying next thing you know, the police brought my momma out the house in handcuffs. Mom had tears running down her face as they put her in the police car. Things started happening really quick. My two uncles and my grandpa pulled up just as the Police were getting ready to take me, Rico and Poody into SRS custody. My uncle Mick (my favorite) stopped the officer and told them that they were there to take me, Rico and Poody. The officers agreed but said first they need me and Rico to come to the police station to make a statement. As the police car pulled off with my momma, I looked on her face, she made eye to eye contact with me and I could feel her pain and sorrow. Our grandpa and uncle's escorted us to the police station and thats when I found out what happend, poor Rico had just walked in on a bloody scene. Prior to the day of the accident, my momma and Toni had gotten into a huge argument which turned violent. Toni hit my mother so my mother had kicked him out the house. She (mom) didn't want to have anything to do with Toni after his abuse and when she put him out he left some of his belongings. That next day while me and my brother were outside playing (poody was to young to be outside so she was in the house with momma) there was a knock on the door. When momma looked out the peep hole it was Toni's sister stating she was there to pick up Toni's belongings for him. Well as my mother was opening up the door for her Toni busted in the door as well. Toni had been standing to the side of the door where my mom couldn't see him just by looking out the peep hole. Toni barges his way in and wanting to talk things out with my mom but my mom didnt really want to hear that because he had already become abusive. Toni's sister said that she had to use the restroom. While she was in the restroom, Toni tried to pleed his case and when my mom denied him, he became enraged. He slapped the shit out my momma and she ran to the kitchen, grabbed a knife and told him to stay away from her and get out of our house. Toni thought she was playing and he charged at her and the knife went directly thru his heart. His sister came out the restroom, down the stairs, all to find her brother dead on the kitchen floor with one fatal stab wound to the heart. In the police interrogation room I couldn't tell the police anything except the fact that I hated Toni and he was mean me, again my grandmothers passing took a huge toll on my family and no one was ever the same especially my momma. Women scorned and abused is who momma became.

CHAPTER

3

....

1987–1988

ME, RICO AND Poody went to live with my Grandpa and my Uncle Mick. Momma had all three of us children by the same man but it had been years since we had saw our daddy and for all we knew he was probably incarcerated just like momma was. Uncle Mick was always my favorite uncle he was the youngest out of 5 children and he had no children of his own. After grandma passed things spiraled down hill a bit. The utilities began to get turned off and there was very little food to eat. I remember some nights, we had to eat can goods straight out of the can when the lights would be off and sometimes when the lights were on we would have to eat things like bread, cheese and sugar on top and put in the oven until brown UGH GROSS but if you were hungry you had no chioce but to eat it. I made a vowel to myself that I won't ever feed that crap to my children, but aye what can I say I survived it so it wasen't to bad. Don't get me wrong even though times were hard I love my grandpa and my Uncle Mick for what they were doing for us and I knew that they would do it again if they had to and I know in my heart that they were struggling and only doing thier best.

Things weren't always bad some days were good and we would eat great. I remember how Poody would always wait until grandpa sat down and started eating to tell him that she had to use the bathroom and grandpa would get so mad and lose his appetite. Grandpa would always ask Poody, "Poody, do you have to use the restroom before we start eating"? One day we were eating Gates bar-B-Que and grandpa asked Poody if she had to use the restroom and Poody said no. As soon as grandpa got comfortable and began to eat here goes Poody, "Grandpa I gotta boo boo". Grandpa yelled "God DARNIT, girl I asked you"!! I could hear grandpa cursing up under his breath. He was so disgusted that he no longer wanted to eat his food. Poody was bad and she knew what she was doing, if grandpa didn't want his food that meant more for Poody. I would laugh to myself on the inside because grandpa was Indian so he would turn red like fire. Everyone in the family would say that grandpa gave Poody the perfect nickname. Poody stayed into something as a kid, she was more like a little boy than a girl and I prayed to God for Poody to be a girl. Grandpa would take all three of us up to the Prison at least once a month to visit momma. The Prison was in Topeka so it was about an hour drive from where we lived. I would really look forward to those visits and it seemed like it took forever to make it there longer than an hour I must say. It was exciting being able to go see momma and spend a little time with her but the hard part was always leaving her, I could always see the tears build up in her eyes as we departed from her. When I visited with momma I would talk to her about things like what was going on in school and she would be so happy to see us giving us plenty of hugs and kisses. Rico and I went to the same elementary school. I was in the first grade and Rico was one year behind me in Kindergarten. It seemed like every morning when I made it to school I would run into the same two little boys who would say to me, "Your momma killed my Uncle". These little boys taunted me. They would be all in my face yelling these things to me and it would eventually make me break down into tears. I felt threatned. I didn't have any control over the things that had happened and yet I suffered threw this very dark situation at hand. I began to act out in several different ways at school. I would have a fight almost every day with a girl named Kia. Kia and I just did not mix like salt and sugar. I would sometimes tell my teacher that I did not want to go outside for recess so that I could stay in the classroom and be fast and sneaky. Me and this little boy would plan to stay in the classroom together while everyone else went outside for recess and while the teacher and the other students were outside, the boy and I would ease off into the classroon closet to kiss and hump on one another. I must admit that I became very mischievious. In the mornings before school Uncle Mick would have to comb my hair (so you can imagine how I must have been looking which was a hot mess). We had a neighbor who lived in the Duplex beside us and she had two daughters. Our neighbors name was Mrs. D. Mrs. D would look out for me from time to time she had noticed the mess my hair was becoming and my hair was to long and pretty to be looking the way that is was becoming so she would braid my hair and put beads on the ends for me and I loved how Mrs D braided my hair. that was really nice of Mrs. D but what I really needed was a mother figure My MOTHER. There is nothing in life like motherly love. Being that it was Poody and I whom were girls we really need our mom to be there for us in many different ways and Poody was just to young to realize it. Our hygiene, our hair, our clothing just life itself we needed our moms guidence. One of my Uncles named after my grandpa Uncle Eric had a girlfriend named Alicia and Alicia. Alicia had a daughter that was 5–7 years older than I was and her name was Shannon. Shannon would always tease me saying "Is someone sucking on your boobs because you are starting to grow titties? I would look at Shannon crazy and laugh to myself. I would always go over to Shannons house because I loved being around her and Shannon was like a big sister to me but this one particular night would be a night for me to remember because it would be my last night at Shannon's house. Shannon and I were watching Cujo when I feel asleep. I was awaken out of my sleep later that night due to crying and yelling. When I finally focused my eyes I remember seeing alot of blood and Shannon was crying. Alicia mad sure that I went back to sleep. The next day Alicia took me home. I heard later on the details about what happened and why I was no longer allowed over Alicia's house. Shannon was supposed to walk to the store that night for a gallon of milk and come straight back home. According to Alicia, Shannon was gone away from home entirely to long and probably got caught with a boy. Alicia decided to give Shannon a beating that she wouldn't forget HECK a beating that I won't forget. Alicia beat Shannon so bad that she busted Shannons head open, and then took Shannon to the hospital where Shannon had to get stitches. If I'm not mistaken that night Alicia beat Shannon with a bat and it seems like Shannon also had a broken arm or wrist due to her mother Alicia's attack on her. I felt so bad for Shannon because I heard it and it was terror and all because Shannon got caught with a boy. It was sad. After that episode Uncle Mick would not allow me to go back over to Alicia's house with Shannon. I liked Shannon a whole lot because regardless of our age difference Shannon was always someone that I felt comfortable around and I could talk to Shannon about anything. I always looked forward to going over Shannon's house spending time with her and Shannon also loved to play in my hair like I was a "Black Barbie".

CHAPTER

4

••••

"When It Rains It Pours" My Story

"MUSIC PLAYING AND the sun was Shinning" the beginning of spring and the flowers were blooming. My mother got released from prison sooner than later. It just so happens that she was convicted of Manslaughter and she got out on Self-Defense "Murder Chose Her I Guess". Anyhow, That was one of the happiest days of my life in my younger years. I was so excited to be back reunited with my mother and not to mention momma picked up about 30 or 40 maybe 50 extra pounds that went to her butt because mommas figure was 5'8" 125 lbs but with this extra weight momma had that went only to her backside I was very observative of mother. Everyone was excited for momma to be home and we all showered her with love. When she was released she was out on Parole. One day Rico and I were outside playing with some of the neighborhood kids as we would usually be playing around with our friends whom lived across the street, and up the street being normal kids in elementary school, when Poody came running outside. Poody was about one years old still in a diaper only Poody was outside running around wildly and butt naked. I tried taking Poody in the house when one of the neighborhood boys came running with a bucket of worms and he tossed them right on the top of Poody's head. I was furious at that point and I started beating the little boy up fighting him screaming at him and all of the neighborhood kids gathered around holding me back from beating the boy up. When I say all the neighborhood kids, there were anywhere from 7–12 kids out side at this point. I managed to break loose from the children and I grabbed Poody and took her in the house. As I took Poody in the house, furious, I wondered why or how did she make it out the house naked in the first place and where were the adults?

We were still living at our grandparents house until momma got back on her feet. This little boy who lived behind us use to always bully Rico, he was a little white boy I won't ever forget it. The little boy would hit Rico and Rico would run from the little boy. That is until one day momma saw what was going on. Rico came running fast after the little boy hit him and started to chase Rico home when momma said yellin at Rico, ("UH UH, Rico you better turn around and hit his ass back or I am going to beat your ass")! I watched and I saw Rico stop running, turn around and punch that little boy right in the nose. The little boys nose started bleeding and he ran away crying. After that day momma didn't have any more problems with Rico defending himself and Rico didn't have any more problems with that little white boy bullying him anymore neither. We use to stay out late at night catching Lightnening bugs and playing Hide-And-Go-Seek. Once, we found a bullet outside so we went, found a brick and we threw bricks on the bullet trying to get the bullet to rickochiet "Thank God That Plan Didn't Work". We were living our lives as siblings and just being mysterious children injoying our mother being home. We had a little swimming pool that we would play in and swim in while getting wet with the water hoose when it was warm outside. Things were getting a bit rocky though. As the seasons changed things began to change as well and all wasen't so good. One day Rico and I were crying mad because we were forced to walk in the cold snow to get momma a pack of cigaretts. Back then in the 1980's children could buy tobacco products out of the store for thier parents as long as you brought a note from your parent with you. Rico cried all the way to the store that day it as a long long cold walk and things were beginning to take a turn for the worse.

CHAPTER

5

....

1989

I HAD A childhood friend named LaRonda. My mom and her mom were bestfriends so LaRonda was always over my house and she and I were around the same age so we had alot in common as children and one day we were simply playing being girls, being children. LaRonda and I jumped around in the bed laughing, playing and singing. Simon says "little girls laughter". We were together alot while our parents left us alone to play and alot of the time LaRonda would spend the night over with me and we would sleep together. LaRonda had a little brother named Kevin whom was around the same age as Rico and they would hang together as well. LaRonda and I would Being that my mom and LaRonda's mom were close friends we grew up together and we experiement together most nights when we were left alone. We would do things like kiss each other, hump each other and we were being to take our expierments a little bit further with touching one anothers private areas. One day we decided to take our experiements to the next level which was oral sex with one another and that was the day that momma caught me right in the act. Momma beat the urge to experiement right out of me (so I thought for the moment) I didn't want to look a LaRonda physically after the beating momma gave me. I then knew definitly didn't ever want momma to catch me in the act.

Momma's new boyfriend Ricky came into the room with us. Ricky had only been around maybe once or twice prior to this night so I didn't really know him as a person but he came into this room were me and LaRonda were playing and Ricky turned off the lights and closed the door in a really sneaky kind of way. Us two girls continued laughing and jumping in the bed when I felt Ricky get in the bed with us quickly. LaRonda and I were about 7 or 8 years old at this point. We continued to laugh, jump and play when I felt LaRonda stop and start giggling differently. I felt Rickies hand touching me, it made me kind of nervous but LaRonda and I just kept jumping and playing. Next thing I knew Ricky was tongue kissing LaRonda in the mouth. Then Ricky grabbed me and put his tongue in my mouth. We just continued to jump around and play while Ricky kissed LaRonda again went back and forth. LaRonda laughed and played so I went along with it but I couldn't believe myself GROSS filthy Ricky just kissed me in the mouth as I thought to myself. Ricky finally got off the bed, turned on the light and left out the room like nothing happened. LaRonda and I laughed and giggled about it afterward but I couldn't help but feel disgusted on the inside knowing that Ricky was going to be a pedophile and knowing that I would have to be careful and watch myself around him if momma was going to have him around. Shortly after Ricky and momma met, we ended up moving with Ricky. First we moved to Lawrence or Leavenworth. It seemed very far away to me and wherever we were there were a bad case of skunks around there. I was in the third grade. Ricky had some ways like Tony because he would alway take Rico to the store and different places with him. I honestly think that Ricky was trying to mask the fact that he was a fucking child molester on the low.

"I want to spread a message to all of the children in this world who are being touched inappropriate, kissed inappropriate, hurt, or manipulated in any one of these forms or fashions TELL SOMEONE!! SPEAK UP, all it takes is someone that you completely feel comfortable around tell them, SPEAK UP TALK YOU HAVE A VOICE TELL!! Please my dear child tell someone don't make a mistake like I did and hold it in TELL SOMEONE that you (YOU) feel comfortable around meaning your teacher, a friend, a friends parent, an uncle, a big cousin, a grandmother ANYONE or call 911 and tell the police just make and effort to tell because if you hold it in things can or will get worse or even worse things can remain the same. These were the days when I first realized that my mother was on drugs. I wasn't quite sure what drugs were, but I knew that there was something wrong because my mother's appearance and attitude was starting to change. I have had asthma every since my mother concieved me and it was proven at birth and my asthma was starting to worsen. I was sick every single Halloween for the next three years. When I would experience an asthma attack Rico was my backbone. Everytime I would get sick and go into an asthma attack Rico would be right there to help me. That also seemed to be the only time that momma would stay home with me, when she knew that I was very sick. Momma and Rico were the only ones that ever made me feel better during my sickness. One night momma was sleeping, it was late at night maybe 1 or 2 o'clock a.m. I was laying in the bed watching the Cosby Show. I could hear Ricky get up and get into the shower. For some apparent reason I was not at all sleepy that particular night. As I was watching T.V, I heard the shower turn off and instead of Filthy Ricky going back in the bedroom with my mom his nasty ass came into my bedroom with me wearing only a towel. I tried not to look directly at him so I kept my eyes glued to the television. Ricky layed down right next to me, I was nervous more than I had ever been in life. He layed down right next to me wearing only that towel wrapped around his bottom part of his body.

Again I kept my eyes glued only on the Cosby Show but I could see Ricky in my paricular vision. I WAS NERVOUS!! As he layed there I could see him clearly out of the corner of my eye. Ricky took the towel completely off of him exposing himself as he began to masturbate. I saw his dick big and hard which really scared me because I hadn't ever in life saw a grown mans penus. As his dick was getting harder and he had gotten aroused he tried to get on top of me. I kicked him up off me and said no in a slight whisper. Ricky lay back in the same position as before and started back jacking his dick off (masturbating) for a minute or so I couldn't move I was completely stiff as Ricky jacked off beside me. After a minute or so went by he tried the same trick twice. Ricky tried to climb his nasty black ass right back on top of me in a sexual position. I kicked and pushed him up off of me, then I ran as fast as I could run into the room with my momma. I tried my best to wake momma up real quick I shook her, "momma, momma get up"!! Ricky busted in the room and said," get out of here don't wake your mom up let her sleep". Ricky was nervous and I was ANGRY!! Fucking pervert I smell a skunk! I left my moms room that night went to the kitchen grabbed a knife and then went back into my room to continue watching "The Cosby Show". If Ricky came his perverted ass back in my room I had something under my pillow with his name on it. As I continued to watch The Cosby Show I can remember thinking how good Rudy's (Kesha Knight Pulliam) life was being famous. Rudy had the good life and here it was me a beautiful black little girl who had to fight off perverted pedaphiles. I kept asking God "Lord why do I have to suffer like this". When I grow up I want to be an actress and then I can make money to support my children and protect them from evil people in this world. I had Big Dreams as a child that I was willing to persue only I didn't think that Kansas was the place for my Big Dreams to manifest. As a child I was always told by many different people, especially on picture days that I was beautiful and had a very pretty smile. How come I didn't feel so beautiful?

WHEN IT RAINS IT POURS

Momma got us an apartment (Townhome) in Gateway. In Gateway we had alot of friends, some I still remember till this very day. One trajic day stands out very clear to me. It started off as an awkward morning for Rico and I as we walked to school that morning Rico and I got chased by some dogs on the way to school. Rico was running so fast that day that he ran across a very busy street without even stopping to look both ways. I remember praying to God that no cars were coming driving fast as they usually would on that street in the morning and God heard me and answered my prayers that very morning. I looked to the sky and thanked God that Rico made it across that street safely (sighs of happiness). I just couldn't help but feel uneasy this whole day during school. Rico and I were walkers and everyday we kept our same routine as for as meeting up and walking home. This day it was different as we approached our Townhome. We noticed immediatly that something bad was going on as we saw the Fire Department in front of our buliding. I was quickly approached by a news Lady with a microphone to my mouth asking me did I live here in this apartment. I remember only thinking about my mom and something being wrong as I took off running yelling were is my momma!! Someone stopped me from being able to run inside that apartment it was a Fire Fighter who stopped me so I yelled at him where is my momma? Momma came from no where and said, "Our apartment caught on fire baby." As a child I faced so many disappointments. Momma what happened to out apartment? Momma didn't speak about it right then and there but she later explained to me that she had fallen asleep with a cigarette lit and it caught our whole upstairs on fire. I felt sad and disappointed but at the same time I was relieved that Poody and momma were safe. I started to feel like my momma was letting this drug addiction get the best of her and it was costing our family more than I could bear. I started being ashamed and embarassed of my momma. All of my neighborhood friends saw what had happened and people had even saw my face Live on the News. I remember thinking, "Lord I want to be famous one day but not like this Lord". This was definitely not a good look for me, not to mention the boy that I had a huge crush on lived close by me and witnessed our apartment being burned up and he tried to comfort me telling me that everything was going to be alright. I was so ashamed that I wished that I could hide from the whole world and just cry, cry cry like a baby. One thing I though, I might have faced these disappointements with my mom but now as an adult I RESPECT MY MOM THREW THE STRUGGLE and WOULD NOT disrespect her NO MATTER WHAT and MY MOM has MY BACK SHE'S MOST DEFINITALY A RIDER FOR HER FAMILY and I WILL GO HARD FOR MY FAMILY MOST DEFINITALY MY MOMMA.

CHAPTER

6

· · · ·

I PRAYED SO much. "Lord please hear my prayers. What did I do to deserve this treatment? Do you love me Lord? I love you Lord and I believe in you. All I ask for is to be in a normal home with my family normal, away from Child molesters. Lord I pray that I become an actress one day so that I have money and my children don't have to struggle like I'm struggling Lord. In Jesus Name Amen.

So here we go again. Now we are moving to Missouri with Filthy Ricky and I do not want to be around his STANKING child molester ass!

"Momma can we pick up our cousins so that they can spend the nightwith us?" We always wanted to be around our cousins Keeda, BeBe and Tya'. Those were our favorite cousins because we were all around the same ages. Keeda was the oldest, then BeBe, then Me, then Rico, then Tya then Poody and we all grew up together. My mother and thier mother were also close friends so they made sure that they kept us close together as cousins growing up. We moved into a hugh 7 bedroom house on a street called Bell. Our home was huge but we didn't have much furniture or food in the home so we had to make due with what we had. Us children had to always fix our own food and sometimes we had nothing but some pancake mix and syrup. We would make one big plate of pancakes and say, "Rub A Dub Dub Thanks For The Grub, NOW DIG IN!" Poor Rico was the only boy out of the 6 of us and he was not fast enough when it came to us girls so he always got the least amount of food. One time grandpa sent Rico some birthday money (3 dollars) and we teased Rico about his measly 3 dollars that grandpa sent him until Rico would just cry. After grandma passed away, I think that it was too much for grandpa to bear so grandpa packed up and moved back to his home town Washington NC. Poor grandpa, he lost the love of his life which was my beautiful grandmother and our family was slowing tearing apart piece by piece. Like a shirt, that shirt will be in perfectly good shape until one of the threads unravel. That's how our family was and Grandma was that important thread needed to keep the family together. Us children always found something to do productive in order to keep ourselves occupied. We had many of different home made games to play amungst one another. When we would get wet with the waterhose outside I would laugh at BeBe because she never wanted to wear a shirt while getting wet (she was a TomBoy). At times we would get just down right bored and we would begin to fight one another and it was always BeBe and I fighting or Poody and Tya'. Momma would get really mad when we would all fight and she would then take our cousins home. One particular time momma decided not to ride with Ricky to drop the girls off at home so it was me, Keeda, BeBe, Tya', Rico and Poody and this day things took a U-Turn (something happened). Instead of taking the girls home we took them to the Projects where my Aunt would hustle at plus we had plenty of family down there in "The Projects". I had a big brother who also lived in the Projects he was my brother on my dads side and his name is Bobby but we all call him Tommie Gunn. These were the worst Projects THE BRICK JUNGLE. Tommie Gunn was also related to Keeda, BeBe and Tya' he was also thier cousin his mom and thier mom are sisters CRAZY SITUATION. It was fun to us kids in the Projects because there was plenty of children down there and it gave us a chance to be kids but the danger that lurked in them Projects were unimaginable. 6-26-15 for instance here's a situation of what goes on in them Projects, a woman witnessed her son get shot and killed right there in her face and she had some of her other children right there with her as well. This is most definitly "The Wild MidWest". The things that my own two eyes have witnessed in those projects are truely unbearable and I will touch on some things later in my story. Were I'm from we "Tell The Truth Shame The Devil", I'm all about TRUTH. So, as we were dropping Keeda, BeBe and Tya' off in those Projects one of our Big Cousins Ox Head happened to be down there and the kids told Ricky to pull over and drop them off with Ox Head. Ox Head watched as all of us children got out of the Van with Ricky. Obviously, something didn't look right in cousin Ox's eyes so we all ran up to Ox Head and greated him. Ricky got out of the Van as well and I heard Ox ask, "who the fuck is this strange dude bringing all my little cousins to the Projects". I answered, "my momma's bitch ass boyfriend". Ox stood straight up and went and approached Ricky saying, "hey what's up CUZ, who are you?" Ricky didn't not reply to cousin Ox as I watched everything very closley. I heard Ox repeat his question again and this time he was face to face with Ricky saying," Aye Cuz, I asked you a mutha fuckin question, who are you? You've got all of my little girl cousins with you, so who the fuck are you cuz? Again Ricky ignored Ox heads question. Next thing I saw was Ox pull out his gun then BANG! Ox busted Ricky upside the head a couple of times with his pistol (he just pistol whipped Ricky and I was loving the scene) until little Rico jumped in the middle on Ricky and Ox yelling, "Stop don't hit him NO, that's my momma's boyfriend STOP!" I screamed at Rico, "move out the way Rico!" I grabbed Rico and pushed him as hard as I could for him to move out of harms way. "Get out of the way Rico before I beat your ass! You don't have anything to do with this and Ricky should have just answered cuz Ox. Fuck Ricky I HATE HIM!" I saw Ricky bleeding badly from the face and I didn't care. Ox head stopped beating Ricky so Ricky ran and got in the van. I dreaded getting back into that van with Ricky but Rico had ran behind Ricky and gotten into the van so I grabbed Poody and we all got into the van and drove away from the Projects

July 2nd and 3rd
2015

As I am writing "My Story" things are steadily occuring within my life and around me so I am keeping a personal documentation of all of these things taking placc because again this is my life "My Story" and I'm giving you all of me and these are the things and situations that are most important to me. I want you to have an insight on my life and some of the things that are going on in the K. I want ya'll to visualize this dark cloud that is trying so hard to take over but I also want you to see just how God works. Today I feel like I have almost lost my bestfriend due to some petty bs and I've been friends with this female for a very very long time. When I love, I love hard but this time I really feel like this girl has crossed the line and we rarly ever have any confilct at all with one another so I really need to analyze the situation which ANALYZING is something that I'm GREAT at LIKE YOUR REALITY TV WE DO THIS FOR REAL IN THE K. Let me tell you what happened which was the straw that broke the Camels back. Candy (my bestfriend) and I started working at a new job together this week for a Janitorial Company. I already have 2 jobs so I only considered this job to help Candy because I agreed to take her back and forth to work. Well Candy and I were working for this married couple helping them clean these buildings. Being that I already had two jobs I decided to go ahead and stick it out although it turned out to be a huge pill to swallow. However anything is possible when you involve God in it first. I had been very exhausted so I wasen't very talkitive, I just wanted to do my job and get it done right so that I could go home and get a few hours of sleep before work so I wasen't very happy or enthused about my situation. I still remained Kosher and i didn't talk behind Candy's back or try to make her uncomfortable although I knew that this job would only be temporary for me until Candy could find other means of transportation. I was only doing this job to help my best friend gain some sort of employment, I HATED THE JOB PERSONALLY. To make a long story short. Candy went and told the owners of the job Allen and his wife Tee that I was talking to her about quitting the job without giving them any notice. Candy told Allen to keep that information about me quitting confidential but of coarse Allen called his wife Tee (my manager) with his concern and Tee obviously called me. I assured Tee that if I decided to quit the job that I would indeed inform her first and yes infact I was indeed thinking about quitting in August but I would let them know before hand. Alan was very pleased with my work and he became irritated with Candy's gossip and trouble making so Candy was fired from the job the very next day. July 3rd my mother was hired to fill in Candy's position. Candy had also went and talked about my mom smoking Crack to Alan and that was none of his business what my mother did in her recreation time. Tee told me everything that Candy said behind my back and I believe Tee because Tee didn't know about me or my life only Candy did. The same knife Candy tried to stab me in the back with turned around and stabbed her. Gods plans for me and my life are way more powerful than Satans wicked games. This is why I rock! My black is beautiful. I'm steeing my mark in this world and I'm making a way for my family. I am telling you my struggle which has lead to my strength and for that "MY BLACK IS BEAUTIFUL". Although Candy did me wrong, I'm not going to judge her we are all human and we make mistakes but right is right and wrong is wrong and she's like family I'd rather love her at a distance.

CHAPTER

7

· · · ·

SO HERE WE go again moving to a whole other side of town with Ricky still in the picture. "The child molester". This time we moved to some apartments in the inner city of KCMO. Again, Ricky being the maintenance man we always seemed to have a free place to live other than the times when Ricky and momma would physically fight and we (me, momma, Rico and Poody) would be homeless or end up in a shelter. I hated Ricky!! Ricky was like a snake, looking and seeking to whom he could devour. Ricky preyed on the weak women, who were on heavy drugs with children (little girls particulary). Time and time again momma would have to tell Poody to quit sitting on Ricky's lap. My sister was a hard head little girl, she didn't have much guidance but, Ricky being a grown man (The Adult) shouldn't have allowed my sisiter or any other little girl for the matter to sit on his lap being that he's a full grown man. I know grown men to this day don't let any little girl, not even thier own daughters sit on thier laps. I've realized that some people in this world have hidden agenda's, incidious agenda's and it's sad that some parents allow these type of sick people in their homes around their children without considering the harm that they are possibly putting their children in and I don't know about you, but to me, personally. Everybody is a suspect. I have very little trust for people becuase of everything that I've seen through in life. The pedophile usually end up being the closest one to the family because they watch and they prey on whom they believe to be weak. Currently I have any biological daughter I have all boys and I still don't trust anyone male or female. I am scared that I would murder a pedophile for taking my childs innocence and I Pray to God everyday to help my heart because as of now my feelings are like concrete. I have a cold heart when it comes to pedaphile because of the things that I have experienced and from my experience I realize that a child molester has a real sickness in the mind and instead of those type of people being locked down in mental institutions for very long periods of time, the system gives them a slap on the wrist sending them back into society to Prey on the innocent, our children "The weak". So, us as parents have to strenghten our children. We have to stand up and fight for what is right and what we believe in, as a people who have to protect our children and other children of the world because the children are our future and we as guardians have to protect these children fron harms way because the devil is always at work. I've been through Therapy a couple of times and trust me no amount of therapy can heal, remove, or cover up the deep scars and wounds that I have embeded in me from my past. Finding yourself all over again is a whole other process after being tramatised (your innocense being taken) a the healing process is a day to day process. I struggle day to day fighting those demons that once attacked me. So I pleed with you mothers, fathers, grandparents, aunts, uncles, cousins and friends PLEASE watch over our children of the world. Not only are the children our future, they are our present (our now) and when they hurt it can also hurt our future. Don't trust people because they are your family, trust no one but God because he's the only one without sin, who's not going to leave you or forsake you and everyone born on this earth was born in sin," Everybody is a suspect". Be aware. be cautious and mosrt definitly be prayed up. It takes a lifetime to get to know ones character because people change like the season. Repent of your sins because that is the best thing that you as a human being can ever do and be sincere. Anyhow, back to "My Story".

So, we moved into this apartment in the inner City of KCMO and once again but this time worse MOMMA WAS NEVER AT HOME. Weeks would go by and I would not see my momma's face or even hear my momma's voice. Alot of times I would just pray to God that my mother was safe because I didn't know if she was dead or alive for leaving us for so long. Stress for me instantly became a natural state of being. I had a couple of music Videos that were recorded on our VCR Tapes that help me make it threw those hard time. Music is "Food For The Soul". My favorite VCR Tape to watch was Tupac "Brenda's Got A Baby". That video by Tupac somehow touched me to my soul and also had a very huge impact on me because I made a vowel to myself to not be another "Brenda" and I would fight with all my might to not let Filthy Ricky take my only thing keeping me MY INNOCENSE. My favorite movie at this time was "Juice" and those were my favorite VCR movies that I would watch to get me by my hard days and Rico always watched along with me and Poody. I had to watch those type of videos to keep from being bad and watching the Porn VCR tapes that were obviously left thier for us to watch if we got bored. I was 10 years old, we times got to boing the Porn movies got watched but they seemed very disturbing so I couldn't watch then very long and Rico would try to gross me out and remind me that they were there. Rico became very interested in Rap and making beats so Rico would make Raps and Beats to keep himself entertained. Us children didn't have any guidence that was until I meet a Lady who lived in the same apartment complex that we were in. That woman's name was Darla. Darla was a very kind hearted woman, a woman of God. Darla was "Heaven Sent". As a human we can pick up good vibes and bad vibes. Darla was definitly a Godly woman. Darla would gather lots of the neighborhood children and have Bible Study. Darla would also feed us food directly out of her kitchen and she would sometimes let us spend the night over her house as long as we went home and showered first. Darla taught me the very most important thing in life and that very special the is "The Lords Prayer". "Our Father, whom Art In Heaven, Hallow By Thy Name, Thy Kingdom Come, Thine Will Be Done, On Earth, As It Is In Heaven. Give Us This Day Our Daily Bread And Forgive Us Our Trespass, As We Forgive Those Who Trepass Againt Us And Lead Us Not Into Temptation But Deliver Us From Evil, For Thine Is The Kingdom The Power And The Glory Amen." The only reason I didn't tell Darla right then about Filthy Ricky was because I knew that if I told, I would go to a Foster Home and be seperated from my siblings. I knew SRS would no just like everyone knew that my mother was on drugs. I had comfort in knowing that Darla was there Praying for me and with me just like Grandma would do. I would rush to that house and take a quick shower before perverted Ricky came home and rush to spend time at Darla's house because I couldn't wait to get away from that "Hell House" that I tried so hard not to call home. Darla's home was like a "Safe Haven" for me and I would take Poody over there with me sometimes. Being that momma was gone away from home for weeks at a time when she came home I knew that her and Ricky were going to fight. Ricky would be lowkey mad that momma stayed gone away for so long so he always wanted to argue and fight with her when she came home strung out. I remember one night in particular because it was honestly my breaking point. Momma came home and sure enough her and Ricky started physically fighting. I shouted to the top of my lungs, jumped up and ran storming out of the house hiding up under the stairs. I heard everyone stop arguing and they began to run out of the apartment looking for me when I heard momma quoting "Messin up my hair". Momma was strung out and she just kept saying that Ricky was "Messin up her hair". When I could no longer hear momma or Ricky, I ran back into the house, into the bedroom and I plugged up the iron. I told myself at that point that if Ricky hit my momma again or did anything wrong, I was going to hit him as hard as I could with that hot iron across the head. I WAS HEATED and looked to me like momma's hair was already messed up from the time that she walked in the door!! No matter how mad I was at momma, I wanted to fuck Ricky up if he thought that I would just stand by why he fought my momma. We had some neighborhood friends that we became really close to, the boy was Rico's age and he had two little twin sisters, we called them Stinky, Buffy and Woody. Buffy and Woody were the twin sisters and they were adorable, one of the had some minor health problems but they were just so cute. Stinky became Rico's bestfriend. Being that Stinky was around Rico alot we devoloped a kid crush on one another and became boyfriend and girlfriend. Stinky turned out to be my real first kiss. Rico continued to make his beats and raps and his was getting really good. Rico has a very good unrecognized talent to this day if I were a Producer with a NICE record lable I would sign Rico but these days all Rico does is work work and more work to provide for his family. Rico was not the type of kid that liked fighting unless you made him really mad and Rico was starting to get into some things dealing with the project neighborhood kids around and being unsupervised. Back then it was either fight or get beat up by momma. One day Rico was outside and he had an altercation with another child and the little boys mother tried to hit Rico so Rico told momma and a huge neighborhood fight almost broke out because set aside momma's drug habits momma was a beast when it came to her children and momma wasen't always Missing In Action. I remember another incident when Rico beat two boys up at once, I watched and hid at the same time. I was scared but I watched as Rico beat both the brothers up at the same time. Rico hit one he fell, then the other one ran up and got knocked out to. Although I was scared and hid, I wouldn't dare leave my brother, I was plotting on a brick or something if he needed me, Rico stood on his ten toes though, "like he was taught. STAND YOUR GROUND". Momma taught us one very important thing and that thing was survival. I remeber momma got me a new bike. I wanted to ride everyone on my bike. Momma told me not to ride my heavyset friend on my bike but I didn't listen to momma, I tried to ride that heavy girl on my handle bars when the accident happened and I ended up with a chipped tooth. I also had another incident that I am also scarred with to this very day. I was outside climbing the tree when I asked a friend to hold the branch of the tree for me so that I could climb higher. She let the tree branch go and I fell out of the tree and scarred my arm for life. It seemed like when I hurt myself I really hurt myself. I was told that "A hard head, makes a soft behind", that's what the old folks told me. I was most definitly hard headed. Rico and I started having more serious fights with each other. I would always scratch Rico up when we were smaller but now the fights between us were becoming much more physical. One day Rico and I were fighting so hard that I busted Rico's nose. Momma was furious with me that day and she gave both Rico and I a beating and of coarse I had to get my whooping first. I cried until Rico got his whooping, that's when it all became funny to me and the whooping didn't hurt as bad as it seemed. When Rico and I would fight we would always try to involve Poody in our conflict and try to get her to chose sides and not talk to the other one. It seemed like I had to always fight for Poody because she was the youngest and I wasn't going to let anyone hurt my little sister "I prayed for this sister so I felt obligated to protect her. One day it was this little girl around my age trying to fight Poody like I was going to let that happen. I blacked out. I was in an whole other part of the apartments when a group of children came running to find me and tell me that a girl was fighting Poody. I went running and when I came into contact with that big girl and Poody I blacked out and choked that girl so hard that she was choking as I talked to her while choking her telling her "You better not ever touch my little sister or I will kill you! Do you hear me!" She couldn't answer because I was literally choking the life out of her when I came back from my black-out surrounded with about 15 other children watching, laughing and yelling for the fight. There were some other music that kept Rico and I occupied like "Vanilla Ice" or "My Hoopty", or "I need Love LL" or "Getto Boys" or "NWA" or "Bus Stop" and "Jodice" Kris Kross.

CHAPTER

8

· · · ·

WHEN IT RAINS IT POURS

IN SCHOOL MOST of the time I would wonder if my teacher even cared enough to realize my situation because it was very obvious that thier was something going on at home with me. I understand that it is hard to pay attention to one child in particular but in cases things can also be noticable to the eye. Some teahers also show favoritism but I'm not sure if this was at all this was indeed the case. I was always interested in certain activities such as: music (chior) and dance at this point also Teather Ball. I actually for the first time in my little life was able to play an Instrument. I didn't get the instrument that I wanted. I played the Clairnet when I actually wanted to play the Violyn. Although, I did not want to play the Clairnet I decided that I was going to learn how to play some type of instrument so I put my all into it. My lungs weren't really good with me having Asthma but I remained determined because that intrument felt like a peice of mind and "Melody". My first song that I learned how to play was "Hot Cross Buns". There was something about that year that was soon about to change. At times I felt so bad and like everything in my life was going bad other than my siblings and all I knew was that I had to protect my family "By Any Mean Necessary". I had a family that needed me and I was going to strive for my family and try my hardest to protect them. I couldn't go to school and tell my teacher what was going on at home, I had to push forward try my best in the morning to comb my hair and Poody's hair and get us dressed because momma was not there half the time to do it. I had to Pray first and sit back and wait for a change to come trusting in The Lord. I would get bullied and talked about very bad by some of the other children not to mention this curl that I really didn't like in my hair. I felt like I was the "Ugly Duckling" do you remember Duck Duck Goose. I had not ever in my life felt so bad before and honestly the kids were very mean. I would sometimes cry because it was so bad. Momma had taken me to get this curl that I surely didn't like and that day at the "Beauty Shop" momma thought she had lost me because I had went over her friends house after the Beauty Shop and she didn't know where I was. It was too much! One day at school briefly, I was being normal. I thought that this other boy in class was cute but I didn't ask like I thought he was cute because I knew my situation and the other kids were already being mean to me. The kids were laughing and talking about me, when the cute boy particapted in the laughter and conversation about me. They laughed, pointed and other things as I started to cry one of the "Pretty Girls" got mad and she actually stood up for me. She said out loud to the other children "Don't talk about her (me) and that's not funny!" The pretty girl also began to cry so I knew that her heart was ginuine and she was actually hurt by the other children picking on me and that girl changed my out look on alot of things from that very day forward and that was to most definetly "Stand Up For Myself First and Farmost". I will not every forget that Beautiful Person as she touched my soul to this very day. I didn't think that people could feel another persons pain until this very day. "There was soon to be a Flood that was going to change my life forever". I didn't see it coming. That was also the moment that made me realize that "although what you may be going threw may seem like your going to die and it's the end of the world, thier is always someone out there who is fighting battles and going threw worse." That Beautful girl who stood up for me that day is a brave girl for many reasons. I went to school stronger every day after that day but, a couple days after the incident where that girl stood up for me had a situation. I went to school as if it was going to be a normal day when I got to class they quickly called the Pretty (Beautiful) girl to the office. 10 minutes later our classromm was getting swarmed with SRS and Police looking people. I knew that the "Pretty Girl" was a bit bigger than me and she was taller than me looked more older than I did or at least more mature. Turned out that my classmate was Pregnat. Pregnat by her Step-Father!!!!! We are only in the fifth grade, I haven't even had a menstrual, Our teacher is looking very hurt now. All this time I've been watching "Brenda's Got A Baby" so many thoughts flooded my head after the disturbing news. It was alot to take in, here I am crying about being bullied and I'm standing up and fighting Filthy Ricky when my "Soldier my Beautiful Classmate" was going threw a battle even more vicious than mine. Here it is I'm crying over kids calling my momma a Crack Head and teasing me because of the situation, fuck NAW I'm fighting back and even harder!! My classmate who stood up for me to my Bullies and here it is she's pregnat by her Step-Father her own momma's husband, I'm fighting to save my verginity from filthy Ricky, it was to much to endure. I have wondered about this Beautiful Person ever since so that I can tell her thanks and Pray for her acknowledging her for her very presence. We were at a school called D.A Holmes at that time and we made up a dance routine in the class and danced in a group together outside for a huge program. Just when I thought I had enough and couldn't take anymore here it was my own classmate. Sometime I wish that I could fight for her like she fought for me with my bullies. It is so sad how a mother (a parent) a person could let something like this happen to an innocent child. How are you moms not aware of what's going on in your household? Crack? Meth? No drug should be that important. Your home is not big enough to be unawre of what's going on in the next room with your innocent children that you chose to bring into the world. Aren't you here to serve and protect as a parent? It's these monsters inside the home that we as people need to be aware of instead of the unknown so much. I am going to expose you MONSTERS, it's bad enough of Demons and evil spirits but the ones whom need to be more focused on is the living one whom roam the four walls in the homes of the innocent. The human monsters are far more dangersous than unliving ones because they also lurk at night seeking to hurt, kill, steal, and destroy and those are the ones you trust (your not trusting any spirits). Protect these children because these are the ones who can't protect themselves. I have always been one to say that "Seeing Is Believing". Teachers I do understand that it's not your job to look into peoples homes but it is your job as mandiated reporters. So, are you teachers really doing everything you can do, like going an extra mile instead of also being some of the predators? A real teacher builds relationship with thier students wanting them to succeed a Monster Teacher sits back lurks and Preys lusting over ones child instead of teaching. Let's all please truely make a difference.

When It Rains It Pours But Prepare For The Flood

I dont want to paint my momma out to be a bad person because my mother is a Scorned Woman and she's a Warrior. My mom is a strong Black Woman whom was born into sin just like the rest of us who has a dark past but also believes in the Glory and Power of The Lord. My mom has been hurt because she lost a wonderful mother at a very early age. My mother is the only girl in a family of 5 so my momma was raised rough around boys all her life and that just how my momma is. My momma is definitly like one of my best friends and in hard times my momma always has my back good or bad, (that's my momma). I love my mom and she's my number 1 chicka. The bible say's to Honor thy mother and father. God is whom I fear, I fear no man. My momma is the not different from some of ya'll mommas.

CHAPTER

9

....

EVERYDAY WASN'T ALWAYS as bad as others. I prayed to God every-day that this pedophile would just stay far far away from me. I would have company sometimes. I had a friend who would come over and spend the night with me. Although, her mother never met my mother, I wondered if she had things going on in her home or something because "Why can she spend the night over and not have to do the Parent Check Thing." Most parents want to meet one another before they send a child with someone they don't know. Me, I'm going to protect mine I want to know and meet before I just let my kids go spend the night in unknown places. Anyhow, I had a friend and she spent the night with me from time to time and everytime she spent the night 'Ricky would want to sleep in the bed with us. I would make sure that she slept on the side with Ricky because I knew what he wanted to do with her. Me and my friend never actully talked about what happended with her and Ricky but I always wondered what happened. All I know is that I would fall asleep and Ricky would be on the side of her touching her in inappropriate places and we would wake up the next morning and drop her off at home like nothing ever happened. All I knew was that I had to protect myself. It felt horrible having Ricky preying over us. Ricky would try to pretend that everything was okay the next day. He would take us out to eat at places like "Shoney's, Texas Toms and stuff like that, Ricky was a 'Trick and I wasn't going for any of his nasty tricky ways. He took us to Mississippi, and places like that. Christmas was good sometimes. I remember one Christmas we had bags and big bags of gifts. But for me, I wasn't buying none of Ricky's mess. I saw old Ricky for who he was and still is to this very day, A PEDOPHILE. One day momma had been gone all day and there was this lady who lived up the hall in the apartments we lived in. The lady her name was Tiffany. Tiffany was a white woman I liked her she seemed nice to me. I guess somehow being that momma wasn't at home Tiffany seemed to be keeping the maintance man "Ricky" company. Well momma must have got a drift somehow about it I think it was Rico. Rico had his way of letting momma know when another woman was in the presence of (Filthy Ricky). So one day momma came home from somewhere out the blue and us kids Sparkle, Rico, and I was in the house along with Tiffany and Ricky and just so happened that Ms. Tiffany and Ricky were in some kind of compromised position and "bam" momma hit Tiffany in the eye and Tiffany went running down the hallway. Rico and I laughed so hard as Ms. Tiffany went running. But the whole time within me I was hoping that momma could just beat the heck out of Filthy Ricky. A couple days later me, Ricky, Rico, Poody and momma were at the store when look who walks out. Tiffany and she's wearing black shades with a fat black eye. After that day I didn't see much of Tiffany and I don't think that she saw much of me.

WHEN IT RAINS IT POURS

I HAD NOT even began to reach full puberty when my body and my life began to start going threw all of these different types of changes. If it was not one thing—it was another. I'm no where near adulthood but by nature I was being forced to be an adult and learn adult responsibilities. I didn't know how to take care of my siblings, I was a child just like them, me and Rico were only 11 mths apart and I sometimes felt like his mother figure. I had to learn how to cook, clean, comb hair, hand wash clothing, and wash my own ass. On top of all of these things I had to learn how to protect myself from a Sexual Predator who lerked and waited for my weakest time so that he could attack. Rico, Poody and I were tired of being left home alone all the time so one night we realized that Ricky was about to leave us home alone so, we snuck in the Van and hid waiting on Ricky to leave the house. The Van that Ricky owned was huge. So big that it had a bed in the back of it so Ricky didn't even notice that we were hidden in the far backseats on the floor behind the seats. We were all 'as quiet as a mouse' as Ricky drove the dark streets of Missouri, preying on valunerable women.

As he drove slowly slowing down at times, scoping women, he approached one woman that was walking. We listened quietly as we clearly heard Ricky speak to the woman saying, "Hey what's up? Do you need a ride?" The walking womans response was to Ricky was clearly, "Hi do you you have some crack?" As she stopped in front of Rickys driver side window. Ricky said," No. I don't have any crack but I do got some money. But, first I want some of that pussy". At that very point Rico and I couldn't keep quiet and we busted out laughing HA HA HA HA HA HA. We scared Ricky so bad that he pulled off quickly from the walking lady scared of someone being in the Van without him recognizing he quickly took us home. Filthy Ricky knew that we were on to him and all his nasty, filthy ways. Rico had a soft heart when it came to Ricky because Ricky always did things for and with Rico so Rico did not see Rickys nasty filthy ways so I had to expose Ricky for who he really was. I had my own personal ways of showing Rico and this was one way that began to work. However, momma still was not hardly ever at home and things were getting worse and worse. Me, Rico and Poody were all outside playing as usual with the neighborhood children when I heard an ambulance quickly approaching our apartment complexes. I couldn't always watch Rico and Poody close because I was also a child and I would sometimes get side-tracked myself. I remember a group of children run to me yelling, "Come on! Come on! That girl busted Poody's head!" I didn't think twice as I got up and ran following the children and the sound of the ambulance. All I remember is thoughts that I didn't know if I was speaking out loud (I'm going to kill whoever did this to my sister!!) What happened, who did it? I remember approaching the ambulance asking questions as they asked me questions like where is our mother? The ambulance wouldn't let me into the ambulance because I was to young so I had to sit back, wait and figure it out. I didn't know who butsed my sisters head but I most definitly wasn't going to let it slide without retaliating on whoever, whenever. I was lost and didn't know what to do all I hoped and prayed was that the SRS didn't get involved and momma would soon show up. Momma showed up as usual and rode on the ambulance with Poody as we allowed them to the hospital.

WHEN IT RAINS IT POURS
BUT WHAT ABOUT WHEN IT FLOODS

One major purpose of me writing this book is to help save someone. How can I save one's life if I can't even save myself first? Last night I watched a show on a Profit called Norsradamus and he predicted alot of major disasters happening in this world and we have some major disasters that he predicted to happen in 2018–2019. People you really need to wake up! It's 2-20-2017 and for the last few years I have had a occuring dream like God is trying to warn me of something that is going to happen in this world. I don't know why but, I have had several dreams that have came true. I know that I have a special gift, I'm just unsure of how to use this gift of mine. Narstradamus was a man with the same girl as me but he had other gifts along with the gift of predicting major disasters. God gives certain chosen people these special gifts. I'm just the messenger. I keep having dreams that I have an underground hiding for my family because we are under attack. Other people have already started building thier hiding underground because they also have the same gift as I do. War is not for away neither is the end of the world and either your going to prepare for the battle or your going to sit back and forfeit the win (give up and lose without fighting). I will use my very last breath to save someone especially a child from waisting precious years traveling the same road that I have traveled. I am fully aware that I'm not perfect and not one of us is but, God created each and everyone of us in his own image making no mistakes. I believe in God (The Creator) he giveth and he taketh. Thier is a song that I really like because she sends a particular message to the young children the song is by Lauren Hill called "Doo Wop That Thing". Look at the lyrics to that song because it has a powerful meaning. Now I would like to talk a little bit about "That Thing". Do you realize how "That Thing" can tarnish your life for good and your very existance and all it takes is ONE single time. See we all have some type of agenda on a daily basis, some of us have a more Incidious Agenda. Truth is that thier are good people in the world and thier are bad people. Now, this is how deep "That Thing" can get sad but true yes it only takes one time of sex protected or unprotected that if that other person is infected can give you an infection and (STD) that can and will change your life forever. STD's are real and some of them are more harmful than others, so harmful that it can touch your very soul. Your body is definitly "Your Temple" it is were your soul and spirit reside. Once you mess up your Temple you condemn (destroy self) because you only have one Temple you will be scarred for life. "That Thing" can destroy you physically, mentally, emotionally and spiritually. I'm going to tell you a story that happened a couple of months ago and then I'M going to tell you a story later on about how I almost had my temple destroyed because of "That Thing". My story gets very deep at times but again I'm working for the Lord to save his souls, so I will take my very last breath and use it to save a soul. I have traveled a dark road and I want you to make the right decision and not take that horrible road that I was once on. Call on Jesus and he will always lead you to the narrow road and take you off that dark path. Remember "All things that glitter ain't Gold". Sometimes thier is death at the end of that dark path but if you believe in the Power of Jesus you can and will be saved. The devil is here to Kill, Steal and Destroy and he seeks whom he can devour. The devil has no love for you but he loves to see you hurting. I "Tell The Truth Shame The Devil" because I love to see the Lord Triumph over the enemy. A few mths ago I was chillen with a few friends when this one guy came walking past. The guy walking past use to always try to have sex with me but I always went the other way for some reason. This day everyone was smoking getting "Lit" when one of my home girls was trying to smoke with the guy walking past. I declined and didn't want to be involved because this guy had gotten weired over the years smoking PCP and I knew that something was wrong with him and I heard roumors of him having herpes (he had the nerve to try to have sex with me and this rumor about him I TAKE HEED). Anyhow, they were all smoking getting (Lit) when the guy started chanting, "Kill Em All" then he started scratching his balls like he was trying to dig something really bad off of him and he didn't care who was watching. That very situation right there was confirmation for me that just maybe (some rumors could be true)I had my momma with me and she started getting nervous because the dude then began to hide behind the trees aiming his hands like he had a rifle and was trying to kill something. It takes alot to scare my moms but this day she was nervous and ready to go.

I no a female who use to come around and talk to me and one day she told me her story. The woman seemed to be lesbain due to her appearance but she had a story that let me know why she was like she was. This story came from the horses mouth (the woman). she told me that the very first time she laid down with a man and had sex, she got up with Genitile Warts. I could not believe my ears because it's a sad situation but IT'S THE SAD TRUTH. "That Thing" can get very messy really quick. Seeing is believing. Kids these days see sex as a necessity when it is not and it's always best to wait you save the best for last. Education should be a childs number one priority in life. Look at some of these new cartoon, the cartoons promote sex and violence which is not appropriate for our children so us as parents have to be aware of the cartoons our children watch. Us as parents have to make sure that we install the right things into our children. We have to set an example and lead the right paths for our children because "That Thing" can make them feel like thier dying inside every single day for the rest of thier dear percious lives. The truth is that "That thing" can wait and if it can be respectful and wait on you then "That thing" is just not for you because "that Thing is only looking for "One Thing. Now, I don't want to make it seem like all things are bad. There is a simple key to every door. instead of searching for "That Thing" find yourself first and let "The Right Thing" find you. For every good woman, thier lies a good man. In the Bible it says that woman was created from a mans rib. God made Adam first then he made Eve. Now think about it, God made us from the Rib, which happens to be located at the side of our bodies. Ladies we are suppose to walk beside our husbands not in the front or the back of him. We are supposed to walk on beside him with love, honor and respect. How much respect do we honestly have for ourselves if we live our lives day to day chasing after "That Thing". We as a people need to first establish whom we are within meaning: educating ourselves, God First, family, home, goals, self preservation, and learning what it means first to deal with our own iniquities. there are many things that we can continue to learn as woman and young women of today. We need to honestly learn how to love ourselves first and learn what God has set forth for our lives. In the 1800's women had to learn how to sew, use the washboards, garden, clean and women of color had to Pick cotton. Thier were outhouses instead of toilet stools. Sometimes I write "My Story" while I'm at work and my client brings "Joy" to me. My client does lots and lots of reading and she is the one who told me about the 1800's and how thier were no sanitary napking us women had to use towels and rags and had to wash the blood out of the towels by hand. She also told me about the Castles and how the bowel movements would run down the walls (GROSS). When I speak, I speak from experience and that's just who I am. I really want the women of today to open up thier eyes to life in general and realize that thiers a reason for every season. Everythiing happens for a reason. I need 100 strong women and men to work with me on building an underground tunnel for our families to perpare for a time of famine, a time of disease, a time of destruction. Repent of your sins everyday. We as a people have to do better. I was always told that "If you knew better You'd do better". I'm giving you some knowledge and it's coming from true life experience.

WHEN IT RAINS IT POURS

As I write "My Story" I realize that I am under attack. Were living in a Spriritual Warefare good vs evil and I am fighting with the Angels against evil. "My Story is going to change someone's life. Some people say that, "You Need to Leave The Past Behind You" again those are the ones that wish the dirty truth would just stay swept under that dirty rug. I have a question. How do you purify dirty water? Me writing "My Story" is a healing process for me. I ask God to lead me. "My Story" is a step in my path of deliverance. So many things have been taken away from me and my life, so many people have been removed from my life but again, "everything happens for a reason". God knows his purpose for me. Again, I am under attack. I have allowed things to resurface in my head, heart and life that I've tried so long to hide and keep under that rug. This goes back to my question. How do you purify dirty water? I ask because I am unsure and no question in life is ever a bad question. I do know that I have been threw "The Shaking, The Beating and the Pressing-: Jacquline Carr". I do my research because seeing is believing. I believe that the process of purifying water have certain methods. #1-Flocculation, #2-Sedimentation, #3-Geration, #4-Ion-exchange, #5-Reverse Osmosis. Did you know that Water is abundant in many locations but can contain impurities, disease and even parasites. I want to clean my spirit and soul and in order to do this cleaning I have to take 5-steps just like the 5-processes of cleaning water. "My Story" is one of my processes that I'm taking. Now I know that some of you are wondering, (What does Purifying water have to do with purifying your spirit and soul?) I only speak from experience and to be fully able to save someone else, I must first save myself and remember I am under attack Spiritually and mentally. I'm not writing this for only myself, I am writing to save souls. Now back to those 5 steps of purifying water and the first step being #1 Flocculation meaning:—To form into Flocculent masses; as a cloud or a chemical precipitate; form aggregatedor compound masses of particles. So, flocculation are rich nutrients and are usually spread on agricultural land. #2 Sedimentation:—and increase in the amount of hydrogen; a decrease in the amount of organic matter. #3 geration (I couldn't find the definition so I'm clueless or Geration). #4 Ion Exchange:—are the units that replace calcium and magnesium ions from wateror also known as water softeners. #5 Reverse Osmosis:—the process in which pure water is produced by forcing waste or saline water through a semipermable membrane. My life, my mind, my body, my spirit and my soul are the 5 things that have been contaminated by sins and the wicked ways of the world that just like water NOW has to be purified and cleaned. I have to find 5 ways to purily MYSELF within. Now, if we take a look back into the bible when God made Adam and Eve look back at the life span of those people back in those days. Some people lived to be 800 years old and more. These days you are lucky if you make it to see 18 years of age. It's called change. The times, people and the seasons have all changed. We as people can take 5 steps in our lives to purify ourselves just like the process of cleaning water. I am going to list 5 steps that I have came up by myself for me that will indeed help me to purify me life. Now, I am definitly no Scientist this is only what I believe that the Lord is speaking into me. # Following the 10 commandments; just like flocculation it is rich in nutrients and not hard because God spreads his word all over the world and it is for us to live a healthy life. #2 Eating and living healthy lives;—Like Sedimentation. #3 Repent of your sins ; like Geration only pray without cease. #4 Love everyone; like Ion exchange except soften your heart, humble yourself and do not be quick to anger. Be the puppet master not the puppet. #5 Change your ways of thinking;—like Reverse Osmosis you have to reverse you way of thinking (out with the bad, in with the new). You are always going to have some type of bad thoughts but be aware of the bad and replace the bad with good. Rebuke the Devil and don't give the devil any victory GIVE GOD ALL OF THE GLORY. Rebuke the devils wicked plans that he has for your life and believe in a higher power.

Once you realize the power in prayer and the power that God has over everything on this earth, Satan will lose his power over you. Rise up people and Serve The Lord Almighty. "No Weapon Formed Against Me Shall Prosper". If you truely believe in Gods word (Read The Bible) you have nothing to fear except God himself. Fear The Wrath Of The Lord! When it rains, it pours but, be prepared for the flood. For the Wrath of God is the only thing that One should fear especially when your not completely right within (purified). Fear the Lord Jehova and purify yourself, cleanse yourself from all dirt and unpurities. Cleanse yourself from your iniquities for the Wrath of the Lord has yet to come and Norstradamus perdicted alot of things and in his (Norstradamus) story they describe it in detail so people please get into knowing life's history and what is really going on in this evil world.

"One Two Freddy's Comin For You"-Film Freddy Kruger

Remember that chant when you were a child? Only me, I would hear stories, disturbing stories such as this one. A group of us in a group discussion, "One night as I got ready for bed as I would normally get ready for bed waiting on my husband to come home later during the night. I had my night lamp on, the room door was closed and I began reading my Essence Magazine when I heard some footsteps. I looked at the clock and it was not yet quite time for Dave (the huband of the lady talking) to get home from work so I assumed that he just made it home early on this particular night. I had a window open so there was a slight breeze that came in and the room got cold. I continued to read my book waiting on Dave to enter our room when all of a sudden the footsteps stopped. I continued to read for another minute or two when I began to wonder if Dave was trying to play some sort of prank on me when the breeze came in again this time colder and harder and the footsteps started up again. This time as I began to yell for Dave, the bedroom door slowly opened and I looked down to continue reading when the footsteps completely stopped and the room turned freezing cold. When I looked up there was a HUGE dark shadow standing right at the foot of my bed and when I began to scream, the dark shadow grabbed my squeezing my throat and that's when I began to pray and Rebuke the Devil". These were the kind of stories that I had to listen to and indure not to mention my Aunt Fee on the Gooding side being possessed. Aunt Fee was evil and for some reason I don't think the she liked Poody because one day we caught a Cab over to Aunt Fee house and during the Cab ride Poody had to boo-boo really bad so she had an accident and used the restroom on herself. Poody was only 3 years old at this time and as soon as we walked into Aunt Free's home she greeted us saying "Look at ol ugly ass Poody". I would get teased at night by my older cousins at the Goodings, they would say things like "ha ha you have to sleep on the floor anow your going to get attacked by the mice and they are going to swing off your ponytails. My cousin Tonya wouldn't tease me though she was one of the good Goodings, Tonya had a good soul. I felt bad for Tonya because she had to live in that house with all of those demons. Little Free had a baby so she was always attending to her baby because I rarely seen her. Some people like to characterize demonic possession as being Scitsofranic but I know better than that. The devil targets Pastors families and my Uncle Ulysis is a Pastor who's family was indeed targeted by some of the most evil inscidous spirits that I had ever experienced.

WHEN IT RAINS IT POURS
BUT PREPARE FOR THE FLOOD

As I write this book "My Story" it seems like the further into the book I get the more harsher things become and I am faced with a harsh reality of my past and it HURTS so bad. I ask God to forgive me for my own iniquities. I have a very dark past and still I "Tell The Truth, Shame The Devil". Just when I have found the light in my life, here I go right back down this dark past of mine unleashing and reopening those wounds that have once already started a healing process. Some days I can even smell the smell of rotten flesh as I write when I'm home alone. I rebuke Satan. I have lost many of my loved ones and not due to death but due to Truth. I thought that the truth will set you free? I feel like a prisoner in my own mind. I'm praying that when I complete "My Story" I will be finally set free. Free from a horrible past that I have hidden within me for so long. I will be greatful, greatful to know that I have inspired someone else's life. Greatful to know that I have stopped someone from going down a dark path, greatful to know that I have stopped the enemy right in his tracks. Greatful, that I have stopped a Sick Pedophile right in his tracks before he offended an innocent child. Greatful that the Lord blessed me with another day at life to be able to tell "My Story". Greatful knowing that every single one of us was created for a special purpose in this world. I want people to know that you can do whatever you want in life if you put God first and put your mind into accomplishing your goals and dreams. Don't ever let men or women discourage you because I have been told many of times that I would not be good enough to do something that my heart truely desired. Prove people wrong by your actions and show kindness. Always love yourself knowing that everyone goes threw something and not everyone can keep it 100 with themselves. What dosen't kill you only makes you stronger and always remember that. Strive for the best. Know that God has a purpose for your life. Again, I am going to lose many of my loved ones because I am speaking out about things that happened in my life but in reality, if they really loved me then they be happy that I'm purifying myself for me first off. They would appologize to me for hurting me and making me feel the way that I feel. I am woman enough to apologize to anyone that I have ever hurt or harmed right here in front of the world. The ones who hurt me badly have not apologized and they talked badly about me as if I hurt them. Family always are the ones who hurt you the worse in life and they say that they love you? What is love if it has to hurt? No pain no gain? Just because you have the same blood as someone it dosen't make you have a Real, genuine love for a person. Look at the bible Story "Cain and

Able". This is my healing process and I pray that I'm guided by the Lord because I love my family no matter what I went threw and for my family I will go an extra mile. My birthday just passed recently and I'm getting older and wiser. No more parting all the time, i'm changing as a woman. Guess who I met on my birthday. The one and the only Jerry Springer!. I took pictures because so many times before technology wasn't like it is now and pictures were easy to loose like my picture that I took ith Russel Simmons (lost memories). I have met lots of famous people in my lifetime and now it is time for me this "Diamond In The Ruff" to shine like the diamond that I am. I am a Leo, a Queen and my essence as a woman stands for so many things. My very exsistance means more than a billion bucks because I have a purpose in life. I was blessed by the Lord to have many talents and I vow to use those talents to the best of my advantage. I speak only from my experience. Where I have been broken, the Lord has molded me. When at times I was blind, the Lord opened up my eyes to see. On the rainy days I learned how to walk threw the mud, play with the bugs and endure. Purified water washed me and cleansed me in order to prepare for the flood.

Years ago I reached out to you Steve Wilkos because your Show is so real. I love the fact that you expose people for who they really are threw Lie Detector Test. Being a Pedophile is a sickness and Steve you expose that "Sickness". Unfortunatly "My monster/My Pedophile who hurt me" would not respond to your phone calls when you would try to contact them. So that left me in a situation were again I was unable to speak out to the world to tell "My Story" so that I could have closure. So Steve, this is my way of speaking out and hopefully you can find a way to tell "My Story" without the pedaphile in attendance because they won't show and maybe we can promote "My Story" on your show to help save lives or maybe you will notice me Steve and just help me spread "My Story" to the ones going threw the STRUGGLE and even the ones who are not so that they are AWARE. If we can I'm here for you Steve because I know that you are all about saving lives and Steve Wilkos, I support your Show and may God Bless you. I also have some wonderful ideas that I would love to share with some producers such as a new Lion King Movie. But hey who knows what the future holds, I have doors opening up for me so I may be your new face in the Spot Light, who knows what God has in store for me. The one and only Monique from "The Parkers" the Show is coming back to KCMO to do another Comedy Show. I attended one of Monique's Comedy Shows before and I JUST LOVE HER LIFE. I love Monique because she stays herself and she don't change up wether you like it or not she definitely has #NoFilter and I did not know that Monique also has a story VERY similar to mine so I can FEEL her heart ache and pain REGARDLESS of what any CAST has to say about her I SUPPORT MONIQUE and RELATE to her feelings and HER STRUGGLE IT HURTS WHEN YOUR OWN FAMILY HURTS YOU. My life has been 80% grey which came with all the rain and the flooding. That made me appreciate that 20% sunshine just that much more. It always seems like when you've had to much to bear here goes something else. Just when you thought that your plate was full the waitress comes in with some dessert.

CHAPTER
11
. . . .

WHEN IT RAINS IT POURS

I FEEL LIKE i'm on a "Merry Go Round" pack up and move, pack up and move is all I have ever known. So this time we are moving. I am in the mist of reaching puberty, I am growing up very fast and way to soon and I am just now completing the 5th grade going to the 6th. Momma just told me, Rico and Poody to get our belongings together we were moving to Kansas with our Aunt Chante but until then we would have to stay over Aunt Fee's house a bit more often until the move. I loved my Aunt Chante she has a daughter with my Uncle on my moms side but to Aunt Fee's house we were. My auntie Fee has a daughter named after her Fee and the Gooding side of my family. Days prior to this decision for us to move with lil Fee a few things had taken place or lets just say a cat (pedophile) got let out the bag. Something big just hit the fan so alot of secrets were about to be aired out. A few days prior to us moving with lil Fee were were all over to my Aunt Fee's house as usual with my cousins "The Goodings" When I had an appointment at the Beautician to get my Curl reformed. Back then in the NWA times 'Jerry Curls' were in style. As I was getting ready for my hair appointment, Poody was outside running her mouth to all of our big cousins "The Goodings". All I remembered hearing was someone shouting saying, "HE DID WHAT TO YOU!". I was rushed to the beautician and this was the day that momma lost me and didn't know were I was at she thought that I had been kidnapped. Momma had instructed me to go over to her friends home after my hair was finished but due to all the commotion of what Poody had just let out the bag momma forgot what she had instructed me to do and everything was "A MESS". When my hair was finished I told the beautician to drop me off over my moms friend Sheila's house were Sheila was fixing dinner so she mad sure that I had food to eat until momma came to pick me up. Momma didn't know that I was at Sheila's house so I spent the night there. As the night went by I had wondered what did Poody say at the Goodings house to make everyone so upset. As the rain fell from the sky that night, I felt tears began to roll down my face. Momma forgot all about me and something big was going on. I can remember the song "Thriller by Micheal Jackson" playing on the radio and I hated that song because that song always played when it started to thunder really loud and the song is general was scary to me. The next morning momma came to pick me up and I just remember her hugging me tight telling me that she thought that I had gotten kidnapped. Momma must had forgotten what she had instructed me to do after I had finished at the beauty shop. Maybe it was the drugs that made momma forget about me or maybe it was what Poody had said the day before that made momma forget but anyhow momma seemed to be a wreck. I had to make it to my brother and my sister to figure out what was going on and what was all the commotion before I left. I felt lost and left out by this time and hurt because momma forgot all about me, not to mention I was definitly confused. Me, "momma where are we going?" Momma answered, "you are going back to your Aunt Fee's house and I want you to watch over Poody and Rico until I come back to pick ya'll up". me, "but momma, I want to go with you, I don't want to stay over Auntie Fee's in that demon posessed house".

Momma, "NO! You cannot go with me ignore your Aunt Fee she is sick. Ya'll are going to be alright. I will be back to pick ya'll up later". I was sick of the bullshit was all I could think about in my head and fine I can get to Poody and figure out was said to my cousins, we finally made it to Aunt Fee's home and it was a slight relief because at least I could be a kid at Aunt Fee's and besides I knew that all of the answers to my questions were finally about to be answered. My cousin Fee had two children now and was about to give birth to her third child. Little Fee had her first child at the age of 14 years old. My aunt and Uncle had a huge house on the corner of 5th St, they need that big house because they had 8 children (a huge family). My 4 boy cousins names are Cecil (aunt Fee's rape child), Little Ulysis, Derrick, and Rob. The 4 girls names are Little Fee, Pray, Tonya and Neicy. Out of the girls Tonya was and still is my favorite and out of the boys Derrick was and still is my favorite. Rob had some strange issues, he would stand on the corner with his headphones on and a 40oz of Colt 45 or old English in his hand talking and laughing to himself as he listened to his headphones. I was so embarassed by Rob and I tried to keep my distance from him because I could tell that he was "Sick In The Head" but other than that Rob was cool only because he would let me drink liquor such as "Wild Irish Rose" Little Ulysis would have us children run down to the corner store and moon the store people every sing night that we spent over the Goodings. I loved my big cousins. Growing up in life your cousins are always your best friends first. Poody had confided in the Goodings and told them that Ricky did something to her. She told the Goodings that Ricky made her perform sexual acts! Ricky's nasty ass couldn't get me so his filthy ass went messing with my little sister and made Poody perform sexual acts on his STANKING BLACK ASS. I was furious to hear this because I felt like killing Ricky with my bear hands. I had tried so hard to protect Poody from that slimy son of a bitch Ricky. I didn't tell anyone what was going on because I didn't want to go to SRS custody and end up seperated from my siblings. Ricky couldn't get me so he went after Poody. I SHOULD

HAVE BURNED HIS BLACK ASS WITH THAT IRON when I had the chance!!. I thought for sure that I watched over Poody well when momma was always gone but a slimy mutha fucka will always find a way like a snake to slither in. So my family being mad explains it all. Now we have to move with Auntie Chante' and my uncles might end up killing Ricky. Cousin Fee had her own house after a few more weeks went by and we waited until it was time for us to move with Aunt Chante'. I was sad because momma was not going to move with us. Fee would complain about us moving with Auntie Chante instead for moving with her because she was getting her own home. Fee had small kids and with me being the oldest I knew that I would have an even bigger responsibility and Fee had gave birth to the baby that she was pregnat with. Auntie Chante only had one child which was my Uncle's daughter. All I knew was that I wasn't going to live in that haunted house on 5th St. SRS would have to come and pick me up if anyone thought that I was moving into a home with snakes and demonic forces!. Auntie Chante' was my Uncle O.G's childs mother. We called Uncle O.G, uncle O.G for a well known reason and I knew that I would be safe with my Auntie Chante' and wouldn't have to fight with the seen and the unseen. Uncle O.G had my grandma's first born grandchild named Bre'. Everyone would say that Bre' and I looked alike when we were children but that's only because "Beauty Is Within The Bloodline". Bre' and I were both dark skinned small petite little girls with this big beautiful smile so I can see why people think that we looked alot alike. Me Rico and Poddy went to live with aunt Chante for that summer before school started I remember because my cousin Bre would always get mad at us "Me, Rico, and Poody while we were eating and say "Stop Smacking". I guess to her we were "Smacking Our Food" Well, we hadn't had a good home cooked meal in years it felt like Bre was the only child so she was spoiled and didn't know how it felt to have nothing and she didn't know what we were going thru as kids, but she was kind of mean sometimes to us and it felt like she didn't care. Bre's friends would always say that me and her looked alike and we would just laugh about it. My aunt Chante' put a perm on Poody's hair and Poody's hair fell out when at that point there was a huge issue of how aunt Chante' was raising us. Aunt Chante' actually did good with us. I remember things like random showers, cleaning, good meals and most of all being safe and comfortable. Bre got to do alot of things that I didn't get to do and that was because her other side of the family would take her out and do family things with her like family outings, skating, movies, The Fun Factory and I felt left behind at times, but I realized that was life and my auntie wasn't a bad woman she loved us as her own nieces and nephew. Again though it seemed like people were trying to make aunt Chante' out to be a bad person. All I know is that someone said aunt Chante' over processed Poody's hair so that's when we went to live with cousin Fee. Rico was mad and he didn't want to move because he had a little girlfriend across the street. She was a white girl and I liked her. I remember going across the street to play with her and in her basement (Rico's girlfriend the little white girl) and she had a real big water bed. We had lots of fun over that house across the street. Her parents would let us go over and play in the swimming pool, water balloon fights we would have a ball all until, (Poody's hair got over processed" that's when we went to live with cousin Fee. Rico was bad and mannish, I think he was over humping with the little white girl across the street. So much for that summer. It was the best in years and it felt good to have a mother figure around and not having to watch my back from Filthy Ricky. Such a breath of fresh air I thought…

CHAPTER

12

....

**WHEN IT RAINS IT POURS
BUT BE PREPARED FOR THE FLOOD**

SPEAKING OF AIR, i can't breathe. "Heavy Breathing huh huh weeze". Auntie Chante', "Lady Bug! Are You alright? It looks like your chest is going to cave in and you are looking pale". Me, "No auntie-(heavy breathing) I can't breathe. Aunt Chante "Did you take your asthma medicine"? Me "Yes~(heavy breathing)but, it, didn't, work. Aunt Chante' "Come on Lady Bug, I have to take you to the Emergency Room NOW"!!

As a child I was hospitalized more than alot of children my age. I was born with asthma and allergies. I hated asthma. You never know how it feels not being able to breathe unless you have this terrible lung condition. I couldn't live a normal childhood for the life of me and everytime I thought my asthma was going to get better it just got worst. "Lord Please let me grow out of this". Rico, had Broncitis but he grew out of it. Rico was my backbone he always helped me out when I was sick and I took advantage because it always made me feel better especially when momma wasn't around to care for me.

~ Nurse can I pease go home. I don't want to stay in this hospital. Nurse "Sorry Lady BUG but your oxygen is way too low and the breathing treatments aren't working fast enough so we're going to have to keep you and treat you with some Steroids to see if you get better. "Me, but I do feel better. I just want to go home. "Anutie" It's going to be okay Lady Bug the nurse has to do her job. Your going to be okay. I have to go back home with the rest of the kids but I will be back tomorrow and I'm going to see if I can get intouched with your mother. I love you, get some rest, the nurses are going to take good care of you and I promise I will be back tomorrow."

~ This asthma don't love nobody. Lord please heal me from asthma.

CHAPTER

13

••••

WHEN IT RAINS IT POURS

COUSIN FEE, "LADY bug (justice), Rico and Poody",pack your clothes you all are moving with me. I just got my new house. Aunt Chante' "Your momma said you all have to move with Fee and her husband so get your things together babies and remember aunt Chante' loves ya'll. Cousin Fee 'Come on ya'll, I got my own house and you all are going to be okay. Lady Bug(Justice) your the oldest out of all the kids so I'm going to need you to babysit while me and Bone is at work (Bone was cousin Fee's Husband that I didn't know and didn't want to no after being around Filthy Ricky). I have to go to the SRS building because your mother is giving me custody of ya'll until she gets her stuff together. Aunt Chante' "If you babies need me for anything I'll be here just call me because ya'll could have just continued to live with me but, this is what your mother wanted. Me, "Come on Rico and Poody let's get our stuff. I wondered where was my momma at. She's just going to move us and not going to tell us. Oh well, we're going to be together and that's all that matters. Plus cousin Fee is going to get custody of us and I'm going to get to be the oldest again. Fee had three kids this time the first was a boy and his name was Kevin, but we called him "Scooby", next there was Tiffany, but we called her Tee Tee, and then there was Cash, but we called her Boodah along with her new Husband Bone. I was the oldest child out of all the kids and at this time I was 11 going to be in 6th grade, Rico was 10 in the fifth grade, Poody was 5 and in the kindergarten. Scooby was 4 so he wasn't in school, Tee Tee was 3 and Boodah was 1. There was 6 of us kids in the home and then Fee. Fee had just got her a house on 7th St. and it was just about time for a new school to start so I hoped for a better school year than those I have had for the last 3 years because living with Filthy Ricky was 'Hell' momma was never home so my hair was nevr done and hygiene. I just wanted better. Fee would go to work sometimes and I would have to do alot of babysitting which really didn't bother me because I was use to being the oldest and having to look over my younger siblings. I liked living with Fee and the first month was smooth sailing. Fee had finally got custody of us and school was just now about to start. We were all getting use to our new routine. Me and Rico took turns washing the dishes we had chores now and we had to live by those chores. I had to go to the laundrymat with Fee she was showing me how to cook, clean, and she even showed me how to do hair. Our landlord lived next door to us, she was a nice old Lady her name was Ms. Brown. She had a alot of cats in her house. Some days I would go over to Ms. Brown's house and talk to her although I was allergic to those cats. We had got to know alot of the neighborhood kids and Rico had a cute friend that I liked and he liked me so we called ourselves having a lil crush on one another. I remember Ms. Brown would fix us cakes sometimes and cousin Fee would take the cake but when Ms. Brown left cousin Fee would say "I'm not eating this cake with all these cat hairs" and we would laugh and laugh about it. Poor Ms. Brown, she didn't realize that the cats hair were getting in the cake. Instead of Fee talking about the cakes she should have just helped me and Ms. Brown fix the cakes but to each its own. One day Ms. Brown came over to bring us a cake, and it was hot outside and Ms. brown had on what looked like 3 or 4 sweaters(shirts) so I simply said Ms. Brown it's too hot outside and aren't you hot with all them shirts on. 'Remind you that Ms. Brown looked to be in her 70's or 80's she was a little frail old lady who was fragile and loving. Well, Ms. Brown said "honey, I'm not hot, I've got on 1,2 and as she made it to lifting up the bottom of that 3rd shirt, "Bam" a titty was hanging down there on her stomache, and we just laughed and laughed for days. After that I felt kind of bad so I would really go help Ms. Brown from time to time, and I think that she was slightly embarassed. Everytime I would see Ms. Brown afterwards she had certain kind of shyness to her. Tia and Tamara Mawery had a song that I liked listening to called 'Yea YEA Yea' so everytime that song came on my mind would pretend that I was in the actual video with them because I really did and do need me some Studio Time. Cousin Fee would always laugh at my singing but I didn't care because I was jamming in my own little world. Cousin Fee loved Mary J. Blige 'What's the 411' cousin Fee even wrote her own songs. Music was our life. One night all the younger kids were outside playing and me, I was in the house with cousin Fee Bone was at work or something. Cousin Fee smoked weed and I knew what weed was me and Rico use to sneak mommas cigarettes and go outside and smoke them from time to time so I knew what smoking was. Cousin Fee rolled up a joint and lit it and passed it to me and I smoked it. That night I had to wash the dishes as usual and I didn't like washing all them dishes because it was alot of them. After I washed dishes I started getting a stomache ache so cousin Fee told me I could sleep with her because Bone had to work overnight as usual being that he was a Storm Chaser so Fee had men on the side that I began to be aware of but the other men in Fee's life had mad respect for Fee and her marriage so they only came around when requested and Fee didn't like to sleep alone. Cousin Fee said she didn't like sleeping with the younger kids because they slept too wild and I could sleep with her everynight to keep the little kids from getting in the bed with her. I didn't mind sleeping with cousin Fee because she was cool and she let me smoke weed now at the age of 11 I felt kind of grown up. That night me and Fee listened to the music, smoked some joints, talked and laughed until I Fell asleep. I remember tossing and turning then I woke up in the middle of the night and had to vomit due to my stomache ache but after that I felt good and back to sleep I went.

CHAPTER

14

····

WHEN IT RAINS IT POURS

MY SKIN FEELS like I have bug bites and I am itching. I hope that I don't
get sick again and wind up having an asthma attack, hopefully I don't have
the Chicken Pox. Me, "yelling, Rico, can you please make me a sandwich
and get me a cup of Milk with it pleeeze brother I'm feeling sick". I love my
lil bro Rico, he is always there for a sister in the time of need. Knocking on
the Front door door. Hey, it's my Uncle Mick. Uncle Mick. Me, "Hi Uncle
Mick. What are you doing?". Uncle Mick was always my favortie and I
knew when momma was messing up that Uncle Mick would be there and
have my back knowing from experience. Uncle Mick replys" I'm moving
in with Fee. I've missed you all so much." I had a sudden sense of relief of
not feeling so well even though it looks like I indeed actually have a case
of the Chicken Pox which I got due to Scooby just weeks ago having the
Chicken Pox now they were passed along to me. Me, "Well Uncle Mick I
have to stay away from you, I have the Chicken Pox". Uncle Mick was also
always there for me threw hard and bad times, he is the youngest out of my
moms siblings and also probably one of my moms favorite brothers. Uncle

Mick didn't have any children of his own but Uncle Mick worked hard for his money working as a Chef/Cook at one of Kansas finest at the time resturants. Uncle O.G was also one of my favorites, he is the oldest out of momma's siblings and he is the Bread Winner hustle wise although Uncle O.G was always in and out of jail because he's the TRUTH a real O.G (Hustla) and one of a kind a true CANNON and he kept them "Money Bags" so the Police was always on my Uncle. My mom has 4 brothers and she's the only girl. Uncle Mick and Uncle O.G were my favorites and I have one Uncle whom was adopted out that looks just like my grandpa but I don't spend much time with that uncle and the other Uncle is named after my grandpa which is my Uncle Eric which is Keeda, BeBe and Tya's dad. Uncle Eric and I didn't always see eye to eye but I love them all. I began to feel a sense of security when Uncle Mick moved in with us. Fee is my big cousin and all but I would have to see how things were going to turn out with her because I was coming out of a strange situation and glad to be away from filthy Ricky. I was ready to be over these Chicken Pox, the summer was coming to an end. I have to be presentable for school and now I had Fee in my life to help me keep up with my hair and Fee is good at hair. I liked Fee she seems to be down to Earth. I had been getting bullied in the Missouri schools so now I'm back on my "Stomping Grounds" and I feel like the "New Kid On The Block". I began to change in so many ways and I also made a vowel to stand up for myself. I wasn't about to be bullied by no one else. One day my big cousin Kat came over to Fee's. Kat is Fee's niece so I expected Kat to be around and I knew that Kat was also a bully and I was done with being bullied. Kat came over one this particular day up to Kat's old bullying ways but on this day I didn't feel like that pretty little girl. No more shyness. All that scared to fight went away dealing with Filthy Ricky. I'm not taking no more losses is exactlly what I thought. Kat has a brother which happens to be my most favorite boy COUSIN. Me and Kat were playing as usual when all of a sudden Kat started getting physical. I kept it in my mind that I was not going to throw the first punch.

I simply told myself on this day "if Kat gets out of line, IMMA BEAT HER MUTHA FUCKIN ASS". I don't feel to good dealing with the chicken pox and extra shit moving from here to there. All I want is some peace. Sure enough Kat had to indeed "Try Me" and the fight was on and poppin. All I remember is playing with Kat when Kat tried to size me up and hit me. I snapped like an automatic. I had Kat on the bed beating her ass FULL THROTTLE STRAIGHT PUNCHES, when Uncle Mick busted in the door and yanked me from Kat's head. I beat her up and then I beat her down. I had enough of Kat and enough of running, those days were over. Pretty or not I sure felt everything but pretty and that's when a Lioness training began session. Uncle Mick found the whole thing to be halarious. All these years of Kat bullying me. NOT TODAY BITCH. I love Kat but enough was enough. Kat, your brother is the one who taught me how to hit hard. I would always ask Kat's big brother (my most favorite)," cousin D-Block can I hit you as hard as I can?" Kat's big brother D-Block was a big dude and I looked up to him because I knew his strength. D-Block would let me punch him to test my strength and every time I punched him I would think about punching Filthy Ricky and get stronger and stronger. Rico was into making beats and rhymes and was very good at it now. Rico had an awesome sense of talent and I felt a sense of protecting my family and even harder because Filthy Ricky had touched Poody and I wanted to "Kill Ricky" Ricky I'm going to find your NASTY FILTHY SOUL and pow. "There's plenty of Ricky's lurking".

CHAPTER
15
. . . .

WHEN IT RAINS IT POURS
BUT PREPARE FOR THE FLOOD

ALARM SOUNDING BEEP beep Beep wake up it's time to get ready for school.

This was going to be a better year," is what I told myself I made a friend she lived up the street from me and her name was Toya. There was a goup of kids down the street that would walk up on our block from time to time and a particular lil boy caught my eye. I was shy so I always spoke to him but that was all I did, I would say hi to him and give him a little smile from time to time. Us kids knew how to have fun, we would make up games to play. I was learning how to do my hair better thanks to cousin Fee and I would also have to comb 2 more heads along with me and Poody I had Tee Tee and Boodah. Tee Tee was my baby plus our real names were similar. Tee Tee was dark skinned like me and she was a little feisty baby with an attitude and I loved it. I would baby Tee Tee and Boodah alot because they were much younger then me. It seemed like cousin Fee was starting to smoke more weed with me so I felt a sense of responsibility. One day while me and Rico was on the bus stop waiting for the bus this little boy kept on harassing me. I think he may have had a crush on me but Rico wasn't having no boys' messing with his sister and neither was I so Rico beat the boy up and told him to leave me alone and from that day forth I never had problems with that little boy again. Although there was another boy on the bus who I think had a crush on me and I would make fun of him because his head was shaped like 'half a moon' so we called him 'Mac Tonight' like the McDonalds commercial. By this time I was starting to get a little mean to other kids because I have been bullied so much that the shy little girl in me was starting to transform. I wasn't so shy and easy to bully anymore. I had to learn how to stand up for myself. I felt kind of like I was being mean for calling that boy 'Mac Tonight' but I wasn't really into boys and I wasn't looking for a boyfriend unless it was one of my brothers' cute friends. Plus, the boy was flat out harassing me so picking on him was the only way I could think to make the boy stop like me although it didn't work he just kept having his crush on me and I thought that was so adorable someone still found me attractive. Cousin Fee would listen to a lot of music, party all the time and smoking but I didn't care because she was at home and she let me be me. We would dance around the house like we were at a party. Cousin Fee made sure she taught me the things that I would need to know for survival. Cook, clean, and do hair that was our thing. Fee even taught me how to make homemade cookies from scratch. I always said that someday I wanted to have kids of my own, get married and be a surgeon (Doctor). Fee would say that boys only want one thing and when they get it, they leave you and if you don't give them that one thing (sex) then there off to the next girl who is willing to give it to them. I would listen to Fee and her advice although I wasn't interested in having sex. I knew about sex and humping, kissing and things like that but I wasn't interested in actual sex although I had humped on several occasions. I humped boys at school and I had humped a couple of little boys who came around with family. I remember when Filthy Ricky tried to have sex with me. Ricky had a big size D from my stand point from what I had seen and I defintaly was not interested in no man putting something the size of that in me UGH the thought was horrible. Fee told me that sex didn't hurt and that sex felt good but of course I didn't think much of it I would rather stick to humping if I needed some entertainment. I was learning myself as a young girl. One day I had to pee really bad and I crossed my legs to hold my pee and as I was rocking I felt a sensation in my clitoris that felt so good so after that feeling I practiced crossing my legs more repeating that same motion so that I could master that feeling on my clit. I had also humped with a girl before but action intercourse was just something that I knew in my head that I wasn't ready to explore. I wanted to give my virginity to someone special one day. I really liked my boyfriend in Missouri and now that we lived in Kansas it was hard to see him but being that he was Rico's bestfriend I knew that I would probably get a chance to see him one last time and I did. Rico kept intouch with him and he came over to spend the night. Now, I thought I was ready to let him take my virginity? Let's see how the night would play out I thought. We planned everything perfect and everyone was now sleep. I felt his hand touching my body as I started feeling my clitoris begin to harden a thump as in a heartbeating motion and my heart was pounding. His lips touched mine and we began to kiss, his tongue entered my mouth and all that I could think about was (ewwww GROSS, his mouth tasted like Churches Chicken eww boy breath). We kissed for a little while longer then, we began to hump one another body to body when one of the younger children started to wake up. We automatically stopped what we were doing, as I felt his penis began to harden. I was so scared and I really think that he was scared also so we stopped being curious, kept our innocense and fell asleep. The next morning we looked at each other and all that we could do was smile at each other with this curious grin on both our faces. We both wanted each other bad that night but the timing wasen't right for us. That was the last time I saw Stinky. Rico and I always teased each other but rico knew that he was indeed my right hand man. I honestly think that Rico faked being sleep that night just to see that if I was going to be bad enough to loose my verginity to his friend, but nope it didn't and wasen't going to happen that easily. I had it made up in my mind that I was not ready to experience that part of life and it was a thrill just being that close and being able to explore. It seems like every night after that Fee always wanted me to sleep in the bed with her as long as she knew that she wasen't going to have any company. I liked sleeping in the bed with Fee because she would laugh with me and talk to me all night about everything and plus I didn't have to sleep in the room with them annoying little children. Uncle Mick had his own room. Uncle Mick worked most of the time but, when he wasen't at work he was always in his room resting. Fee had a couple different male friends and kids fathers that would come over from time to time and I knew that Fee was having sex with them I could always tell by her reactions and thiers even though Fee was married to Bone she was thinking that I didn't know what she was doing but I watched everything because she never knew when Bone was going to pop up. Fee also had a friend named D that would come over from time to time. Sometimes Fee would have me out in the streets with her in the middle of the night looking for D when Bone was at work. When all of the smaller children were sleeping in thier rooms Fee would roll up a *Joint* and she would let me smoke it with her and we would talk about the birds and the bees. Uncle O.G came over to Fee's house alot or we would all go over to his house. Uncle O.G's house would be LIT, he had an after hours at his house. Uncle O.G's house was set up like a Club at the bottom part where he had a bar, a dance floor and a huge sterio system for parties (That was the party Spot for the adults). Uncle O.G would always come threw with *Money Bags* and he would always give me and the other children money. This was around the time when some of that *Dirt* started coming out from under that old carpet. Things that were done in the dark began to come into the light. I began to hear alot of things about

Uncle O.G and cousin Fee. I didn't really know if I should believe what I was hearing BUT God gave me ears so I couldn't help it but to hear, I also had eyes to see. Rumors began to surface (or truth) that uncle O.G and Fee had been having a sexual relationship for many of years. I heard that Uncle O.G had to literally tie cousin Fee to a chair and call her parents because she was flipping out on Uncle O.G behind thier sexual encounters (I began to wonder because one of Fee's children actually looked like Uncle O.G). I couldn't believe my ears because Uncle O.G and Fee are first cousins so this rumor was a bit much for me at the time, plus I'm a child who has already been threw to much in my life and all I wanted was a peice of mind. I didn't now what to do or say all I knew was from experience and that was to always *Keep my eyes open to everything and BE ALERT*. I had to keep opened eyes and ears to every situation. Fee was the *Party Girl Type* although she still managed to handle her business at home. Fee had me and she knew that I had her back as far as monitoring the children at home while she partied. Fee always had a *Big Butt* so the men would always call her Big Booty Fee. Big butts ran in our family because momma was skinny with a big butt. Fee would also dress in small, fitted clothing which would expose her shape and would draw alot of attention to herself. Fee talked to me about alot of things as if I were in her age range. I listened to alot of what Fee had to tell me because I knew that she was showing me the ropes and giving me alot of knowledge and I love her for that. Fee continued to smoke weed and drink with me, I didn't mind smoking because I needed something to stimulate my mind and smoking weed made me feel more responsible, a sense of adulthood. I was transforming into a young woman quickly. I don't recall Uncle Mick being around me when Fee would give me alcohol and drugs so that's why I knew what Fee was doing was wrong because she most definilty didn't do it around my Uncle Mick. Something wasen't right about this picture but I couldn't quite put my finger on it at the moment so only time would tell.

CHAPTER

16

· · · ·

WHEN IT RAINS IT POURS

SOMETHING WAS WRONG with the house that we were living in next to Mrs. Brown so, Fee decided to move down the street and stay on the same block that we were on. There were neighbors that were in all of our age ranges. We had one family that lived next door to us that we got along with really well and Fee had started having a secret affair with one of the men next door to us. We had a Pear Tree in our yard and we loved picking the pears off the tree and eating the pears. I had met a friend around my age on the opposite side (my neighbors). I really liked this particular little girl because it was obvious that her parents kept her secluded and she seemed to be kind of spoiled or (well kept) like her parents were very over protective of her and she was really nice I liked going over her house spending time with her. Our neighbors on the other side of us where Fee began to build her secert affair with one of the men were very welcoming to us and our family began to get close to thier family again cousin Fee became real close to them also being that she started having relations with one of the guys who lived there while Bone would be gone alot of time Chasing

72

storms when he had a Storm in his own home anyhow. I ended up getting acquainted with one of the little boys on that side and he became my boyfriend, his name is Buddy. Buddy and I would flirt very innocently. Buddy knew that I was shy and I think that's what made him interested in me. Buddies aunties would tease him about him having this big crush on me and I would Blush. Buddy would always ask me if I wanted anything from the store when he would go and although I might have wanted something I was always to shy to say yes. Even though I really wanted something from the store I was to shy to say yes and admit it. We (all the kids) would get a chance to stay outside late at nights playing Hide-N-Seek and other games that we wanted to play. Buddy had some little girl cousins and one of their names were China. China was so pretty and I would baby her up and call her my *play daughter*. I told Fee that one day I wanted children of my own. Fee would respond by telling me that "boys aren't shit and all they want is one thing SEX and if you don't give them SEX they wouldn't like you no more and they would leave and go be with the girl who is giving them sex". She would also say that if you did indeed give the boys sex that they would get you pregnat and run off anyway and leave you all alone with a baby to raise by yourself. Fee knew that I had a boyfriend and she was okay with that. Sometimes Fee's secret affair would get drunk and pass out in Fee's room butt naked on the bed. One day I didn't realize that Fee's secret affair was in her room and I walked into Fee's room and there her secret affair was DRUNK in the bed butt naked, dick everywhere sleep. I would of coarse shut that door to Free's room quickly and not open it again without knocking first. I was mad about what I had saw and I most definitly didn't want Poody or one of Fee's daughters walking in that room seeing what I had saw. I told Fee that I saw her man naked and Fee had addressed that situation (issue) with her secret affair and I began to be alert on what was going on in our household once again because I didn't trust any man and definitely had to stay aware for me and the small children and Bone coming home while Fee had became very careless in her marriage. After that incident Fee broke off her relationship with her secret affair saying that he wasn't nothing but a drunk. I stayed into my music because music was food to my soul. There were songs like "Whoop There It Is", "Rump Shaker", "SWV Weak", "Toni Tony Tone Lay Your Head On My Pillow", "Xcape", "DJ Quick", "Mary J Blidge" and more. Fee would have lots of parties and I was remained Fee's designated babysitter. "My childrens grandma told me one thing yesterday that makes alot of sense:—You can take away a childs innocense but one thing you can't take away from that child is the childs memory and that's FACTS". Back to "My Story". Fee would ask me to sleep with her alot after she dumped her drunkin secret affair. One particular night Fee had went out to a party and all of the younger children were sleeping. When Fee came home I was still awake, Fee peeked in my room to see if I was awake and when she saw me awake she asked me as usual "if I wanted to sleep with her" (It is so hard to tell "My Story" it hurts and it's horrible but, it's the TRUTH and only God can judge me and I'm working only for the LORD my God and My Savior so I will continue). My answer was yes as usual because I didn't feel anything different. Usually Fee and I would talk the night away and I would always be the first one to fall asleep. I got myself together to sleep with Fee and I looked forward to our conversations and sometimes Fee would roll up a "Joint" so that we could smoke it together. This night was very different as Fee and I started to conversate while smoking it must have been a little while since I had last smoked with Fee because I fell asleep before we could have much of any conversation and it was what woke me up while it was dark in a dark room that changed my life forever. I remember hitting the joint for the last time and when I woke up my panties were off and I was recieving oral sex from an unknown person. I began to scream but it was not hurting me and it was not a rough touch and my Clitoris was hard a fully throbbing so my scream turned into a slight moan a I reached to feel the head of the intruder. I felt hair and at this point I began to get nervous because was this intruder Fee and if so why would my own cousin hurt me in this manner? If it was Bone where in the FUCK IS FEE and why THE FUCK IS BONE EATING MY PUSSY. It was hard to scream and they began to softly eat my pussy where all I could do is close my eyes grab thier head and get me a nice nut before I fell back to sleep realizing that I was a SQUIRTER. The next morning when I woke up I felt for my underwear and they were on the side of me as I hurried and put them on all confused about what I had just experienced and not to mention when I got out of bed wondering what had happened to me in the middle of the night break-fast was being cooked and Bone was indeed at home leaving out the door and Fee was up happy as ever cooking a huge breakfast for the famliy. Fee started the conversation like this," So, Justice, "how did you sleep last night, you fell asleep before I could get a word in?". I have been curious about some things and I don't know for sure if I can talk to you about them but I will talk to you later about them". I answered Fee, "Yeah, you can talk to me cousin. I am going to use the bathroom and I have to get dressed. I felt my clit jump from last night as I ran into the bathroom to gather my thoughts". The night before night was really weird and I felt different the next morning. I didn't stop the intruder I actually participated not knowing what else to do but it all felt very mush so wrong. The sexual activitiy (oral sex) lasted for half the night. I was in the 7th grade. I couldn't believe what had just happened and I began to feel nasty and ashamed. Fee is my cousin, my big cousin and my Guardian what if it was her? If it was Bone where the fuck was Fee and why did she let him do this to me. It was hard to tell whose head it was because Fee had a short haircut and Bone had short hair that was usually braided in plats but it wasn't braided this morning. I felt sick to my stomache afterwards just the thought of being with a family memeber was sickening to my soul. I knew that it wasen't right to be with your cousin in this type of fashion but I was confused and didn't know if it was Bone or Fee who had just ate my pussy so confusing that it made me lightly squirt on my first experience *It hurts so bad to tell My Story right now at this point*. I felt violated and down right disgusted. How could I!!

I fought filthy Ricky off all these years but now I have become weak. Fee is my big cousin and I knew that this shit right here was not supposed to happen Fee was suppose to be protecting me so I blamed her for the whole incident then she kept me under the influence. Now all of those rumors about Fee an uncle O.G began to dawn on me and clearly had to be aware of Fee and Bone and take heed to those rumors about Fee because she was wild. Now I had to make a huge decision because if I told anyone what had happened Me, Rico and Poody were going to go into Foster Care because we didn't have anyone in our family who wanted to help momma take care of us, not to mention that it had been months since I had seen or talked to my momma. I felt like I had been set up for a failure. How could I allow this to happen!?! I began to get mad at God because this was way to much and it was so hard for me to bear. My prayers didn't seem to be paying off because it was just one bad situation after another. I thought that God was supposed to protect me? My heart was breaking and I began to give up on prayers. This was the most time when I needed God, I can't go on any longer being a child who has been forced into incest. I was definitly at my breaking point but I had to stay strong for my siblings. This fucking Nasty Bitch Fee and her dummy husband Bone I WOULD KILL THEM BOTH! I became enraged in anger, I'm going to have to KILL someone to earn my respect! Fee kept me intoxicated so that she could take advantage of me! I felt like a target for pedophiles. I needed my momma now more than I had ever needed her. Momma wasen't there and I didn't think that God was there either. Fee and Bone continued on with thier life like none of this had happened. Fee continued to go out and party more now and make sure that I was in her bed when she made it home. The activities between the intruder and I happened frequently but each and everytime it was when Bone would come home after Fee would ask me to sleep with her on those particular days and It happened frequently but I could not ever guess if the person eating me was Fee or Bone because they kept thier identity hidden and didn't hurt me just gave me some really great head. I began to get frustrated even more because I was always stuck babysitting small children EXTRA children than before and Uncle Mick was always at work. I began to get mad and mischievious. I would make the small kids fight one another all the time for my personal entertainment. It wasn't fair to me or any of the other children because I began to take my problems and issues out on them and I know that hurt my little cousins and Poody. I always had to clean, cook, babysit, comb hair and now I had to please Fee sexually. Things that were going on with Fee and her life began to unravel and seep out from under that rug. Fee had three children at this point and two of them were supposed to have the same father (the youngest looked like Uncle O.G but the adults most definitly didn't mention that). Scooby and TeeTee were suppose to have the same father so when thier father would come over to visit he didn't really want to deal with TeeTee only Scooby and I didn't really understand why until one particular night. I would tell TeeTee to go and talk to her and Scoobies dad but when she did he would put this weird look on his face (like Maury I AM NOT THE FATHER). I found out why really quickly when one night Fee thought that I was alseep and she brought a strange man in the home and he went to TeeTee and picked her up saying "Is this my baby Girl". I tried to play sleep but that man was definitly not Scoobies dad that everyone thought was TeeTee's dad as well. I saw that strange man in the dark and this strange man was most definitly capable of being TeeTee's dad so why was Fee playing both? Turned out that both men are cousins that's why Fee tried to keep things secret SHE WAS SLEEPING WITH COUSINS!. I was shocked and felt bad for having TeeTee approach Scoobies dad like he was her father to. I was a kid and I only knew what I either saw for my own two eye or what the adults told me to believe. Fee's older brother would come over from time to time (Little Ulysis) and he was always a fun and wild type of cousin but this day he was CRAZY. Cousin Ulysis was high off of PCP and he was WEIRD, LOUD and ANIMATED. Ulysis was yelling some weird things aloud this day and he wasn't the same big cousin. Ulysis came over one day and as I got up off the sofa to go into the bathroom Ulysis followed me, Ulysis was on PCP so I stayed away from him (Ulysis) because that was definitly not MY BIG COUSIN, Not the cousin that I knew and would "Moon" the corner store with. I kept a distance from cousin Ulysis at that point because he had changed up on me and that was not the Big Cousin that I knew and loved. I began to see a very darkside of the Goodings and it was far from pretty but I love my cousins to this day. That darkside on the Gooding side was looking a bit scary but they are my family so I was willing to stick it out the long way with them. One day my Uncle Eric had been drinking and he came over to Fee's house tripping with me, calling me out of my name and some extra shit. I had to be alert on my 10 toes at Fee's house there was to much nonsense going on. My sense of security began to fade away. Remember, my mother has 4 brothers and she is the only girl. My momma has a younger brother that had been adpoted out of the family for whatever issues that my grandma and grandpa were having but my uncle would come up Kansas to visit the family on occasion. My Uncle's name is Rob and he moved to Witchita KS but he came up here to visit his bloodline from time to time. This particular time would be a time that would scar me and Rico's brain permanitily. Rico and I witnessed this night for our own two eyes and remember "The eyes don't lie". So, Uncle Rob was up here in Kansas visiting us at Fee's house, the grown-ups had been partying, smoking weed and drinking. It was getting late and everyone was LIT (fucked up) and all of the smaller children had fallen asleep, all except for Rico and I. Uncle Mick was there and he was also awake and Partying enjoying his younger brother being home in Kansas. Rico had ran him some bath water so that he could take a bath before going to bed and I was up watching T'V when the whole scene occuried. Fee went into the bathroom where Rico was about to get into the bath tub in a DRUNKIN MOMENT (feeling herself). Rico and I began to peek into the bathroom, I looked threw the door keyshaped peekwhole and there was a slight crack in the backside of the door or on the floor wher Rico could see into the bathroom and we

(Rico and I) watched as these bazaar events took place. Remember Rico and I saw these things with our own two eyes now. Fee came into the bathroom, took off her clothes where she was butt booty naked and fell on the bathroom floor so hard where the Iron that was sitting on the iron Board fell off onto the floor and almost knocked Fee upside the head. Fee lay there on the bathroom floor and the commotion was so loud that Uncle Rob must have heard it and came running in the bathroom to check on Fee and make sure that she was alright. Uncle Rob tried to get Fee off the floor but Fee wouldn't let him. Fee instead reached up and started to rub Uncle Rob's penis. Uncle Rob pushed Fee's hand away from his dick and told Fee to stop it and get up off the bathroom floor and that she was drunk. Fee told him to leave her and let her lay there. Uncle Rob tried again to pick Fee up off then floor, then tried giving Fee her clothing. Fee denied uncle Robs help and began to rub his penis again. Once again uncle Rob pushed Fee's hand away from his penis. Uncle Rob tried to gather his thoughts when Fee again began to rub his penis and I saw uncle rob began to get a hard on and sat down on the toilet seat. Fee rubbed Uncle Rob's penis pulling it out of it's pants and she started sucking Uncle Rob's dick. Rico and I watched as Uncle Rob tried to fight but then had no more fight as he enjoyed the feeling that Fee was giving him. Uncle Rob and Fee had sex after uncle Rob couldn't resist and after Unc was done he reached into the tub where Rico's wash rag was, grabbed it out and washed himself off and left the bathroom. I busted out laughing HARD as I saw the look on Rico's face being disgusted. Uncle Mick walked in and caught us looking in the bathroom and yelled at us to stop peeking and lay down. (UGH) Rico your towel as I giggled before uncle Mick almost scared the black off me. Rico and I had saw everything at that point and we both knew that Fee was definitly not to be trusted and I wondered who was the intruder who had eaten my pussy multiple times in Fee's bed. When Uncle Mick left the room, I peeked back in as Fee hurried to get dressed, I heard uncle Rob say that he was about to go and I hurried up to act like I was sleep because I was definitly not sleeping with Fee's triflen ass. The devil was at work was all that I could think. Fee was running threw the family and I knew that those rumors weren't only rumors about Fee and Uncle O.G this bitch Fee is a FREAK maybe Fee had a demon in her or maybe Fee went threw something trajic in her own life with her brothers (who knows) but this shit with Fee was real and I didn't feel like I could talk to her about what happened to me in her room like a big cousin because she looked like me to be the intruder so it angered me and I began to treat Fee like she was indeed the intruder after I just witnessed her with my own uncle and the things that happened to me happened in her bed and the lips felt soft like that of a woman. Buddy remained my boyfriend and I really had began to get close to him without sex but sexually curious. Fee ended up letting all of us go on a trip to Oklahoma with Buddy and his family where I had alot of fun and we got to go to the Car Show and the Rodeo. Buddies family had taken a liking to me and I really liked his family. I planned on letting Buddy take my verginity in Oklahoma BUT things didn't play out that way. I wanted to tell Buddy about what was going on at Fee's but I was to shy to open up to Buddy. Fee scared me from having sex and I wanted someone who would love me for the person that I was and someone to respect me because Fee or Bone had already taken my innocense and I wasen't ready for intercoarse, not when Fee told me that he would only fuck me and leave me. "I needed Love like LL Cool J". I had things on my mind and Buddy had to get to know me a bit more before I gave him something that I felt like was already being taken. After we came back from Oklahoma and got settled in a bit at home my old cousin Kat came over for a visit. I wasen't worried about old Kat because I knew that if Kat even thought about it I was like a firecracker A BIG ONE. This time Kat didn't want to fight me, Kat wanted to fight Rico. Kat tried to beat Rico up and that was my boxing partner. I started to beat Kat's ass just for all of her bullying ways but Rico could stand his own ground and if he really needed me I had his back. I had something else in mind for Kat though this night and Kat and Fee both knows what happened and that Justice only speaks FACTS since Fee had a sickness. Kat liked humping me also when she didn't want to fight me so that was the payback. I wanted Buddy to take my verginity NOT FEE OR BONE. I felt like TRASH but I felt a little better when I got Kat involved. I was FED UP with Fee and all this sick bullshit! I began to rebel in so many ways. I felt like Fee and Bone had got the best of me, I wasn't supposed to let this shit happen NO! I had a best-friend at the time. I call her my Twin Bestfriend because we have been friends since her birth. My Uncle Mick and her mom are bestfriends for 18 years or more. When she was born her father named her after me because he liked my name and again I was *The beautiful Black Diamond*. Justice is by Twin Bestfriend that I grew up with from birth and her moms name is Dime. Anyhow, Justice wanted me to spent the night over her house with her this night and Fee would not let me when the rug got flipped up and things unravled. Fee wouldn't let me be a child and I had enough with Fee and her bullshit. Justice had a brother named Squirt. Squirt and Rico were around the same age. Fee wouldn't let me go over Justice's house. Free said that I had to stay home and babysit. Fee only wanted me to stay home because she wanted me to sleep with her or Bones and fulfill her needs but that filthy bitch had another thing coming and I was about to snap. I couldn't take any more so when Justice, Dime and Squirt left us that night after a visit that went so good but ended up so bad because I couldn't just BE A KID I exploded on Fee. "My Story" is sad and true. I was 12 years old at this point and my life was like a horrible movie. I haven't even ever had my first period yet. I had to play a role to keep my family together. I wanted to KILL that bitch Fee and her husband Bone, take the kids and run off to no where land. I was FED THE FUCK UP. I wanted to run away from home and just get away from everyone ALL MY FAMILY!. I was about to be a fuckin REBEL and I wanted me a GUN to name the bitch BETTY. I was a *Diamond In The Rough* indeed. Fee or Bone was not going to get away with this bullshit, over my dead body. Fee knew within her heart that I wanted to kill her and my heart went cold. Fee started saying some fucked up shit to me, things like (my momma didn't love me that's why I was there with her) or things like I was Fat and had cellulite like one of her friends. Fee started getting really messy and I was seeing a very dark side of Fee. Everyday I thought about running away from home. Fee was having sex with two of her "So Called" kids fathers and neither one knew that she was sleeping with the other. She would just use both of them along with everyone else for her own benifits when one day one of her daughters dad let Fee use his "Rental Car" Fee asked me to ride with her and although I didn't want to I rode along whe we didn't even make it down the street and Fee was smoking her cigarette and fire dropped in her lap and BAMN she wrecked the car right into an electric pole. I jumped out of that car so quick! All I could imagine was the wires to the pole falling in the car and electrocuting Fee for her evil ways. I jumped out the car and took off running back home. Fee was on some other shit and I didn't want to be any where around her when the WRATH came. I prayed harder and harder when finally Fee got a female friend named Chris. Chris was a heavy set woman and she had a beautiful voice. Fee and Chris would sing together. Fee could sing really good but Chris had a Gospel voice that could make the Angels listen, her beautiful voice made her a beautiful person to me. Chris had some sisters around my age but they lived up in St. Joe. When Chris and Fee's voice would combine they made a great melody. Fee would try to get Chris to do things like go to the clubs and party with her. Fee's father is a Pastor so you know what they say about the Pastors children *them are the worse* and the devil always targets the strong families. It's a spiritual warefare going on and I've been at war for many and many of years as you can clearly see. Repent of your sins people. I felt just as guilty for participating in this world of sin. I could have ran away from Free's house but I sacrificed for the sake of my siblings. I remembered what and how my grandma taught me to PRAY no matter the circumstance. I prayed for my cousin Fee and I prayed for people or things to occupy Fee so she couldn't target me. I also prayed to God for me a bestfriend, someone that I could talk to and open up to about my situation. I prayed that God would take me out of that situation before I pulled a MURDER. I prayed that my momma would get herself right and come back for me and my siblings and take us away from all the madness. I prayed that God would put a STAR in my famliy that would be solid and shine like a diamond taking my family away from the hood away from the struggle. I just wanted a better life for all of my family even the ones who had hurt me because I didn't know what they had been threw that made them this way. I wanted my family to get right with God first because if my grandmother was here she would want me to PRAY and she would protect me so I knew that I couldn't give up on my only protector GOD ALMIGHTY. I was begining to learn right from wrong and what Fee or Bone was doing to me was very very WRONG.

17

····

WHEN IT RAINS IT POURS

BUT BE PREPARED for The Flood (I messed this chapter up a little needs good edit)

Speaking of *Flood*. I find it real weird that I can't recall the *Flood* of 93". They say that it rained for 30 days. Why can't I remember all these days of rain when I knew that I was flooded with pain and I most definitly didn't like the rain. The rain meant that I had to stay in the house all day and normally Fee would be home all day as we are MORE STRESS. I think that cousin Fee was so scared at this point. Fee was scared that she was about to feel the WRATH of GOD for everything, ALL her wrong doings. Me, I'm a *Prayer Warrior* (that is what my Pastors call me). Sure indeed I prayed and prayed day in and day out no matter the situation, good days, bad days. I prayed for a change to come within my life and my family. I prayed that God would make a way for me and my family. Fee or Bone was having thier way with me taking advantage of me. It's a reason why I can't remember that Flood and it was God. God heard my prayers when at that time I didn't quite realize that God heard me. My attitude was becoming a bit rebellious. So we ended up moving into another house. Fee had also developed a friendship with a lady named Carol. Carol had three children whom were all around the ages of me, Rico and Poody. Carols youngest daughter actually has the same birthday and same age as Poody. Carol was in a relationship with my Uncle Eric. Carol always had her children around us and although they seemed kind of weird in a sense we actually became very close to Carol and her children. Fee was still up to her Freaky ways. Fee began having threesomes with her sons fathers sister while Bone was storm Chasing. Its was some Jerry Springer shit going on with Fee. Fee would have her babies daddies sister named Jackie and Jackies boyfriend sleeping in the same bed with her at the same time. Fee's girl-friend/sister-in-law Jackie also had a sesual relationship with my Uncle O.G. I knew that Fee was getting out of control and I tried to stay far away from Fee plus I had the baby all the time. I loved my baby cousin so much and I wanted to protect him from everything that was going on around him I wasn't a mother yet but I had experienced motherhood. Fee, had given birth to a new child and the father was a mystery until the birth was it Bone or D or God knows who and I always had to babysit and the baby had gotten really sick and she would just leave him on me to babysit almost 24 hrs a day. I didn't know anything about newborn babies and this baby became sick. I was babysitting as usual when he started choking and couldn't breathe. I saw him turning purple and patting him on the back wasn't helping him breathe so I held him in the air by one leg patting his back until I heard him able to enhale and exhale properly. I was so scared and my nerves was bad, all I knew was that I was going to protect this baby and he was so cute and adorable and innocent. Fee's baby felt like (My Baby) and I was going to treat him like I had given birth to him and protect him from everyone even Fee. I got frustrated at times because I always had to babysit and I had no real life of my own. Free was lazy, she could be sitting right in the room by the T'V and call you from all the way in an opposite room to turn the T.V for her. Fee thought that she had some built in maid services. It was always, "make me a glass of water, wash the dishes, fold, the laudry, comb the girls hair!". Sometimes I just wanted to snap and say," FAT BITCH GET IT CHA DAMN SELF!" The shit was nerve wrecking and didn't make any sense, I felt like Fee was taking my kindness for a weakness. That bitch Fee was most definitly pushing my buttons and my fuse was about to blow. I began to get into dancing alot. Dancing would help me take my mine off of my stress and I was a really good dancer. I was frustrated because some of the kids on the block began to go around teasing me saying that "my uncle Mick was gay". I would get really mad when the neighborhood children would call Uncle Mick gay. I would stand up to the kids saying "my uncle isen't Gay he's just feminine". I had not ever saw Uncle Mick with a girlfriend around but I damn sure didn't see him with a man either although he did have a gay male friend for a really long time now. I observed Uncle Mick, uncle Mick liked to cook and clean like us females but he didn't dress like us or wear make-up or any weird shit and I really didn't care about his sexuallity personnally because he's my favorite. I just thought that my uncle was a CHEF, he is a very good cook. Well, I didn't care if uncle Mick was gay, straight or whatever I knew that he wasen't SICK, he wasen't a Pedophile and he didn't hurt me. I was going to love my uncle either way straight or curved because he showed he love and I would beat a kids ass for teasing me about my Uncle Micks sexual preference. We ended up moving to a new home where Rico and I had to walk to school at West Middle. This time Rico, and I were going to West Middle School. Rico and I had to walk a good distance to school and we would have to walk threw the graveyard. We (Rico and I) would walk threw the Graveyard every morning. It was the graveyard where grandma was buried but grandma didn't ever get a headstone for her grave so I did't know exactly where grandma's body was located but, I wondered and I had a sense on security in that graveyard that I didn't want to walk threw. Rico and I would try hard not to disturb the dead. Every morning I would ask Rico the same question over and over again, "Rico, Does my hair look alright?" Rico would always let out a sigh of irritation, "huh—it looks just like it did yesterday". Rico would reply and I would Crack Up Laughing. At Middle School I became moe interested in sex because all of the girls were talking about it, plus of the things that I was being exposed to in my home. I met a boy friend named Mike, we were not boyfriend and girlfriend just friends to the point where Carol's daughter named Thea was dating Mike's big brither Steve "R-I-P MIKE". Thea and I had became really close friends and I would confide in her. There was a girl a western named Meeka and everyone would say that Meeka and I looked like we were sisters. I wanted to be in Drill Team so bad that year at school but Free didn't let me. Free tried to say that my grades weren't good enough but Free was lying I had A's B's and C's no D's or F's and my grades were always A's and B's until the past couple of years. Fee just did not want me to be active in school fearing that I would expose her or Bones little secret. I wanted to be active like all of the other students. That was the year when R-Kelly came up to our school and I missed him thankful because R Kelly must like them young and for that I KILL FOR MINE. I told myself that day forward that I was going to meet as many famous people in this world that I wanted to and would not let Fee or anyone else hold me back. R Kelly had alot of great songs at this time and I wanted to meet him at that point though GOD saw my best interst. One day at school I had a terrible stomache pain and when I went into the bathroom, I saw blood. I knew that I had just now began puberty and started my period. I always heard people say that "once you start your period, you are able to get pregnat and have babies". Although I wasen't sexually active with boys (I kept that thought In mind). When Fee made it home from work that day I told her that I had started my period. Fee seemed to be in shock. But before Fee had came home I had went into her bathroom to find a sanitary but all Fee had was tampons so I tried using one and I was hurting so badly that I had to tell Fee what was going on. After I told Fee what had happened she got all emotional and hurried to get me some pads instead of that painful tampond. I couldn't sit with that thing in me. One night after that free had tried to fight me because I had got into trouble at school, Carol held me back and I was extremely mad because I wanted to fight Fee but Carol Kept sayin no don't let them Fight, no Justice Fee is pregant. I had thoughts of Fee telling me that my own momma didn't love me and that made me even more mad and the fact that Fee was not just trying to give me a whooping which it was to late for but Fee was trying to Fight me like I was a grown woman. Fee was full of drama and I didn't want that bitch putting her hands on me in any kind of way anymore. I would sleep with Fee just to keep her from bitching with me. I had for some reason became scared of sleeping in the dark. I had saw alot so I wanted to sleep with the lights on. I would have nightmares where I would wake up crying in my sleep. For instance, I would have dreams that some kind of monster was chasing me, or dreams like this one "I'm at home with my family members, when a fight breaks out. I have to protect myself so I grabbed a knife to stab my cousin but they don't die so I have to keep fighting harder and harder. I try to run and hide in the house. I lock all windows, doors etc but my cousin just keeps on coming back and manages to get in the house, so I have to jump out a window in order to get away. In some of my dreams I would get shot in home invasions and survive. I would have all kind of crazy dreams. Some dreams would be like demonic forces were trying to attack me. Do you know the feeling when your sleeping but it feels like your awake but you can't physically move your body? They say during their time it's a witch riding your back that's why your awake but you can't move like being paralized (demonic Forces at work). These kinds of things began to happen to me so I became scared to go to sleep at night with the lights off or I felt like I needed to sleep with a weapon close by me. I felt like I had to get away from Fee because when Bone came home the same thing kept on occuring night after night. Uncle Mick was living in the basement but he still worked all of the time so I think that he was unaware of what was going on in the home with Fee. I remained in constant prayer. Fee had also been sleeping with one of Carols cousins Albert who would wear these tight pants where you could see his dick print and Fee always talked about how big his dick was but he was ugly as fuck and I thought that it was completely disgusting. Fee slept with Dee on the low and Dee was possibly her childs father. I hoped that the baby was Dee's because Dee was cool and he didn't make me feel all weird when he came around and I didn't have to wonder in the middle of the night when Bone came home who was supposed to be a Husband who was never at home to tame the WILDNESS in Fee. Fee knew who her childs father was going to be because if the father of the child was Carols cousin that was going to be one ugly baby. I had to witness all of these things going on and not to mention I was coming down with a sore throat. I had this white puss on my tonsels and I didn't know where it was coming from. I went to the doctor and whatever medicine the doctor gave me healed me. I tried hard to stay away from Filthy Fee but it became hard because this year she always had me secluded. My friends were the one's like Dime's Daughter Justice and Carols Daughter Thea which was a bit older than me. Justice came around every now and then but when she did we would always have alot of fun. My cousins BeBe, Keeda and Tya' would come around. I continued to have asthma attacks from time to time but not as much. I was starting to figure out what had indeed trigger my asthma attacks. I didn't like being in the hospital but at this point anything was better than being in the house with Fee and all of those responsibilities. I got a peace of mind when I was in the hosiptal. Momma would come around from time to time but I couldn't tell her what was going on because she was on drugs and I refused to put Rico and Poody in a fucked up situation back in the dope house with momma. One time before Rico, Poody and I had to live in the Dope House with momma and somebody almost got killed. Momma almost killed this old mad throwing a full blown 50lbs pickle jar filled with sugar across the room at the old man's head. I never saw a 70 year old mad duck down so quick in my life. I most definitly not going back to that. Uncle Ulysis had a Church and we would attend his Church most of the time with the Verse family. I had another friend that I grew up with because her dad and my grandpa were very close friend and her name was Nedra. Nedra's dad's name is Mr. T and him and grandpa were close friends for a long long time since Sunshine Bisquits. grandpa had moved back to North Carolina after grandma passed and I missed my grandpa. Nedra is a really good friend but I didn't confide in Nedra. I felt like I couldn't get that close to anyone at this point and Fee made sure that I stayed secluded for the most part. I was secluded so bad that I can't remember that flood of 93". I bet that Flood scared the shit out of Fee but she continued in all of her filthy ways so she wasn't scared enough. Fee kept me closed up and away from other people but she made sure that all her desires were met when necessary. Fee tried to be like R Kelly and "Keep It On The Downlow" but she was scared not knowing when this BOMB would blow right in her face. Fee didn't know when I would explode and I was really ready to explode on her because I had been getting molested in her custody but no one cared to do anything about it. Every year it seemed like we had to move homes and this time we were going to new grades and the worst school in Kansas at the time Northwest Middle and Fee's younger sister had got adopted out but Fee was making arangements to let her younger sister from Knob Knoster moved up here in Wyandotte. But before Neicy moved up here we moved in this other house where I met *Fly Guy. Fee let her babies father (Scoobies Father) sister Jackie and her boyfriend move in with us. Jackie had a son around Scoobies age named Tay. I would make Scooby and Tay fight sometimes but other times they would just fight on thier own after they got threw playing all day. Scooby was hyperactive and he would keep me entertained doing things like kirate' and the splits. It was funny because I thought that the splits was for the girls but not when it came to karate' and dance for boys back in those days. Scooby knew how to dance and knew how to fight as well. I began to get a thrill out of watching the kids fight as long as my babies weren't losing the fight. If my little cousins began to lose a fight with the other cousin I would just break the fight up and start over training them for the battle. Jackies boyfriend would come over to Fee's house with this huge yellow Pithon Snake wrapped aroung his neck and God knows I don't like snakes and if there is one thing in life that I absolutely hate that would be a SNAKE. I stayed away from Jackies boyfriend because I knew that the snake is the devils serpent and bad things lingered around a serpent. There was some weird shit going on with Fee, Jackie and Jackie's boyfriend. My hair began to fall out during this year due to all of the stress I had endoured so Jackie made me a hair appointment at her beautician. I was at that beautician all day and night and the cosmetologist there cut my hair in a short style that I definitly didn't like and I was very disappointed and even more frustrated. I wanted to look at least half way decent for my new boyfriend *Fly Guy* but as usual, something went wrong with that house and we ended up moving to a new house again. This time Rico, and I were going to West.

Jackie had a son around Scoobies age named Tay. I would make Scooby and Tay fight sometimes but other times they would just fight on thier own after they got threw playing all day. Scooby was hyperactive and he would keep me entertained doing things like kirate' and the splits. It was funny because I thought that the splits was for the girls but not when it came to karate' and dance for boys back in those days. Scooby knew how to dance and knew how to fight as well. I began to get a thrill out of watching the kids fight as long as my babies weren't losing the fight. If my little cousins began to lose a fight with the other cousin I would just break the fight up and let the start over training them for the battle. Jackies boyfriend would come over to Fee's house with this huge yellow Pithon Snake wrapped aroung his neck and God knows I don't like snakes and if there is one thing in life that I absolutely hate that would be a SNAKE. I stayed away from Jackies boyfriend because I knew that the snake is the devils serpent and bad things lingered around a serpent. There was some weird shit going on with Fee, Jackie and Jackie's boyfriend. My hair began to fall out dur to all of the stress I had endoured so Jackie made me a hair appointment at her beautician. I was at that beautician all day and night and the cosmetologist there cut my hair in a short style that I definitly didn't like and I was very disappointed and even more frustrated. I wanted to look at least half way decent for my new boyfriend *Fly Guy* but as usual, something went wrong with that house and we ended up moving to a new house again. This time Rico, and I were going to West Middle School. Rico and I had to walk a good distance to school and we would have to walk threw the graveyard. We (Rico and I) would walk threw the Graveyard every morning. It was the graveyard where grandma was buried but grandma didn't ever get a headstone for her grave so I did't know exactly where grandma's body was located but, I wondered and I had a sense on security in that graveyard that I didn't want to walk threw. Rico and I would try hard not to disturb the dead. Every morning I would ask Rico the same question over and over again, "Rico, Does my hair look alright?" Rico would always let out a sigh of irritation, "huh—it looks just like it did yesterday". Rico would reply and I would Crack Up Laughing. At West Middle School I became more interested in sex because all of the girls were talking about it, plus of the things that I was being exposed to in my home. I met a boy friend named Mike, we were not boyfriend and girlfriend just friends to the point where Carol's daughter named Thea was dating Mike's big brither Steve "R-I-P MIKE". Thea and I had became really close friends and I would confide in her. there was a girl a West named Meeka and everyone would say that Meeka and I looked like we were sisters. I wanted to be in Drill Team so bad that year at school but Fee didn't let me. Fee tried to say that my grades weren't good enough but Fee was lying I had A's B's and C's no D's or F's and my grades were always A's and B's until the past couple of years. Fee just did not want me to be active in school fearing that I would expose her little secret. I wanted to be active like all of the other students. That was the year when R-Kelly came up to our school and I missed him. I told myself that day forward that I was going to meet as many famous people in this world that I wanted to and would not let Fee or anyone else hold me back. R Kelly had alot of great songs at this time and I wanted to meet him. One day at school I had a terrible stomache pain and when I went into the bathroom, I saw blood. I knew that I had just now began puberty and started my period. I always heard people say that "once you start your period, you are able to get pregnat and have babies". Although I wasen't sexually active with boys (I kept that thought In mind). When Fee made it home from work that day I told her that I had started my period. Fee seemed to be in shock. But before Fee had came home I had went into her bathroom to find a sanitary but all Fee had was tampons so I tried using one and I was hurting so badly that I had to tell Fee what was going on. After I told Fee what had happened she got all emotional and hurried to get me some pads instead of that painful tampond. I couldn't sit with that thing in me. One night after that Fee had tried to fight me because I had got into trouble at school, Carol held me back and I was extremely mad because I wanted to fight Fee but Carol Kept sayin no don't let them Fight, no Lady Bud Fee is pregant. I had thoughts of Fee telling me that my own momma didn't love me and that made me even more mad and the fact that Fee was not just trying to give me a whooping which it was to late for but free was trying to Fight me like I was a grown woman. Fee was full of drama and I didn't want that bitch putting her hands Dee's because Dee was cute and he didn't make me feel all weird when he came around. Fee knew who her childs father was going to be because if the father of the child was Carols cousin that was going to be one ugly baby. I had to witness all of these things going on and not to mention i was coming down with a sore throat. I had this white pus on my tonsils and I didn't know where it was coming from. I went to the doctor and whatever medicine the doctor gave me healed me. I tried hard to stay away from Filthy Fee but it became hard because this year she always had me secluded. My friends were the one's like Dime's Daughter Justice and Carols Daughter Thea which was a bit older than me. Justice came around every now and then but when she did we would always have alot of fun. My cousins BeBe, KeKe and Rudy would come around. I continued to have asthma attacks from time to time but not as much. I was starting to figure out what had indeed trigger my asthma attacks. I didn't like being in the hospital but at this point anything was better than being in the house with Fee and all of those responsibilities. I got a peace of mind when I was in the hosiptal. Momma would come around from time to time but I couldn't tell her what was going on because she was on drugs and I refused to put Rico and Poody in a fucked up situation back in the dope house with momma. One time before Rico, Poody and I had to live in the Dope House with momma and somebody almost got killed. Momma almost killed this old mad throwing a full blown 50lbs pickle jar filled with sugar across the room at the old man's head. I never saw a 70 year old mad duck down so quick in my life. I most definitly not going back to that. Uncle Ulysis had a Church and we would attend his Church most of the time with the Verse family. I had another friend that I grew up with because nher dad and my grandpa were very close friend and her name was Nedra. Nedra's dad's name is Mr. T and him and grandpa were close friends for a long long time since Sunshine Bisquits. grandpa had moved back to North Carolina after grandma passed and I missed my grandpa. Nedra is a really good friend but I didn't confide in Nedra. I felt like I couldn't get that close to anyone at this point and Fee made sure that I stayed secluded for the most part. I was secluded so bad that I can't remember that flood of 93". I bet that Flood scared the shit out of Fee but she continued in all of her filthy ways so she wasen't scared enough. Fee kept me closed up and away from other people but sghe made sure that all her desires were met when necessary. Free tried to be like R Kelly and "Keep It On The Downlow" but sghe was scared not knowing when this BOMB would blow right in her face. Free didn't know when I would explode. Every year it seemed like we had to move homes and this time we were going to new grades and the worst school in Kansas at the time Northwest Middle and Free's younger sister had got adopted out but Fee was making arangements to let her younger sister from Knob Town moved up here in Wyandotte. But. This time Rico and I were going to the worst middle school at that time in Kansas and Fee's younger sister was going to be moving up here shortly. Fee's younger sis was darker skinned than me and she was raised in a small town. Neicy moved up here eventually. Neicy would do things that irritated me so I would threghten to beat her up. Neicy was the sneaky type. Neicy and Rico thought that they were slick and they would hump at nights. Fee ended up divorcing Bone and got a boyfriend name Dame getting another boyfriend and Dame ended up moving in with Fee. I had to be alert about this whole marriage and divorce that Fee had done but things were changing and I wasn't sleeping in the bed with Fee as much so I felt a little bit more safe not knowing if they got divorced because of something happening to me but I didn't trust anyone and I had to protect my cookies but Fee was getting kinda more out of control in some aspects. One day Fee wanted us to play strip poker with her and her boyfriend came. Rico wasn't into Fee's shananagians so Rico declined Strip Poker but Neicy and I took the invite. At the end of the game everbody ended up naked all except me of coarse. Fee would make the naked person stand up in front of everyone else and spin around to show off thier naked bodies. Although I had won the game Fee still made me get naked infront of everyone which I truly think was unfair. Fee just wanted her new boyfriend to see me naked is what I though about the whole thing but she said that it was to make sure that it was our own little secret. I was appalled that Fee's new boo Dame went along with the whole strip Poker thing Dame seemed like a "Good Guy". I had saw Dame naked and i looked at him completely different kind of in a disgusted and ashamed way. I told myself that I would fuck him up if he tried any perverted shit with me and I meant that. When Thea would come over to visit we would sometimes play truth or dare so one day I dared Thea to fuck Scooby and Thea did that as everybody watched the live sex scene. That was my very first time watching an up close and personal sex scene. I actually saw Scoobies penis going inside of Thea as Scoobies penis was white with Thea's cum. Thea was four years older than I was a Scooby was about 6 years younger than me. One night I was curious about scooby and scooby would always start trying to sleep next to me at night and hump on me. this night I was curious and I gave Scooby a little Scooby snack. Afterwards I felt ashamed and I didn't want to feel this way so I stayed far far away from Scooby. I didn't want to experiement with my own little cousin and someone was doing things with me. I felt very bad and I made a vowel to myself not to be that curoius or weak minded. Scoobies mom and step dad was scorning and scarring me and I didn't want to do the same thing to my little cousin. I had to fight this force off of me and I perpared myself for a fight. Fee brought me and Nicki some of the smallest skimpiest outfits that she could find for us to wear. I called my outfit a "Shoop" outfit because it was like the outfits that Salt, Pepper and Spinder-ella had on in the "Shoop" video. my favorite cousin Fee's sister cut my hair in a cute Bob and this ugly duckling began to transform into a beautiful swan. I wore that "Shoop" outfit on the first day of school my New Hood Middle School and all heads began to turn and guess who came back around "Buddy" and he didn't like my transformation. Buddy walked me home from school this day and on the way home from school I was turning grown mens heads and Buddy exploded for the first time this day in a fit of rage. I had found out later that Buddy had been playing me and since I did't give him the Jewel he went looking elsewhere for a "Diamond". After that I figured that Fee was right about boys and I was going to show Buddy just what he was missing. Buddy couldn't get my Jewel (my Cookie) and he was on the hunt for anything with opened legs. Buddy had been my boy-friend for years and I really wanted Buddy to take my verginity but I had my eyes set on new things and Buddy did to. I had met a guy friend named Gerd and Gerd lived a couple of houses down from me. my cousin Derrick had gotten married to a lady named Kita and Kita was always over Fee's house with Derrick they had a beautiful little daughter together. I loved my cousin Derrick because he was a cool cousin and he would work on music with Rico. Kita caught Gerd sneaking in my window when Nicki was in the room sneeking Gerd in but Kita was cool and didn't tell on us. One night Kita got drunk and tried to fight Thea saying tghat Thea was trying to fuck my big cousin Derrick. Fee was cheating on Dame with multiple men and told me not to tell Dame but one day I did. I told Dame what Fee was doing behind his back and Dame went off on Fee but guess who Fee came back to ME so I had to be cautious about what I said because at the end Fee always had the last say so. I didn't care about Fee being mad at me I wanted to kill her anyway for violating me. Our first week of school at Northwest Rico, Me, Neicy and a friend on the block named D got suspended our first week of school. This was my first time ever getting suspended in my life and I was in the 8th grade. This is why we all got suspended. We were walking to school the day before our suspension when a bus full of kids rode by and began to throw rocks and apples outside the window hitting all of us, so the next day we were all perpared for the battle. When a bus rode by we all threw rocks and bricks at the bus when we heard the bus window break. turned out we bricked the wrong bus and glass got into a girl's eye and the security had watched the whole sceneral. In the first housr of school I heard my name being called on the intercome to come to the office. I was in big trouble and I got suspended. We bricked the wrong Bus and hit and innocent girl. I was mad because I wanted that bus who bricked us and turned out the the bus we got hit by was a bus full of Wyanditte High School kids. We all got suspended for 5 days and almost had to have our parents and guardians responsible for the girls doctor bills. I felt bad for the little girl because she didn't do anything to hurt me. I was mad, bad and rebellious. this was going to be rough year I thought, not to mention someone got beat with a hammer before school that was one of my classmates in school who did the beating so I knew that I was going to be dealing with a rough group of children. I met a couple of good friends this year in school male and female. I also had my eyes set on a new boy a

"Fat boy who was the big class clown" named DeShawn. I liked his smile the most and that's what attracted me to him. One day we were all in class and everyone started choking and I began to choke and almost had an asthma attack. DeSawn had sprayed mase and it had everyone choking. This was when I met Candy. Candy would always laugh at DeShawn's jokes but I didn't find this mase thing funny at all and Candy was a little to jokeable when it came to DeShawn. Candy sat next to Deshawn and she would always wear this bright red lipstick. We ended up moving houses again but we were in the same school district. Candy was in the same walking distance as I was so we began to walk home from school together. Candy was the complete opposite of me. Candy was light skinned, and petite. I was dark skinned and thick. But, for some reason ALL THE BOYS would follow Candy and I. Candy began to walk to my house sometime after school and I would also walk to her house sometimes. Candy and I got a thrill of all the attention that we were getting while we were together so we started dressing alike. Fee started letting me go to the Clubs with her. I went to real adult clubs on late nights. I would get into clubs like The Motorcycle Club "Black Angles", 20 Men. Although I was in middle school I didn't ever get carded Fee always got carded. Fee would put makeup on my face and it would make me look older than my real age and I had a body like a grown woman wearing a size 13 in women. Free got a kick out of the older men trying to holler at me. Carol and Chris would also go on occasion with Fee and I. They say "Birds Of A Feather Flock Together" Carol had some hidden secrets as well that were about to surface.

CHAPTER
18
....

WHEN IT RAINS IT POURS

THEA AND I started becoming real close and began to open up to one another. Thea had a shocking *Real Life disturbing Story* of her own. *Sad Truth* but, Thea told me how her and her siblings had just before they met us recently gotten out of foster homes and Carol had just recently gotten custody back of her children. I couldn't believe my ears because Carol seemed like a normal woman with a normal family just slightly on the weird side but normal. Carol didn't appear to be on any type of drugs Carol was a heavyset woman that was nice looking to be heavy and she seemed to be nice. Fee would tease me saying that I was giong to have cellulite like Carol if I didn't slow my eating down (bitch I eat so much to clam my STRESS LEVEL that your inflicting)-is what I thought when Fee would say fucked up shit to me trying to emotionally destroy me. Anyhow, Carol was hardworking and normal from what my eyes could see so I couldn't understand why was Thea just now getting out of Foster Homes. I asked Thea, "Thea, why were you in a Foster Home?" Thea gave me specific details about her life and what had happened to her SO SEE PEOPLE

99

THIS STUFF IF REAL LIFE WAKE UP!. Thea told me how her own flesh and blood BIOLOGICAL father child molested her very frequeltly and how he would make her perform oral sex on him occasionaly. Carol wouldn't divorce Thea's father once Thea's story came out so SRS took Thea and her siblings, finally Carol decided to divorce her husband Thea's dad and Carol got her children back. Carol woul not divorce her husband and was sexually abusing her own his own children even after the FACTS. Now how interesting is that "Birds Of A Feather Flock Together" Thea had endured years of being sexually abused by her own biological father and her own blood mother wouldn't leave thier father for the sake of her own children NOW HOW CRAZY. This is "My Story" but Thea's Story plays apart in my life so I can't dwell on Thea's Story as Thea has a strong STORY to tell that is all so real. POW a bullet was fired because I told Thea "My Story" about what Fee or Bone was doing to me and I told Thea everything. Thea's Story inspired me and made me love her even more and not judge her for what she had done with Scooby because Thea had a strong Story behind her. Thea couldn't believe her ears once she heard "my Story". I told Thea that I did indeed want to get away from Fee but I didn't want to have to go to a Faster Home away from my siblings. Thea assured me that she would tell her mom only to try to seek me some help. I told Thea not to tell her mom because her mom and Fee was friends and to just let me figure it out but Thea didn't listen to me and she told her mom anyways. Several days later here we go, Carol and Fee set up a huge family meeting where Fee sat right there in my face. I denied telling Thea that because I knew that Carol had gone about the situation in the wrong manner but I was somehow glad because Fee aslo knew that I would expose her ass at any given time and I wasen't playing anymore. At the end of the day I knew that I had to go home and face Fee and she was definitly going to be a bitch. I didn't care if she acted like a bitch just as long as she didn't try to put her hands on me. It's hard for me to tell you these strange details about my life but it's me and I started to change becoming rebellious. I did things that I to were ashamed of being that it was done to me but it's the harsh reality of life. I ask my little cousins for forgivness because I would sometimes watch as they began to hump one another along with fight one another. I know that I raised my little cousins rough but I was also raised rough and I didn't know how to deal with my anger and for that I apologize to each and every one of them on the Gooding side because I love all of them even Fee after she let harm come my way and NOT apologize to me. I took my anger out on Fee's children instead of taking my anger out on Fee and I apologize. I started to see my faults and it mad me began to protect my little cousins just as if they were my siblings. I showered them with some love to fight good against evil. I didn't want to be anything like Fee or Bone and I wanted the best for my little cousins I would protect them something that Fee didn't show me. I'm a prayer warrior and I began to fight those evil demonic forces with Good doing towards the ones hurting me.

19

....

WHEN IT RAINS IT POURS

WE ENDED UP moving once again but in the same school district. the home that we moved into was owned by one of Fee's flings so he rented the house to Fee. Our landlords name was Mr. M. Mr. M had a son that was fine as wine. He was looked mixed very light skinned with natural curly hair and I caught Mr. M's sons attention and he caught mine as well. Mr. M's son would come over and visit me from time to time and I remained a vergin (In my Eyes). I would have to walk a longer distance in order to get to school but I was so glad that we didn't have to switch into a whole other school district this time. Candy and I became really close and she didn't live to far from me but Candy would always say that I lived so far away. Candy and I continued our walks home from school with one another and we started getting close. Candy had a big family like mine only they were all brothers and sister. Candy had one sister and 5 brothers so there was 7 of them and Candy was the oldest child like myself. Candy had two younger siblings around Rico's age and we would all walk home from school with one another in a group of us. Candy always made sure that we had matching shirts so we dressed alike and she became my bestfriend. Fee would not ever let me spend the night over Candy's house and Candy would have to help me clean up my whole house in order to for me to be able to go down to her house. Candy would spend the night over my house ever blue moon because Candy always had to watch over her younger siblings just like I had to always watch over my younger siblings and little cousins. Candy soon became my confidant because I knew that she saw my frustrations. I confided in Candy and told her everything that was going on in my life and I told Candy the truth. Candy also confided in me about her situations. Candy felt like I did because she had to be so responsible, babysitting and not getting the chance to be a child so Candy and I found positive activities to do with our younger siblings. We found fun things to do like "Make Plays" and act out scene's. Since there were so many of us children we could split up into groups of two and have some very interesting Play's going on. We would also do talent show's and singing contest. Sometimes we would also have Beauty Padgents and Make up Dance Routines. Fee would always feel free to talk to Candy and I about things like "Sucking Dick" but Candy knew that Fee was "Sick" so we laughed it off and voweled to not EVER SUCK A DICK, like Fee until we were married with children. We tried ignoring Fee but Fee was always up for volenteering a sexual conversation. I took a liking to "Queen Latifah"—(You Don't Know Me From A Can Of Paint) and U.N.I.T.Y. I was Thick and Fiesty with a bad attitude. Candy and I began to notice the sexual changes in our bodies and all the boys at Northwest started *flocking to us*. We had a couple of boys who would harass us everysingle day on the walk home so we began to *Crack Jokes* on the boy for our own entertainment. We used to call one of the boys *Copper tooth*. Copper Tooth has changed for the better though. One boy would actually follow me home and harass me and he happened to be the *popular Boy* that all of the other girls really liked because he was in middle school with gold teeth in his mouth but (I didn't have an interest) I didn't see him like the other girls did and I didn't particularly like dark skinned boys although Buddy was dark skinned but it was something about Buddy. Candy and I met a couple of friends in Candy's neighborhood one name Tara and one named Breayi and we would sometimes go over thier houses. Candy and I did everything we could in order to stay away from our own homes and the things that were going on in our homes so we met friends with nice houses that we could have relaxing teenage girl fun. I began to have a Crush on the *Class Clown* DeShawn and DeShawn didn't live to far from Candy and I. DeShawn lived on 15th so, I would persuade Candy to walk with me to DeShawns house with me from time to time. Candy and I would make dance routine up off groups like TLC "Creep". I was a big dancer and I became good at dancing. Fee would teach me new dances like "The Perculator" and I became good at doing the splits. I learned how to do the splits and bounce and twerk with it. Fee also knew how to dance so she kept me up to date on all the grown up dance moves. I had a Big love for Dance In Me. One night Candy and I managed to sneak to a Party that was being thrown at a recreational Center for teens so Candy and I went and we dressed alike. They Played songs like "If There's A Blue Bird On My Shoulder" Candy and I were the life of the Party as we danced wild and Sexy all night. Candy liked Red and I liked Blue so we were "Set Trippen". The party was hype as they played artist like DJ Quick, E40, Ice Cube, Master P, Hot Boys, T Pac all of the Hip Hop artist. We had so much fun and "All Eyes Were On Us". Candy and I knew then that we knew how to turn up the Party and I started getting really curious about having sex. Candy and I would talk about getting our virginities taken and how we wanted to be together when we did it so that we could have our first experience together. I definitly noticed that I was catching the eyes of many different boys but I had my Crush and that was Deshawn *The Class Clown*. I was mad at Buddy because I had heard about him threw the streets and several different females who were dating him. I also met a boy at the swimming pool "Parkwood" and he had "Pretty Brown eyes that had caught my attention. I almost gave this boy my verginity but I didn't I wanted to be cautious and make sure that it was the right timing. Since Buddy moved on, I moved on. Maybe Fee knew a little something about these lil nappy head boy's is what I thought. I would talk Candy into going to Deshawns house with me frequenlty. Candy and one of DeShawns boys started getting close to one another. One day was the right day so I let Deshawn take my verginity while Candy has Deshawn's friend occupied. candy and I planned to both have our verginity taken on this day but Candy reigned on me. I thought that Candy was actually letting DeShawn's Friend so I actually really let Deshawn and it hurted so bad. DeShawn was working with a nice package to be a *Big Boy* I had to get on top in order for him to enter me and it was so painful. I got a thrill because I knew how to ride a dick like a pro. DeShawn busted my Cherry because I bled a little after sex with DeShawn and I was definitly not going to tell Fee's noisy ass what I had done it was non of Fee's business. It became a thrill to me so Deshawn and I had sex several times after that. Fee must have smelled the sex on me because she quickly became aware of my plans. I felt like my business was none of Fee's business and I had lost all respect for Fee. Fee's baby looked at me like I was his mother because I always had him on my hip and my side. I fed Fee's son, clothed him and bathed him. When I went places I would have Fee's son with me so much that people questioned if he was my son. during this time my grandpa had finally moved back into town. I could always tell that my grandfather was still mourning over my grandma. I could see it in my grandfathers eyes. My grandfather had been drinking so much alcohol and I could tell because one day my grandpa was so drunk he fell right in front of me. I know that something was bothering grandpa because he would not ever let me see him in this condition. My grandpa was a nice looking man he was half blooded Indian with green eyes and his mom was full blooded Indian so, I knew and felt my grandpa's pain. grandpa went to the doctor after that fall and the doctor told him that he couldn't drink anymore that he has Surosis of the Liver due to drinking and if he drunk any more liquor that it would kill him. I spent the night ove Keeda, BeBe and Tya's house one day, the next morning we all got a disturbing phone call. I broke down crying ALL of us kids broke down crying my grandpa had taken his very last drink. Grandpa was heartbroken because my grandma was no longer here the family was seperated and I saw and felt my grandfathers pain. I wish that I could have helped my grandpa. My Grandpa was the provider a STRONG man who had taken GREAT care of his family all until Grandma passed, I wanted to keep this secret about Fee and Bone because I don't like to see my family hurting. BeBe and I became alot closer and we would talk about having sex with boys. one day I snuck this boy that I had a crush on into BeBe's house while BeBe's mom was gone and I had sex with him in my cousins basement. It hurt even worse than sex with DeShawn I had a full set of nails on when I started and when I finished I was missing a whole 5 nails. I got an even bigger thrill but I had worse things on my plate and a sad Funeral coming up. We had to plan a funeral. Aaron Hall came with a song called "I Miss You" and memories of my grandma began to surface now my loving grandpa drank himself to death mourning over grandma. Fee's boyfriend Dame had a group of friends who made music and could sing thier hearts out when combined together. Fee also had a gift in music. BeBe and I both became rebellious and we would sneak drinks out from her momma's Bar at home. BeBe's mom was a *Hustla* and the first time I ever saw an actual BRICK it was over my auntie's House. I began to connect with my brother Tommy Gunn on my dad's side of our family when BAMN another move and another change was about to happen. I was hit with the news very shortly after grandpa passed away. Uncle Mick was taking Rico, Poody and I because momma was back in Prison and we were moving to North Carolina where they were going to Bury Grandpa. they were taking Grandpa's body back to Washinghton NC after is Wake. Being that my Grandpa was going to be buried in North Carolina Rico, Poody Unlce Mick and I got packed and ready to attend a funeral also looking for a place to move in North Carolina. Momma was transported in shackles to the Wake for grandpa and I remember when they brought momma in the Funeral Home. We had a long bus ride to North Carolina but we got to ride threw New York and I got a chance to see the Statue Of Liberty so I was excited. Besides us traveling to Mississippi with Filthy Ricky, I hadn't been outside of Kansas and I had a lot of daily in North Carolina that I knew nothing about. Uncle Mick seemed different. I wondered why he was taking us away like that from Fee. I was excited to be getting away from Fee but I had Candy and Deshawn in my life my bestfriend and my boyfriend. I started to Pray to God that I got pregnat by DeShawn so I wouldn't have to leave Kansas. Uncle Mick was very persistant on getting us away from Fee. I was confused and sick and tired of moving every year for the past 6 or 7 years I have been moving somewhere new every single year. My big brother Tommy Gunn was now in contacft with us. I just wanted to make sure me, Rico and Poody were all together. I had also had a baby that I had been raising since his birth. It was alot I didn't want to leave Lil D he was like my own son and Deshawn, how would Deshawn take the news and my bestfriend. My grandpa died and now we had to move out of town. I needed some stability and things were far from stable.

CHAPTER
20
····

When It Rains It Pours
But Be Prepared For The Flood

THIS WOULD BE a new year 'I told myself). no, Fee, I'm in a different state and I'm still with my siblings. Uncle Mick had us our own home waiting on us, not to mention that Uncle Mick was coming out about his sexuality. I didn't care about Uncle Mick's sexuality and I remain to look at him the same but this explained alot. This was the reason I never seen Uncle Mick with a girlfriend. This was why he didn't have kids. I wouldn't have known Uncle Mick was gay unless I paid close attention. I was older now going into high school Uncle Mick never engaged in any hugging, kissing, or sexual activites with male or female around us kids I guess it was just intuition or *friends of Uncle Mick's* like one of them were manly but him and Uncle Mick would be closed up in one room together too long and if they weren't doing drugs they were doing something. I got the chance to meet two of my females cousins and we became close(I still keep in touch with them on facebook). One of my cousins' Cheeka, we would play double dutch(Jump Rope) together. I quickly became popular in lil

N.C. and I grew close to two female friends one was white and black(I'm not racist) Me and my two friends' keep intouch. One's name is (Berta the white girl) and (Tiff the black girl). I spent more time with Tiff because she lived close by me. Me and Tiff would go to the store and steal us matching outfits so that we could dress alike. Me and Candy lost contact. I became very popular with the boys' and one night I snuck out the house and took Poody with me so that she wouldn't tell Uncle Mick on me. We went to this Beach Party. In North Carolina they listen to alot of East Coast music artist like 'Biggie Smalls, Craig Mack, Method Man, ODB, Dog Pound, Lil Kim, and things like that (Sugar Hill Soundtrack) we had alot of fun that night, but when I got home about 2 am and tried climbing thru the window Uncle Mick was right there waiting on me. I always got into trouble in NC again I had grew rebellious and I liked to have sex and smoke weed. Fee had given me all these bad habit. Uncle Mick tried to sign me up for finacial assitance due my asthma and Fee was so mad at Uncle Mick for taking us that she lied to SSI about the severity of my asthma. Things were getting bad Uncle Mick was always at work so I would sneak neighborhood kids in the house, I would have sex on abandoned school buses, on my back porch, on the bench in the backyard. I was having sex with multiple boys' some protected and some weren't. I started picking up alot of female enemies and that's when I started to have really bad serious fights. I was known for fighting and Tiff would sometimes be right there fighting with me. I was becoming completely out of control for Uncle Mick and not to mention I had been awaken out of my sleep several nights by unknown intities. It happend on three different occasions over a 4-month period. The first I remember cleary I was in a blank sleep when something would tell me to open my eyes. When I opened my eyes there by my dresser stood a black figure of a female staring at me. I only say the complete figure of this girl. I would put the covers over my head and began to Pray (I rebuke you Satan in the name of Jesus). When I pulled my head out of the covers (heart pounding) the figure of the girl was gone. The second time it happend it was almost the same thing it was in the middle of the night I was in a blank, sound sleep when something told me to open my eyes. When I opened my eyes this time it was a little boy running toward me as if he were going to jump on me. 'It sounded like he was giggling'. I put the covers over my head quickly and began to pray. The third time it was different in a way although it was in the middle of the night and I was in a blank soundless sleep. Me and Poody shared rooms, Rico had his own room and so did Uncle Mick. This time when something told me to open my eyes I saw shadows 3 or 4 shadows flying over Poody while she slept. I was so scared But I didn't no how to tell Uncle Mick what was happening. All that I could do was Pray to God that Me, Rico, and Poody got sent back to Kansas, and if not with Fee with another family member. I wanted to talk to Uncle Mick about what Fee had done to me but I still didn't know how or who I could talk to. Momma would get the chance to call from time to time and I would talk to her but I didn't feel close enough to tell her how I truely felt plus I was mad at momma because if she was there none of this mess would have happened (or would it because it almost happend with Filthy Ricky). I was in so much stress that I continued to smoke. There was a little boy who came over to my house and he wanted me to try some of this weed called *chocolate Tied* he rolled it and I smoked it. I was so high and scared that I thought that I was going to die. I never felt so high in my life. Rico was so mad at me I couldn't even cook dinner that night I was so high that Rico had to cook. Uncle Mick made me a doctor's appointment because he found out that I had been sexually active and damn I didn't know it but I had a sexually transmitted disease called 'gonorrhoea'. I knew who had given it to me. It was this attractive boy. Tiff knew about him and told me that he was known for *burning girls* I didn't want to listen. I was promiscuous and I had to bump my own head. Uncle Mick was becoming very frustrated with me and the last straw was when I got caught stealing at Walmart. I had over $300 dollars worth of clothes that Uncle Mick had to payback and that was it Uncle Mick was fed up not to mention all the holes in the walls at home, the broken windows. All because I had fights with about 10 kids in 10 months. We stayed in NC with Uncle Mick when enough was enough and he sent us back to Kansas. I was happy, I thought that we were going back to Fee where I could be grown. (Fee treated me like I was an adult). But was I in for a big surprise. That year I was so bad, even in school and I didn't pass the 9th grade. I continued making dance routines I had one to 'Let Me Ride That Donkey'. I love my cousins in North Carolina and my favortie two were Cheeka and Shelly. I spent more time with Cheeka and she had told me that one of the guys that I had became involed with was possibly our cousin and that was crazy but I had friends fast up there in North Carolina and I had to stop with all these boys beause one might be a cousin and I'm definiltly not another Fee. I was just living my life. Those spirits were scary and I witnessed them with my own two eyes now I know for facts that there was another life out there that I knew nothing about and Spirits and Intities are real.

CHAPTER
21
....

**WHEN IT RAINS IT POURS
BUT BE PREPARED FOR THE FLOOD**

I WAITED AT the Airport not knowing what was ahead of me. We had usually taken the Bus and this time something was different. I was sad because I had met my cousins and seen their faces, they were my family. Not to mention the fights that Tiff and I had together she was most definitly my rider and I built bonds. I had to leave Tiff all alone to fight the battles that we had in play and I most definilty wasn't a runner. I couldn't believe Uncle Mick! He was actually sending us back to Kansas and he wasn't coming along with us. Uncle Mick had drove us to the Airport and left us not telling us anything. when we got off that plane we were greated by an SRS lady who remembers me until this day because I had Lot's of questions for her and I wanted answers. I knew in my heart that we were going to a Foster Home and I wanted to take my siblings and RUN. Now matter how nice that SRS lady tried to be I was fueled with anger. I began to cry for the first time in a long time I cried. All the bullshit I had endured to keep me and my siblings together my own Uncle. I kept saying to myself that Uncle Mick should have just left us with Fee threw the struggle at least we were together. I knew that we were going to be seperated. This year I was going to be a BEAST just because I DIDN'T GIVE A FUCK ANYMORE. I was going to REBEL and didn't care who liked it because at this point I was hurt and felt like I didn't mean nothing to anyone. I felt like God didn't hear me so I was going to make him hear me. I knew that a Foster mom wasn't going to genuinly love me for me so I had FUEL TO MY FIRE. I wasen't going to show NO LOVE all my LOVE WAS LOST. I had lost about 30–40 lbs and I was looking great but I felt a MESS. I was like a flower who began to blossom and I would make sure to live my life the way I wanted to no matter who liked it. I was about to ruffle some feathers and I was going to go to war behind my siblings. I looked at that SRS lady and told her that she better be lucky if I didn't RUN. The K is My Turf and If I Don't Like Something IMMA STAND UP!

CHAPTER
22
....

When It Rains It Pours

RICO, POODY AND I were now in Foster homes. Turned out Poody and I foster parents were mother and daughter so Poody and I would be able to be close by. Rico's foster mom ended up being a white lady that had all boys and she seemed to be a nice woman, I liked Rico's foster mom, Rico wasn't placed to far from me so we were going to be able to go to the same High School High. I didn't pass the 9th grade because I acted out badly and the studies in North Carolina were different like we actually studied the real story behind "Bloody Mary". Rico and I were going to be in the same grade this year but the school schedule didn't have Rico and I in the same classes. I would always look for Rico in the Hallways of High School because it was a big School. The Foster home that I was in consisted of about 6–10 girls all ranging in the ages of 13–18. I was 15 years old and I got along well with most of my Foster sisters but thier were some that we didn't quite click together. I took a liking to 3 of them in particular and thier names were Downy, KeyShawn, LaShawn and sometimes Tierra, ATL, and Tionna. ATL and I didn't always get along. Our Foster mom's name was Mrs. Jenie and I don't think that Mrs. Jenie liked me to well. Mrs. Jenie would tell the other girls that I was a "Dirty Leg" because of the way I dressed I guess so I kept my distance from Mrs. Jenie and again I don't think she liked me. I knew Mrs. Jenie was only in it for the money she looked like that kind of lady but she also looked like a well kept and knowledgeable lady. Mrs. Jenie had raised her daughters very well. Downey had her own car that Mrs. Jenie had helped her get so I would always ride to school with Downey. Downey also had a job and I wondered how was Downey working because of her age. Downey and I were the same age I had just flunked 9th grade. Downey was only in the 10th grade so how was Downey working at Wendy's? You have to be 16 to work. Mrs. Jenie was altering peoples Social Security Card or something in order to get the girls jobs at early ages. I analyze and pick up on things pretty quick especially when I need clothes and shoes myself. I knew that something fishy was going on in Mrs. Jenie's home while she had the nerve to lable me calling me a *Dirty Leg* she was doing Dirt of her own. Mrs. Jenie didn't want to be responsible for clothes and shoes she wanted you to work for your stuff because the little money the State was giving us for clothing and shoes was not enough. Mrs. Jenie altered things so that you could fend for yourself. I didn't like that idea so for me it was going to be back to stealing my clothing to get by. One day I was looking threw on of ATL's book of Obiturauies and I saw a real close friend of mine. It was Fee's daughters uncle Billy R.I.P Billy. Billy was a few years older than me, he can't be dead is what I thought! What happened while I was gone? I felt confused so I confirmed with ATL if this was indeed a real Obiturary and she confirmed to me that Billy had indeed died in a fatal car accident. Billy was still in high school. I became so sad for Billy because I had just recently lived close by Billy before moving to North Carolina. My heart jumped out of my chest it felt like as I read threw Billy's Obiturary. I had only been gone away for 10 mths. and this happened. When ATL told me Billy's Story I almost cried. Billy was driving fast an hit a tree, his insides came out of his body due to the impact of the car accident.

I was floored (Shocked) and hurt all at the same time. I couldn't wait to talk to Fee to see what had happened to Billy. Fee was working on getting me back into her custody and she blamed Uncle Mick for taking us. Fee said that Uncle Mick shouldn't have ever taken us like that. But little did I know that Uncle Mick took us because of his suspensions of me being molested. Why didn't Uncle Mick just talk to me I would have told him everything because I trusted him? I didn't want to go back to live with Fee but I didn't want to have to live in this Foster Home. I wanted to be with my siblings though. This was when I also found out that my friend Mike was dead and gone but not forgotten R.I.P Mike. I needed to smoke some weed to clear my mind from all of this terrible news. I would go on visits to Fee's house. One day on a visit to Fee's my Uncle O.G gave me a couple of joints to smoke and they were mixed with HASH. I saved those joints and one day while Downy and I were on our way to school I smoked one of those joints with her. Downy and I would usually smoke together on our way to school but this joint uncle O.G gave me was something different. We were both high as fuck when we made it to school our eyes were red and one of our friends who became close to us he always knew when we had been smoking he blurted it out "Ya'll High then A mutha fucka". Jared was his name and Jared was loud and attractive. Jared would always be waiting on Downey and I so he could crack jokes. Jared had a crush on me and I had a crush on Jared. Some times Jared and I would take our jokes way to far. I would see an ugly girl coming down the hall and I would stop her and say "Hey, My boy Jared said, What's Up? Can He get your number?" I didn't like being so mean sometimes because I knew how it felt to be teased, now I kind of felt like I was bullying and I couldn't be *The Bully*. One day our joking almost took a turn for the worse and I almost had to fight the girl which I didn't hesitate to fight at this point but it was all jokes and the one getting joked didn't find things so funny. One not so cute girl came walking and as usual I tapped her to tell her that Jared liked her when the girl got really mad at me and almost wanted to fight me. I learned my lesson and I brought all the joking to a minimum. I had mad several friends at Wyandotte not to mention Candy also went to Wyandotte. Candy and I had gotten back cool but it seemed like Candy hardly ever came to school. I got into the hang of skipping school. I would skip school, smoke weed, come back to school at lunch time and leave school again until the end of the day. Downey didn't skip school as much as I did she would skip every now and then. Downy and I had a few mutual friends one named Montai, and one named Kalisa. We would also hang out with Montai and smoke weed alot of times. We would also hang out over Kalisa's house alot. When we were at home at Mrs. Jenie's house I hung out more with KeyShawn. KeyShawn and I would walk to Fred's Store and Grocery alot. Everytime KeyShawn and I walked together we got plenty of attention from guys and some were grown men. One man in particular would always try to holler at me everytime he seen me and his name was "Yellow". Yellow Boy had plenty of females he was the neighborhood rapper. It was fun and I liked walking with KeyShawn getting that attention. I had a couple of different boys that I started being sexually attracted to and it became a game I had 3 Kevs. One Kev I would have sex with after school and we would turn all the way up and I would fuck him and some of his boys but he liked me on the other hand and we would talk about having a baby. I got tired of his friends lusting over me like some stray dogs so I brought my girl KeyShawn along to help me tame the boys. The other Kevin was my boyfriend at school Kevin but he would pick me up after school while he hustled and we would vibe toghether listening to Master P and we also would talk about making a baby together. The other Kevin lived across the street from Fast Freds so I caught him when I felt that thrill and wasen't occupied. I began to pick back up my relationship with Deshawn so we also started our sexual relationship back up an Deshawn would pull up at that Foster home with his Best friend Philly and they would pick me and Keshawn up. Philly was Deshwans bestfriend and I had known Philly threw Deshawn. Philly kept a Clean Monte Carlo with beat, Hydrolics and he went to Schlagle High

School. KeyShawn and I liked going with Philly and Deshawn. I liked smoking weed and having sex. I was out of control and no one was going to stop me. I was finally getting a chance to have fun and enjoy my life and NO MORE BABYSITTING. KeyShawn smoked weed with me but this day the weed felt different and I was beyond high. I had found out that Philly and DeShawn had been lacing our blunts with "Wet, PCP". Key-shawn and I were so high that we just wanted to go home. We didn't want to hang out with Deshawn or Philly. I started staying away from home more than normal. I liked hanging with one of the Kevs in particular because he was about his money we called him K.D. K.D became my boyfriend and he "Made The Money". K.D would pull up on me with some of his homies and we would get hotel rooms or be at smoker houses. K.D was my new thang until one day at school K.D got on some real dis-rtspectful shit right in front of me. I wanted to snap and beat some ass when I saw another chick all on K.D kissing him. I knew from that day that I had to keep it G. I was not going to be the mistress or a side chick. Boys weren't loyal and I most definilty was going to get my thrill and bounce to the next and let them bounce to the homegirl definilty not a hater. Buddy made his way back into the picture and this time I was ready for Buddy. I had waited for Buddy for years and when we finally had sex it was worth the wait. Buddy had a big one and he knew how to use it. I looked past the pain and I wanted to give Buddy a ride that he would never forget. I wanted to show Buddy what I had learned and what he had been missing, what he couldn't be patient and wait on. I wanted Buddy to know that I really did indeed love him and that I was going threw some things of my own. I wasen't ready for sex when I had Buddy but now I was more than ready. Bebe and I would make bets as to who can smash the most boys. i thought that BeBe was going to be lasbian but she actually talked to me about fucking and we made bets. I was keeping my bets however I think that Bebe was just lying about what she was doing. I was always truthful about my acts and had had several, many different boys, I was rebellious and didn't care about what people thought about me only God can Judge me. My family didn't care about me so I thought so I was going to do what the fuck I wanted to do. I remained mad at DeShawn for lacing my blunts. One of Buddies cousins started coming around me and his name was Mel. Mel would be high on PCP when he came around and one day he did something that almost got me in deep trouble. Mel came over one day high off PCP he knocked on Mrs. Jenie's door and I opened the door for him. Mel busted all up in Mrs. Jenies's home with his dick on hard and began to hump the air and put a condom on. I tried to get Mel out of Mrs. Jenies home when Mrs. Jenie's daughter that is a Sheriff pulled right up in the driveway, out the car and walked right in on what Mel was doing. I was so furious because Mel and I hadn't ever had sex prior to this so why did he act like this knowing that I was fucking his cousin Buddy? I knew that Mrs. Jenie didn't care for me to much and she had this big pretty home and now this bull crap. I tried to assure Mrs. Jeanie's daughter that I wasen't doing anything wrong it just looked bad. Mel had his dick all out with a condom on it but I was fully dressed so thank God Mrs; Jenie daughter looked at the evidence first. I didn't want to get into any trouble with Mrs. Jenie althught I didn't want to be there anyways. Mrs. Jenies daughter (Shay) made Mel put his dick back in his pants and get out of that house. I thought that she was going to tall on me but she did not tell. I was relieved because I actually didn't do any wrong doing in Mrs. Jenie's home but after that I was curious. I began to bribe Downey out of the alarm code to Mrs. Jenie's house. Mrs. Jenie trusted Downey not me. So, I decided that I was indeed going to skip school and have sex in Mrs. Jenie's house because I was tired of Mrs. Jenie referring to me as a *Dirty Leg* heck I didn't know what a *Dirty Leg* but I was gonna show her a Dirty Leg. Downy finally gave me the alarm code and I put my plan to skip school into motion. I snuck one of Deshawns boys in from school and had sex with him right in Mrs. Jenie's home. I eventually snuck Mel back in there to and he got the bidness. I knew that I was digging myself a whole but I didn't care at this point. I didn't like being judged by people so I acted out. Instead of judging someone you should first get to know that person. I felt like Mrs. Jeanie didn't love me she judged me the very day that I walked in her door. Some foster parents be all about that "Ol Mighty Dollar". Even though I was a young teenage girl I did pick up on vibes and when someone did not like me so instead of being quiet I acted out. I would sympathize with the other girls about thier situations. We would watch movies like "Waiting To Exhale" or "Sparkle" and it was shows like that, that got us by and passed time. I didn't like SRS because it was all about money and not genuinely about the best interest of the child. Some of the girls would tell me thier stories about how they didn't get molested until they went into the Foster homes and it was sad. It was like you take a child from a bad situation but you put them in a worse situation. SHOUT OUT TO THE MOVIE MAKERS OF "Beaches 2016" I've heard some horrible stories with the girls in the Foster Homes. Maybe I could have a "Talk Show" to touch on some of these sensitive subjects. They take what's in the dark and try to sweep it up under the rug, just call me your "Clean Up Gal", I'm going up under that old dirty rug and cleaning some things out. I have become a good fighter due to all of my altercations growing up. People knew me and very few tested my temper. One day Candy called me out of the clear blue because thier was a group of girls outside of her grandma's house in The Projects trying to fight her and her friend. Candy and her auntie Q pulled up on me and picked me up so that I could come and help them fight. When I pulled up all the females who were gathered around ready to fight knew me and everybody backed up off of Candy's grandma's house and backed up off of Candy and her friend. Candy's auntie Q was amazed at the crowds reaction once they pulled up with me. "I heard someone in the crowd say, DON'T GET QUIET NOW". Wasen't you bitches just talking shit! Now who came to fight who. Lady Bug is here and I'm with my team now who wants to fight? It was so funny to me because I didn't know that I made such an impact on people. At that point I became even closer to Candy and her family. that night I went back to that Foster home knowing that my time there was going to end fast. After that, I knew that Rico was getting moved all the way to Leavenworth KS and I knew that my behavior would get even worse because he was like my son. My bay bro and I didn't play when it came to my siblings. I started getting closer to Candy. candy would have parties at her moms house. I always looked up to Candy's mom because she always wore cute little clothing, she had a banging body and always had a dude with a TIGHT ride. I found out that Candy had also lost her verginity. Not only did Candy lose her verginity Candy was pregnant and I could not believe my ears. I started having a sexual relationship with Candy's older brother Mackie. I had wondered why Candy hadn't been coming to school. I started to pray to God for me a baby and I wanted a baby with DeShawn because he had taken my verginity. One day after school I went to see Candy and she had given birth to her baby and I had to be around my BestFriend. Candy had a BEAUTI-FUL baby girl, when I held Candy's baby she made my heart melt because she was so beautiful. Candy and I had alot of catching up to do.

CHAPTER
23
. . . .

WHEN IT RAINS IT POURS

AFTER THEY MOVED Rico far way far away from I really didn't have a sense of understanding. Rico was my baby brother, I raised him basically because mama wasnt ever at home. I got moved into a girls home because I couldn't tolerate being called anyone's dirty leg. The girls home that I was in consisted of about 10 girls diiferent color, religions, Ect. I made friends with alot of the girls there. Some of the staff members were easy for me to get along with. This was actually better for me I didnt have someone looking down on me or judging me. I missed my brother and sister so much though. I made friends with alot of the girls there some of us called ourselves sisters. We had to do things in order to keep ourselves busy so we did things like make dance routines. I loved dancing and was good at it so I orchistrated alot of our dance routines. I choose a group of girls around 3 or 4 other girls who could dance good and we would always dance, sing and laugh just to keep ourselves doing something positve. I still had the urge to smoke weed so I would sneak and find a way to get weed. I went to the same high school so I had alot of the same friends. Us girls always found girly things to do to keep ourselves looking good and up with the latest trends. Growing up in group homes we didnt have alot of money to spend so we had to improvise. We learned how to do french manicures and even full sets of nails on each other nails. I knew how to do hair good because Fee had taught me alot when I was there with her and not only that Fee was fighting to get me back in her custody. I would go over Fee house sometime on the weekend. I knew that although Fee was messed up in the head that she loved me and I was her little cousin and she was still trying to help me out. Fee knew I hated being away from Rico and Poody. I even think at some point she may have regreted what she had put me threw but I had to figure out how I could get out of the system and get my life together. I wanted to be grown so I didnt have to deal with certain things. I wanted kids of my own so I could build a life of my own. I knew that I was going to act until I got my own way. We would get bored and play Demonic Games like 'Light as a feather stiff as a board'. We would try to get people to float in the air with our minds Instead of playing "Bloody Mary" in the mirror we would call "Lucifer". Some of the white girls didnt believe in God they believed in 'Black Magic' or whatever it was. I always kept my christian belief I knew deamons were real because I had saw spirits in North Carolina so I didnt like playing with the dark side, I aways used percaution. We also dicovered 'The Pass Out Game.' I would make some girls 'Pass out' but things started getting really serious and scary. Girls started acting possessed by deamons spirits. I got scared so I left that game alone. I rememberd playing with the "Ouji board" with Fee sometimes but again I wasnt into the Black Magic. I knew that demons are real and I didnt want to play around with that too much, I was rebellious but not stupid, although I acted out fighting alot and smoking weed. Someone told that I was smoking weed because I started having to drop random drug tests. I also knew how to outsmart a drug test. I started plotting ways that I was going to run away. I was getting older and I didnt want to be in any group homes until I was 18. I had a mind of my own and one way or the other I was going to get Fee from SRS. One night me and three other girls that were my friends there were Annie, Shalissa and Lacreasha a friend we planned on sneaking out of the group home just to get away for a little while. We weren't going to run away we just wanted to sneak out. So we planned. We knew what times the staff would come to check on us in the middle of the night so we all put clothing in our beds to make it look like we were in our bed sleeping and we climbed out the window. Once we escaped it was like a breath of fresh air. It was late at night and we all managed to sneak out the group home. None of us had a plan but me I was the mastermind and I knew that we needed to steal a car to get wherever it was that we were going and just as we walked up a dark street I approached an old station wagon and when I looked in the window of the car the keys were right there. I couldnt believe my eyes. We all hopped in the car, I was the driver and we drove off into the dark night. We were excited we couldnt believe that we managed to get that far and now we didnt no where we wanted to go from there so bam, I ditched the car and called called my big cousin to pick us up and we went back and snuck into the girls home 'safe and sound.' It was a huge thrill, we all got away with it and didnt get caught now that was only the beginning. I knew that I could run away if I wanted too and that was going to be my next move because I had to get away from this group home. It was embarassing having a big white van drop me off for school in the morning. I had all this family but yet and still I felt like no one loved me "The Dark Child". I had people at school questioning, "why was I getting dropped off in that Van?". I didn't want any of my friends at school to know that I was in a group home, I refused to get bullied and thier were already girls at Wyandotte who were Bullies and who would try to slick bump you in the hallways. I knew how to fight and I was not scared to fight and would fight if i had to. I just wanted a normal life, a normal family and was that to much to ask for? I had grown to have a temper. They would always bring in a new girl that would get on my nerves and that's when the fight would be on. I wasn't going to take anyones shit. Sure enough I had my mind made up and that was I was going to fight for what I wanted in life. I wasn't going to let anyone come and steal what little bit I had, my happiness or my joy. I was going to always stand up for myself and fight. The nice young lady in me had been ripped away from me. I once was shy but I had quickly grown out of that shyness. My body had developed and I had a mind of my own that had developed along with my body. Staff tried to persuade me into having a breast reduction but DeShawn along with other male friends of mine said that I didn't need any type of reduction and that by boobs looked good the way they were. I wanted to be free from the SRS system because the system didn't love anyone and they were all about the money. I didn't want to be an asset to the system especially when I wasn't happy and I wasn't physically seeing any of the money from the system personally. I had to continue to steal my clothing in order to have decent clothing. The system wasn't helping me at all besides having a roof over my head and some type of food in my stomache. I didn't seem to be getting ahead in school and in my studies because I skipped school everyday. As soon as that big white van dropped me off in front of my High School, I would began my own journey for the day. I would skip school, smoke weed and have sex if I wanted to. DeShawn and I would have sex from time to time but I wasn't faithful to Deshawn because I didn't have trust for anyone and I wanted to have my fun. I didn't want to stay into school because I didn't have proper clothing, shoes or hair maintance. I wasn't secure so I would find ways to make myself feel secure. The Security at school began to know me by my name because they started to notice me skipping school almost every single day. The Security would began to call my name out loud if they caught me skipping but, I would laugh them off and continue my day. Security couldn't help me and I couldn't go and live with them in their big, nice houses. So, I did what I wanted to do and not what was expected out of me. Times were hard so I had to be tough. I didn't want to listen to anyone I wanted to learn from my own experience *Experience was always my best teacher*. I had to live my life for me and find a way to reunite with my siblings and at that point I didn't care about anything else but that. I also started taking a liking to some of the staff members in the Group Home, the ones who felt like family and that didn't treat me like a number (a dollar sign). You can always sense good people from bad ones. Time was beginning to get the best of me and I knew that it was a matter of time before SRS moved me into another place. Again, you never raelly know what kind of people you were going to come into contact with, some are good people and others are bad. Me being a Leo, I feel like a true Lioness in this Jungle so I was very territorial. I didn't mix so well with some people especially liars and loud mouths wether in school or at home it didn't matter you could not just make me fit in with everyone. I could get along well with most but being that I had developed a strong personality thier would always be one girl that would test my temper. when I got mad everything would go black and it was like a blackout, I would snap and attack at any point when need be. I wasen't a bully and I didn't like bullies. I was a straight forward person although I had my ways about me. I got into alot because I had always hung around the males and females would get mad at me about "Their Boyfriend". For instance, I had a friends boyfriend who liked me. I tried to resist my friends boyfriend but men also have thier ways around things and things happened. I ended up having my sex with one of my friends boyfriend at her house when everyone fell asleep. I tried to warn my friend about her boyfriend. My friend wasen't all the way 100 because she was sleeping with her own sisters boyfriend so I knew that if she wasn't REAL with her own sister, then how the fuck would she be able to keep it 100 with me. I confided in Downy about having sex with our mutual friends boyfriend and Downy went right back to our mutual friend and told her our little secret. I apologized to my friend and I admitted what I had done with her boyfriend, I most definitly wasn't a punk of any sort and I most definilty wasn't a liar. Although my friend was doing her own sister wrong I just didn't feel right for what I had done and we almost had a fight but I don't think that my ex friend really wanted to fight me. I didn't mix with females really well because I hung with the boys and the boys knew how to manipulate and sometimes things would happen that always weren't supposed to happen, that's why I say *Experience is the best teacher* and I was indeed in my learning points. I was also learning not to trust all females and some of the ones that you called your friend weren't really your friends. Downy was switching. Although I was far from perfect, I still knew how to be 100 and real no matter the situation I was not going to lie to someones face. I was going to be Real and Honest no matter the consequence and I'm still to this day that way and that's one thing that I have yet to notice in many people because now and days people lie to get by *fake it until they make it*. NOT ME I'm real to the core and if a person don't like it then they don't like me. I kept Downy as a friend they say "Keep your enemies close and watch your homies". Candy and I had sort of lost contact after she had the baby but I still considered her to be my Bestfriend. I ended up having a bad fight at the Group home and the police was called and I was taken to JIC which was Juvenile Intake Center where they kept me until they could find me somewhere else to live within the next couple of days. I was in JICV looking for a way to excape and breakout of there. The next couple of days I was sent to a different Girls Home and I wondered to myself what this experience would bring. I was going to be *The New Girl* all over again but at least again I was in the same School District. Getting moved from place to place wasn't seeming to be that bad because I started to become very popular and it seemed like when I went somewhere new all the girls were waiting on me to come like they had already heard all about me upon my arrival and some of them I had already known from pervious Foster or Group homes or maybe even school or just because Kansas City Wyandotte CO was small to me now and I mad myself known in the TOWN. I was cool once I had gotten situated in the new Girls home and the Staff members there were even better. One of my favorite Staff reminded me of a family member because she was so down to earth and her name was Earley. Early would ride us around the City in the Big White Van and I no longer felt embarrassed. We would have fun in the Big White van and I got to smoke weed on nice occassions. One day we were out in the Big White Van at a popular gas station when this FINE chocolate, sexy dark sinned dude with all CRUSH DIAMONDS in the front of his mouth started trying to hollar at me. He really wanted me and he gave me his cell phone number and when he smiled all those diamonds were shining like the snow and he was so sexy kind of like DMX in his younger days 'Belly" but better. I didn't know what this guy as FINE as he was has saw in me but he wanted me and I really digged his SWAG and the way that he approached me was very unforgettable so I took his name and number, they called him Damu. I had quickly found out that Damu had a wife who was one of our staff member who had happened to be one of my favorite Staff members that I looked up to whom had treated me like family. Again I had built relationships with people and staff and they would confide in me and tell me stories of thier lives. I really liked this particular Staff member named Sherie. Sherie had told me *Her Story* and I did not realize that her dude that she had always talked about was indeed Damu. Sherie had just lost her one year old baby due to a heart attack and Sherie kept all of her babies belongings after he passed in her trunk of her car. Sherie told me the story of how her baby passed away after he had been running a bad temperature before he went into a convulsion losing one of his shoes. I was appalled that Damu was infact the childs father and how he had approached me not knowing that I indeed knew his wife. After I found out the details to Damu I threw his phone number away and did not ever call his phone. I felt so bad for Sherie and I could still see her pain and how she was struggling behing her baby passing away to the point where she rode around with the babies belongings. Sherie had my back and I most definitly wasn't going to cross her even though Damu was FINE AS WINE. After that day Sherie had taken me to school on day when DeShawn was all out the window trying to holler at her. I laughed to myself as Sherie turned DeShawn down right there in my face, after that I told Sherie that Deshawn was one of my dudes but I wasen't faithful to him. Sheria found Deshawn to be disrespectful and she said that I deserved someone better than DeShawn. In my mind I said that Sherie deserved better than Damu but I didn't want to tell Sherie about Damu giving me his phone number just days before because I knew that Sherie was still hurting behind her baby and I didn't want to stress her even more about a messy dude, Damu had tried to holla at me and I was only 16. Little did I know, Sherie's husband Damu sold big drugs and years later Sherie had got indited by the Feds along with Damu. Damu later died in the Feds due to a heart attack R.I.P Damu aka Dino. Shortly after I began to have fights more and I was getting into a lot of Beef with the girls at school. I started feuding with the *Blood Bitches* and one of them was Buddies cousin who thought that she was about to bully me because the TWO LITTLE man wanted me. I almost had a big fight and I got suspended until we had a parent teacher confrence. My favorite Staff Early had to take me up to the Principal's Ofice to get me back into school and to have a confrence with Buddies cousins and their mom along with the Principal. Buddies cousins and their mom knew exactly who I was and that meeting almost turned into a group fight right inside the principal's office. Early had almost got into an altercation with Buddies cousins mother because things were said and things elevated quickly. Things were getting out of control and that's when Fee had stepped back in and had gotten me back into her custody. Rico, Poody and I had all moved back with Fee but that same week of me leaving the Group Home my favorite staff Early was on her normal morning routie, she had taken the girls to school in the Big White Van and when she returned back to the girls home she had found my two close friends dead in the car right around the corner from the girls home. Early had found Mel (Buddies cousins) and his big brother both shot up and dead in the car R.I.P Mark and Melvin. Early was also good friends with Mel and his big brother Mark which is how she spotted thier car and aproached thier car to find them dead. Things were beginning to get Real in the K. I had friends whom I had knew on personal levels who were now losing thier lives to senseless crimes. I thought that I was to young to be witnessing some of these strange, grewsome, grimmy things that were occuring amungst me and my life but aye it all started when I was 5 years old and my Grandma passed away. I had reoccuring nightmares that would repeat themselves after my grandma passed away. I didn't like having them bad dreams and I took heed to everything going on around me. Here it is I am back living with Fee and her children. I was happy because I had missed my little cousins they were all my babies although Little D was really like my baby and I missed that little boy so badly. Little D was getting bigger, he had this sandy redish brown hair with these big pretty brown eyes and a light brownish skin tone. Little D was about 2 or three years old at this point so he was walking good and everywhere I went Little D was with me and everyone thought that he was my son. He had long braids so some people would think that he was a girl but he didn't look anything like a girl he was just a handsome baby boy. Fee was working and it seemed like Fee was getting off into different drugs like PCP and Cocaine maybe even Crack. One day after Fee had got off of work she was smoking some PCP and she passed it to me to make me smoke it with her and that kind of angered me a little. I was 16 and Fee was yet and still trying to expose me to Bull Shit. Fee would have different male friends come around some who were friends with her boyfriend and one of the men liked me, he was 29 years old, his name was Ant. Fee insisted on me messing around with Ant knowing that Ant had a girlfriend and children at home. I wasn't very interested in Ant I had my eyes on another one on Fee's boyfriend friends name Rich. Rich was my type and I thought that Rich was Fine As Wine. however Rich didn't really pay me any attention I was young. Free insisted that I mess with Ant so I did just for the Thrill. I fucked the shit out of Ant and Rode him to the point where he told me in words that I fucked like a grown woman and that I indeed fucked him better than his woman at home did.

Ant told me that I rode dick like a grown woman and that added fuel to my fire. I knew all about sex at this point and whatever I didn't know Fee laced me up with GAME. Fee taught me everything, she told me how to grip a dick with my pussy and how men loved it when you could use your pussy muscles. I knew how to RIDE IT really well which was my favorite position and Fee would always talk about how Doggystlye was her favorite position. I used the game Fee gave me to the best of my ability. I had sex with Buddy one day right in Fee's front room and I loved it because I really still had deep feelings for Buddy. DeShawn and I would have wild parties with his best friend Philly. This was back when Master P, Mia X, C-Murder, Silk The Shocker and Mystical were HOT. On occasion DeShawn and I would have sex right in front of Philly while Philly and one of his chicks would have sex so we would have big orgies. One night while having an orgy with Philly I was riding DeShawn so hard (to one of Master P's rap songs) that I broke down the couch that we were fucking on and the condom broke that DeShawn had on. My favorite big cousin Kat's big brother D Boy (my Favorite big cousin)and his wife lived right next door to us at Fee's house. Rico, Poody and I spent alot of time at my big cousins home. I would also hang out with Downy at times even though she ratted me out I could stand on my own 10. I got along well with Downies family and they treated me like family so we would throw big parties and stay out late drinking and smoking. I started going to school more because I was back at home with Fee but I skipped school so much and began to have fights at school so much that I got suspended for a whole school semester so I had to attend an alternative school. While at the Alternative school, let's just say some classmates got bored and curious one day and decided to set the school on fire. One of the male teachers there became furious and he choked one of the other students up on the wall and made the student cry. That same student that got choked by that teacher later caught a murder charge for killing an innocent little 10 year old girl "It's REAL in the K". Once I got back into Wyandotte I tried to do better for myself but I knew that all of the 12th St blood bitches did not like me because I hung around the 12th St Blood dudes and I wasn't going to back down to NO ONE on a bad day. I was cool with all the dudes blood, crips and Folks. I had a couple of Leo female friends that knew how to fight like I did and they wouldn't back down either thier names were D and Cassidy. I also hung around Monta and Candy from time to time. For some apparent reason Fee started watching me closely. I used to sneak Fee's weed roaches but at this point I became aware that Fee was using different drugs so I had to watch out smoking her weed roaches. Fee had also started liking DeShawns older brother and they had sex. I didn't like the fact that Fee was trying to get to close into what I had going on because that would put her right into my business. I began to sleep a little bit more than normal, I was thinking maybe I smoked to much weed or I was getting comfortable being back at Fee's. One morning Fee made me get up and she said that she was taking me to the Health department because she thought that I was sleeping like I was pregnat and that I needed to go and get checked out just to be on the safe side. Fee made me get up and go to the Health Department. I didn't really think anything of it so I got up and went by myself to the Health Department. Fee was tripping, "I thought to myself as I got dressed not worried about a thing". I was going to prove Fee wrong and I just wanted Fee to mind her own business. I had to urinate in a cup and wait in the room waiting on the nurse to come back into the room. I remember having to answer all types of questions about how many sexual partners I had and so on. I had to get a STD check because I was indeed sexually active with multiple guys. I was honest with my nurse about everything although I didn't mention the wild parties and orgies that I had been involved in. I just wanted to get myself broke in so that sex wouldn't be so painful because I still experienced pain while having sex. I had been having some entertaining sexual encounters and I had even had a switch up with Buddy and his cousin with Downy and I. Buddy was turning out to be disrespectful so I was going to play his game and not show any feelings or emotions. The nurse walked back into the room so all of my thoughts went blank. The nurse stated saying, "'I have your test result in and your pregnacy test is positive which means that you are definitly pregnat. We have to start you on some prenatal vitimans immediatly". WHAT!! My heart skipped two beats and my mouth went so dry. I was flooded with emotions all at once. I couldn't believe my ears or what I had just heard. the nurse confirmed my test again making sure that I fully understood what she had just told me nurse, "Yes you are indeed pregnat and we are going to need to get you scheduled with your regular physician to start prenatal vitamins. I am going to give you a letter of pregnacy to give to you parent". My ears felt stopped up and I couldn't hear straight as everything became blurry. Fee just ginksed me, that bitch! How am I going to take Fee these papers? For once and a lifetime my prayers had beed answered. I knew that DeShawn had got me pregnat that night that I broke that Couch down in that basement while we were having an orgy but I didn't know how I was going to tell DeShawn that I was pregnat because he wasn't my only partner. As I walked back to Fee's house I felt like a changed woman. I was happy but sad. I wondered to myself "How the hell did Fee know that I was pregant?" As soon as I entered that house Fee was waiting on me to enter the door. Fee was waiting on me with this curious look on her face. I took a deep breath and I handed Fee the papers that the nurse gave me. Fee yelled, "I KNEW IT!! Who is the Father?" I told her DeShawn is the father and she grabbed the phone and began to call DeShawns home. I hesitated because I wanted to be the first one to break the news to DeShawn, Fee was adamant and she wasn't playing no games at this point. She called DeShawns house and asked to speak to DeShawn's mother. Fee was mad and I didn't understand why that bitch was so mad. Fee and DeShawns mother had some STRONG brief word with each other and there was a brief silence that envaded the room. I wanted to cry myself to sleep. I felt like this was a dream but I was fully awake. The next few days I was very cautious because I had alot of enemies at school who wanted to fight me. I was good at fighting but I didn't want to fight while I was pregnat and put my child at risk. I went into the restroom and I noticed that I was spotting about to bleed and I knew that this was not at all normal being that I had just found out that I was indeed pregant. I was pregant and I had just found out that DeShawn had been skipping school with one of those 12th St bitches whom I didn't get along well with. There was about to be a fight. One of my DAY ONES D which is a Leo like me tried to calm me down because I had told her that I was pregnat and she knew the 12th St bitch and D knew that them bitches didn't fight fair but I wasn't scared and I was ready for the drama. D followed me as I searched the hallways of Wyandotte in search of DeShawn and that 12th St BITCH. I ran into one of the bitches who thought that she was tough, the bitch had already had 2 children in the 10th grade. D knew that I was pregnat so she tried to mediate the situation, I wasen't scared of nare bitch and was not going to let my guards down. D told me to calm down, I listened to her but if one wrong move was made by DeShawn or any bitch I was going to go Full Throttle. God had other plans for me and I felt myself calming down as I approached one of the females. I was already spotting so I had to be easy and not let my emotions get the best of me. I wasn't about to let DeShawns FAT ass disrespect me either, but I listened to D because Deshawn or that hoe ass bitch wasen't worth 50 cent. I wasn't going to risk my baby but I was going to let DeShawn have it in a different manner. When I got home from school that day I told Fee about me spotting and about what was going on with DeShawn, Fee made me a Dr. appointment. I went to the doctor and found out that not only did DeShawn give me a baby but he also gave me Clamydia a STD. I dropped out of Wyandotte and Fee enrolled me into a G.E.D program. I was greatful that Fee had my best interest and Fee had my back no matter what. I was going to be able to get my G.E.D and finish school earlier than what I was supposed to. Although Fee took me through some changes, Fee still had my back when I needed her and that meant alot to me. Fee is my big cousin and I forgave her for what she had done to me

EVERYONE makes mistakes and I was far from perfect. I didn't want to go to school anymore. I needed to be away from Wyandotte and the hate and most of all I needed to relax so that my baby could be healthy. I prayed to God for a healthy, normal baby. I wanted to know who DeShawn was fucking and how did this STD come about. Although I had been sleeping with misc. people I had used protection. DeShawns mom seemed to be excited, this was going to be her first grandchild. I was oly 16 years old. DeShawns mom and dad are married and had been together for many and many of years. Although DeShawn had an older brother DeShawn was the first to have a child on the way. I was also the first one of my mothers children to concieve a child. Fee ended up dropping some news on me that I wasen't prepared for. Fee said that she was moving to St. Louis with her new boyfriend which happened to be my momma's ex boyfriend. I WAS CONFUSED BY THIS NEWS. That was weird! I already had to be aware of Fee's weed roaches and now she was indeed fucking behind my momma. I couldn't understand why the heck Fee would just decide to up and move. Fee told me that I couldn't go to St. Louis with her and that she wasen't even going to take her own children with her. Fee had just gotten me back out of SRS Custody but now this news and on top of it all I'm pregnat. Fee told me that I could move with whoever I wanted to move in with. I was 16 pregnat and I had to make some huge decisions for myself and my unborn child. Fee said that she was NOT sending me back into SRS Custody and I Loved Fee for that she was letting me be me. I wanted to live with DeShawn and his family. I was only 16 but, I knew how to survive on my own. I could also move with Downy and her family if I needed some where to live. I had my options but now I began to worry about my little cousins. Where were Fee's children going to live? I knew that Scooby had a good dad I worried about three of Fee's children in particular. My baby lil D. I could not leave this little boy again he really needed me. What about Rico and Poody? Why was Fee doing this? Fee had picked up a new habit "Crack" I hated Crack. Crack is what had my momma gone and now Fee.

Fee was beginning to change on me so I had to come up with a master plan and QUICK. I stayed with Downy's older sister Cindy for a brief moment when one of the little homies witnessed his own mother get shot in the head by her boyfriend and I couldn't take it. I moved in with DeShawn, his partents and his older brother. After I moved in with DeShawn things began to get bad amungst us two. DeShawn had a neighbor who he was fucking and I had found out all the information that I needed to know about DeShawn threw his Bestfriend Philly. Philly had an interest in me after that Orgy night. Philly wanted to fuck me and he told me all about DeShawn and DeShawns ways and where the Clamydia came from. Philly confided in me and told me everything about DeShawn. Philly told it all and me being young and dumb I went for it and I fucked the shit out of Philly giving him a ride of his life. Philly always had the nice Monte Carlos's with beat and hydraulics so I showed Philly how a real RODEO queen got down in the K. I was young, dumb hot headed, and full of anger. Philly liked the way I fucked him and it was our little secret until I decided to expose DeShawn. I told DeShawn about Philly out of a fit of RAGE and things BLEW up. Not to mention DeShawn started doing more drugs and DeShawn became angered I added fuel to the fire and DeShawn started becoming abusive. The Bitch that DeShawn was fucking next door kept on calling DeShawn and I was feeling very much disrespected and things were about to BLOW UP!

I'M IN THE K—I'M IN THE MIDDLE OF THE JUNGLE
I'M A LIONESS—I'M A QUEEN—I'M A WARRIOR

I'm going to be all the way truthfull with you as much as I can without the Feds watching and stalking. I'm getting into my grown up years and things weren't always pretty and I've played with "Pandora's Box". I have to keep some things secret and some things are "Priceless" so I can't let you in on everything but believe me "When It Rains It Pours But Always Be

Prepared For The Flood, I'm Lady Juice I'm From The K and I was Built straight from the MUD-Diamond In the Ruff". The System is FUCKED UP! They give a Pedophile a slap on the wrist but harass all the Drug Dealers. The system set's you up for a failure quickly to give you a Felon and try to cripple your Skills for Entrepreneurship. They don't want to see us make it BUT LADY JUICE REFUSES TO FAKE IT! I will speak TRUTH. I have been threw it all, I pray for this young generation I want better for ya'll. I don't do POLITICS they don't want a Felon to vote but when times is always hard All I want is a boat so I can soar far far away from here Tupac seen "DEATH AROUND THE CORNER"—I Rebuke THE DEVIL YOU HEAR!. Men try to use thier tastosterone to intimidate us women, BUT I STAND UP FOR MYSELF it's women like me who give men a beginning. Men need to protect thier families instead of cause so much pain I ASK THE LORD TO SHIELD ME AND PROTECT ME FROM THE RAIN. Why are you young boys shooting up peoples houses killing innocent children I'M FED UP, I pray to GOD ONE DAY YOU TAKE THESE COWARDS AND ALL THE REAL MEN STAND UP. Real don't do a drive by, we handle the shit face to face STOP ALL YOUR RUNNING TALKING LIKE YOUR A GANGSTA handle the shit grow up like MASE. Master P said always look a man in the eye before you kill him THAT"S REAL so why do COWARDS shoot threw windows and do drive by's you cowards ain't made of STEAL YA"LL WEAK and broke that's why ya, mad because you was always a joke well lol look at the system they don't want you to vote. Quit being the puppet and be the puppet master remember theres someone looking down on you don't be a lil basterd BE A MAN. A REAL man leads his pack well in the right direction you little boys have been mislead by a mom who didn't no much and probably wanted you dead (abortion). I will be glad when people can come together and the whites stop feeling superior, if these things in life had happened to you it would expose your true interior. I live for the children and pray that these pediphies get exposed my life I'm living is for the youth when you Cougars are getting to old. Why focus on prostitutes and not the Trick Daddies-passing STD's out like that's the new Grammy. The System ain't shit. *NWA FUCK THE POLICE* ya'll are killing our youth guess what I'm LADY JUICE I will expose THE WHOLE TRUTH. People are still racist and not all cops are bad but growing up in the K you'll learn that your own family is the first to hurt you, they don't want me to tell MY STORY but I straighten my Crown and move like the Queens move. Beware there is a dark cloud hovering over Kansas City, I pray that cloud away because everything that glitters ain't Pretty. As far all these reality TV shows I must say I love me some Hennessy she rides for her siser and it reminds me of me and POODY but I will not ever have respect for the ones who don't respect thier own parents ON REALITY TV LOOK WHAT I'VE BEEN THREW AND I STAND STRONG WITH LOVE FOR MINE. We need a reality show to expose all the FAKE, again I'm LADY Juice I tell the Truth I'm Coming STRAIGHT FROM THE K. I would like to send a special SALUTE to MONIQUE and Queen Latifah those are two women who I am quite sure have had to uplift other women on several occasions and Eddy Murphy, Ice Cube, Tyler Perry, Martin Lawerence, The Waynes Family (I love your because you're a talented FAMILY) just inspirational people. I have learned to send a SALUTE instead of all the BEEF they want you to engage in. The movie "Beat Street" was popular. I made plays as a child that was also my form of Art. Hard work and faith. I'm a figure 8, again a "Diamond In The Ruff" and I am the TRUTH. I would like to send a huge SALUTE to some of my favorite actress Vivica Fox, Angela Bassat, Holly Berry, Cicley Tyson, Felicia Rashaad, Lauren London, Nia Long, Tisha Cambell Martin, Trisha Arnold, Whoopi Goldburg, Queen Latifah, Jada Pinkett, Lisa Raye, Kimberly Elise, Geena Davis, Tika Sumpter, Jamie Lee Curtis, Vanessa Williams, Taraji P Henson, Janet Jackson, Loretta Devine, Whitney Houston (RIP), Tisha Cambell, Megan Gooding, Keisha Knight Pulliam, Da Brat, Robin Givins, Gabriel Union, there are so many more Saulte Female Artist Tamela Mann, Jacquline Carr, Justice Cobbs,

Monica, Kelly Price, Mary J Blidge, Laren Hill, Adina Howard, Kelly Rowland, Gladis Knight, SWV, Beyonce, Fantasia, Riahanna, Trina, Cierra, Eve, Foxy Brown, Brandy, Aliyah (RIP), Toni Baxton, Mariah Carey, Shania Twain, Alicia Keys, Excape. I have many SALUTES.

CHAPTER
24
....

WHEN IT RAINS IT POURS

I GRADUATED THE top 10 of my G.E.D. class in College. I got my G.E.D. in two months top 5, and I was one month away from giving birth. The Catholic Ladies "The Nuns", loved me. At the college they said "I am a very intelligent young lady", not to mention De'Shawns mothers deep involvment in the Catholic Religion. I ended up going to the girls home for Pregnant Teens but I ran away from there to go be back with De'Shawn and his mother. I wasn't going to give birth to my child living in a girls home when I had a decent woman whom excepted me and De'Shawns unborn child. I was finished with school I just had to stay out of trouble and not risk getting caught by SRS. I was labeled a run away. By law, shortly after I graduated, I gave birth to a 6 lbs 7 oz 19 inches healthy baby boy. It was 3 or 4 in the morning when my water started leaking. That was when De'Shawn and I rushed to the ER. The birth of my son well besides the fact that I didn't an Epidural so besides the pain medication in my IV I felt all the pain. While my babies head was coming out I felt the sense of my vagina started ripping so instead of me continuing to push, I stopped pushing and started screaming. The pain was agonizing. That (giving birth) is the worst pain I have ever felt. Due to the fact that I stopped pushing I (my vagina) squeezed my babies head and eyes. Lil De'Shawn Jr was born with blood clots in both of his eyes. Other than that he was a healthy baby boy who was born looking exactly like De'Shawn so their was no need for a Paternity Test, the proof was right before our eyes. After the birth of lil De'Shawn, me and big De'Shawns relationship went down hill fast. I didn't want to get pregnant again but I got on a pregnacy shot (depo) to prevent getting pregnant. De'Shawn, the baby, and me lived with De'Shawns parents and older brother but the fact that De'Shawns parents were around didn't stop the fact that all De'Shawn and I did was fuck and fight. I knew in my heart that De'Shawn was cheating on me and it hurt because I was being faithful to him. At this point all I wanted was a happy family but the more drugs De'Shawn use, the more fights De'Shawn and I would have. De'Shawn would come home at 2 and 3 A.M. with an argument waking me up out of my sleep arguing almost every night and it was instant when he came home with glitter on him and a females hair hanging from his facial hair and that sure wasn't mine and where I'm from that was nothing but evidence of him and his cheating ways. Not to mention one day De'Shawn was mad at me and spit his pop in my face (the ultimate disrespect). I knew that when I turned 18, I was leaving De'Shawn I was going to be determined to find my own apartment. Pooh Pooh, (lil De'Shawn) and I were leaving and big De'Shawn was not going to be welcome to come along. Not to mention that "That Buck Tooth, Big Booty, Bitch from next door kept being disrespectful calling the house phone. I was appalled by De'Shawns behavior. l had lost all my baby fat my body bounced right back into shape right after I gave birth and I was looking and feeling like a million bucks. Other than the stretch mark I had aquired. I was super sexy dark skinned curves shaped like a coke bottle. I couldn't believe that De'Shawn had all this at home and would still cheat. I became FURIOUS! I was faithful for the first time in life. Not to mention once again only this time a different friend of De'Shawns came to me with all the info where, when and how De'Shawn was cheating. I wasnt going to give in because I knew all of De'Shawns boys had a crush on me but when he offered to eat my pussy (that turned me on). I had to get off that Depo shot (pregnacy shot) my hair started to falling out fast along with my weight loss. The shot lasted 3 months and I knew that I had to be caution. Everyone said that after your first baby its easy to get pregnant again fast. One day De'Shawn and I had been arguing and the arguing turned physical. I didn't want to fight in front of my baby but De'Shawn pushed me to the limit and it *flashed* somehow lil De'Shawn got knocked on the floor and I lost my mind I ran to the kitchen and grabbed a knife De'Shawn ran to the restroom and locked the door really fast and BAM I stabbed that knife through that bathroom door about 3 or 5 times. I had to stop and think before I did something I might regret. I thought about momma and that innocent. I thought about putting Lil De'Shawn through what I had witnessed as a child. Big De'Shawn had became a very abusive physically and mentally and I couldn't take very much more abuse. I was a ticking time bomb not to mention now we were tearing up De'Shawns parents house that they worked hard to build from the ground up. I used to say bad things and wish bad things on De'Shawn, he hurt me. I wanted him to feel the pain I felt. I felt bad, I wanted him a place of my own and to get away from De'Shawn. I didn't want to live this way. I was feeling very disrespected. I wanted a true love. I have not once in my life condoned a man hitting a woman. Men have the upper man clue. You are by nature physically stronger than woman so why hit and abuse your woman. I am a fighter and life itself had already taught me how to fight back. Love yourself first. I was onces insecure about the way I looked. These ways were different. Some say "The Blacker The Berry ". I had something within me that made me fight for what I loved and for what I wanted in life. I was being torn down and broken apart. I remember when Old School Mates "Females of Course", would come over to De'Shawns house to act like they were visiting

De'Shawn and his mom but really wanted to see my baby to see if he looked liked De'Shawn and he did. My pooh pooh unfortunately looked liked almost just like De'Shawn. Eventually and quickly when De'Shawn saw that all his cheating ways was about to catch up to him. He gave me a nice sized diamond ring. I was a diamond in the ruff and I knew it because diamond are a girls bestfriend but my heart was truely broken and not to mention pooh pooh was three months and my minstrual hadn't showed up for the month. I couldnt stand the sight of De'Shawn, his smell, and everything about him began to make me *Flash*. I didn't want anything to do with him. Another doctor and another positive pregnacy test not to mention De'Shawns brother rubbing all of this in on the both of us. De'Shawn and I knew that his big brother wanted the best for his nephew. I prayed to god that this next baby would be a girl. De'Shawn gave me a nice diamond ring and a nice unborn child. Things weren't perfect but I prayed for things to get better and I knew that as long as De'Shawn remained on drugs we had no chance and I already already began to come up with a plan. I was almost 18 in less than a year I would get my own place. 17 two kids. The Block De'Shawn lived on was a party block. There was a little girl named Shaka who would always come visit me. She was a pretty little girl and had big pretty brown eyes and she would come and visit me at Deshawns because I tried to stay in the house as much as possible, I couldn't go outside without getting harassed by some cat chaser. The dogs were out and I was like PREY. I needed a female friend that I could hang with from time to time. Poody ended up getting adopted by our Uncles Girlfriend which happened to be Fee's friend Carol. Carol adopted Poody and Carol lived in a house right up the street from DeShawn's parents so we were all in the same area. Poody and I were close by so we stuck together and decided to have a "Joy Ride". Poody was around me and Poody was beginning to get into some things of her own. Poody and Cloey was born on the exact same day but they are two of a kind. Cloey is Carols youngest daughter. Somehow, Poody and I ended up in a stolen car and along came Cloey. We wanted to go on a "Joy Ride" for some reason I was big and pregnat so we went on a Joy Ride, The Police got behind us and we jumped out and ran. Cloey wasen't into drugs, I couldn't believe that she had got into that stolen car with Poody and I but Cloey was a rider and wanted to come along. Shortly after I found out that I was pregnat for the second time and things began to take a turn for the worse with DeShawn and I. One day I was at home at DeShawn's mom and dads house when the phone rang, of coarse I answerd, "Hello". female speaking, "Can I Speak to Deshawn?" Me, "Bitch NO you cant and why the fuck are you still calling this phone hoe? female speaking," He still fucking me and we just fucked last week". Me, "Bitch you said you fucked him when? Well You A dumb hoe I got the RING BITCH so quit calling this phone." female answering, "well bitch fuck you and I'm still going to fuck him". Me answering, "I'm pregnat did DeShawn tell you that, and as a matter of fact bitch if you want it, YOU CAN GET IT!" I slammed the phone down in a fit of rage. DeShawn's mom was sitting right there and I honestly forgot that moms was sitting right there. I wanted to cry so bad but I didn't! I was so hurt and I did not want DeShawn's mom to witness this pain behind the same nasty bitch that burned DeShawn and almost caused me to lose my baby from stress. I tried to gather my thoughts as I stormed out of the house and decided to take a walk to a friends house. Her name is Monica, Monica was Downy's close friend also. I called Monica and she told me to come to her house. DeShawns mom told me that I could leave the baby because she saw that I was fueled up. I told her that if DeShawn came back to have him call me. I would be at Monica's. DeShawn had just brought himself a brand new car for the first time ever with some money that he had got back from the state. I knew that when I saw DeShawn's face that it was going to be a fight since he couldn't control his miscellanous AND IT WAS WAR TIME. As I was walking down the street on my way to Monica's, I could hear a car pulling up besides me. It was DeShawn! I had a stick in my hand as I was walking for my protection from the stray dogs. Deshawn pulled up next to me with

his windows rolled up. I told him to roll the windows down! DeShawn
didn't roll his windows down so I hit his window twice when the whole
window SHATTERED. DeShawn pulled off very quickly. I made it to
Monica's to tell her what had just happened when DeShawn came pulling
right back up. I ran to DeShawns car and started punching him threw the
window when Deshawn managed to grab my arm and held my arm tight
as he stepped on the gas. I ran with the car trying to beat my arm away
from DeShawn when he hit the corner and I went rolling on the hard
concrete. I hit that concrete hard and all I could think about is IM PREG-
NANT! I was scrapped up badly and bleeding. DeShawn had just dragged
me with his car while I was pregnat with his child. Monica's Father Big Will
came and pulled up quick and got me off that corner and also gave me a lil
25. I love Big Will to this very day RIP because things was about to get
GANGSTA REAL QUICK!. Big Will had saw everything that had just
happened and Big Willy wasen't about to play no games (Big Will always
teased me calling me THAT LIL BLACK GAL, I love Big Will he always
showed me love day ONE a BIG MAN WITH A BIG HEART) he pulled
up in that big Van and told me to get in. By this time DeSahwn had pulled
off. I got in that van and Big Willy handed me the STRAP and we went
looking for DeShawn. ONLY GOD KNOWS (If I had found DeShawn
This Night!) We searched for about an hour and no DeShawn No where
he didn't even go home. Monica wanted me to come back to her house that
night but I had some unfinished business that I had to attend at DeShawns
house. I was hurt but I didn't start bleeding from the vagina so I knew that
my unborn baby was okay by the GRACE OF GOD and my baby was
going to be a SOLDIER like his momma A WARRIOR. The next day I
called that hoe who had broke my family up, I wanted to fight her since she
had all that mouth over the phone and she was bold enough to come over
DeShawns when she pleased regardless of me so I wanted her to REALLY
MEET ME. I told her to meet me on the Church parking Lot. While I
talked to the HOE on the phone I could hear her cousins all in the back-

ground taking shit like they were going to jump me but aye I had enough ass whooping to go around. I was so mad at this point that I could have fought 10 bitches and came out swinging for the 11th. Plus, I knew that within DeShawn's heart he loved me and wasn't about to let a group of females jump me and fight me unfair. I prepared myself to walk up on the Churches Parking Lot to fight her fair and square, I wanted this home-wrecker for once and for all. DeShawn, his big brother and some other people were up on the Churches Parking Lot all sitting out, chilling there as normal when I made it up there On my way up there I had a brief discussion with the girl next door whom had also recently had a fight with DeShawn's whore and lost the fight, I told her if she wanted her payback to come up to the Church Parking Lot. She declinced and I strapped up my Sneaks and took off mad noticing that I had a full Set of nails on my fingers that had already went threw war with Deshawn. I made it up on the Church Parking Lot. About one minute later I heard a car full of females pulling up. That's when my eyes made it to the hoe that I came up there for, the hoe who kept testing my woman hood and my family. DeShawn was sitting on his car and I was standing in front of DeShawn. I pushed DeShawn across the car and told him this was because of him! I told that hoe to get out of the car! I heard all them other whores in the background saying, "Awww Shit Deshawn this is ALL BECAUSE OF YOU". The bold little hoe got out the car and the FIGHT was on. I beat that bitch up so bad as non of her punches connected with me I fought her blow for blow given by me and everytime I hit her she hit the ground, once she got up she began to rip my shirt off my back along with my bra and my titties where every-where when Deshawn tried to get in the middle. Deshawn tried to grab me and I fell to the concrete, the hoe tried to run up on me when I fell but DeSahwn pushed her. I jumped back up ready to fight even more mad because DeShawn had made me fall. DeShawn took off his shirt and wrapped it around me because he didn't want everyone to see my titties and when I looked down I saw blood falling. I knew that the hoe didn't get one hit off butt when I looked at my hands, I was bleeding from my finger nails where they had split in half from me being so mad balling my fist up punching not realizing that my fingers were injured. I beat her ass and my blood was on her. I had got my nails done and fucked myself up as well as fucking that hoe up. I was so mad that I didn't feel anything until after the fight and I was so mad. That hoe's cousins sure didn't try to help her after that ass beating that she had got but they were all talking shit like they were going to jump me. After I beat the hoe up none of her cousins wanted to fight me. I heard them yelling at Deshawn blaming him for thier cousins ass beating. Everytime I knocked her down after a punch I let her get back up to square up again and her cousins did not want that beating for themselves they weren't fucking Deshawn. I was furious and Deshawns big brother was CRACKING THE FUCK UP! Big Bro called me Tyson after that fight. I felt a small sense of relief "Another One Hits the Dust". I knew that hoe was a dunnnnnnn hoe and I wouldn't have to worry about that rat anytime soon. I still had this grudge with deshawn that was not yet settled. I was really going to fuck with Philly now and whoever else that I wanted to fuck with because Desahwn made me look like a complete fool and I was hurt. I was a figure 8 shaped like an hour glass and time was ticking on DeShawn and I. I knew that DeShawn loved all of this COLA but it was about my respect and my I had fallen out of love with DeShawn. I need to hurry up and get away from DeShawn because I felt an sense of evil coming amongst me and I knew that it was bad to hate and kill. So, I ended up moving back out to Downy's sisters house and Downy had just gotten her own apartment. I had fallen out of love with Deshawn and I had an application for an apartment that I was going to turn in as soon as I turned 18 so that I could get my own apartment. I was also going to sign up for some Housing and government assistance as soon as I turned 18. I had to have a plan because I was a runaway with about 6–8 months before I turned 18. Times was getting hard. I had a baby, no job and a baby on the way, I had to find a way to support my children. DeSahwn was no help. We had needs like clothing and shoes hygiene, food and misc. expenses. i was determined to find a way so one day it was Me, Downy and a mutual friend of ours named Erica that I had known from middle school. We all went to the store with intentions of stealing. Downy was scared so Erica and I did the stealing. I had my son Pooh Pooh with me because I needed his diaper bag to be able to steal more items for us. While we were in the store stealing some secret shopper spotted Erica stealing which automatically made them watch use 3 because we all came in the store together. We got caught. I got caught with 300 dollars plus woth of items. All because of Erica being MESSY Downey didn't take anything so she got released and I told Downey to take Pooh Pooh to his grandma DeShawns mom. Lil Deshawn is a grandma's baby so she didn't mind ever looking after him and Deshawn's mom always had my back. I knew that because I was a runaway I was going to have to go back into SRS custody, something that I dreaded. They took me into a group home I saw my favorite staff member Early and she told me the exit door with no camera and I ran and had my momma pick me up until I mad it back to my baby. SRS was looking for me and making threats so I turned myself in only because they SRS made a deal with me not to take my baby and that me and my child would be able to go to the same home together. Pooh Pooh and I ended up in a Foster Home in Olathe KS with a nice white woman. I loved the Church that we went to Called Christian Center it was perfect for Pooh Pooh and I. The church had activities for teenagers and everyone was so nice and welcoming. I was allowed to have visits on the weekends to DeShawns parents at this point SrS didn't seem all that bad and the caseworkers seemed to have a heart. I really liked my Foster mom although I found it odd that she was taking baths with one of her adopted 5 years old mixed little boys. I found that one thing about my Foster mom very odd because I didn't take baths with Pooh Pooh and he was my own child. "Different Strokes for Different Folks". I couldn't quite grasp the fact of what was going on so I didn't come back from a pass one night. I was only mths away from being 18 so I hid out until i turned 18 and I got the phone call that I had been waiting for. I had gotten approved for my own apartment in the same complexes that Erica and Downey also had apartments in so it was about to GO DOWN IN THE K.

CHAPTER
25
....

WHEN IT RAINS IT POURS

I FINALLY GOT moved into my apartment. De'Shawns mom made sure that I got furniture, she went thru some agencies to get some help for me and her grandson. I brought my own bed room set brand new cash. I meant what I said De'Shawn was not moving in with me. I had got to a point where I almost hated De'Shawn. I didn't like having sex I tried to have sex with a couple of partners besides De'Shawn, but my baby just didn't let me enjoy sex. I found out at my doctor's visit that I was having another boy, so I prepared myself. I had started getting a little closer to Erica as a friend and Downey remained a friend although I knew (keep your enemies close but watch your homies as well). Once you crossed me I kept a close eye on you. Before I moved out of De'Shawn's moms house I had met someone whom I liked alot, he came over one day with my favorite male cousin Kats big brother D-Boy. I had always been close to my big cousin D-Boy growing up. He had one of his friends with him one day he came to visit me at De'Shawns and his friend liked me and I liked his friend. I would leave from De'Shawns with Pooh Pooh in his stroller, walk a few blocks away and meet up with D-Boys friend T-Money. T-Money was a hustla and he got money. When I got my apartment D-Boy and T-Money would always come over and we would have a good time. T-Money met me when I had just turned 18. I had a few friends so De'Shawn really wasn't an option not to mention I had almost lost my apartment because of De'Shawn,& Downy's cousin G.O. One night I had a house party and there was a robbery gone bad. De'Shawn had just showed me that he was a dumb criminal. I let De'Shawn spend the night one night and again 3–4- or 5 in the morning my water went gushing everywhere. This time I refused to have a natural delivery I wanted an epidural. I went to a different hospital this time to give birth and there was a mirror on the top of the wall where I could see myself giving birth. I was so excited 6lbs. 11oz 21 inches a healthy yellow baby boy. My baby was so cute he was bright yellow almost mixed looking with some good curly hair. Pooh Pooh's hair wasn't this good and he wasn't this yellow but you could still look and see that indeed De'Shawn was the father. I called my new son Tay. Erica had also just had a baby and her baby's dad turned out to be my ex high school boyfriend Kev. I didn't know how to take that because me and Kevin had tried many times to have a baby. Oh well (I thought) I wasn't going to let a piece of dick get in the way of me and Erica's friendship. Dick is dick. Me and Erica went and got our first tattoo together on our necks. I got chocolate with some black cherries. Erica also showed me how to sell dope. I had to get money and a 9 to 5 wasn't going to be the way with two babies. Me and Erica shared the same drug habit weed & wet. Now we also shared some of the same serves. Erica would always get smokers cars and I needed some transportation so I jumped right in the game. I had met this dude named Taz threw Rico. Taz and I became a couple, we would get money together and get high together, not to mention I kept T-Money because he was a hustla. T-Money had a girl at home but she wasn't a friend of mine so I let him worry about his chic at home, it was obvious that he wasen't to worried the way that he would eat, my pussy. I wanted T-Money for myself and I liked his Hustlin ways so if it meant that I was fucking him to take him from his bitch then I was up for the challenge. Taz was going to be something temporarily someone to get my mind off DeShawn and I wasn't ready to settle down just have a lil fun. Taz always wanted to be around me and I didn't mind that because Taz was a good guy, a provider and knew how to get money. There was something about Taz that I didn't like and I didn't quite no what that was because he didn't show me any bad intentions. DeShawn had blew it completely, during one of his raging moments about Philly and I Deshawn told me that he had sex with Poody my one and only sister. I didn't believe that Poody would do me like that so Deshawn called Poody on a three way call to verify that he had indeed had sex with my little sister. I knew that DeShawn was mad at me for having sex with Philly but my little sister was taking matters way to far. I would not ever have sex with Deshawns big bro so why would he hurt me like that. I was so hurt by this information that I vowel to not ever have sex with DeShawn every again in life although I would have to somehow forgive Poody. I confided in Philly and Philly and I became real friends. Men are always so quick to say, "Bro's before Hoes" although I was hurting, I refused to let some dude come in between me and my sister or even me and my friends. I wasen't married yet, I remember Fee told me that I would never get married. I wanted a husband. Any man that had slept with my sister after sleeping with me was most definitly not husband material. I was done with being faithful to men until my Mr. Right came along. I was going to Hustle like the Diva that I am FULL THROTTLE FOR THE CASH. God first then I had to get to the money. DeShawn didn't know how to get money but Taz and T-Money did so I had a few tricks up my sleeve. Yellow Boy had moved to texas but he came back to KS to visit and I was finally 18 and grown up. Yellow Boy had been chasing me since I was 14 and I had a fetish for Yellow Boys and Bowe-legged ones. Yellow and I ended up hooking up and having sex for the first time. I told Downey my little secret, Downey went right behind my back and told Taz. Downey had crossed me for the second time.

Downey told Taz on me and decided that she had a few tricks up her sleeve. Downey decided to hook Taz up with a couple of her friends and one of those friends had just went out to the club with Downy and I days prior to her fucking Taz. Once again I felt betrayed, not only by Downy but by Taz as well. That's when the fire began to burn bridges. Once again Downey had crossed me and I was beginning to think that Downey was a little bit jealous of me which added fuel to my fire. Taz wasn't going to leave me not when he had been introduced to my RODEO. I tried putting Taz out of my house and he wouldn't leave. Taz fucked Downy's friend named Ricca. Ricca and I ended up having some strong words verbally which turned into "Meet Me So We Can KNUCKLE UP". My adrenaline was pumping. Ricca had pushed my buttons, although we were not close friends she had crossed me. Ricca had been in my home and during our argument Ricca had said that she was going to call SRS on me and anyone who knew me knew that I didn't play when it came to my children. I STILL PLAY NO GAMES WHEN IT COMES TO MINE! I was supposed to be at Erica's babies birthday party with Pooh pooh and Tay but instead Ricca was calling and pushing my GO buttons. I rented out one of my smokers cars me, Poody and Downey got in the car together and Rico and Taz followed us. I was on my way to settle this Beef with Rica fair and square Drastic Times calls for Drastic measures. As we pulled up to meet Ricca to fight, there was a huge group of girls all standing outside in Silver City Apartments about 10 females deep which meant we were out numbered. I didn't care because I came prepared just in case. Ricca was taller than me and thicker than I was but I didn't care, she wasn't the first to be bigger than I. Soon as I pulled up and parked the car I spotted Ricca in the crowed of females. Ricca immedialty started walking to my car and I could see that she was holding something red in her hands. I yelled, "Bitch your gonna spray me with mase"! Before I could finish my sentence Ricca sprayed me in the face with mase. I hated mase and I had asthma no time for the bull shit so I jumped out the car and went straight for Ricca. I went for Ricca Full

Throttle like a PITBULL. As I fought Ricca we were both swinging but I managed to grab Ricca and got her down on the ground. At that point I climbed up on top of Ricca punching and scratching her like a wild LION that couldn't see but I could feel. I was squinting as I fought but I needed to get my eyesight so I got up off of Ricca. I heard Rico's voice asking why was I fighting with my eyes closed as I tried to find my way to someone so that I could get that mase out of my face. I heard everyone yelling and the crowned was mad becasue thier team player had got her ass beat real quick. Ricca got up off the concrete and ran fast into her apartment. Taz and Rico tried calming me down but the group of girls were getting out of hand and they were mad because whatever had just happened I left thier homegirl LEAKING, BLEEDING. One of the girls were so mad that she tried to run up and hit me but Rico stood in the way and she punched him and that made me furious as we argued with the crowd. Rico and Taz finally got me to calm down and get in the car to take me around the corner to get some bottles of wter to get the mase out of my face and to bring me back in case bitches wanted a round two. As soon as I flushed my eyes I went straight back to Ricca's for round two. When I pulled back up Ricca was so scarred that her big ass wouldn't come back outside. I wanted the big bitch who had swug on me though. I wasn't done for the night bitches had me fucked up and I was FULL THROTTLE FULL OF ENERGY. Later on that night Erica and I made a special trip back down to Riccas house after we got the babies straight. Erica and I wanted to have our own little celebration. A couple of days later Erica and I both recieved restraining orders in the mail. I was beyond mad that punk ass, hoe ass, bitch Ricca. **** My apologies but I wanted to stop and say GO KC the ROYALS are the CHAMPS!!!!!!! WE WON KS GO ROYALYS THE BOYS IN BLUE!. I support KC ALL DAY and it's winning season. Thier might not be enough room for a REAL woman with STRETCH MARKS in the spotlight BUT KC IS DEFINITLY IN THE BUILDING THIS YEAR BABY. I'm One of KC's AUTHENTICS KC SALUTE... Now back to "My Story". Ricca was the bitch who started this fight now the bitch is putting restraining orders against a young lady. Ricca started it and I finished it. I was good at finishing things by this point shit I just needed my Champion Belt. "I wanted so bad to be mad at Downey, I felt so betrayed by Downey again. Taz and I continued as a couple because he wasn't going anywhere and that fight with Ricca and I had brought Taz and I closer. Rico started having sex with Downey's big sister and it was strange because Rico was younger than I was and Downy's big sister was older than me. Rico was only 17 and a run away. Poody was still with Carol and when Poody wasn't around me Poody was getting into some things of her own. DeShawn lived right down the street from Poody and Philly was right around the corner from Deshawn. Poody knew that I was intimate with Philly even though Philly was DeShawn's bestfriend. I found out that Poody had also been having sex with Philly. I was frustrated because Philly tried to act like he wasn't having sex with Poody whenver I came around. Although I had Taz, I didn't want to commit to Taz, not when I was fucking other men and he was capable of also fucking other women. I had a thing for T-Money at that point but Poody turned around and fucked T-Money behind my back. I was furious but dogs will be dogs. T-Money and my favorite cousin D-Boy would always come over my house on the late nights and raid my refrigerator like "Fat Boys' d Boy would always bring some Meukow (a coniac with a black panther wrapped around the bottle) and everytime I drunk that alcohol with them I would drop my cup in my lap. I had alot of fun with them two. Even though T-Money was showing his hoe tendencies I had a soft spot for him. T-Money would always tease my baby when he came over saying that my son looked like the Dinosaur "Not The Momma" and we would laugh and joke. Even though I knew that T-Money had a girl at home we took a genuine liking to one another, we had a bond and when it was me and him IT WAS ME AND HIM no matter who he had at home. I had a neighbor who had moved in upstairs right above me and I would always hear her and her dude fighting to the point where it would make me think of fighting with Deshawn and it was disgusting and nerve wrecking. I began to get better at making money and my clients started accumlating. I quickly began to accumulate on Diamonds and Gold. I had 14 and 10 karat on every finger along with multiple gold chains. I was getting a name for myself and I didn't quite realize it. I became very popular and everywhere I went people knew me and if they didn't they wanted to know me. I had one client that I really didn't trust because he always wanted credit and I didn't like giving out any credit I DON'T PLAY WITH MY MONEY not when I had my own habits and expenses. I was sceptic when it came to this client but I trusted him with credit even though I really didn't want to. I figured that he would give me my money because we all lived in the same complex. I was new to the game fresh off the porch so I had to learn the ropes. I learned the game fast. It was time for dude to pay me my money and he was hiding out until one day. I caught dude walking and Rico was around me so I told Rico the play so that he was aware. I approached dude and asked him about my money when all he had was some lame excuses. I wanted my CASH BAMN—BY ANY MEANS NECESSARY. I told Rico he play and if I said it the I meant it. Rico and I are a TEAM A1 since Day 1. Rico already knew the plan so when I approached dude for my money and he had excuses, I HIT HIM IN THE MOUTH thats when Rico tried to jump in as I gave dude a combination of punches Rico came in on the Licks. I grabbed dude by the shirt because Rico wasen't playing with dude and almost knocked dude down the stairs but I was pulling him back up into the punches when his shirt ripped off his back and he began to pull out a weapon. Rico and I took off running in a THRILL OF THE MOMENT. I knew that if anyone else owed me any money that it wouldn't be nothing nice. Rico and I laughed at the incident for days and I also learned a valuable lesson in the Game NO CREDIT. A feen will say anything in order to get a quick fix and I didn't have any hand outs. Momma didn't no that I sold Crack which was mommas drug of choice so I never wanted to deal with Crack because I saw what it did to my momma. I didn't want to sell that poison to my momma and I was only doing what I had to do to make fast money. Momma was soon to find out my new lifestyle that I had quickly established. I had to do what I had to do because Deshawn was not supporting me at all when it came to taking care of my children. If I wasn't having sex with Deshawn he didn't want to give me any money and I was not going to bow down to Deshawn not after he had sex with my sister and I meant that I was standing on my own 10. I would not ever take my children away from thier father or thier grandparents I was just not physically into Deshawn and his no good ways, I was done. Pooh Pooh was a grandma's baby and I love the bond that they have so I would not ever come in between that, you have to always cherish your memories with you grandparents. Anyhow, meanwhile, Downey had her own mess going on. Downey had ended up getting into a huge fight where her eye got messed up and when I was trying to go and help her fight my momma was over my house and wouldn't let me. Momma tried her hardest to keep me from fighting especially when it was not involving me. WAKA "I GO HARD IN THE MUTHA FUCKIN PAINT". When I start there's no stopping me 50 "Many Men". Downey had alot of issues of her own grow-ing up that were simualr to mine but also intense so I sympathized with Downey alot. I started noticing my jewelry coming up missing. I had so much jewelry that I didn't wear it all at once so I started to peep game. For some odd reason Downy's momma always wanted to use my restroom when she came over and that's exactly where I kept my jewelry. I was furious when I put two and two together and figured out who had been stealing from me. I told Downey that her momma couldn't come over my house anymore and she was lucky that I have respect for my elders. Downey's mom was one of my clients but after this day I just wanted her thieving ass to stay far away from me. I was a single parent trying to make a way for my family. I had to do what I had to do to make my paper and I wasen't going to the stores to steal anymore I was 18 and capable of now going to jail and those were chances that I didn't want to take I would rather sell dope and take those chances. Soon after Downey had that fight she recieved an eviction notice. Again me "the Good Samaritan The Loyal Real Friend, I let Downey move in with me. Downey had an uncle by marriage which was her aunties ex husband who worked for the City and he would always come over and try to flirt. He had money and was willing to Trick some Off but he just wasn't my "Cup Of Tea/ I DONT DO TEA I DRINK JUICE!" Downy on the other hand started sneaking and sleeping around with her anties ex husband "Nasty Trick" Gangsta Boo. Erica had a baby by my Ex dude K.D from high school. Even though Erica and I were both aware of K.D we became close friends and Erica became my club partner and we would have so much fun together. The moment I let Downey move into my apartment things became out of order. I tried to keep my apartment clean for the most part but things quickly became cluttered and my apartment became a revolving door. Shortly after and innident had happened with DeShawn and one of Downy's cousins with an attempted robbery then the office became aware of what was going on. The Office manager basically gave me an autimanium. She (The Office Manager) told me that either Downey had to leave my apartment and get off the premises or I would also get evicted. I had a big heart and I just wouldn't listed. I didn't want to follow someone elses rules and I wanted to be the Boss of me. Taz had also moved in with me but I remaind discrete with T-Money. T-Money noticed that my home was becoming unorganized and he wanted me to put Downey out. Downey was also having a descrete relationship with my cousin D-Block. I didn't judge Downey because I had a few discrete relationships with a couple of her family members also. As a result of me having a hard head I ended up getting evicted. the manager of the apartments really liked me so she told me that if I just moved out that she would not put an eviction on my record so I could be able to get my act together. I was cool with the managers decision but I had no where to move. I had a house full of furniture that DeShawns mom had helped me get threw her church and I was losing everything. I had come into contact with one of my cousins that I didn't get a chance to grow up with and she had a daughter around my age and they had a huge house with just the two of them. My big cousin was sick with Lupis, although I didn't grow up around them they were family and my cousin had a big heart and was more than willing to help me all she had was one daughter around my age. My big cousin was willing to take me and the two boys in and even Taz. I could not believe myself or that they were real genuine people in this world. Downy was the cause of me losing my place for me and my babies and I seriously doubt if she would have done the same for me. I knew then that I was REAL to the CORE and that people like me were hard to come by and my cousin CeCe had just taken me and the boys in which also showed that she was a genuine type of person. *Be Aware Of The Ones you Have In Your Circle, Find Out Ones's Motives And Where Ones Loyality Lies" Some people are all for themselves.

CHAPTER
26
....

When It Rains It Pours

I HAD MET my cousin CeCe and her daughter and her daughter Kay once for the first time when I was about 13 years old. Cousin CeCe had a terrible disease or cancer called Lupis but since the first day I met my cousins I took a liking to my cousins. I met my cousin Kay back when I was 13 when we were supposed to go skating one night together everyone loved skating back in those days and I hadn't had enough practice to be good at but I loved to skate. I found out that threw Kay and CeCe I was related to one of Kansas hottest rappers in our time "Rich The Factor" so I knew it was GANGSTA and TALENT all threw my bloodline. Although Cece was sick with Lupis that woman had a heart of gold. You could not ever go over Ce Ce home leaving hungry because CeCe FED everyone and made sure that you left with a full stomache. Cece house was like a mini Mansion and she only had one child Kay. Cece welcomed me and my family into her home. Taz and I felt welcome there. Taz and I had to find ways to keep money in our pockets so along with our hustle we added in something that would help us make more money and we added another product to our

160

hustle. We started smoking *LoveBoats* which kept us lovely and on our grind. PCP aka Wet had become one of the more popular drugs going on and every since Deshawn and Philly laced me I tampered with it from time to time. *Love Boats* made my sex drive sky high and the thrill of sex was great when I smoked. Love Boats would boost up Taz's sex drive and it gave him stamina and we would fuck all night 12 hours of exotic sex and fun. Kay loved my baby boy Tay, she thought that he was the cutist, chunkiest baby that she had ever seen. Kay had just found out that she was pregnat so she would always wish for a boy whom looked like her adorable little cousin Tay (my baby). Pooh Pooh spent alot of time over his grandparents house because DeShawns mom had him so spoiled that it was sometimes hard for me to deal with Pooh Pooh because he was just a grandma's boy, Pooh Pooh would sometimes just cry and cry for his grandma. Taz had Tay spoiled as if Tay was his own biological child. At this point Taz really seemed to be a great provider something that I wasn't getting from DeShawn so I wanted to keep Taz close to me and try to be a good woman even though I didn't know that if I was ready to settle down. I wanted things to be right and I had already been threw so much. Poody would come over and visit me alot. Poody had became close to D-Boys wife and she would make up these dance routines, she even went to Detriot with D-Boys wife. Poody was making moves and I was raising my two children. Poody was only 13 and 14 years old and was already having sex and partying like when I was her age and I had already been through now Poody was beginning her stages of GOING THREW. We had a "Hard Knock Life" as Jay Z would say. It was hard growing up in the K. Poody had even started having sex with a much older man who was in his late 30's or early 40's. Poody was growing up way to fast and although she was adopted, she lived her life however she wanted. Poody's birthday was coming up and the older man that she was messing with happened to be a DJ so we planned a huge party a CeCe house. Kay and CeCe were down with the party as long as things didn't get out of control. Kay had alot of male friends whom she had known from her block. Kay also had an older male friend who was in his 40's who she would call for money and Kay was younger than I was. I felt left out when it came to having a "Sugar Daddy" I wasn't quite into "Sugar Daddies". I knew that I could get anything that I wanted and needed from Taz. Taz made sure that I didn't want for anything. Downies old man kept chasing me and I was dodging him. I was completely disgusted by old men, plus I saw how the old men had more game than the young ones. Old men didn't want to have to come off 3 and 4 houndred dollars for sex let alone conversation and all I had for an older man was conversation baby. I felt like Old mens breath STANK and I didn't want any parts of that. If I couldn't talk an old man out his pockets by my conversation then I didn't want what was in his pockets either way. We had Poody's Party and it was packed to capacity. It was alot of kids Poody's age at the party and I had fun dancing around being me, managing things making sure that everything was being ran smoothly and making sure that none of them younger children were getting to drunk and carried away. Poody was very wild so I had to watch her because she showed her wild side that night. Kay reminded me alot of Jada Pinkett Smith. Kay was absolutly BEAUTIFUL in my eyes she didn't have a flaw. I always told Kay how beautiful she was but for some reason I felt like Kay was showing this jealous streak. Kay also completed me alot on my apprearence like my hair, my butt, my body and things like that. Kay would say that I was *Thick* and that she wanted to be thick. I would say that Kay was Perfect with no stretchmarks and beautiful dimples in her cheecks with a beautiful skin tone just like Jada. Despite some of Kay sways I took a liking to her. I didn't like alot of disrespect that I would see when it came to Kay disrespecting her own mom but that was family business but again I witness Kay literally calling her mom bitches and things like that I didn't approve of. No matter what my mom put me threw I would not ever call my momma out her name, put my hands on her in a bad way none of that I would treat my mom with respect no matter what. I would not let no one disrespect my momma and that's just how I feel. I tried to talk to Kay about her disrespectful ways when it came to her mom but Kay wouldn't listen. Kay had so many excuses for being disrespectful to my cousin and I didn't like it which made me act differently towards Kay. Kay would also say things like her mom slept with her boyfriend but to me that was bullshit and just Kay trying to justify why she would be so evil to her mom. Cece had a house right across the street from a popular Car Shop and all of the KC hot rides would be up there. Nice cars meant BALLER ALERT. Kay started acting like the jealous type and she was getting mad because Taz was always at home with me and when he wasn't he was bringing me money home. Taz made sure that he came home to me every night and I don't think that Kay liked that because she was pregnat and didn't have her babies dad there with her every night. One night as I waited on Taz to come home Kay was up to some tricks. I was in bed waiting on Taz when one of Kay's male friends came running in my room trying to hop in my bed with me real quick to play it off. Kay had other male company when her unborn childs father popped up on her so now Kay had to use me as a crutch and I didn't like getting used in that manner. I was furious as I thought to myself, "Damn Bitch, now what if Taz came home and your nigga is hiding out in my room ". It was a messy situation and not to mention Kay's dude really started trying to put his mack down on me. It was to much going on and I didn't have time for any messy situations. Kay got the situation together really quickly. kay had a smart mouth and liked to start alot of shit talking like a drama queen and the only drama I was interested in was my own. Months later Kay had her baby and named him after my son Tay and my ex Taz. I was kind of confused by Kay's naming of her son but it was all love. Shortly after, Kay and I had a huge arguement and I couldn't deal with her mouth without giving her these hands so before I put my hands on my little cousin I decided to move out with me and my new family in order to keep the peace.

CHAPTER
27
. . . .

WHEN IT RAINS IT POURS

IT WAS A hard time. I had two boys and homeless. It was hard moving house to house. I was no longer in SRS custody so I knew that I had to make some better choices in order to protect my children from going threw all the heartache and pain that this life can bring. I felt like Downey owed me she was the reason why I had lost my apartment and Downey had now gotten her a new apartment so Taz, the boys and I went to live with Downey. I didn't care what or how Downey felt she owed me and she acted like she didn't want us coming to live with her. I began to have a change of heart about alot of things I felt like the devil was on one shoulder and My Guardian Angle was on the other shoulder. I knew that I didn't want to sell dope to my momma but she knew that Taz and I sold dope so I came to a realization that momma was going to get her dope wether I sold it to her or not so I had to make a deep decision knowing that I was in a situation and I needed the money for my moms grandchildren and I. If I didn't seel her the dope then she would just go put the money into someone elses pockets and momma wanted me to GET THE MONEY. Rico was always out at Downy apartment and Rico was still in a relationship with Downy's big sister. Rico ended up getting Downy's big sister pregnat so Downy and I became like family. Downy had also went behind my back and hooked Taz up with one of our mutual "White Girl" friends from the group home so I felt betrayed and Downey and Taz were being decietful to me so I also had a few tricks up my sleeve. things started becoming physical between Taz and I something happened at Downey house and I became so mad at Taz that I put all his clothes in Downy's bathtub and I poured bleach on everything clothes shoes and all. Downy's apartment smelled like bleach for the next two weeks. My temper was beginning to get worse and I had just gotten out of an abusive relationship with DeShawn. I knew that my patience was getting thin and I didn't to want to make the same mistake that momma had made "One stab wound to the heart ONE MAN DEAD". I remembered that look on mommas face when the police put her in the backseat of the police car and drove her away from the crime scence and that look on my mommas face played in my head for many and many of years. Momma once again" A woman Scorned and I had to witness that horrible day along with my siblings. I knew that abuse in a relationship was that I had a 0 tolerance for. Basically I had taken my mother as one of my clients, growing up my mom always had my back and had me serves which meant I had my clients, rental cars, jewelry, etc. One time momma came with me A rental car and the car happen to be a stick gear. I lied and said that I knew how to drive a stick because I wanted the transportation. So while I was driving Downey was controlling the stick. We burned out the clutch of that car before we made it five blocks away. Mama was leery about bringing the cars to me after that (at least the ones that weren't automatic). Mama became one of my loyal customers and of coarse like a family we worked together. One day particularly it was a cloudy day "When It Rains It Pours". Momma had gotten me a rental car, of coarse I paid for it. I went to pick Poody up. Poody was always my Ridah. Poody had a friend with her and Downey wanted me to come back and pick her up. Taz wasn't at home so I was trying to get out in traffic to make some MOVES. Poody and I always listened to our music LOUD and got our roll on. I mad it back to pick Downy up and we got ready to leave. We were all excited to be out of the house enjoying ourselves. Poody got into the passenger seat and Downy and the other two passengers positioned themselves in the backseat putting Poody's friend in the middle because she was the smallest. It was a cloudy day outside and it didn't say that it was going to rain on the forecast so things seemed weird but I didn't let weird things stop my day. I wanted to enjoy my day rain, sleet or snow. As I drove away in the mist of the cloudyness it began to slightly sprinkle. As I approached the highway which was 18th st espressway headed towards 18th st (The City) I turned the music up and put my foot on the gas *All Gas No Breaks*. As the car mad a slight shift I looked at my speed limit. I was going 65 miles per hr in a 55 mile per hour speed zone. I was just getting on the highway so I was trying to pick up A little speed. I turned up the music as a popular song came on the radio and I pressed on the gas a tad bit more. I quickly felt my steering wheel shift hard as if someone had just grabbed my sturing wheel. The steering wheel was shifting hard and out of control left and right where I could not hold the steering wheel steady using all of my strength so now the car was going out of control. I tried to press on my break as everyone began to scream. The break was stuck and there wasn't anything that I could physically do everything had spirraled out of control just that fast. At this point all I could do was hold on and listen to the screams trying my best to control the vehicle. I couldn't understand what was happening. I couldn't control the steering no matter how hard I tried and I couldn't press the break. the car began to weave left and right. This was some type of nightmare. I thought in my head when the next thing was a huge crash. We smashed right into the median. The backseat passengers were all screaming in pain and terror as I lifted my head. My fingers were locked holding that steering wheel. I looked over to my passenger and Poody was knocked out due to the impact on the side that she was on was the side that I had wrecked on. I didn't see any blood so I began to shake and slap Poody in order to wake her up. I was praying to God that my sister was alright as I shook her. I was scared, mad and confused all at the same time. Poody opened her eyes while the backseat passengers continued to scream. I was scared because I knew that I didn't have a drivers license. I heard the ambulance and the police sirens so Im knew that help was on the way. I called Taz to tell him what had happened and to have him come and pick me up. Everyone began to exit the car but Poody's friend that was in the backseat couldn't move. The Police pulled up and they asked me for my name, I gave them a fake name due to my license. The officers asked me if I needed medical attention and I declined thier help but Poody's friend couldn't move so I knew that something really bad had just happened. The ambluance came and the passengers were all rushed to the hospital. Taz picked me up and we rolled away from that scene. That was my first time being the driver in an accident and I was absolutely terrified. I knew that something had just happened that wasn't all my fault. the car that I was driving was a rental car from enterprise and it was a brand new Kia when Kia's first came out. "What went wrong"? We made it back to Downy's and my momma was really shaken up by the whole accident. I had a bone sticking straight up in my finger. I knew that my finger was indeed broken but I couldn't go to the Hospital. Everyone was sore and bodies were hurt. Poody's friend had to be rushed into surgery she had a broken Pelvis Bone. I was so sad for Poody's friend and I didn't know what to do in order to help her. I wasn't suppose to be driving without a license so thier was nothing that I could do but stay in the house and away from smokers cars. Later on I found out that the car's axel had broken on me and the accident was not at all my fault but I was indeeed driving a faulty car. That wreck was out of my control. I was scared and I felt like my life had just flashed right in front of my eyes. From that day forward momma also took cautions before bringing me rental cars. I thanked God for saving me because I knew that God had just spared our lives. I was driving 70 mph in a 55 mph zone so I knew that things could have been worse. Things began to take place at Downy's house so I didn't want to be there so me and the boys went to move in with Erica. I got along better with Erica. Plus Erica wanted the boys and I to move in with her but she did not want Taz to move in which was fine with me because Taz and I had been going threw some things and I need time to find me. Taz wasen't faithful to me and I wasn't faithful to Taz. Although Taz and I liked being together we both realized that we really needed to be apart at this point in time. I wasn't ready to settle down and neither was Taz. When feelings get involved with emotions, other things come into play especially along with Fedility. I agreed to move with Erica, Erica was my party Buddy and Erica and I shared more of the same interest. Erica kept a clean home and I liked stability and organization. Erica also knew how to Hustle, we got high and were still able to maintain with all of our daily functions which was something that Downy lacked in. Erica would also keep her appearence up to par which was also something that Downey lacked. I had put a couple of applications in so I was waiting on a few waiting list to get me my own place. Taz and I kept our relationship we just no longer lived in the same home. Anything I needed Taz was right there for me and the boys. Erica's son and my son were maybe 5 or 6 months apart so we both had small children. Erica was still in the apartments that Downey and I had moved from so I had to play my cards right in order to keep Erica out of trouble as a friend something that Downey didn't do for me. Erica was looking out for me and as a friend I wanted to be 100 with Erica. erica knew that I had a ton of male friends and so did she so it was now *Game Time*. I would kick it with Philly from time to time over his parents home right around the corner from Deshawn but Deshawn wouldnt know. Philly would have some wild get togethers and everyone would have fun like Celly Cell. Philly kept different kinds of drugs and money and had his male friends and I had drugs and money and had my female friends and we would all get fucked up and party. Money, smoke, drink, and fuck that was our mission. I remember one day at Philly's we were play fighting, me and a mutual guy friend and I acted like I was going to hit him in the head with a can of spray starch and when I swung the cannister it was a trick gone bad. We were all talking shit to each other just having a good time as usual when Lee called me a bitch. I picked up the can of starch to act like I was hitting him but when I swung the can the top of the can came off and the can really hit him in the head and I busted his head on accident. I was scared because it was a game and it happend so fast. When I saw the blood run down Lees's face my eyes got big and I saw the anger in his face. If I wasnt the homegirl in the hood things had a way of going from playful to serious 0–100 real quick. Lee was mad ass fuck for the rest of the day and I learned a vauable lesson about playing. I had a dangerous side. We were all smoking that Juice and sometimes things can get Scary. You had to beware of things like random Orgy's as well because of things could also get a bit on the freaky side. One day me and Erica were down at Philly's when Erica had sex with one of Philly's friends and some bad things about one person just to get what they want from you so you had to beware of things like that you literally had to gaurd your kitty as a prized possession or your prize might have got took. We had alot of fun at Philly's and Philly's had two sisters who would also be in on the fun. Philly's mom had taken a liking to me I could tell by some of the things that she would say to me, I even believed that she wanted me to have her a grandchild. I had alot of fun with Philly behind De'shawn back and especially after De'shawn told me that he had sex with my only sister. De'shawn hurt me with his words so many times that I had been broken and I wanted him to feel the same pain that I felt but I didnt want to have a baby with Philly that was just to far not to mention that Philly was also having sex with Poody but was lying to me about it. Philly was the homie and I was the Home boy's babymomma. Poody would come over and and party alot with us at Philly's plus Poody had met a group males who like across the street from Philly who did the same thing we did with the juice. Me, Erica and Erica's aunt went half on a car which was my first car. We split the money three ways so that it was all of our cars and we had our own transportation without having to rent smokers cars Ericas aunt had also moved in with Erica so that was a plus because we began to all work together. Me and Erica would go in with our money half and half to buy our drugs to sell so we now sold crack and PCP. Me and Erica made a good team although there was one thing I didnt like. One day I noticed my baby crying alot and Erica's son was several months older than my youngest son and Erica's son would pick up his toys in the play pen and hit my son in the head with toys. My son had several knots on his head because of Erica's son and that started making me mad. They were babies but they couldnt even play in the same playpen without Erica's son hitting my son and I got to the point where I wanted to politly spank Erica's baby on the hand for hitting my baby. Attitudes were beginning to rise. Some people say two or more women living together is like a ticking time bomb eventually there will be an explosion and sure enough the saying was true. It all started one night while we were all over Philly's house partying. I dont know how Taz found me but he did. Taz was mad because he was still providing for me and the boys but couldn't live with us at Ericas and we were all partying at Philly's house when someone noticed Tez outside by our car with a gun and he had broken our car window. It was about to be a terrible altercation with Philly and Taz. Taz was mad and somehow he found out that I was at Phillys and he was all in his feelings. I was mad because Taz didnt have the right to come over there disrespecting busting windows out of a car that I didnt purchase on my own. That was what I call a Bitch move. Philly was mad because Taz had that gun out there and there were some words exchanged back and forth by Philly and Taz. I didnt want anyone to get hurt behind me so I left philly's home. Me, Erica and Erica's aunt was mad because we had all put in on that car together. It was a nice little car our only means of transportation and we worked together as a team to get. Remember that was the beginning of that steam of events. I got the window that Taz had broken fixed by De'shawns dad, he put some plexy glass in it until I was able to get the regular glass fixed. It was winter time and we couldn't survive winter in the cold without a window. Weeks later I had plans with a couple of my male friends. I had a few tricks up my sleeve and a few male friends whom I were involved with. Taz was only my top option but I saw alot of things in Taz that I knew in my heart me and Taz would not last. The relationship with De'shawn had scared me mentally. I was scarred mentally anyhow, I had plans to go to the hotel with a friend of mine and a couple of his male friends. Me and Erica had an agreement. Although it was winter and snow was on the ground I didnt want to be stranded overnight at that hotel room I was just going to have a little bit of grown and sexy fun. Erica agreed that she would come and pick me up from the hotel that night. That night I went to the hotel with a male friend named J and his two friends Lunatic and Boo. This night was very weird and turn in to be a night that later lead to a stream of kansas city most remembered events. That night at the room me and J had a very deep conversation that later manifested into a horrible spree of crimes and murders, Have you ever heard of the *Kansas City Vampire*. Me, Lunatic and Boo all smoked wet. I found out that night they did another drug they snorted powder cocaine aka Tony montana. J and Lunatic kept going to the bathroom at the hotel for long periods of time and they were talking about something. I tried to listen at the door but Boo kept watching me and I was the only female there so I was kind of nervous. I kept hearing them sniffling and running water. Finally they came out the bathroom. We smoked a couple sticks then me and J began our time. J asked me to get in the shower with him and I assumed that it was because Boo was still in the room, Lunatic had made a run and I figured J wanted to do some freaking in the shower. I agreed to get in the shower with J although I was starting to get nervous and wanted to go back to Erica's. I played along. Me and J got in the shower together and thats when J began to open up to me in conversation as we both washed ourselves up. J told me that the devil had been talking to him and Lunatic and telling them to do some crazy things.

He explained to me a situation where something happend and he was running threw the woods barefooted as the police chased him and Lunatic. He just kept saying that the devil told them to do it. I wanted to change the conversation. I was just getting more nervous and just wanted to get J's mind off of whatever it was that he had been thinking about so I began caresssing his body and we had some hot, steamy conversation in the shower When we were done with that I called Erica to come and pick me up as we agreed and Erica did not show. I was furious!! I had to stay in that hotel room all night with J after the devil had been speaking to him. I wasn't at all scared I was more mad because me and Erica had an agreement that she didnt keep and now I felt like she abandoned me. The next day I recived a phone call some apartment through HUD had an apartment for me and I was excited. I was so ready to move out of Ericas home especially after she left me in that hotel room with J all night. I prepared myself for my new apartment it was going to be a new start for me and the boys and I did not want anything to jeopardize it. I found out how hard it was to live with other people and I was so ready for my own place. Pooh Pooh was going on three and Tay was two they needed their own home and own space plus Taz was excited because we could finnaly be back together as one. Taz hated the fact that I had moved with Erica and he couldn't move in ericas home with me. Once I finally got all my paper work filled out and found out where we were moving, my mouth dropped. The projects. I had family in the projects but the projects were not safe at all. The projects had a huge crime rate alone down on 1st, 2nd and 3rd street. Oh well, I thought. It was better then being homeless. I would just have to learn how to take the bitter with the sweet. I was ready and trained to go.

CHAPTER

28

....

WHEN IT RAINS IT POURS
BUT PREPARE FOR THE FLOOD

WE DO THIS for real. I for the first time ever got stuck in them *PROJ-ECTS* and I knew that I didn't want to be down there. Society gave me no option all because I didn't have any income so I was a black female no income stuck in the projects no options. I was excited just to be able to have my own though. Erica and I were unable to reach a mutual agreement about how we were going to split our product and our car that we had all went in on and brought together. Something went wrong quickly between Erica and I and we didn't quite see eye to eye. Night time hit, I had our product that we went in on and Erica must have thought that I was a weak chick. As I continued my night of moving in trying to get settled in my new apartment Erica, her aunt and her aunties husband pulled up in OUR car in front of my home. Erica was mad and obnoxious stating that I should give her our product. I simply tried to reason with Erica and tell her that we needed to sit down and reach a mutual agreement about our small assests when quickly things took a turn for the bad 0 to 100 real quick. Before I continue *My Story* I wanted to give a shout our to a Comedian that I was blessed and able to attend that has now scarred me for life with on of his jokes. A Comedian that I was able to see up close and a little to personal with his (Ball/Nut Sack) joke. Thanks Arnez J for scarring me for life lol. I loved your show and had a wonderful time but what an EYE POPPER. These are my life experiences. I was cute that night Arnez so I bet your a bit shocked by *My Story* but aye in a *Diamond In The Rough*I love Comedians and thier hard work they put in to just get people to laugh and put thier daily lives to the back of thier minds for a coulpe of hours and one of my favorites is Chris Tucker and Mike Epps but I really love Eddie Murphy and Martin Lawrence also God Bless all you people who go out and work hard for THE PEOPLE and dont look down on THE PEOPLE who support you. Alot of these rappers/artist get besides themselves forgetting that it's your fans who BRING THE MONEY but ya'll make it and accumulate money then get disrespectful and beside yourself forgetting where you really came from and how you made it there. People don't no how to support people after they have made it to the top so I have some mixed feeling about things these days. Now back to *My Story* Erica pulled up outside of my little project mouse infested place with some beef up her sleeve with the same car that I had invested my money into in an uncivilazed manner. In the car with Erica was her auntie weighing 350–400 lbs and her aunties husband. the whole situation didn't look good. I came to the door in order to resolve the situation at hand when things got all out of control 0–100 REAL QUICK. Remind you that Poody, Rico and Taz were all there with me helping me and the babies move into our new home. Erica left my porch after I tried talking to her and she went to the trunk of the car and grabbed a Crow Bar. I was busy trying to talk things out not noticing that Erica was trying to really BEEF. Erica tried to hit Poody in the head with a Crow Bar while Poody's back was not facing Erica and Rico caught everything while it was happening. Rico grabbed that CROW BAR and Erica got slung to the ground. Poody realized what had just happened and that Erica was trying to attack her so Poody automatically started fighting Erica and the fight was on. I ran outside NO MORE NICE LADY while Erica and Poody fought I ran up and started fighting Erica's fat ass auntie. I was hitting Erica's auntie and she wouldn't fight me back until I hit her one good hard time and the fat bitch football tackled me. I fell to the ground and I noticed Poody run to help me. Poody was on Erica's aunties back swinging from her back as I managed to get to my feet. as I got back up I noticed one of Ericas cousins approach the scene and hand Erica's auntie a gun. I saw the gun being handed so I hit Erica's auntie with all my might and she dropped the gun to the ground. Erica's aunt's husband tried to hurry up and retrieve the gun from the ground but Taz had things governed. Taz pulled out his little 25 (gun) stepped on the gun that was on the ground and pointed his gun to Erica's aunt's husbands head and made him get up saying "I got two 25's now". Everything got quiet and quick as Poody and I began to argue with Erica and her aunt. I was MAD. Erica tried to hurry up and jump in the car and Taz began to kick out all of the car windows as Erica and her little crew piled up and burnt out from the scene. We had two 25's (guns) and the projects were back quiet as the mouses that roamed the apartments. It was pitch black outside and no one called the police so I went in my house, closed the door, and fired me up a stick out of the bottle that Erica and I had purchased together. Taz and I smoked good that night and enjoyed each others company to the MAX that night. Our adrinaline was pumping and we were all excited about what had just taken place. I wasent scared of the Projects from that point on and I had to be a WARRIOR down there in that battle field. We all knew from that point on that we had to all stick together and we were all ready for war with our two 25's. We were in THE HOOD and like Master P said "We were all BOUT IT BOUT IT" now let the games begin. The next morning people started coming out of thier apartments talking about the fight that WE had the night before. Although not a soul except Erica's family came out of thier house everybody was watching the fight inside thier homes threw thier windows and they had saw everything as it had happened. In Wyandotte County the news travels faster than an airplane. My big brother Tommy Gunn was born and raised in them Projects so it was time for Rico, Poody and I to get a chance to know our Big brother Tommy Gunn. I would soon learn about this dark could that hovered around the Projects and truely learn what it felt like to "Walk Through The Valley Of The Shadow Of Death". It's real in the PROJECTS and only the strong survive. You have to be a WARROIR and NO LIMIT SOLDIER in real life to make it threw. I'm cut from that cloth and CONCRETE so you cant just break me and I don't give in so it was time for war and God had me covered in THE BLOOD.

CHAPTER
29
....

WHEN IT RAINS IT POURS

IT'S OFFICIAL AND now I'm in the Jungle im a LIONESS built for this type of environment. It seems like im not alone in this jungle because I started quickly picking up on my surroundings. Turns out that my Best Friend Candy also lives in the Projects just on the opposite side of me. I lived right in the middle of the Jungle which was the worse part to live in and the part that Candy lived on was the not so violent side. Turns out that Candy had been having herself a sexual relationship with someone close to me and she or I didn't even realize it. It was my brother from another mother Tommy Gunn. Candy knew that I had a big brother she just hadn't ever met him. Candy didn't know me as well as she thought she did. We call my brother Tommy Gunn(Tommey Gunn) for various reasons. Tommy Gunn is a Leo like me and we look alot alike even though we have different moms he looks like my dad and I look alot like my dad as well. Tommy Gunn and I look alike and we also act alike in alot of ways he's just a male and I'm of coarse female BUT DONT GET MY FEMMINE TWISTED. Tommy Gunn and Rico became very close and Rico and Tommy Gunn had something going on with Candy and her little sister. This dude named Hamp that DeShawn and I both went to school with and were mutual friends with also lived down there in the Projects. Hamp had always had a thing for me in high school and I had been knowing Hamp since middle school but Hamp lived down there with his daughters mom and when he saw me he would try to get at me but I had Taz and wasn't going anywhere until I said so. Hamp was always one of those kids in school who knew how to fight because he had a "Cleft Lip" so he got teased alot and would beat kids ass alot to. Hamp was cool and he was one of DeShawns friends. I called Hamp "A BEAST" because of his whole demenor. Although I knew that Hamp had a temptation for me I thought that it was cute and I ignored him. I liked a RUDE boy, a protector, a GOVENOR, a BEAST like me in this jungle. There were several other people that I was soon to meet because Tommy Gunn knew everybody and had alot of family down in those Projects so I met alot of important people fast. If you were Tommy Gunns family you were my family. Tommy Gunn was always at my house because we had years of catching up to do. It was time for my siblings to get close together and know one another on a more personal level. One of my BIG homies that I knew from school and he was also Poody's adopted moms Carol's nephew he lived down there so we got really close his name is Big Russ. Big Russ is a Leo like me so we became close friends quickly. I began to hear about all the dark tales that lerked about in the projects. The stories were heart breaking and scary, all the murders and all the BLOOD SHED. It was real down there in the Jungle but there was also some love. Cousin Ox also lived down there and his sisters that I grew up around. My Auntie made alot of money down there in that alley before she passed away so alot of family and people still hung around down there in the Alley. Taz and I started to argue more and more but we remained a couple. Poody lived with her adopted mom but she was always over my house with me. I had my habits and Poody also started picking up on some of those habits. Poody was only 14 years old at the time, I love my little sister but I didn't want her picking up my habits. Poody was doing things that I hadn't even done before and I was now a grown woman. Poody started smoking PCP and she also started stripping in the "Crap House* located in Missouri and her dance name was *Rolex*. I began to wonder how in the fuck was my little sister getting in into these types of places doing these types of things. Poody had a really nice body like Beyonce at the age of 14 *Nothing Personal to Beyonce* but we were doing things in the K and we didn't grow up with a SILVER SPOON. Poody was all natural and very beautiful but she was young and my baby sister whom I didn't want living this kind of lifestyle so early in age. Poody and I would always have Twerk Off contest and everyone loved to watch us and record us. Being that Im the oldest with two children I had morals and stretchmarks but people always thought that I was a lovely sight to see. Thick, chocolate and shaped like an hour glass or coke bottle beautiful inside and out. I was confident in myself and my body but I had my flaws that DeShawn had installed in me from his verbal abuse but I didn't let those flaws bring me down I knew exactly who I was as a woman and as a person. I quickly began to build my circle of associates. There was a couple of apartments/townhomes that were getting broken into down there in the Jungle so I had to quickly learn who was who. Mostly everyone was family although there were some haters whom you had to be aware of and keep an open eye of your surroundings. I began to know my next door neighbors. Winter was over and Spring was approaching so there were more and more people coming out. Everyday was a party. Taz and I stayed on our HUSTLE. Lots of Tommy Gunns family and friends always came around so everyone knew me as thier CUZ. Momma was always at my house and we kept product, different types of product. An old friend of the family (my moms and uncles friend) would come around alot and I didn't really trust him because him and my big cousin lil Ulysis had already had a terrible altercation so my big cousin Ulysis had been locked up in Prison for alot of time. Where im from you TRUST NO ONE. The families friend name was Kev and Kev was always lerking. Even though I had product I had to be aware of the LURKERS. Kev would always come over trying to buy product but he knew that I smoked so he always wanted to smoke with me and I didn't like that because I had my own shit and could smoke by myself whenever I wanted to plus Kev also smoked crack and he liked mixing CRACK WEED and WET (PCP) I had whatever Kev wanted but I wasn't for no BS. Kev was BUFFED and looked like he worked out because he had big huge muscles but again something had happened were lil Ulysis had beaten Kev with a crow bar so I didn't trust NOTHING because in the JUNGLE people had motives. Kev was like a snake to me and I don't like snakes. I knew what was going on I best believe that I was TRAINED TO GO, so i kept a close eye on old boy Kev. Rico and Tommy Gunn were like night and day but they got close. I raised Rico and Rico was not a cheater Tommy Gunn on the other hand had plenty of females. Rico was the husband type because he had a big sister like me always in his ear. Tommy Gunn on the other hand I don't no but it was ALL LOVE either way. I couldn't judge Tommy Gunn for his ways because I hgad ways of my own. I started to build a closer friendship with Candy now that we were all grown up and didn't have to deal with ADULTS being in our way. I would go over Candy's house alot and conversate with her to build on our friendship and catch up. Candy and I were complete oppsites but when were together we just leveled each other out. Candy had two little girls now and I had two boys. Being that Candy lived on the quiet side of the JUNGLE her house was more peaceful than mine. One night Candy and I decided to go out to the club. We went to a night club and that's where the FUN began. We took some pictures together while we were inside the club and the pictures came out GREAT! We took some beautiful pics together so it was no wonder why ALL EYES WERE ON US. Candy and I THE LIFE OF THE PARTY once again. All heads turned when we stepped in. The night went so well that we got invited on someones "Party Bus" at the end of the night. Candy and I made a deal that if we came to the club together than we would leave the club together.

everything was going good on the party bus until someone got mad. Something happened and it happened fast. I was ready to go home because I knew that I wasn't doing no fucking I had Taz at home and I was most definitly not looking for a one night flight. Candy had alot to drink and I could tell because of her behavior. I could tell that Candy was drunk because of her movements but she was a grown woman so I let her handle herself. Something happened that almost got us put off the Party Bus. I had to maintain that's why I didn't drink any alcohol and I wasn't about to let anyone take advantage of me because I was drunk NO WAY. We made it off that Party Bus safe and we laughed about the whole incident the next day but I told Candy about herself and her drunkeness shanangains. Again everyday was like a Party. There was a Night Club up the Street from where I lived so I went to the night Club on occasion when I need a piece of mind and time to think. Seems like the dark tales would always surface involving unsolved Homicides and people were mad about thier loved ones being murdered in cold blood and nothing being done about it. I started putting popular names with faces. There were some people down there who I associated with that put in serious work. I quickly became aware of what a Hood *Birthday Cake* was all about and if your from the hood you know exactly what I mean (hit with a brick) down in the BRICKS. Nothing sweet about it I tell you. There was some real evil lurking down there in the Brick Jungle. I had also just dogged a bullet. Remember when I told you about me being stranded at the Hotel room when Erica was supposed to pick me up and dude talking about the demons talking to him with J, KC Vampire and Boo. Breaking News just hit the town. The Police discovered some dead bodies in the basement of KC Vampire's home. Bodies that had been eaten on and hidden in the basement of his mother's home KC Vampire is also known as "the Kansas City Vampire". When this story hit the news my heart dropped and I felt a sense of heartache and disquest mixed with anger and rage. I was just recently stranded with this dude and now this horrible crime committed right after J told me that Demons were talking to him and KC Vampire. I know that something was bigger to this crime than would ever be heard because DEMONS are real. I was hurt because the body found was that of a neighborhood boy that I knew who lived around the corner from DeShawn not to mention KC Vampire's mom's house where the bodies were found were also right around the corner from DeShawn's house KC Vampire's mom's house. There was a dark cloud hovering not only around the Brick Jungle but also around Kansas and things were hitting to close to home. DeShawn was close to KC Vampire and days before the bodies were found in the basement Mark tried to Get DeShawn to help him go to his house and unload a huge Chest so heavy that it took two grown men to lift. THESE ARE FACTS IM LADY JUICE AND TELL YOU NO LIES IM THE TRUTH A WARRIOR IN THIS JUNGLE A SURVIOR AND I THANK GOD YE THOUGH I WALK THROUGH THE VALLEY. Days before they found Freds body ate up in KC Vampire's basement Poody and I was walking from DeShawns and Fred was trying to be cute on his motorcycle in front of us both and fell off the motorcycle embarassed. That was the last time I saw Fred. SICK and SAD but the Devil is REAL people. *My Story* is true facts and I can back everything I say. KC Vampire didn't appear to me to be some type of serial Killer but he killed many of people. It was sad and I had heard just about enough. I had to be aware of my surroundings. I had yet to see a dead body and I didn't want to so I was walking on egg shells trying not to crack one. All those bad dreams I had been having over the years were making me aware. I just wanted happiness and to live a normal, happy, wealthy life like Kisha Knight, Raven Samone, and Janet Jackson not here in this Brick Jungle fighting roaches and rats. There has to be a better way is all I thought and I was going to PUSH for mine. One day I was outside when I was approached by one of Tommy Gunns cousins who also calls me her cousins named Dimples. Dimples was a Stripper. She approached me talking all this talk about how I would make a great Adult entertainer so on and so forth. I told Dimples no I would not and that I had Stretch Marks on my stomache but she insisted that my stretch marks weren't bad and that she saw worse and that I would be a Great ENTERTAINER. I knew that I had potential but not this kind as I thought to myself only because of my stretch marks. I told Dimples that I would talk that idea over with Taz first to see what he had to say about all of that business. That night at home I had a deep conversation with Taz about how Dimples approached me and the whole conversation. Taz agreed that I had the body and the looks for it also I could dance but Taz felt like me Dancing for a living would open up doors to a whole other world. I assured Taz that if I did indeed consider Adult Entertainment that it would simple be professional and he had nothing to worry about that he had my best interest and would have to put his trust in me as a good woman with good intentions. I was unsure of exactly what I was saying but I didn't want Taz to be someone who couldn't put his trust in me although I wasn't certain if I wanted to conduct myself in that manner. I need extra money I had two children to feed. I had to think about all this Dancing yea I liked to dance but dancing in front of strange men naked was just not going to be right in my eyes. I had plenty of things that I didn't like doing and momma being my personal customer was one of them. I loved my momma and didn't like providing drugs to her no matter the struggle. I had to make a decision and quick. I talked to Candy about it to see what she had to say. Poody was already Dancing at clubs without a license and we were true Queens of Twerk we just didn't make videos for the world to see which is why I didn't feel comfortable dancing infront of a bunch of THIRSTY HOUNDS. Adult Entertainment was a whole other ball game and I was unsure because of my spiritual ways and beliefs. I thought about it long and hard for about a week or two but Dimples also lived the the Brick Jungle so she made sure she made a mention everytime she saw me from that day forward. I needed some excersise I thought first. I was shy and I didn't belong in no Strip Club with all that I had been through with PERVERTS!. I had a shyness within me. I needed to practice in the mirror. All kinds of thoughts ran through my head. I danced for this one guy who was the neighborhood Trick Daddy who had been trying to get me for the longest but he was older and I didn't like older men. I danced for him one day he took me to his home and tried to flirt with me and make me strange offers that I declined so I decided since he had lots of money and lots of women that he had a good eye for talent. I wanted the opinion of another man other than Taz to give me an honest opinion. I had a small area to dance in but I did a small dance for the man his name is Mink. Mink was not enthused with my little dance performance and he told me that he didn't think that I had what it took. I was to shy and could barely dance in front of him so how would I be able to move a whole crowd of HOUNDS. Mink's comment had just added fuel to my fire and I wanted to prove Mink wrong and I knew that I had potential no matter what he said with his trickin ass. I made my decision and I took Dimples up on her offer. Dimples worked at a Strip Club named Gus Goldmins. Gus was a little Italian Man, I went to the Club to meet Gus. Gus gave me an Intent to Hire application so I went and got my Adult Entertainment License. I was hired and it was just that simple. I had been wearing Stillitoes since the age of 15 so I didn't worry about walking in skinny heals I was a PRO at that. All I had to do now was learn how to "Dance Like A Stripper". Poody and I practiced at home everday before my first day at work and that's when Dimples began to give me the game and knowledge that I needed to no in order to succeed. Dimples laced me with game, she *Sprinkled Me like E-40*. Dimples had a close friend that worked with her prior at Gus Goldmine and her friend had ended up having sex with Eazy E THE RAPPER who had just died of aids so there was alot of things going around and it was getting real. I prayed to God because I was a believer first and farmost and I didn't feel comfortable going down this path no matter what potential Dimples saw in me. Everthing that was going on in my life I prayed every single night. Never in a million years did I think me LADY BUG stripping ENTER-TAINING. Dancing came natural but this getting halfway naked because

I damn sure wasnet going to get nude OVER MY DEAD BODY!. This was to much and my spontanious ways were catching up all because of what one single person doubted me on REALLY. It was to late to turn back I had already went through the process can't get scarred now. I remembered when I was a little girl and would dance to show off for my big cousins to show them that I had skills and could dance and entertain them. I always danced for the Goodings and they enjoyed dancing with me it was talent all in the family. I prayed for God to watch over me at all times because I was now entering a new real life situation something that was all new to me. Growing up Grandma taught me how to Pray first and that's all I've ever known. The struggle is to real and I will always put God first no matter what. I had to learn ways of survival. I wanted and needed better for me and my family. Experience was my best teacher because momma and daddy won't always be around. Fee taught me how to survive even though she scarred me physically and mentally I looked up to her alot but when she did that to me I couldn't look up to her anymore I felt angered. Fee taught me from experience to Trust No One and I lost respect. I had to only trust God and his plans for my life and know that God and only God could protect me. I called on my guardian angle my closest means of comfort. I didn't really want to entertain a group of men but something about it made me curious. My decision was made and the application was final. It was time for me to get on my grown woman and get to the business THE MONEY. DeShawn didn't give me one fiflty penny Taz helped me within my boys and provided. Taz took full responsibility as a man. I had to hope for the best but prepare for the worse because somthing in my heart didn't want Taz for a lifetime not when T-Money was in the picture. I was taught to "Never Count Your Chickens Before They Hatch". I felt like I was in a trap so I had to play my cards right. I stayed high so that I didn't have to face the harsh realities and to keep the mind of a Hustla and business woman. Like "Players Club" I was going to make the money. I knew that I had to really get ready to fight temptation and advances. Sin is real and so are Heaven and Hell, repent of your sins and turn from your iniquities trust me I'm still learning. Ask God to Guide you when somethings we dont seem to understand. The devil comes to Kill, Steal and Destroy. You body is your TEMPLE. In the darkest places if you find light God is that light. God knows us more than we know ourselves. Writing My Story has shown me THE STORM that I went through and made it out of. God is not done with me yet and I have a testimony. My Story is real life and I don't care about any kind of fame. I fear God and his wrath. I'm focused on making it threw the Gates of Heaven not trying to be something that I'm not. I want to save souls, I have been through a fight and it's been a battle that I'm still fighting God made me a fighter for him his WARRIOR. I know that your eager to hear about my life as an entertainer but only God can Judge me and I know your judging my personal character but you didn't walk in my shoes and some have walked in worse shoes I just THANK GOD that I'm able to tell you. My story is a apart of me and this is what I lived through. I want you to grab your children close and cherish them knowing that children are a blessing from God and God works miracles and I've seen Gods works and how the Blood that Jesus Shed is so powerful. Mothers you need to raise your sons to be MEN and take care of thier females not bring them down. How to work honest jobs and stay in school and put God first. It starts at home do ya'll see what went on in my home now before you judge me on my decisions look at what I grew up going threw at home first. Parents it's time to do better and trust me you are going to see how not perfect I am but the difference is that I strive for better and I know how to love my neighbor. Momma is a woman scorned that murder found her. I am a woman STRIVING and DRIVEN WITH DETERMINATION. It's about self respect KNOW YOUR WORTH. Living the Stripper life is definitly something that Im not proud of FAST MONEY AIN'T ALWAYS GOOD MONEY. I didn't have one piece of stripper clothing so I had to go to Pricillas and go shopping plus adult entertainers got a discount on clothing. I got a couple outfits and a pair of shoes to last me until I made some dance money to buy more. I need prayer and motivation. I want to say this about Kansas City as I'm sitting here watching the news and there was just a homicide down in these apartment I lived in as a kid called Gateway that momma set on fire when I was a child. Gateway is a set up there is only one way in and one way out of there. There have been several unsolved homicides down there in Gateway R.I P to one of my close friends Lil Red who's homicide remains unsolved and I would love to help his mother solve with any information I could help out with. I wish that I could help solve Cold Cases that's what my heart desires because I don't like senseless crimes especially black on black robbery kill-ings. How dare you young boys who are you to Judge. I got a story of some young boys like you who kill/murder. I'm going to show you how God works so when you think you've out smarted God look what happens watch as I tell you my story REAL LIFE EVENTS. GOD IS REAL!!. STOP THE KILLING GOD IS GETTING UPSET WITH PEOPLE also you rappers need to stop promoting so muck killing and violence especially if your not really living that life it's called FALSE PROFITS. YOUR SOUL WILL BURN IN HELL FOR ETERNITY if you think your the last JUDGE. GOD IS THE CREATOR. As a mother it hurts me seeing other mothers losing children because you lil boys are cowards. CHICAGO WAKE UP GODS WRATH WILL COME FOR YOU. A woman brought you in this world how do you take another womans child from her? It's not only you Chicago I'm talking to the WORLD NOW. Watch HOW GOD WORKS MY STORY IS REAL FACTS REAL LIFE and GOD IS REAL and who gave you LIFE and if someone didn't love you and protect you, you wouldn't be able to grow up and kill. Look at the babies killed while they were young or the ones aborted BE GLAD YOU GOT BREATH AND STOP TAKING YOUR BREATH FOR GRANTED BECAUSE GOD CAN STOP YOUR BREATH IN THE BLINK OF AN EYE -AN EYE FOR AN EYE, I've seen it happen with my own eyes which is why I'm scarred to blink wrong I FEAR THE WRATH

ONLY, NO MAN! Where I'm from I was taught as a female to knuckle up and call it a day because at the end of the day theirs a tomorrow. Cowards go and shoot up a house in the middle of the night aiming to kill innocent people. Real men stand up for what's right like "Common" the definition of a real MAN. A real man works honestly to provide for his family. A real man protects his family and does good for his family like GRANDPA. Grandpa worked everyday to provide for his family to see a smile on his families face. I love my Grandpa and he is the definition of a GOOD MAN. God made men first for a reason. You young boys are messing up the generation and that's why thiers so much evil and hatred. A man that really loves a woman will respect and honor his mother. He will again PROTECT not HURT or KILL. He will show respect and love to women in general. Boys stop hurting women its time to grow up and be men WOMEN its time to raise MEN not COWARDS it starts at home stop covering up for your childrens mistakes and start correcting the mistakes properly. Everyone has a purpose in life. God wants his souls to go to Heaven not hell and you young men are letting the devil win because he THE devil has filled you with anger and made you think that a Gun is your power whe honesty if you cant use your gifts that GOD gave you (Your Two Hands, your BRAIN First) how can you think that you can make it to heaven. Have you felt the FIRE. FIRE don't feel good, play with fire get burned. Blacks have already suffered enough do a background check our ansetors were SLAVES and were always hated by another human race now why do we hate our own skin color so much? To my white people I LOVE YA'LL, why could ya'll ever have so much hate in your heart to feel superior and better than the next and filled with so much HATRED. Do you know were hatred leads you (TO HELL). God created everyone EQUAL how are you whites better than me because I'm no better than NO BODY WALK-ING THIS EARTH. Hate will lead you NO WHERE BUT IN THE PIT OF HELL. You people can let hate consume you I REFUSE to. I will love those who hurt me and let GOD handle the his people accordingly. God knows I pray for everyone SLAVERY DAY'S ARE OVER and it's sad that white people ever though of some HATRED AS SUCH CONDEMING YOUR OWN FAMILIES SOULS. It's hate and I am here to make a change. I love you white, chinese, mexican, Itilian, BLUE, BLACK, GREEN, ORANGE, YELLOW or PURPLE. We are Gods creations and we make the world go around. Show love and STOP evil ways (there goes my book) because people are so quick to anger and hate until you feel the wrath of GOD. I pray everyday for this world to be a better place. My family is mixed up with different races and mixed children are so beautiful because all things are beautiful when you come together as an equal as ONE. I've seen alot of hate with mixed children coming from the white side of the families DO YOU NO THAT GOD WILL TAKE YOUR VERY PRECIOUS BREATH. Some of you white people have so much hate in you that you will HATE your own flesh and blood because of the color of thier skin when its a PRECIOUS INNOCENT CHILD. White people you wonder why your own children kill you look at the hate you have within your own hearts ITS NOT FAIR. I pray for better, role models, for more love in the world. I pray this DARK cloud away from KS. I PRAY THAT YOU DEMONIC EVIL FORCES MOVE AWAY BACK TO THE PITS OF HELL MOVE IN THE NAME OF JESUS!!!! It's WAR TIME GOOD VS EVIL I'M A WARRIOR IN CHRIST THE BATTLE IS THE LORDS AND MY HEAVENLY FATHER WILL WIN THIS BATTLE I DECLARE BY THE BLOOD JESUS SHED. Lord have mercy on these people's souls and my own in. In Jesus name AMEN.

CHAPTER
30
....

WHEN IT RAINS IT POURS

MY ADRENLINE WAS racing and pumping hard. Im in the dressing room of the Strip Club and it's my first night. Dimples is doing everything in her power to make me feel relaxed but I'm nervous as fuck with all these naked bitches around me. I can't relax for nothing and my heart was racing. I had not came up with a dance name so all the girls are asking me, "What's my dance name going to be." The only thing I had in mind was Chocolate which I had tattooed on my neck. I kept hearing naked bitches asking me "What's your stage name" but all I could see was titties and ass and it's making me even more nervous because not one single female was ashamed of thier bodies and it was a normal thing for them to be running around naked no worries. I had to breathe and brace myself. Dimples introduced me to all of the other dancers and the girls were all welcoming towards me. We all laughed and talked as we got dressed. Everyone helped me try to figure out a stage name they were all trying to get me to chose something other than Chocolate. A couple of the girls recommended that I be called *Peaches* because I had big nice sized titties. I had double D breast and I was insecure about my breast and didn't want anyone to call me peaches, melon or any thing of the sort plus, there was a dancer that worked at the club prior to me working there and her dance name was Peaches so that was a NO for me I didn't care what those dancers were talking about. I was the new thing poppin and I had standards and couldn't be cloned. I was a Diamond In The Rough and I had a mind of my own. I told them other girls that they would not call me peaches and that they would respect all this thick milk chocolate and my dance name would remain Chocolate until I decided on another name for myself. I observed the other girls and I observed myself and my swag as well as thiers. We were all in our dance uniforms, of coarse I was the last one to get dressed and leave the dressing room. I was nervous and I had to analyze the whole scenery. The air was filled with smells of multipule perfumes and lotions. I was ready to leave that dressing room a changed woman, not to mention the customers had started accumlating in the club and the manager needed girls on the stage to entertain. As I walked out of the dressing room I took a deep breath, Lights/Camera/Action. I walked to the bar and took a seat as I tried to keep my legs from shaking and feeling light on my feet. I wanted to watch some of the girls perform to see what Strip Dancing was all about before it was my turn to take the floor. The thought that someone said that I wouldn't make it in the industry just kept dwelling in my head when Dimples interrupted my thoughts. Dimples started conversation with me saying, "aye cousin, so how do you like it so far?" My answer, "Im nervous cousin." Dimples, "Girl your going to do a great job and you look great. You need to find out what loosens you up. Do you need a drink?" Me, "No cousin I don't want to drink I have to analyze the scene. Drinking will make me even more nervous and I have to walk in these heels. Girl my legs are already shaky". Dimples laughed at me and said, "Don't worry cousin you look good with your thick ass and I got you just watch me and I how I move through the club. When it's your turn go to this Juke Box and chose whatever three songs you want to dance off. you can go last since it's your first day. Dont be scarred just watch me it's easy". Me, "Trust me cuz I'm watching everthing. let me get an Ice water that might help me to relax. Bartender may I get a glass of ice water?" Bartender said, "I have a glass of Ice water coming up". I felt like all eyes were on me even though I wasn't on the stage. There was some customers who were trying to make conversation with me but I was trying to watch as Dimples began her performance. I watched Dimples closely as she began to perform. I listened to her music being played closely. Dimples loved dancing to slow music "H-Town" to be exact. Dimples was in her own zone as she groved to the music. Dimples would do things like make her butt cheeks jump left cheek right cheek, to the beat of the music (this was Stripper Dancing) I knew how to make my butt cheeks jump. I knew some of the moves and I thanked God that Gus Goldmine did not have a pole because I did not know how to work the pole. I knew some of the dance moves just from dancing at home and in the Clubs. Time went by I was in a daze and it was now my turn to take the stage. I just remember hearing a voice saying, "Chocolate, it's your turn". I walked from the bar to the stage nervousness set back in. I had set my songs at the Juke box and everything was moving so fast. My song started to play. I cant remember my first song but I know that it was a fast song maybe something like "Ludacris—Fantasy" or "Drunkin Masters—50 niggas Deep". I chose two fast songs and one slow song by "Drew Hill—Beauty". I looked at myself alot in the mirror as I danced trying not to focus at all the eyes that were focused on me. I tried to focus on me and my sexyness as a Stripper. I blocked everyone out literally. My first two song were fast songs so I felt out of breath a little as I reached my third song "Beauty". I was releaved when my third song came on because I had danced so hard my first two songs. I began to sweat bad, I was nervous and my heart was pounding. As my third song played I relaxed and I finally built up the courage to actually face the crowd. As I turned to face the audience all eyes were definitly glued to me. I began to understand why Dimples had danced off slow songs. I felt exhausted like I had been dancing all night. I danced slow not removing any of my clothing but I however showed a little bit a skin (Not to much). When the third song was over I got off the stage so quick, went straight to Dimples to ask her how did I do? My heart was pounding and my body was trembling. Dimples replied, "Cousin, you didn't go collect your tips. You have to go around and politely ask for your tips". I was completely embarassed that I had to go around and ask men for money. I had to make my money so I did as Dimples instructed me to do. Dimples walked around with me letting the regular customers know that it was my first day. Some of the men told me to relax and that I looked good. I noticed that all eyes were on me. The next girl was on stage and I wanted to watch her so I knew what I was up against. I sat down to watch and Dimples sat down besides me to keep me company and to conversate with me and give me some Stripper Knowledge. Dimples told me, "Cousin you are going to have to mingle with the customers, that's how you are going to make your money. Watch me cousin, I'm going to show you the ropes. Were gonna GET THIS MONEY!" I watched Dimples as she did her thing. I also had a few men who were eager to talk to me so I began to loosen up and mingle with the fellas. I began to get bored with conversations quickly so I went back into the dressing room to get freshened up and to get a piece of mind. I noticed that the other girls were all in the dressing room also refreshening up and changing thier outfits. I only had two outfits and I wore my favorite one first. I knew that I had to step my game up and make money so that I could stock up on my attire. the other girls quickly began to mingle with me one in particular. I wasn't a big cigarette smoker but I decided that I would smoke a cigarette and maybe get me a drink to bring back in the dressing room to sip on. I noticed that some of the other girls had drinks in the dressing room. Gus came to the dressing room and told us to get back out in the club area thier were clients building up and we needed to get to work. I began to catch on to things very quickly and see how things were run. Before I knew it my turn had came up again to dance so I had to quickly rush to the Juke Box to get my song in order.

Dimples reminded me she said, "Just remember cousin, you always go after me so when you hear my songs starting, go to the jukebox and get your songs ready ahead of time and you'll be just fine". I responded, "Okay cousin I got it". That night went better than I intended it to. Before I knew it Taz was there to pick me up from work. There was a gay Club across the street from Gus called Soakies. I counted my money as soon as I made it home. Taz and I counted all the money that I had made together. I did better than what I had expected and our tip out was 25 dollars per night so I had to be wise, loosen up and GET THE MONEY. I managed to make enough money to buy me a few more Dance outfits and I had money to also put with Taz to build up our products. I felt relieved that night. My body was sore so Taz gave me a wonderful massage that night to ease the pain and we got high of some product (Juice and weed/ Loveboats) and had sex for about 4–5 hours straight before I made it to bed. Taz and I would always fuck until the sun came up so that wasn't anything new to us. Taz and I were night owls. The next day I went and purchased a couple more Dance Uniforms plus a Garder Belt because my money accumulated really quick. Plus I had to go to family dollar and stock up on hygiene and feminine products to prepare for my work week. I had in house babysitters so the boys were taken care of. DeShawn was unaware of my new job at that point and it was none of his business. The next day at work I got my schedule. I had to work 4 nights out of the week to start off with. The second night after work my whole body was sore like I had just fell down 20 flights of steps with my stillitoes on! I was so happy that I didn't have to work 6 or 7 days a week. Being an Adult Entertainer was not at all easy work *Hats Off*. Dancing was fun and I had a point to prove. I had survived all week and I was doing better each day. It seemed like everyone in the Brick Jungle was aware of my new career. Dimples had private shows lined up for us and I had no clue about any of it but Dimples was orcasterating alot of business for us. My first Private Show was for some well known Bondsmans in KCMO. I didn't believe that I was ready for private shows this soon in the game. Dimples assured me that I was definitly ready, so I went along with what Dimples thought was good. The first Private Show was really wild and I saw alot of things. I was on my menstrual so I didn't really want to perform. This was my first time having to perform being on my menstrual and I was new to Entertainment. Once we made it to the Private Party it was packed to capacity. As soon as I walked in the door there were a couple of females on the floor putting on a FREAK performance. One was smoking a cigarette with her pussy and the other one had both her legs behind her head and they were both BUTT NAKED NO CLOTHING ON AT ALL. The two girls began to perform oral sex on each other right there on the floor right in front of everyone and the crowd was going wild and money was flying from everywhere. We went in the dressing room provided to us in order to get ready to put on our performance. I had put a tampon in me to stop my bleeding as I got ready. It was my turn to dance and I was doing really well all eyes again were on me. I was dancing for a PERIMEDIC (ambluance worker) and I peformed on this particular man. I decided to lay the man down and Get on top of him like I was riding him in a rodeo show when I felt something and looked down and all I saw was blood. I jumped up off the man and ran right out of that room into the bathroom. I didn't understand how I bled through that tampon that quickly. I told Dimples that I was not dancing anymore for the rest of the night and I would just watch everybody when the man came knocking at the door wanting to talk to me. I let the man in to apologize to him for what had just happened. the man assured me that everything was alright and he was definitly not mad he had saw worst things happen. He told me about his career as a Perimedic. The man was very comforting to me and he told me how beautiful I was and how he really wanted me to come back out on the floor just to keep him company personally. I felt alot better about myself. He was genuine and he was not mad at all he actually had alot of respect for me and he was very mature about the situation that had just taken place. I had alot of respect for that man because he was different and he was a real MAN. I also realized that I had a few drinks that night which had thinned my blood. The perimedic offered me another drink and he had a deep conversation with me about how beautiful I was and how I deserved something better than dancing for a career and I asured him that Entertainment for me was only temporarily. I told him that I was new to the industry and the *Stripper Lyfe* was definitly not a lifetime option for me. I got fully dressed and began to watch some of the other girls perform and make thier money. I saw some great entertainment that night. The female dancers were not at all nervous that night and everyone had a great time. It was a good night that taught me a valuable lesson. I would hear other females talk about the stinky females, I was already the type of person who stayed up on my hygeine so I was not worried. If you were a STINKY FEMALE the news traveled around fast and everyone would talk about your business amungst one another. Dancers names traveled really fast and I had people approach me talking about they heard that I was one of Gus's Finest. Different men in the Brick Jungle began to watch me close and make comments like, "Can I get a Lap Dance". I ignored the people and the sexual advances. One night at work this man was there at the Strip Club from out of town. The man from out of town wanted attention from me and only me that night. The man made so many offers to me also he tipped me really well. The man offered me 400 dollars to come to his Hotel Room with him for one hour. I declined the man and his money and he didn't stop the whole night he tried to persuade and persue me. I wasn't in the Club to do those types of things, I had a man at home. Dancing was my job, I was an Entertainer and I was most definitly not about to get into anything unprofessional. Taz was a good provider and I wanted to keep everything on the up and up with Taz. I was definitly not about to cheat with some random even if he offered me 1000 cash. things began to change really quick though. One morning after work as Taz and I woke up as usual after a long night some-one knocked on my room door and Taz jumped up to run to the door to answer the door. Taz and I fucked for hours that night as usual so we both went to sleep naked like we usually slept. I looked up as Taz ran to answer our room door when I noticed a long noticable scratch running down's Taz's ASS cheek. That's when I woke all the way up and began to snap on Taz. I didn't scratch duing sex so where the fuck did that scratch on Taz's ass cheek come from?. I was trying so hard to do the right thing and be faithful to Taz despite our past. Taz began to lie to me saying that he was running from the Police while I was at work and he ran through the woods that's how he got the scratch. Did I have the word STUPID written across my face, I thought in my head as I snapped on Taz? I felt it in my heart that Taz had cheated again. I was hurt and disappointed. Just like what happened with DeShawn, Taz was repeating the cycle that I had already been through. I was fueled with anger not to mention I had just turned down 400 dollars. My womans intuition told me that Taz had cheated on me I just didn't no who he had cheated with. My heart was heavy and I refused to play the fool, NOT ME! How could Taz cheat on me when I made sure to drain his nut sacks when we fucked 4–8 hours straight every single day. I told myself IT'S ON NOW TAZ you have just woke up the BEAST in me. I told Philly that I worked at the Strip Club and Philly wanted to support my moves as a friend. Philly had him a clean Old School on rims, with beat and Hydrolics with a bad ass paint job. Philly would pull up at my house in the Brick Jungle and all eyes would be on me and Philly, of coarse I always rode in the fornt passenger seat with Philly. The night Philly came to the club to see me Perform Taz ended up showing up. I was giving Philly a Lap Dance and all eyes were on Philly and I when I looked up Taz was standing there with this hurt look on his face. Philly was really enjoying himself at that point but I had to play my cards right so no one got hurt. I gave Taz his attention for the rest of the night and of coarse I went home with Taz. Philly and I wanted each other bad that night but I put my feelings to the side and did what a woman was supposed to do. I had particular clients that would come to the Club just to see me perform. One particular client had offered me alot of money in the past that I had declined but now I felt like it was time for me to take this particular client up on his offer. The next day at work I had plans in mind with one of my clients and it was GAME TIME. I decided that it was the perfect time to play the game so the client and I arranged to meet up the next day while I was off work. I was sexually attracted to the client so we hooked up the next day while Taz was out making moves. that client ate my pussy so good I couldn't believe that I let things go this far. Things were begining to move along pretty fast and the money was coming in even faster. I was learning how to dance even better and my body was shaping up fast. Things seemed to be going good and for the better SO THEY SEEMED.

CHAPTER
31
. . . .

WHEN IT RAINS IT POURS
BUT PREPARE FOR THE FLOOD

IT WAS A warm and sunny day. One of my play sisters from the Group Homes wanted to come over to visit me for the weekend. Her name was Meme. I was really close to Meme and I was truely like a big sister to her. Meme had one baby boy and her baby was born with his intentions on the outside (A rare Birth Defect). I was sad because the doctors told Meme that her son would not live very long due to this rare disease and he had already went threw several surgeries to try to help reverse his intentions. I've always had a big heart so it hurt me to witness Meme going threw something like this. Meme didn't do any type of drugs she was just very hyper active. I took on to Meme as soon as we met so I took her under my wing as a little sister. When Meme made it to my house we laughed and talked about some of those old memories being in those group homes together and growing up in and out of SRS custody. Some of the fights we had together fighting together against the other groups of girls. Tommy Gunn and Meme were flirting with each other the whole time since Meme walked through the door. Meme got to spend time with my children. Meme's son had to always be hospitalized so he was not able to come over to my house with Meme. Meme had found a peaceful mind frame dealing with her babies illness so I would just say silent prayers for Meme and her situation with my lil nephew. The night was winding down and I decided to take me a bath and get ready to wind down. As I was cleaning out the bathtub because we didn't have shower in the Brick Jungle only baths Taz rushed into the bathroom were I was at yelling at me saying," Baby Did you hear that! Hurry up come on follow me"! I ran down the steps and outside behind Taz that's when a horrible scene unfolded right infront of my face. The scene from this day will not ever leave my mind. As I saw a crowd building up right in front of my house at a car parked right in front of my complex I ran up to the car to see what was going on. As I ran up to the car there was a guy in the car slummped over and his brains along with a water fountain of BLOOD coming from his head. One of my neighbors was also by the car yelling for someone to go and get her a towel. The neighbors 3 year old son was also right there at the scence so I got mad instantly like BITCH GET YOUR SON AWAY FROM THE SCENE! The Guy in the car was slightly jerking while he was slummped over and the blood poured from his head. I yelled for someone to get the 3 year old little boy and take him in the house. I thought about my children and as I looked around I noticed Tommy Gunn in my door to my house guarding my boys from coming out that door. Tommy Gunn had his nephews governed. I took another look in the car as the boy stopped jerking I saw brain particles everywhere. I just kept hearing people around the car screaming saying, "He shot himself I saw when he did it! He was high off PCP smoking WET! He started tripping in the car by himself and next thing he did was picked up the gun and he shot himself right in the head". I heard the sounds of the ambulance. I ran up to my house, told Tommy Gunn to watch his nephews and I took off walking away from my house I walked around the corner to Candies house. I told Candy what I had just seen. I began to cry. That was my first time seeing a dead body and I was not the same person. Taz kept calling my cell phone but I didn't want to go home not to that house ever again. I finally went home and the story of what had just happened began to unfold. I took a deep breath. Meme was also distraught and she told me that she was never coming over my house again and I haven't saw Meme since literally!. I couldn't believe that such a thing had just happened that close to home. I had to Pray over my home. I had heard all these dark tales about the Projects the Brick Jungle and now I had to witness the horrible things going on and so close to me. It mad me think of "Tupac—Death Around The Corner". I was so sad. Earlier that day I had saw that boy who had just now taken his own life UP AND BREATING. That same day I had been outside and we were all conversating as usual and now this boy laid in front of me lifeless and now I couldn't even recognize his face. I put the whole scene together in my head from everything that was going on earlier that day in the projects. I knew in my heart that I didn't want my children to grow up down there in that Brick Jungle. I was ready to pack up and move but I hadn't even been down there in those Brick Jungle for 6 mths. I didn't understand how my brother Tommy Gunn lived down there all his life I was ready to MOVE OUT!

32

....

WHEN IT RAINS IT POURS

★TELL THE TRUTH, shame the devil★. Past experiences started to get the best of me and I became curious. Experience is the best teacher and I was sure to learn. Taz and I became involved in a sex triangle. I say triangle because triangle's have three corners but it was more like an Octagon or something. I had multiple men and there is no telling how many females Taz had because it really didn't matter at this point. Taz and I tried so hard to be like your ordinary couple but we were far from ordinary. Our relationship became physical and we had fights like two enemies. Things began to spiral all out of order. I kicked Taz out the house every other day because I felt closed in and I wanted my freedom. Amongst our arguement Taz and I decided to have a threesome. I wanted to do something spontanious for Taz's birthday that was coming up. Taz and I stayed under the influence and I countined to work at the club. I had not thought about being with a woman since my terrible experience growing up and I felt like God was completely against. However, old thoughts began to get the best of me. I began to put my plan in motion. I didn't have a particular female in mind because I did not seek that type of thing, I was under the influence so things were very cloudy and seemed to just happen sometimes. I thought about the situation and I felt like it would probably be better for me to do a threesome if I did it with someone whom I had already known for a period of time. Something inside me just wanted to have spontainious sex, wild sex, with a woman and Taz went right along with my plans. I had been exposed to all of these naked women at work that my mind began to wonder and thoughts played in my head of being with a woman. When I thought about another woman during sex with Taz it made my sex drive go high and I wanted to pursue those feelings on an intimate level. I talked about my thoughts and feelings to Downy and it was like Downy understood and wanted to be the willing third party. I didn't have a physical attraction to Downy but she was someone that I considered. Downy and I talked more about having the threesome with Taz and she really wanted to participate. Downy also let me in on a little secret of her own. Downy told me that she had been attracted to me for longer than I knew. Downy told me that one night I had been alseep with her on a couch when we were in the group home together and that while I was sleeping that she was rubbing on my booty trying to get me then. When Downey told me her secret it all sounded to familiar to my ears. WHY DID PEOPLE LIKE TOUCHING ME IN MY SLEEP! Fee or Bone touched me in my sleep. It was horrible but it made my clitorus jump and I became wet as my mind went into action. I knew what I could do to a woman and how much I could please. I asked Downy, "why didn't you just come out and tell me how you were feeling". Downy said that she was scared to approach me due to what I had been through. One day Taz, Downy and I decided that it was time to fulfill our deepest fantasies. Taz and I had our drugs and Downy also like to smoke the Love Boats. We met up at my place. I had one rule for Taz and that rule was "Do not NUT in Downy Taz had to pull Out", I didn't care how good the pussy was PULL OUT! Taz agreed to my terms. We all went to my bedroom where we began to smoke our Juice and Love Boats.

The next thing I knew Downy and I began to rub each others breast. Taz pulled down Downy's pants and panties while I pulled out her breast and began sucking them. As Taz pulled down Downy's panties my other hand touched her pussy. Downy had a fat pussy and it was EXTREMELY wet and slimy. I watched as Taz began to eat Downy's pussy and I got turned off when I actually saw how wet it was but something else turned me on. Next thing I knew BANG! Poody had busted down my door and caught us in the act. Taz jumped a little bit but he kept eating Downy's pussy and I yelled at Poody to close my door! Poody didn't even knock she just busted right in my door. Poody yelled at me saying, "SO, your just going to watch Taz eat another bitch out". Downy was giggling and moaning at the same time. I jumped up, put the knife in the door (that way nobody else could just BUST in) and we continued our threesome. Taz continued to eat Downy's pussy as I sucked her breast. Downy moaned and said that it felt really good. I told Downy that she had a fat pussy. It turned me on so I wanted to taste Downy for myself. Taz came up and I instructed him to let Downy give him some head while I did her. I went down on Downy as she moaned even louder while she tried to suck Taz good. Downy wanted to eat my pussy so I let her while I gave Taz some head. I was turned on Taz wanted to fuck me so Taz and I began to have sex. My pussy didn't want to get wet for Taz for some reason so I stopped Taz and told him that I wanted him to fuck Downy while I orcastrated the whole thing. I sucked Downy's titties while Taz fucked her in order to stay entertained. I reached down and felt Downy's pussy while Taz fucked her and her pussy was soak and wet. I got turned on so we fucked each other for a couple of hours before we ended our threesome. I talked to Downy telling her that she had some good pussy although the taste of her did not quench my thirst. I was amused and didn't think that Downy had that kind of freak in her. Downy was pleased and she kissed me telling me how wonderful of a time that she had. The day went well and we injoyed ourselves except for the fact that I couldn't understand why I couldn't get wet. After Downy left that night

Taz and I fucked until morning as usual. Downy was a bit to much for me as a woman and I wanted great taste so she didn't meet my standards as far as taste but she got really wet and had a really fat pussy. I was confused by the whole thing and it wasen't so bad Taz seemed to enjoy himself. Maybe Downy wasen't to much for Taz and he could handle all that wetness so I let Taz be a man that he was. I'm a woman! A feminine woman at that. I was balled up with emotion. Smell and taste meant alot to me so I thought that maybe that was the reason I couldn't get wet or maybe it was God not wanting me to act out in that manner. Some men are nasty and disgusting and will do just about anything. I had to watch Downy, I knew in my heart and felt it in my heart that Downy wasn't a real friend and that if she could then she would try to take my dude. Downy wasn't so bad when her dude was all on me when Buddy pulled that bullshit and I fucked the shit out of Downy's dude right in her face and he had a little dick. Buddy had a big dick and Downy didn't know what to do with that. I needed to play the game and put a couple of people to the test. I was most definitly going to test Taz because as a Queen I TRUST NO MAN and if Taz could fuck a bitch in my face he damn sure could fuck a bitch behind my back and I was far from a stupid bitch. Taz wasn't attractive enough for me to let him drag me down like I let DeShawn and I was not going to play the fool. Taz was beginning to fail the test as far as I was concerned. I had morals for my life I wanted a Husband one day not no thirsty Hound ready to hump any and every bitch that came on the block. It was time for me to Boss-Up, I paid the cost to be the boss and no man was going to use or abuse me again as far as I was concerned plus** I had options bigger than Real Estate, I'm clocking in on time, while half of you bitches running late**(rhyme time).

CHAPTER
33
····

WHEN IT RAINS IT POURS

MEMORIES ARE A part of life that you have to deal with. I sit back and thought about all the times I've shot guns on New Years hanging out with the fellas, partying having fun good times with Downy's side of the family. Downy's family became like family to me plus they were because I had a niece or nephew on the way. I didn't think about the bad things that we were doing while we were shooting those guns because what goes up must come down we just did it because everyone shoots on New Years. Now here it was I've witnessed a dead body. Things were getting bad. I did what I had to do in order to survive. I had regular customers that Taz knew nothing about. I kept my job at the Club working as many hours as I could to get my mind off the Bull Shit. One night at the club I was approached by this Italian Guy he was clean I knew that he was some type of business man. The Itailan Guy told me that he owned his own Strip Club in Atlanta and he was a friend of Gus. The Guy wanted me in particular and it was like Gus knew it and had made arrangements. This Italian man was very hand-some and looked like he dealt with lots of money and very well kept. I sat down and kept the man Company as he requested. The Italian man began to make me a very serious offer. The Itialian man told me that he owned his own Strip Club in Atlanta and that he wanted me to come to work in ATL at his club and that he would provide everything for me. This man was so serious. He told me that with the body that I had I could make a ton of money in Atlanta. He told me that I wouldn't get anywhere working down here in KS not what I deserved. He was serious about what he was saying to me. I told the Italian Guy (Club Owner) a little bit about my current situation and that I was the proud mother of two little boys and I would not ever leave my children we had a whole life here in KS. I couldn't just up and move all the way to ATL with a complete stranger. I had trust issues and I most definitly didn't need a pimp or anything of the sort. He assured me that he was no kind of pimp and that he saw alot of Potential in me and with my body I could make alot of money in ATL. He told me that he was a business man with plenty of connections that would help me make lots of money to where I wouldn't need anyone. He told me to trust him and that he only wanted to make me Shine like the Diamond that I was and he would provide for me until I made enough money to be on my own. I thought about his advancement for a brief minute or two. I had my babies and I would not put them into that type of situation, Pooh Pooh was 3yrs old and had just started Pre School, I was in a relationship. I declined the Italian man's advancements and continued to work that night. For some odd reason Dimples began to change up on me. Dimples appeared to be hating on me because I was making more money than she was and all of her hatered began to take a toll on me and my job. My dance performance was on it's way to being Flawless and I was getting better fast. One of my favorite cousins on my dads side came up to the Club to check me out, she was curious about dancing her name is Fantasy. I showed Fantasy everything that I had learned as far as Entertainment. Fantsay had the perfect Stripper Body. Everyone would always say that Fantasy and I looked just alike. Fantasy had diamonds in her mouth and she was on her hustle.

Fantasy couldn't danced as good as I could but I was ready to train her to be good as me or better. Meanwhile, I did a few shows at this after hours. I had a specific person attend one of my shows, it was the man who doubted me and told me that I would not make it. That night I was flawless and I had a point to prove. That night that same man who told me that I would not make it in the industry made it rain on me at the club (MONEY SHOWERS). During my performance the man began to appologize to me for what he said about me and he told me just how good of a dancer I really was. that night we ended up having sex and he paid me extra money and that same night I ended up pregnat by him. I had no feelings for this man, he was my trick daddy and now I was pregnat. I had been with Taz plenty of time unprotected. Taz happen to be in jail but he was getting out soon and we were still a couple. I never had morning sickness with any of my other children but with this pregnacy I WAS SICK! Taz didn't have any children and we tried and tried for children. Taz got released from jail and I was pregnat. I could not explain this one to Taz. I wasen't ready for any more children so I thought. My trick daddy who had gotten me pregant had a woman at home. I had to tell him that I was pregnat and when I decided to tell him that he got me pregnat he already knew before I knew. Turns out that he was also having my pregnat symptoms so he knew that he had got someone pregnat. I told him that I wasent ready for children. After Taz got out I went up to the club up the street and had a few drinks. I had a neighbors who lights were cut off so I let her stay at my house. I had been drinking so I was drunk. I came home and went to sleep but when I woke up I woke up to someone in the midst of having sex with me. I thought that someone was Taz but turns out that Taz best friend was let in my house and he took it upon himself to come up to my room and get in the bed with me. When I woke up and figured out who was in my bed it was to late and Taz had walked in while his best friend was getting dressed. Taz was so mad that he hit me in the stomache and liquid began to run down my legs like my water had broken. I was hurt and MAD. I told my trick daddy what had happened and he gave me 375 dollars and took me to an abortion clinic. I was sick when I walked in that clinic but I walked out feeling back to normal but my feelings were hurt. I had done something so terrible. I felt in my heart that I was concieving my first baby girl. I was hurt and I just wanted to die. I felt something in my soul that was very unhappy with my life. Its was time for me to repent and go into deep deep prayers. I do not recommend anyone in life to ever get abortions. ABORTIONS are NOT of GOD. I was hurt to my soul I tell you. I was so disappointed in myself and my actions at this point. As I write this *My Story* it hurts and I pray to God to cover my baby Girl and tell her that I really love her and I apologize to her I'm so hurt and ashamed. My baby girl did not deserve that. I'm writing my wrongs and I apologize and ask that the Lord forgives me. I have to stop my story because a story just hit breaking new and it hurts me to my soul. A childs human remains were just found here in Wyandotte County. This dark cloud over Kansas has to move. I'm so dissappointed when it comes to the system!! Here it is, I would love to help out with Cold Case files but the system won't allow me to help. How did the teachers not no that a child was missing from school, what about neighbors and family noticing that a child was missing! IT BOTHERS ME! Moms please protect your child NO man should come before your child unless that man is your husband and if it's your husband who is hurting your children YOUR CHILDREN ARE INNOCENT GODS CHILDREN AND THEY COME FIRST. Things have to change. It's so sad because you worry about things happening outside of the home when technically sometime things happen in the home first. When things happen in the home children are basically helpless unless they confide in a higher authority someone outside of that home and usually the predator will make it hard for that child that the victim to communicate with anyone outside of the home. Every life counts. Us as people need to open our eyes and ears when it comes to the children. I am supposed to speak up and out!. Children should be loved they are a precious gift from God. Pedaphiles are real, killers are real, thieves are real but guess what SO IS GOD, GOD IS THE REALIST. STOP the violence and protect our children. Lord please remove this dark cloud away from Kansas. I had a talk with my oldest son about what he wants to be in life when he completes school and he said that he would like to be a Police Officer. I will back my soons decision 100% if that's truely what his heart desires. I was looking for my baby to go to the NFL as long as he played football but it's his decision not mine and I want my children safe. Back to* My Story*. Once again I'm in my home minding my own business Taz runs in saying, "Baby baby, come outside and look, you wont believe this shit". As I run outside Taz lead me to this car. The car was rolling slowly down my street right in front of my house. Taz reached in the car putting the rolling car in Park. I looked inside the car and see air bubbles coming out of a guys mouth and the guy is slummped over, blowing spit bubbles. Then, I recognized the guy's face and how I knew this guy named Meechie. An incident had just taken place a couple of nights before this particular day where I was hanging out up on 3rd Street. Now here it is this man lay right in front of Taz and I lifeless. I told Taz that I was calling the police and that this was the guy Meechie from the other night that I was telling him about. Taz shook his head saying, "I know him also. Damn this is fucked up. I just got back on the block and this is what I found not to mention I just saw someone take off running up the hill going towards 3rd st. I shook my head and said, "Damn baby I might no who just killed Meechie". This was crazy and the true meaning of one day your here and the next day your gone. I had a flash back of what had just taken place a few nights prior up on third street that might have lead to this boy being murdered now laying here lifeless. I was up on third street hanging out with all my 3/1 homies when I heard and saw an altercation taking place with some of the homeboys. That's when I noticed a serve pulled up and pulled off really quick. In the hood dudes did not play no games when it came to thier serves thier clientel. One particular homeboy busted the serve and one of the other guys got mad becasue he didn't have any real work to get the serve so he snatched the homeboys crack sack. The homeboy got pissed off real quick for dude snatching his crack sack. I heard the homeboy yell, "nigga you got me fucked up! I want my work back now or its about to be some shit". While the homeboy argueed with the one guy who snatched his crack sack, there was another guy right there named Meechie (who Taz and I had just found dead). Meechie was in the middle of the altercation with the homeboy and the guy who snatched the crack sack. I kept hearing the guy yelling at the homie like, "Man I do not got you crack sack". Next thing I knew, the homeboy swung on the dude knocking him out cold with a one hitter. The guy fell to the ground sleep from the punch and the homeboy went threw the guys pockets and shoes and socks. the homeboy noticed quickly that the guy actually did not have his crack sack anymore and that he had indeed passed his crack sack off to Meechie. The homeboy yelled at Meechie to give him his mutha fuckin crack sack and Meechie took off running as fast as he could and the Homeboy took off running behind Meechie. After they ran off I left the scene before dude that got *knock the fuck out* could wake up. In the hood it was normal to see someone get knocked out like the movie "Friday" and it was actually halarious but finding this dead body was something that most definitly was not funny at all and especially if it was all over a crack sack. The next time I saw Meechie was Taz and I finding his lifeless body. Taz and I watched as Meechie's family gathered around the scene that's when I noticed Poody's best friend on the scene which was a male friend and Meechie was his cousin. It was truely a sad day in the Hood and I wanted to help however I could without being a snitch because I was cool with the homeboy and I knew Meechie's family for a long period of time. This dark could was beginning to manifest more and more.

CHAPTER
34
....

When It Rains It Pours

IT WAS ALMOST time for my birthday to come up. This had already been a crazy summer for me so I really wanted to take time and enjoy myself for my 21st birthday. I had witnessed all these murders and senseless crimes so my heart and soul felt heavy and to top it all off I had just found out that my 15 year old sister Poody was now pregnat with child. Poody had always been a rough child growing up so I knew that Poody was not ready to be a mother yet physically or mentally. Poody was always at my house and she had been involved in a relationship with a much older man who was in his 30's. One day before my birthday Poody and I were at my house as usual when I received a knock at my door. It was one of my neighbors letting me know that someone was cutting on the Fire Hydren so that everyone could get wet and if Poody and i wanted to come out and have some fun in the water. Poody and I had not got wet in the Fire Hydren before so we agreed to put on our bathing suits and come outside for so innocent fun and play. Poody and I were always the life of the Party so we wanted to have fun and entertain not knowing what we were really getting ourselves into. I always tried to explain to Poody that being that she was pregnat that she needed to chill out sometimes and that she couldn't always do normal things because she had a child inside her that she also had to be aware of so she needed to *Chill Out*. While pregnat there was no time for horse play but Poody did not listen to me all the times. Anyhow we went outside to get wet. There were people already beginning to gather around in the water. Before I knew it, a couple of neighborhood guys outside ran up to Poody and I one guy grabbed me, picked me up and ran me to the front of the Fire Hydren that was spraying water. The Guy dropped me in the water and the water pressure was so high that it sent me across the hard concrete hurting and scraping me up across the concrete. I got up quickly trying to yell because all I could think about was stop them before they do Poody like that Poody is pregnat and this pressure can and will hurt her badly. I yelled for them not to drop Poody in there but it was to late and before I knew it Poody was getting up behind me hurt. Poody was 6mths Pregant but her stomache was small and you couldn't really tell that she was pregant. I got furious and I yelled at the guy that had dropped Poody in the water saying, "why the fuck did you just do that bull shit! She is pregnat you dumb mutha fucka!" Before I knew it Poody was also yelling. Poody was hurt and she had also gotten scrapped up by the concrete. Poody punched the guy that had dropped her in then water and he apologized stating that he was sorry and didn't know that Poody was pregant. Poody and I were angered so we went back into the house. Later on that night Poody began to bleed really bad. Poody was rushed to the ER where she immediatly went into Labor that the doctors couldn't stop. Poody was bleeding so bad that the doctors had to let her deliver. Poody gave birth to a 1lbs baby boy and I was right there with her. I saw my nephew and after he was born he was so little I felt hurt in my heart. I left the hospital and 11 hrs later my nephew passed away. Poody was losing so much blood that she had to have an emergency C-Section. My nephew wasn't supposed to be born so early and that blood probably got in his lungs. I was devestated when I found out the news that my nephew had passed away. Poody was furious and turns out that the father of her child wasn't that old mans it was Poody's boyfriend that was a few years older than she was. I couldn't bring myself to go back up to that hospital after my nephew passed so I waited on Poody at home just in case I had to fuck that boy up who dropped my sister in that water. When Poody made it back to my home after she got released from the hospital she had only a box of memories with her which had my nephews footprints, premature babies diapers and some things that the hospital gave her for memories of my nephew. I felt mentally drained, my birthday was in less than a week and so much pain and sorrow. My little cousin Kay came around to try to cheer Poody and I up so we spontaneously planned a trip to St Louis for my 21st Birthday. Kay had her own car so she said that I could drive her car and that we would just stay there all weekend just Me, Poody and Kay. It was my 21st birthday and I had not ever been to St. Louis let alone me drive out of State. I got the information that I needed in order to drive down there and how it wasn't hard just one straight highway so we got our things ready to leave. I didn't want Poody to go because she had staples in her stomache from having a Ceserion not a whole week ago. Poody was not going to let me leave without her and I really didn't care about the opinion of Taz. I agreed to let Poody come along only if she agreed to take it easy and she agreed that she would do so. I planned to dance at a couple of Strip Clubs in St. Louis and Kay agreed. Kay had never danced before but she was very curious about it and she had the body for it. Kay wanted me to show her how to dance and show her the ropes and how to "Dance Like A Stripper" so I began to dance with Kay and show her the ropes. Kay was very excited about our upcoming trip and our little Vacation was only a couple days away. Although I didn't to much care about Taz's feelings about my trip I knew that he was my man and I had to talk it over with him. -Lord take this Dark Cloud away MOVE IT LORD!! I just found out some devestating news. One of my close friends named J was shot and killed two nights ago. The person who shot and killed J. went and turned himself in to KCPD. Again, I'm documenting events that' also going own as I write because this is my life. I want ya'll to really visualize this dark cloud hovering over KC. the devil comes to kill, steal and destroy. Will it all stop? When will you people realize that it is a higher power than you *The Higher Judge*, *The Last Judge*. Hatred is all so real and it's amungust us. People will smile in your face and stab you right in your back. My heart goes out to the family of J. I knew J on a personal (non sexual) level, someone that I could conversate with. J was a *Pretty Boy* light skin, pretty green eyes and his mom is a retired Sheriff in KCK. The man that took J's life left innocent GODS children without a father. J was a dad with a life of his own and he didn't mean anyone any harm. It's almost like black people are becoming endangered spicies. I pray that you young men of the future wake up because it's not fair to let the Devil win, if you want to fight-fight a good fight and protect these children, provide for your families by working HONESTLY, love your mothers and children. MY GRANDFATHER was a PROVIDER for his family! Wake up young men before the real victim is YOU and you wake up in a pit of HELL SOUL BURNING FOR ETERNITY and you cant get out no matter how much you scream and ask God gor forgivness. Hate is REAL no matter the COLOR and PREDJUDICE is HATE and it's REAL. Love is also real so people we need to learn to LOVE. Back to my Story as I calm my soul because there is more to come you haven't heard everything yet. I consulted with Taz about my spontanious trip to St. Louis and Taz agreed just like I knew he would. I assured Taz that I would be on my best behavior. Friday night came and we were all ready to go but there was a couple things that bothered me and one being that Poody was going and she wasn't healed up. The other thing was that none of us had any money and we were going out of the State with less than 100 dollars all put togehter. We were admit on going on this trip so it was time to Get To The Money Makin. I drove us down to St. Louis after I got high and had to make a stop because my mind was racing. When we got to St. Louis we ended up in a well known area where their were these Huge Clubs. We knew that we didn't have very much money to get into the high priced clubs so we went to a small Strip Club were Kay and I didn't have to pay a tip-out and we could make all our money. Kay and I danced while I made Poody sit down and watch and help me keep track of the money. Kay was showing her wild side that night and she had a ball. At the end of the night we met a Group of dudes who insisted that we stay with them for the night instead of going to a Hotel room so that we could save some money. I observed the group of guys because we had money and I had to watch all my money. However, Kay had really wanted to go with the guys and save our money so that we could possibly make more money from the group of guys. One of the Guys names in the Group was Goldie. I remember Goldie the most because he had a mouthful of Gold teeth and he stayed up geeking all night. We agreed to stay with the group of guys and I knew that I had to watch Poody close but we explained the situation with Poody to the guys and the guys really liked Poody and I so they wanted to make sure that Poody and I were very comfortable. When we make it to the Trap House with Goldie and his friends Poody and I were ready to lay down and relax for the night so they took us to our designated area in the basement of a house that was a nice spot for Poody, Kay and I could all sleep. Kay was not ready to go to sleep however Kay had a hidden agenda for that night. Goldie had some drugs that he snorted and I didn't snort anything up my nose so I wasn't interested. Kay insisted that I take a line with her because it was my birthday weekend. I agreed to only try one so that Kay would leave me alone and let me go to sleep with my sister. I went to the area where Kay and Goldie had been and some of the other guys were getting in relax mode while others were up snooping. I approached Goldie in a playful manner and made jokes. I was curious however because I knew that cocaine was a white substance and this was a brown substance and Goldie appeared to be crushing a pill or something up in it. Kay insisted that I try one and I watched her as she did one. Goldie told me the instead of the white it was brown and gave me the utensil. I did one line and it burnt the heck out of my nose so bad that I declined anymore with a sign of irritation. I was upset and I knew that I had to watch Kay. I was sleepy though and Kay was not. I insisted that Kay lay down with me but she declined and she wanted to party with Goldie. I went in the room where Poody was laying and I lay next to my little sister as Poody and I feel fast asleep gripping our earnings. When Poody and I awoke the next morning there was a altercation so it seems like were weren't asleep for 4–6 hrs. Kay was upset and screaming. Kay started yelling, "Someone stole my money and I'm not leaving here until I get my money"! I didn't have time for no extra drama and bullshit plus we didn't have a gun or any protection with us so Poody and I told Kay that instead of trying to fight some full grown men we would just give her some of our money that we had made. Poody and I were kind of mad at Kay but I was more focused on us getting on our A game and not having any more situations like that. I didn't come all the way to St. Louis to play with my life or to bull shit around I came to get paid and not take losses and Kay needed to step it up. I knew from that point on that no matter how exhausted I was I had to keep an eye on Kay because I wasen't giving Kay or nobody else any more of my hard worked for Cash and I most definitly was not giving up this Precious Diamond that I had between my legs. Later on that night we ended up at White Castle because White Castle was so packed it was like a Car Show. Poody and I ended up running into a very nice group of guys while inside of White Castle and we decided that this was the perfect group to leave with and it was my birthday and I wanted to enjoy my night. The guys all had thier own cars that were very nice cars that looked like they could be show cars. My guy friend that I got in with had a drop Top Mustang clean and new, Poody left with a guy in a Benz, and Kay left with a Guy in like a Porsh or something like that. We ended up at my guy friends home which had a huge outside pool and jacuzzi set up very nicely with his Mansion that he lived in. My guy friend and I had a long nice friendly talk that night. Turned out that he was a business owner who owned his own Pool Installation Company installing Pools and jacuzzi's. This guy was FINE AS WINE FORREAL and he was very well mannered. I explained to the Guy that I didn't not want to ever be a mans one night stand and that I wanted a husband one day and how I was in a relationship at home It was my birthday and I was enjoying my time with the ladies. Kay was again drinking and began to act on the wild side. Kay went to a vacant room with her guy friend and I knew what she was doing. I couldn't wait until Sunday which was my birthday so that I could go home and relax. Kay was getting way out of control and I also wanted Poody to get some relax time. We agreed to spend the night at my guy friends home plus Poody's guy friend was also understanding and liked Poody and wanted his time with her. My guy friend and I went to his room only with an understanding that I am a lady not a one night stand and that he would have to respect me and my wishes and he agreed so we all went to sleep that night peacefully. The next morning the fellas cooked up breakfast before returning us to Kay's car left by the White Castle. We left St. Louis once we reached Kay's car and talked amungst one another about our experience. I had a ball all besides our first night with Kay's money sistuation. When I pulled up at home Taz didn't answer the front door so I went around to the back door and I was suprised by a coming home Birthday party that Taz had planned for me. I had family there waiting on me to come home my favorite cousin D-Boy was there and the barbeque was almost finished cooking. My babies were ther waiting on thier mother and when I went in my home I was suprised by some nice gifts that Taz had brought for me. Taz had purchased me an expensive new comforter set and not one but two Gold and Diamond rings. One Ring was a Diamond engagement ring and the other ring was all 14 karat gold with a big L for my nickname. I was so excited by Taz and I was even more exicited that I knew how to be a WOMAN a LADY that was far from a HOE and I knew my morals and had respect for myself despite all the things that I had been threw growing up. I saw Love amungust all the bad things going on. I had just lost my baby nephew, Poody and I were so glad to be home and my birthday turned out to be a blessed birthday and Taz showed me that despite that threesome with Downy that he was really in love with me The Queen Leo.

CHAPTER
35
....

WHEN IT RAINS IT POURS
BUT PREPARE FOR THE FLOOD

AGAIN AS I'M writing *My Story* another Tragedy strikes and this one is so close to me as well as J was. It's the beginning of a new year and already two close friends of mine and it's like the devil is at work and this cloud needs to MOVE Lord. I was just in the presence of my friend 2 or 3 days before his terrible homicide. I've know this guy I call Mr. Cole aka (Chocolate Drop) aka Swerv for 10 years or better. the sad thing about this is that his birthday is in 3–6 days. I called the detectives to see what was going on in his case or to possible be of some assistance because I have ran across some valuable information that can help solve the case but the detective on the case is not communicating properly with me. I am so frustrated about this whole situation another friend and another case going cold if it is not solved after the first 48 hrs. My firend was murdered at an apartment that I had just droped him off at 2–3 days prior. he was murdered at 2:30–3:30 Central time. Those are some odd hours and it was snow on the ground it's January. My friend was visiting a mutual so called friend but no one knows anything not to mention a neighbor pics up and completely moves. I knew I had bad vibes about dropping the homeboy off at these apartments/townhomes this was were momma caught her murder case. Mr. Cola got killed at a so called friends home and that same friend did not even attend the Candle Light Vigil. Something isn't adding up plus my sons bestfriend dad lives right there where the homicide occured and he heard the gunfire and got up out of bed that night and he told me everything he witnessed going on days prior and days after the homicide. When Crime hits close it hurts everyone who knew that particular victim. This is scandalas Kansas and you have to keep you enemies close and you homies even closer. GOD DON'T LIKE UGLY AND AINT TO FOND OF PRETTY. Swerv was a good dude and didn't mean anyone any harm he was a likeable guy. Fuck POLITICS what about my friends homicide THAT'S HOW I FEEL, when the DETECTIVES WONT LISTEN—another black man dead huh! God works in his ways LET JUSTICE BE SERVED! NO JUSTICE NO PEACE! Lord I Pray everday "LET THERE BE PEACE ON EARTH". Obama I know that you did alot for the people but it takes more GOOD people than you NO MATTER YOUR COLOR! Wake up HATE IS REAL! We need to come together because when God calles you to JUDGEMENT it don't matter what color you are you have to go MEET THE REAL JUDGE. It's sad and if you kill to steal and rob you will face YOUR DEMONS IN HELL.

CHAPTER
36
····

When It rains It Pours

THINGS WERE GOOD then, things were bad. Taz and I were on a huge rollercoaster ride. We became well known and made money fast with many products and means and ways. Taz had also taken the Police on several dangerous high speed chases with me being in the car without my concent. It was the summer no droubt and things were going well. I had a trick up my sleeve for Taz though because Taz thought that I was stupid. Taz had become more abusive even worse than DeShawn and I. Taz was fucking other bitches and he though that I was stupid when I knew that I was his number 1, I wanted a real man not not Boy Toy but it was playtime for me because i had games to. I had a selection of men to chose from and I also kept one close. T Money and I continued our Love Thang. T money was who I wanted all to myself but we were both involved in a relationship. T Money was a Hustla and a protector and I always had security and fun while in his presence although he was showing some small hoe tendencies of his own. I gave T Money a call and told him that I needed to meet up and talk to him. Taz had been gone getting money and he left me with a whole bottle for myself (juice). Don't get me wrong about Taz because Taz was a hustla and always getting to the money and in doing so alot of hoes also came in to play along with alot of (HOUNDS) men flocking around me. Taz and I went all wrong when our relationship became physical and Taz thought that I would ever settle for a man who beat a woman (I saw what momma went through). If Taz thought that he could just fuck me and fight me then he had the wrong train of thinking. I wanted to fuck with T-Money this particular night and show him how I was getting money and I had the best JUICE going in town so maybe we could team up on some business. Things was going well working at the club so I kept Taz and I afloat. I enrolled into cosmetology and began school along with working at the club. Dimples and I kept bumping heads and I felt like Dimples was a bit jealous because I made more money although I showed her love. Dimples had caused me to lose my job a couple of times because Gus liked Dimples but Gus's son Frankie liked me and he saw what Dimples was up to so Frankie had my back. Frankie liked me genuinely as an Entertainer and he saw that I was professional and just honestly making my money. I had to keep a close eye on Dimples though because there's real love and then there's real hate in this world. I didn't trip off Dimples because there was plenty of money for us both to eat but we didn't quite see eye to eye. Anyhow, I met up with T—money with some plans of my own in mind. T-Money had this crazy bitch that for some reason wanted to fonk with me about T-Money and I was ready to put a demo down on any bitch tryna take my crown. T-Money had been arguing on the phone with the crazy bitch because the bitch had made some threats to me and me personally I don't take threats kindly. I didn't know where this CRAZY BITCH came from. Bitches knew all around town that I was fucking with T-Money. T-Money got off the phone with the Crazy bitch and we began to talk business along with pleasure. T Money and I smoked some Juice that I had and our conversation went really well. T Money really like my juice so I gave him the bottle and we made a small business agreement. T-Money was the D-Boy not Juice Man but I was about to turn those tables for him. That night when I made it home I began to put a few game plans into order. I had to figure out a lie about that bottle and cover my tracks from Taz. I had money and could replace it but if Taz was playing a game so was I. I had to get home and spend time with my babies. I want my babies to understand that if I had to be gone away from home so much I was trying to make a way for them to be taking care of because DeShawn was not helping me provide only God and my children's grandparents along with the help of Taz. I didn't like living in that brick Jungle and I didn't like my children having to live there. I wanted to be with my children as much as possible while we were down there in those projects. I had seen and done so many things that I wanted to just get away. Taz was getting worse and the next couple of weeks was a struggle with Taz. Taz would always rent these smoker cars and when he didn't feed them the dope they would call thier cars in stolen. This day, Taz had picked me up and we were riding when I noticed a police car get behind us. The Officer quickly turned on his sirens. Taz looked at me and said, "We are about to take this Police Officer on a high speed chase". That is exactly what happened. I yelled at Taz because I saw it in his eyes and I did not like that look in his eyes, "No Taz! Please". Taz yelled at me, "Be quiet! I have to focus so pay attention!" This time I was different, I didn't yell the whole time and argue with Taz I simply had his back and watched out trying to help guide him in the right paths. I was terrified, all I could think about was a horrible car wreck happening and I wanted out of that car. I prayed to God that I lived to tell *My Story. We always knew that if you could make it over the water into another State that the police had to stop thier chase. Taz and I made it to Missouri when they had a Cop car over in Missouri waiting on us with the Spikes out trying to make us wreck. Taz noticed the Cop throwing out the spikes so he dogged the spikes as I prayed and we made it past the spikes. That was a close one as Taz and I didn't yell at one another we began to communicate with each other. I told Taz to let me out but he told me why he could not let me out. Taz said that we had to hurry up and go back across the water to Kansas. I didn't like Taz idea but we made it back to Kansas safe and sound. But, that was not the last of our wild High Speed chases with the Law however now I knew how to help Taz intead of yelling however, I didn't want to be involved in Taz's wild Chases and the thrill was gone from me as quick as it came. Taz hustled day and night for me and my children so somehow I felt obligated to help Taz despite his ways he also had good ways and I knew the hustle came with the Police. Living down there in that Brick Jungle made me solid as a brick and prepare me for the street life. There were more shoot outs and more dead bodies. My patience was getting thin. Taz was staying gone away from home even longer so sometimes when he would come home his bags would be packed at the front door waiting on him. I had more male friends than I could count and the situation was becoming a bit dangerous. I had men that were ready to go to war with Taz at any given time to take his place. I had began to grow close to a particular male friend who would spend nights sleeping at the end of my King Size bed while Taz was gone this man was Big Russ and he reminded me of *Bone Crusher*. Big Russ was also aunt Carols nephew(Poody's adopted moms nephew). Big Russ was a Leo like me so we got along VERY WELL BESTFRIENDS fast. Big Russ was heavy set with long braids, brown skin just like *Bone Crusher* and Big Russ knew how to fight just like me and was not scared to KICK ASS WHEN NECESSARY! Big Russ didn't back down from nothing or no one. While Taz would be gone for days at a time probably fucking Downey for all I knew and I really didn't give a fuck if he was I had plenty to chose from, Big Russ was there mostly the times Taz went to jail. He was there for me as a real friend. Big Russ started paying for me to get my hair done every single week and make sure that I was smiling, happy and content. Taz ended up getting locked up so Big Russ stayed around me close to where he slept in my bed every single night. Big Russ had a huge Crush on me but I didn't want those problems because I knew when Taz got home that the problems would occur because Taz was not going to willingly leave me. I kept telling Big Russ how I didn't want to cause confusion in our frienship so I wanted to be strictly BEST friends with him but Big Russ did not want to stop his fantasies about me. One night I decided to see what that mouth was like on Big Russ since he kept offering me. Big Russ ate my pussy for hours and I decided to try to let him fuck. I didn't feel to write so it didn't quite work. I was really wanting this to be a non intimate friendship with Russ and I (Pletonic). Big Russ would like to took me in the eyes telling me how beautiful I was and then I would say someting stupid to get his mind out of the gutter and on business. I told myself that what happened that night with Big Russ and I, I vowed to not ever let it happen again. Big Russ was someone who was very special to me we liked to listen to music together and sing together to songs like (*Brian McKnight-Love Of My Life). Within 3–6 mths Russ and I didn't seperate and our friendship grew strong and although he knew that there would be no more intimacy he still slept in my bed everynight with me and we just layed there and enjoyed each others presence. One day Poody had gotten into a altercation with this female that I went to school with. Poody was younger than me so why would a female my age want to fight my sister so Big Russ and I pulled up on the scene where Poody was located and about to fight. There was a big group of people outside of the female wanting to fight Poody house men and female. Big Russ and I hopped out of the car to see *WHAT'S POP-PIN. Some dude ran up and started talking shit and before I knew it Big Russ knocked his ass out with one hit to the chin. Everbody got quiet and I asked, "Who's next"? Russ, Poody and I jumped into Russ's car and rolled out. That situation brought Big Russ and I even closer as friends. It's crazy how things can happen so fast sometimes. Days later Russ had an altercation with this Guy that I had an altercation with in high school all behind some high school bs and Big Russ beat that dudes ass. However it was time for Taz to get out of jail and it was also Taz birthday time again. When Taz got out he noticed that Russ and I had gotten really close and he didn't like it because I would not let him just run back to me. I had became close to Russ so some decisions had to be made. It was Taz birthday and Taz had been drinking when he pulled up to my home. Taz came inside my home and Russ and his best male friend were there. Taz got mad and there were some bad words exchanged between Taz and Russ. Things escalated really quick and before I knew it Taz and Russ were meeting outside to fight. I saw Russ leave the house first calling Taz outside to fight. Taz took his gun off his waist then Taz went outside after Big Russ. I tried to stop Taz while Russ was outside but Taz didn't hear a word that I said. We were in the Brick Jungle where there was nothing but space and opportunity. When they made it outside no word were exchanged just fist swinging. Taz tried swinging on Big Russ but non of Taz's punches were connecting and everytime Russ swug he landed a punch and Taz landed in the MUD. Big Russ let Taz get to his feet twice but the third time Big Russ had other things planned he was about to fuck Taz all the way up and I couldn't take any more I jumped on Big Russ's back bear huging him with my arms around his neck yelling for him to please stop. That's when Big Russ male Best friend started yelling at me to stop. Big Russ listened to me and let Taz get up. Taz got up quickly and started running for my house that's when I warned Big Russ and told him to hurry up and leave because Taz had his gun at my house. I ran behind Taz begging and pleading with Taz as he made it to his gun. Taz didn't listen he said that it was all my fault and it would be my fault when he shot and killed Big Russ. I cried to Taz telling him that I loved him and killing Russ was a stupid decision and he would go to jail for a long long time over a bad decision. I began to Pray out loud for God to stop that situation and somehow Taz heard my prayers and he had a change of heart. I had to figure alot of things out because I loved Big Russ as a friend and not a companion. I wanted Big Russ there with me to protect me from Taz because Taz and I had been fighting. I had a sexual relationship with a man that was Poody's older mans brother. I wasen't having sex with Big Russ. I had put Taz out and found out that he had went to Downey's so I didn't want Taz, I just didn't want any problems because Taz would act ugly over me. I wasn't fucking Big Russ and T-Money was a hit and miss. I had a older working man whom I would have sex with quite often and that older man had a woman at home so we kept our relationship on the down low. This older man name Ron was getting tired of keeping it on the down low. Ron's brother was fucking Poody and I was fucking the shit out of Ron so good that he had gotten into his feelings and wanted a whole little relationship with me despite his woman at home. Ron even took me to his home that him and his girlfriend shared on occasion. I began to feel a sick feeling inside. I didn't want Russ and my friendship to end so Russ continued to stay at my house with me every night to protect me from Taz trying to put his hands on me. Taz was mad because he gave me all that jewelry I had 24 karat Diamond earrings, rinds on 8 fingers and I was taken care of by Taz and Russ. I had to make me a Dr. appointment, I was becoming sick with a nausa feeling. I made my Dr. appointment and Russ agreed to take me to the doctor and be there for me threw whatever. Taz had began to slowly move on. Since Big Russ and I weren't intimate we were considered BFF I understood that Big Russ also had needs and if I wasn't fucking him I excepted he had to get a nut. One night this female who lived by me had a group of females over her house and I guess Big Russ wanted to have some fun. Big Russ was in and out my home that night so I reminded him that I had a Dr. Appointment the next day and that I had a ride to my appointment but he agreed to be there to pick me up from the Dr. I told Russ that I was scared that I was pregnat by this man who had a girlfriend at home and I didn't feel right and I needed him to be there with me threw evertyhing because he was my BFF. Russ guaranteed me that he would be there for me no matter the situation or my decision. I had just had an abortion about 8 mths ago and I didn't want another baby especially not with a man that was already halfway taken. I had two babies and I was already struggling to take care of them. I didn't trust no nigga especially not one that was bold enough to take me to his job, and his bitches house DISRESPECTFUL ASS DUDES!. I didn't want to break up someone happy home I could not find happiness in bringing unhappiness to someone else. I didn't wait up for Russ to long that night because I knew that he was there with me everynight no matter what bitch he had been involved with. I woke up the next morning and unbelievable no Russ. This was not like Russ he splet in my bed with me every single night for mths now no changes in our schedule. I woke up looking for big Russ that morning because I needed to make sure that he was picking me up from my appointment plus I couldn't believe that some bitch had his attention that hard where he didn't make it back to me. I was furious with thought about how much fun Big Russ had all night so much fun that his ass couldn't even call me to tell me that he would be gone over night. I was furious! I went to my Dr. appointment and got the news that I had expected. I was pregant and FURIOUS! I had slipped up once again. I couldn't believe myself. I called Big Russ' phone a million times after I got that news. Big Russ did not answer his phone and that was fair from normal for Big Russ and me we were way better than that plus he was my ride. I went over Poody's house after my Dr. Appointment to tell her that I'm pregnat by her dudes brother and to BLOW big Russ up he had me messed all the way up! For the last 3–6 months Russ had slep right there with me at the end of my bed now he got a little pussy and didn't no how to check in? My brain was going 100 miles an hour wondering why Russ was not answering his phone for me. What did I do wrong, I kept thinking to myself? I called several people looking for Russ and I kept getting a story about him being with my neighbors and some white bitches. It was a little past 11 am and I made it to Poody's house. When I began to tell Poody about my pregnancy she stopped me in my tracks with some devestating news. I was wondering why everyone was looking so sad because just as I went into my converstion with Poody about being pregant and Big Russ not picking me up from my doctor's appointment Poody broke me the devestating, horrible news that hurts to my soul. Poody said, "Sis Russ didn't come and pick you up because

Russ died last night!" I screamed to the top of my LUNGS *NO AIR!!!!!!!!!!
NO, no Russ is not Dead NO!!!!!! Aunt Carol came to sit me down and
explain the situation and what had just happened. I felt like my AIR was
sucked right out of my lungs. I WAS LIFELESS and everything became a
nightmare to me. i couldn't be dreaming I had just left the hospital and
found out that I was pregnat. Why LORD! Im going to KILL that bitch
next door! LORD WHAT HAPPENED! Big Russ had been taking me to
his brother to get my hair done (yes his brother done hair better than alot
of you bitches)! I was close to Big Russ's family so I called his brother to
talk to him and turns out that Big Russ passes away at his big brothers
home late that night or early morning. Big Russ brother told me that Big
Russ died peacefully in his sleep of a heart attack that night and he wasn't
found until around 11 am because I kept calling Big Russ's phone, it was
getting late and Big Russ didn't sleep in late quietly like that so when his
brother went in the room to check on him he found him lifeless. I CRIED
MY HEART OUT! Russ didn't tell me that he had heart problems. Big
Russ was young no older than 22 years old NOOOOOO! I got instantly
mad at God. God had taken my best friend from me that quick in the blink
of an eye. It seemed like everytime I loved something or someone it got
taken away from me. I could not go on I wanted to cry myself to my grave.
When Big Russ's wake came I was literally the first person right there. I was
so mad because in his obiturary they put some random chick as his BFF
and Russ and I both no THAT WAS A LIE and I was indeed his REAL
BFF. I was hurt and mad at the same time. I will always be Big Russ Best
Friend RIParadise Russell. There was so many things going on around this
time that's it's impossible for me to tell yall everything. But, one day prior
to big Russ passing we were all sitting in my home, it was me, Big Russ, Big
Russ male best friend D, and Tommy Gunn. D had just gotten a phone call
that his sister had just had a fight with her babies father Lil Blue. Lil Blue
and Taz were BFF. Lil Blue was the one I woke up to in th middle of the
night that night. Lil Blue had a baby by D's sister (Big Russ's Best friend).

Lil Blue and his babies momma got into a huge fight were his baby momma D's sister threw a brick threw Lil Blue's windshield. D got the phone call about his sister and Lil Blue putting his hands on his sister while he was sitting in my home so D just kept sayin, "Man when that nigga lil Blue make it down here im going to beat that niggas ass". Shortly after that call D recieved lil Blue came riding down my street with a brick in his window. Big Russ had just left to go make some money when lil Blue comes rolling down the street. D saw lil Blue coming and we all went outside to see what was about to happened as I tried to talk to D and tell him why he should think rationally. Lil Blue rode slowly down my street and when he approached the front of my house D ran to his car and hit him in the face a couple of times. I watched as Lil Blue face looking at me and he smiled. Next thing I heard was gun fire. POW POW POW. Lil Blue shot D right there in cold blood with a smile on his face as Tommy Gunn ran with my babies in the house and I was speechless. D started jumping around yelling that he had been shot and that's when one of the 3/1 Crips showed me what a birthday cake in the hood was all about. D was getting hit with a brick and he was shot at the same time as I yelled at the 3/1 cuz to stop and don't hit him and for someone to call the police as Lil Blue fled the scene. That's how fast things tended to happen in the hood. Back to Big Russ's funeral/wake I said my goodbyes as I prayed over Big Russ soul. *Lord you called your angel home. I'm selfish I wanted Big Russ on this earth with me. Lord you have your reasons and purpose in life for everything. Tell Big Russ that I love him Lord and that I'm mad at him for leaving me and not telling me honestly about his heart condition*Amen. My soul felt heavy with pain so I couldn't stay for the burial plus to let the family put someone else as Russ BFF when I was most definitly his BFF for life. I was HURT and my friends and family who attended with me knew that Russ and I were Inseperatable. I felt helpless and hopeless. I didn't want to keep my unborn child I felt rebellious and I wanted my unborn child up in heaven with Big Russ to keep him company for me until I made it to Heaven. Big russ needed some company from my unborn child. The father of the unborn child did everything to hide from me because he really wanted me to get stuck with having to give birth to his child. I wasn't giong to let his clown ass control the situation so I came to his job with threats of exposing his unborn child to his girlfriend because I knew that would get his attention. Finally my unborn child father gave me the money and I went and got my second abortion. I did my best to hide it from Taz because after Big Russ passed away Taz came right back around. The father of my unborn child refused to leave me alone and Taz had moved back in. One day my unborn childs father pulled up insisting that I talk with him so I agreed. During our conversation sitting in his car in front of my home Taz pulled up and got heated fast pulling his gun out pointing it at me in the car yelling for me to get out of the mans car. I heard a gun shot go of as I took a deep breath and my momma came running out of the house yelling at Taz saying, "You MUTHA FUCKA! You kill me YOU MUTHA FUCKA! Don't point that MUTHA FUCKIN GUN AT MY DAUGHTER I WILL KILL YOU TAZ!"

CHAPTER
37
····

WHEN IT RAINS IT POURS

I RUBUKE YOU Satan and ALL of your wicked ways. "No Weapon Formed Against Me Shall Prosper". Amen. In The Name Of The Father, The Son and The Holy Spirit, I Pleed The Blood Of Jesus!!

It was a beautiful day outside and I decided to get out the house and take a walk. I liked to walk alot for excersice. When it seemed boring inside the house In The Brick Jungle there was always entertainment outside of home. The sun was shining and I was feeling Blessed to be able to see another day in this beautiful world that God created for us. I took a walk and I didn't make it a block far before I noticed my cousin Ox Head. Ox was with one of his friends that I had not yet seen before in the hood. As I talked to my cousin Ox Head as I would usually do, I noticed his friend watching me. I wasn't really into Dark Skinned guys but lately I had, had my share of Dark Skinned and I loved everything about Dark Skin. I had an eye for Beauty no matter the Shape, Form or Fashion. This Guy was Dark skinned with a very nice Athletic Build. He had eyes and a face like the rapper/artist "David Banner" from mississippi. He had a Gold tee, he was sexy as I began to observe his whole frame and demenor. Just as I was ending my conversation with my cousin Ox and began to walk away, I heard them talking quickly and Cousin Ox yelled for me to come back that his friend wanted to talk to me. I yelled, "No, if he wants me then he better approach me like a real man". I rolled my eyes and began to walk off with an attitude as I though to myself "And He Better Not Yell Out Hey Or Im Really Not Going To Like Him". Before I knew it the Dark Skinned had gotten in his "Old School Chevy" I noticed that this was a new car on the block to try to catch me because I started walking very quickly. He pulled up next to me and the first thing he said was, "I apologize for being rude, would you like to go to the movies with me?" I asked him, "What are your intentions with me? I had a little bit of a Jazzy Attitude". The Guy's reply was, "I think that your very beautiful and I would like to get to know you better. Can you please get in the car, I will take you home or where ever you would like to go". I smiled to myself. I was really attracted to this man as far as Physique. He had a body that you would see in "Sports Illustrated Magazine" He was eye Candy and so was I. I got into his car and we had a very long talk trying to get to know one another. I learned that I had not met him before because he was a Truck Driver who drove over the road and when he was at home he lived in KCMO. He was getting out of a relation-ship with this crazy chic but he assured me that she would not be an issue for me and that thier relationship had been over for about 3 mths or better. I told him the truth about my current situation and that I was in an abusive relationship with Taz and that Taz would come and go basically. He told me his name his name was J-Nutt and that he wanted to spend time with me while he was here in town to get to know me better. He was very attractive so I took him up on his invitations. J-Nutt began to take me on real dates. I was fed up with Taz and his bullshit plus he was beginning to move around 'Messy" I found out that Taz had a particular stach spot that I felt was a bit uneasy. Taz's physical abuse was about to stop. Taz thought that he could buy my love with expensive jewelry and that was going to be enough while he fucked bitches and fought me but a real man had found me and by the looks of it he would be more than a protector. Taz had aimed a gun at me and had fired off a bullet into the headlight of a vehicle I sat in. Enough was enough and I would sure Kill Taz before I let Taz Kill Me because by the way things were going they were getting really ugly and its a "Thin Line Between love and Hate". I saw what my momma already went threw and I didn't want to take my children down that dark path with me so I made a decision. I liked the new man (J-Nutt) that God had placed into my life. J-Nutt was a new Big Fish in a Big Sea and J-Nutt was 100% MAN. I talked to J-Nutt about how I felt about men hitting women and J-Nutt assured me that he was not a woman abuser and that he would not ever put his hands on me in that manner and that he would protect me against any man who tried to beat on me. J-Nutt told me his story and he told me that the only woman hit hit was his childrens mom (which was a no no for me) which he completely and honestly explained the whole sistuation and events that lead up to the one day where he physically hit his childrens mom. His story was genuine and I believed him. J-Nutts childrens mom was the only woman that he had ever loved and he had her name tatooed on his arm (Muscle). Turn out that his kds mother and I had the exact same birthday and that was a HUGE BLOW. I'm a Leo, A Queen, A Lioness so I knew how us Leo's were and if he loved this wman like that then I could make him love me the same way that he loved her. It was the beginning of a new Chapter for J-Nutt and I so I had to close the old Chapter of Taz and I. I knew that as soon as I got close to another man its almost like Taz smelled it and would come back running but this time I wan't going to let Taz run back. J-Nutt had to go back over the road and I wanted Taz all the way out of the picture so that there would be no problems or further altercations. Nightime fell and I had a strong feeling that this would be the night that Taz would try to come back after 3 or 4 days went by of not hearing anything from him. I had gotten a call from this guy friend of mine that I had been seeing occasionally only for good sex when we needed. This guy was one of my side chocolate pieces and when we had sex it was like the most amazing experience for us both. My chocolate side piece came over and we did what we always did best FUCK and the package was always well delivered. My chocolate guy friend always drove his Surburban to my house and park outside. Poody, Ox Heads little brother JB and my Uncle Eric was at my house this night. Poody began to bang hard on my room door and my friend and I had just finished fucking. Poody was banging histercally saying Taz is at the door trying to kick my door in. Taz was going all around the house yelling that he knew that I had a dude in my home. I told everyone to be quiet and keep the lights off while I figured out a plan to get Taz to leave. After about 10 min of a dark house Taz quit beating and screaming. I didn't know exactly what Taz was contiplating but I knew that it couldn't have been anything good so I hurried and put my plan into motion. I rushed my friend out of the front door and made sure that all the windows and door were locked while I kept all the lights off. My stomache started to hurt from all of the drama so I went to the bathroom to release my bowls, that when I heard a loud BOOM as I began to take a shit. I looked up and it was Taz! Taz had kicked the bathroom door open so hard and he began to snatch my hand trying to snatch all my rings off my fingers. Taz was trying to take my jewelry that he brought me. Somehow, I managed to get my pants up or skirt down and it was fight time. I hearn a couple of my rings flying to the ground but the fight was on. I was hitting and fighting Taz and so was Poody. Poody had a glass bottle in her hand and she was busting Taz upside the head with it. My Uncle Eric was also fighting Taz trying to kick him down the steps. My uncle managed to throw Taz down the steps and Taz took off running out the door. As we locked all the doors trying to figure out how he had gotten in. Taz had climed threw a window that I had forgot to lock! Next thing I knew Taz was picking up bricks busting out all of my windows from the upstairs to the downstairs. Taz had busted about 10 windows All my windows. I called the Police I finally had enough and couldn't take it anymore now Taz was destroying my property and I had children whom had to live there. I could not afford an eviction and Taz was dangerous. The Officers who reached my home saw all the damages that Taz had just completed. I told the officers everything that had just happened and I also gave the Officers some valuable information about Taz and the product he had and where to find it on him once they pulled him over. The Police was mad that night and they were definitly on thier job. The Officers promised me that they would catch Taz because I knew that if they didn't then Taz would just come back and the fight would be on. Taz went to jail that night and the Poice listened to me and they found the Product. Taz had a little suprise for him while he always got away when the Police couldn't find where he would hide it. When the Poice took Taz downtown to headcourters they had a little suprise for Taz thanks to me. I was disgusted with Taz and he had indeed caused me to much pain. It was my turn to inflict some pain and the Pain that Taz felt that night would stick with him for life and he would think twice about the bull shit that he put me threw. However I felt bad afterwards for telling the police where Taz hid his product but I had to now think about my two children and their well being. I refused to loose my children my children had been threw enough and Taz was messy to the point where my baby had been exposed to some serious product that could have killed him or gotten both my children taken but it was by the Grace of God that I payed attention in specific areas of Poision Control Teaching being in the Group Home for Pregant Teens (I had a bottle of liquid to counter act POISON). I was ready for a change and I wan't going to get that change with Taz in my life I wanted Husband material.

CHAPTER
38
....

WHEN IT RAINS IT POURS

MY RELATIONSHIP WITH J-Nutt began to get intimate and we became really close so I called him Jay. I was very upfront and honest with Jay about everything because I did not want any suprises or any misunderstandings. I didn't want to hurt Jay and I told Jay that I was not ready to settle down although I did one day want to get married and live a truthful, loving, normal marriage under God's covenant. I was not ready to settle down with Jay because my last two relationships had turned out to be disasters and I just wanted time for me to enjoy my adulthood I had been locked down to long in forceful situations growing up. I also confided in Jay and told him everything about me and my past life. Jay was 10 years older than I was but did not look at all his age he looked much younger but he was mature. Jay got attached to me quickly and would tell me how he also wanted to get married on day and live like "The Cosby's". I was a bit uneasy of Jay and I being attached because I wan't ready to settle. When Jay was not gone over the road working Jay was at my home with me. After that incident with Taz breaking all my windows out two months later I got my Sec 8 and I moved out of that terrible brick jungle, turns out they were tearing down those roach and rat infested bricks to turn over a new leaf and turns out my apartment was one on the list to be torn down. I was glad to get away because all the murders, the robberies, I had witnessed more than enough HARASSMENT from multipule people on multipule ends and I was glad to be away from that place although it left me with a scar that wont ever go away. I moved into some apartments instead of getting a house because I wasn't ready for the responsibilities of a house. I liked these apartments because it had Mirrors everywhere all over the apartment. I was confident in my body as a woman and Jay was built like an ATHLETE so I wanted to have some fun and entertainment with those mirrors. I didn't feel compatable with a dark skinned man other than sex but he was worth a try. Within a month or two of Jay and I dating Jay decided to introduce me to his mother and family who he worked hard to provide for. Although I was not ready to commit to Jay, Jay made it really hard for me and I wanted to live alone with my children for a change and I did because of my Sec. 8. I always told Jay to remind him that I was not ready for commitment plus I continued to see T-Money when I wanted to see him. Once I made that business deal with T-Money, T-Money started really getting Money and things were looking really good on that end so me and T-Money had a sexual and business relationship that I was not ready to let go due to Jay. I brought T-Money lots of clients and money because he knew exactly what to do with it and how to double, tripple and sum more although T-Money ws showing HOE tendencies and was fucking more bitches than I had in pairs of panties. I would always be in the Trap house with T-Money while Jay was gone over the road. I was the Queen of the Trap House and it was most definitly like a movie being in the Trap. The things that you would sometimes see in the Trap was better than any Reality Show besides Love Hip Hop ATL that is but we neck and neck lol. T-Money had bitches and I was the Queen so Queens will always come first so I would always witness one of T-Money's bitches flip out screaming mad at him crying because they couln't have him I WAS THERE and they wanted thier turn. T-Money had a cold mouth piece he could eat a peach like me for hours. T-Money was the King at what he did and he did it well knowing with confidence that he was Awesome with his head game and MONEY GAME. T—Money became fasinated with Delta's and had some nice, clean TRICKED out Delta's. One day while T-Money and I was at the Cars Wash (I always rode front seat like QUEENS DO) we had a great day *All Eyes On Us* we were all on Juice and LoveBoats so we were most definelty in OUR zone forgetting that T Money had a whole bitch at home that he also took care of along with providing for me when I needed or wanted him to. Poody was in the backseat riding with T-Money and I and as we left the Car Wash T-Money baby momma/girlfriend at home spotted us out leaving the carwash and T-money was having so much of a good time that carwash that he was unaware of his surroundings. Next thing I knew as we were riding down the blocks BEAT on kicking it I hear a horn HONKING loudly and multiple of times trying to get our attention. T-Money looked in his rearview mirror and noticed that it was his girl-friend. When T-Money noticed, I also noticed and that's when she hit T-Money's car so hard from the back that he wrecked his car into the side of the street THIS CRAZY BITCH "I thought". As we wrecked the crazy bitch quickly jumped out the car, ran to T-Money's side of the car and began punching him hard in the face. T-Monay turned and looked at me and I tried to think rationally plus I didn't want him to HURT her because I had witnessed some things with T-Money already before. I told him, "don't hit her please T-Money she's a female". She started yelling at him and crying stating that he had me in the car and I remember thinking "As long as the bitch don't say nothing to me or think that she is going to come on this side and try to fight me because the fight will be on AIN"T NO PUNK IN MY BLOOD!" T-Money managed to pull of from the scene trying to avoid a fight because I started getting loud and mad and his girl was definitly mad also. We made it back to T-Money's Trap house and of coasre I was not leaving ANYWHERE. His girlfriend pulled up, T-Money made sure he kept us seperated because his girl was a LEO and SO WAS I QUEEN IN THE JUNGLE. It was quiet for a couple of hours but when T-Money finally came out from being with her he went directly to the bathroom and I knew what he had done to quiet his little KAT up! I didn't care because he sure wasn't about to get none of this and I advised him to keep it KITTENS in check. I gave T-Money a disqusted look and told him that I was ready to go home now. T-Money would always find a way to make things up to me because he didn't want to lose me because I was the Queen of the Trap. His girl might have been the Queen of thier home BUT NOT when it came to the Trap, I made The Trap a happy place and I was the Queen of T-Money's Trap and he made sure that his whole team of Shottas knew that and they all had MAD respect for me whenever I was present and they knew not to look at me like they had lust or T-Money would KILL. T-Money had formed a SQUAD and he gave his MONEY Gang a name and it was all love, respect, and loyalty. The Squad was ready with guns and vest and we most definitly wasn't ablout to take any loses. Eventually T-Money would make me count up Black 30 gallon Trash bags full of money. I had to seperate 100's, 50', 20', 10's, 5's, 2's and 1's along with quarter, dimes, nickles, and pennies. I counted everything despite my dislike for math I liked this math and I was all the way honest and loyal an T-Money knew it and trusted ONLY ME. We ended up counting a little more than 50,000 in cash all juice and hustle money. I tried to pursuade T-Money to invest his money in a business something like a Strip Club because I had alot of connect and I knew that he really needed to invest this dirty money into good money and he had some good females on the team Realators, Nurses and some more so we were solid. T-Money didn't listen to me and I came back in about a week and his whole team had gold teeth and diamonds in thier mouth. I was furious because I had helped T-Money reach those achievements and he didn't put any diamonds in my mouth!. I went off on T-Money and cussed him out with some very choice words. T-Money had been having sex with a few females that were close to me and I was helping his ass put the whole orcastration together so I was very dissapointed in T-Money not taking me along being that I was the Queen of the Trap to get me some diamonds I PUT HIM ON FIRST! T-Money became disrespectful in my eyes and he was fucking/sexing my own flesh and blood like fuck me and how I felt!. People became cut-throat and my own family was trying to take my position as Trap Queen and I didn't like it not to mention T-Money seemed to look beyond me. I was becoming a Lady and I had to keep my composure although I was hurting inside and I was most definitly not about to fuck/sex T-Money behind all these random ass bitches I WAS GOOD bull shit ain't nothing. One of T-Money closest friends kept making secret advances at me and I liked the way he moved so I took him up on his secret advances because two could play the game that T-Money was playing. I had sex with T-Money's right hand mand and it felt great. T-Money's little brother also came along and had an eye for me and T-Money's brother was Fine As Wine. T-Money would always get mad when his crew started lusting over me but they saw the dog shit that T-Money was pulling and the dogs were getting tired of being fed bones they needed the meat and wondered why T-Money always wanted me all to himself while he was being a HOE. T0-Money told his member that I was his and that I was off limits or he would fuck someone up seriously. One day T-Money had a new guy friend of his come over and the guy was FINE, yellow, with pretty eyes and he made a loud comment about me saying, "damn! little momma right there is sexy then a mutha fucka with her thick, chocolat ass shaped like a Coke Bottle. He licked his lips at me while he watched me lustfully." He didn't know about T-Money little rule and let's just say things almost went from 0–100 and got ugly. I watched as T-money's laugh turned straight into a frown. T-Money literally snapped on this guy friend of his and I snapped on T-Money, I was tired off all his bs and I told him about his friend and I fucking already! T money was so mad and hurt that he got mad at me and sent me home putting me out of the Trap house that night and I was glad to go. I was so sick of playing T-Money's games. T-Money yelled at me before he put me out saying that I was a Lady and he was a Man, I was not suppose to do what the boys did and he was hurt that I fucked his right hand man. It was time for T-Money and I to have a heart to heart because I loved T-Money and my feelings and his were getting involved and I didn't want anyone to get hurt even worse. Later T-Money and I had some make up sex but I was scarred so I wanted to stay away from the Trap house for a while so that I could focus more on being a Lady and plus I had Jay and I knew that Jay was the type that I had to watch he was 100% MAN. I had to play my cards right being the Jay came in and out of town and sometimes he just wanted to suprise me so he didn't always tell me when he whould be coming into town. Jay made sure that I had money in my pockets when he came into town and I really didn't need T-Money or the bullshit T-Money came with i could get what I wanted one way or the other regardless. Before I left the Trap for a while I had a friend of mines birthday that had came and I had been at the trap. T-Money had told me that he was going to take me shopping at the Mall so I asked him if Erica could come along. Erica and I had gotten back cool and it was her birthday. T-Money took us to the Mall and we BALLED OUT! T-Money had also had some random bitch with him one that I didn't like because she tried to play Queen but at this point I didn't have a fuck to give and I had other things in my mind I wanted Jay not T-Money but T-Money wanted to show me that he didn't want me to leave the Trap and he wanted to spend his money on me so I let him like a BOSS would. This little bitch thought she was now running the Trap and I wanted to beat his ass so bad. I had just gotten a two face piercings getting ready for the 50 cent and G unit concert. I had a huge thing LOVE for 50 cent and I didn't chase rappers but I wanted to meet 50 Cent up close and personal. I didn't fight this bitch that night because of my new face piercings and Poody talked me out of it because the concert was days away. That night after Mall shopping with T-Money I left the

Trap House but little so called friend Erica wanted to stay with T-Money-"I guess she felt obligated, he brought her some shoes". I didn't care because if I had stayed I would have murdered a bitch that night. I went home Erica stayed and when I got home Jay was in town waiting on me. That was a close call I thought as I made it home. that night Jay and I made love and Jay told me how he had been feeling about me really wanting to make things official with me. I was not ready to settle not with all the BS going on with T-Money. That night Jay made me an offer and he wanted me to start traveling in his trucks with him over the road. Jay had a trip coming up going to California and Jay had some connections from traveling so much. Jay told me that he also wanted me to go to Vegas with him because I was more like a Vegas Girl. Jay told me that I could and would blend in well with Vegas because of my style. I was honest with Jay and told him about T-Money. Jay said that if I wanted to live this type of lifestyle then he could show me the money route and help me more than T-Money was. I was excited about Jay and I conversation, I hadn't been to the Bay area and I wanted to go so that I could see what the Bay was all about plus I loved Mac Dre and Messy Marv. I agreed with Jay to go with him on his next run and he was very excited. I wasn't stupid I knew the things that I had heard about Vegas and I wondered what Jay meant about me blending in with Vegas chicks (I know this nigga ain't tryna be on no PimP shit is what I kept in mind). I get my own money and would not ever let a man or woman PimP me NO NOT ME, I lead not follow. Jay also began telling me all these weird stories and how he did indeed have a girl that he took to make money that ended up getting taken by a PIMP. Jay told me all about Lot Lizards so I knew all that I needed to know because Jay laced me up. I yelled at Jay, "Im NO DAMN PROSTITUE!" Jay laughed telling me that he had mush respect for me and didn't mean it that way he just seen potential in me that I didn't see in myself and instead of dealing with little small money that we needed to get and could make BIG money. I felt disrespected so I left the conversation with Jay alone. The next morning as soon as we both Jay and I woke up I heard a car door close and heard people talking that's when I jumped out of bed to look out my window. Jay had gotten up first and went into the bathroom as usual while he drilled me about always being so clean everytime we had sex that he could not yet tell my natural scent as a woman. Jay was in the bathroom and I looked out the window noticing that T-Money, Erica and one of the Shottas was all outside of my house getting ready to come in. I tried to play it off and distract Jay however my plans of distraction did not work and before I knew it they were at my door. I tried to keep Jay in the room while I answered my door but when T-Money came threw the door things got loud because I tried to only let Erica in while T-Money got mad and busted in my door on his own. Jay opened the room door and words were quickly exchanged and Jay was ready to fight. FIGHT was all in Jay's blood but T-Money stayed strapped and I didn't want those problems. Jay had a brother that was murdered and the crime remains unsolved. There was not about to be blood shed on my clock so I quickly found a way to de-escalate the situation. T-Money was so mad that he took my shoes that he had just brought me (I later got them back) I wan't concerned about shoes I didn't want anyone to get hurt. T-Money was crazy about me even though he had just laid up with Erica all night eating her ass I WAS DUN WITH T-MON-EY's nasty shenanigans. Jay had a bad temper and was the type that would beat ass and take names last. I stayed away from T-Money and the trap house even more because I began to sleep a whole lot more and this feeling right here was all to familiar so I made a Dr. appointment. My appointment came and my test results came with it. I was pregnat by Jay. I was so mad and I was not ready to stop smoking my juice to have Jay's baby plus I didn't want to settle down with Jay. I almost broke down in tears as the doctor read me my pregnacy results. I gave Jay the news and I begged Jay to give me 375 for an abortion but Jay was not about to abort any child of his and he made that very clear to me. I told Jay about my drug habit to use it as a crutch but Jay didn't hear none of my excuses. I felt like Jay was trying to trap me and I was unhappy about being trapped. I told Jay that I didn't want a long term commitment with him but he didn't hear that either. Jay set me up I thought or did God do this intentionally? I had tried to make a baby with T-Money on several occasions. I was devestated and even more I was not ready to stay away from the Trap House that I helped come up and climb to the top. Jay knew that I was involved sexually with mulitple men so he tried to say that he was unsure and would need a DNA test because of that incounter with T-money. I was furious but I put things into God's hands. If God kept putting pregnacies in my life I refused to go agaisnt God anymore I could not force myself to get another abortion I was still hurting behind the two that I had gotten. I prepared for my trip to California with Jay. Although I was with Jay's child Jay wanted me to come out of state with him and he promised to protect me. During the next few weeks I planned. Jay is a Taurus so he is very bull-headed and we started now bumping heads more than ever. The Lion wasn't taking any shit from the Bull so the fight was on to try to make this relationship between Jay and I work. I went to Vegas and Cali with Jay and I had some good times and some bad times. Jay made me drive his 18 wheeler on a straight path and It was THRILLING although I was scared. Jay tried so hard to make me happy but I couldn't just shake the Juice I had cravings. I prayed to God for my baby growing inside of me because the first three mths of pregancy were hectic and I couldn't not break away from drugs. I enrolled into College so that I could stay out of the Trap. I needed to further my education so that I could try to make something out of my life. I loved cosmetology but something within me wanted to work at a school being a Secretary/Receptionist. I wanted to someday own my own business so I needed a trade that would help me business wise so I enrolled in Business School. I couldn't afford a Huge College like Hartford, Texas or UCLA. I was smart indeed but I had childen and a whole family that I could not leave. I needed something that would help me with transportation to and from. I had to think logical so I did what I had to do it was me taking a step forward for me and my children. I had attended Cosmetology once before but I got pregant so I didn't complete the program plus all the drugs so I was determined this time for change. I had a gut feeling that Jay would not be my husband because we began to argue alot. Jay did not do any drugs not even weed. Jay had two daughters already so I prayed that my child be a girl. Jay and I began to get familiar with one another's family. I enrolled in College which was a 10 mths coarse and the baby would be here in 10 mths. I started to think about baby names but Jay had already had a name in mind and when he told me the name he wanted if our child was a boy was a really good name and he said that if the baby was a girl then I could indeed name our daughter. Being that Jay had lost a brother to a ROBBEY HOMICIDE Jay had his name chosen and I would not go against Jay's wishes. Jay's brother who got murdered looked almost identical to "Treach from Naughty By Nature". I let Poody move in with me because she didn't have anywhere to live. Poody had also been struggling with PCP. Poody spent alot of time at the Trap House with T-Money and the Gang while I turned into the stay at home type. Poody kept me informed on what was going on in the Trap. Remember the Trap was like a Movie you did not know what you would see like one day all of us getting high in the room and Poody spazed out all of a sudden pulling off some unknown girls wig that she didn't even know and T-Money having to hold Poody down until she came back to normal. Things tended to sometimes just happen like that in the trap. Poody had changed after she witnessed the death of her baby boy and she smoked PCP to cope with the pain of loosing a child. T-Money always somked good with us in the Trap. I was furious with T-Money because Erica told me all about how T-money ate her that night I left her at the Trap. Erica became infatuated with T-Money and started lying about being pregnat by T-money and so did my own cousin Fantasy. I was done with sexin T-Money he couldn't get another piece of chocolate until I said so IF I said so. T-Money was mad that I got pregnat he talked shit about me not being loyal. I did good with showing no emotion once I reached my breaking point. Let me back up a bit and tell you how things went at the 50 cent and G-Unit concert. Poody and I got dolled up for the concert just me and her. As soon as we walked in the concert doors we were stopped by this White Guy that was intrigued by Poody and he stated that he was 50 cent's manager. I told him that if he was indeed 50's manager then to get Poody and I back stage with 50 and G-Unit and the man did exactly as I requeted. Poody and I ended up back stage with "Eclipse" which was a group that performed before G-Unit arrived to the Memorial Hall on 7th St where 50 cent and G-uit performed. As Poody and I walked threw the crowd straight threw everyone with that white man ALL EYES were on Poody and I WE LOOKED AMAZING. We were backstage awaiting 50 and G-Unit. Poody went off with the white man and I waited patiently. As soon as 50 and G-Unit walked in they went straight on stage Poody and I were put right on stage with 50 Cent and G-Unit. I got a chance to be up close and personal. I watched 50's moves closely. As every-one got quiet, I yelled Out, "I LOVE YOU 50!! I was excited as I watched but 50 looked me eye to eye, smiled at me and shook my hand. That night we left the club on the G Unit van with Lloyd Banks and G-Unit. Llyod Banks had a thing for me although I was unsure I had came for 50 and 50 only. I called my cazza fantasy Pop and her crew up to the hotel room where Poody and I was with G-Unit. Lloyd Banks and I had a very long talk and Lloyd was so cool that I told him he looked identical to one of KS ballers. Lloyd really liked me but I could not see myself fucking Lloyd when I had a 50 Cent fetish. Lloyd was cool beans so I thought it over. IM A BOSS SO I MAKE BOSS MOVES! I told Lloyd that if I ever came to New York I would find him. Llyod and I were the same age and he was a really good dude genuinely and I didn't want to fuck 50 I wanted to talk business. Rico had talent and I wanted to put some things in 50's ear about Rico. 50 was occupied so I didn't get to him at the Hotel. But I had a ball, No HOE in me, I wasn't giving up my PIE on a one night stand famous or not! Lloyd Banks and I laughed together, had a good time and I left untouched. T-Money's Trap began very comical and Poody and the gang made up a song called "Dunkin and Movin".

To Be Continued...

LOOSE CANNON

IT ALL STARTED when I played that game with Lucifer back in my teenage years in and out of those Group Homes and now sometimes I can feel him breathe on me I have even felt him touch me, I'm unsure if it's the devil himself but this thing seems to follow me wherever I go. Not to mention the history that lies deep in my family when they label it Bipolar and Schizophrenic: (having a mental disorder that is characterized by disturbances in thought-such as delusion of persecution grandiosity or jealousy and by hallucinations). After all these years I never Knew what these thing meant but my mother has now explained to me that I have a Great Uncle who has been hospitalized for basically his whole life in some type of mental institution because of this awful disorder and instead of them just saying that aunt Fee was just down right possessed by demonic forces they now put this mental disorder name to it. My temper has gotten really bad and I cant explain it, all I know is that I can feel this burning sensation in the *Pockets Of My Eyes* and I remember that Book I read and when the souls in Hell were BURNING in torture and agony; Or was I experiencing this feeling because of how I found Philly and my eyes had saw too much and by the way did anyone take the time to see how I FELT about finding Philly-I was hurt and enraged beyond furious his eyes were open and my mind was open and subject to so many things being that I was under the influence I went North and South within BUT DID ANYONE CARE TO ASK HOW I FELT! I was a real friend and did not leave my friend there like that because I wouldn't want anyone to leave me like that "That's Why I looked a SNAKE IN THE FACE AND CALLED HIM LIKE I SAW HIM"!. Again after Grandma passed in that house I kept having these strange nightmares OVER AND OVER the same nightmares of this Lady with these DARK EYES like DARK SOCKETS around the eyes. These Nightmares, Sometimes these nightmares come into reality. I know is these voices in my head sometimes be of pure evil I asked that you PURIFY Me Lord. I REBUKE YOU SATAN YOU HAVE NO POWER! "As The Rain Falls On My Window-I Tried *Some Things* Just To Clear My Mental—Sometimes Blacked Out—Dark Like The Sky And Lost All My Mental—So See *Those Things* Had Been Ethereal:-an ethereal world created through the poetic imagination ethereal beauty—I Can't Stand The Rainy Days". Oz and I packed up our family and tried to move away from that dark cloud back in Kansas but for some reason strange things and strange people seem to follow. In Kansas I had been with Many Men before Oz and I met and Oz also had his share of women one to which is one now very famous and well known in the Industry for her music so I know this life can be a Mystery. Things can happen so fast some times that you have to watch every single detail and me I've always been just that type because I've been THREW THE STRUGGLE BUT HOW DID I END UP IN THIS PLACE!! I keep smelling this FOUL Smell and I'm feeling something touching me but I don't see It. I can Smell it and Feel it BUT NOW CAN'T see It and I know that it's there. If That MUTHA FUCKIN Maintenance Man would have just left me the FUCK ALONE none of these things would be happening. It's his fault he kept PROVOKING me NOW LOOK SOMETHING happened and I cant remember what happened or how it happened. Again all I remember is that I have had my share of men that's why I tried so hard to change my ways. I had my share of fun but have to GET OUT OF HERE I have Children. Yes I had The Mail Man, The Police Man, The Boxer, The Lawyer, The D-Boy, The Truck Driver, The Business Owner BUT now I have Oz and Oz is all I want and no the path wasn't easy I had my fuck ups and Pandoras Box had been opened but this thing with the Maniac Maintenance Man just wasn't supposed to happen. This mutha fucka came for me and he is the one that was demonic possessed. I'm just Gods Warrior and Iioness, I've prayed to be purified. I don't like when someone puts their hands on me and I just SNAPPED I cant remember because everything went BLACK. PLEASE you have to let me out of here. These walls hold a different type of darkness and my senses heighten when the nights falls. I cant stay another night I have kids. I don't remember all I know is that I blacked Out BIG this time. Oz and I took our family away from this dark cloud. I was at home in our new home that we worked so hard to buy after our investments began to pick up we moved away to get ready to start a family for ourselves. We chose a nice part where we could raise our family in peace so how did the mutha fuckin maniac maintenance man find me. I had just gotten out the shower Chocolate skin glowing immaculate smelling like Chanel and Burberry when I got a horrible knock on our door. Things happened back in that Dark Cloud of a State I have children and a Career "Ya'll let this happen to me!" I'm NOT fuckin CRAZY I FEAR THE LORDS WRATH, He's CRAZY, HE TRIED TO KILL ME AND MY FAMILY and I will Protect my family by any means necessary. LET ME GO!—"Doctors response, Mrs. Cannon can you please tell us what happen again and start from the beginning when you and your family made it here in our nice town". Your safe Now Mrs. Cannon I just need you to start from the beginning because something awful has happened and all we know is that we found you in a pool of blood at your Beauty Salon/Spa/Boutique with a hammer in your hands with this mans blood on it so we need you to tell us everything you can remember from the very beginning mam".

IF HE CANT BRING NOTHING TO THE TABLE
THEN JUST FEED HIM MUD
DON'T TAKE OUT YOUR CHILDRENS MOUTH
WHEN HE JUST WANTS TO BE A THUG
GOTTA WATCH OUT FOR HIM IF ALL HE DO IS TAKE
HIS MOMMA BIRTH HIM LET HER RAISE HIM
RECOGNIZE THE REAL FROM THE FAKE
I RAISE MY BOYS TO BE MEN
DON'T YOU EVER HIT A WOMAN
IF HE HAS NO RESPECT FOR HIS MOTHER
HE WON'T HAVE RESPECT FOR HIS CHILDREN
YOU'LL SEE HE'S FAKE
PEEP THE GAME WHEN HE STARTS
PLAYING WITH YOUR MENTAL
ALWAYS TRUST YOUR BETTER JUDGEMENT
*WOULD YOU BUY A CAR CASH
OR WOULD YOU GET A RENTAL*?
IF HE HIT YOU ONE TIME
IT WONT BE THE LAST
WHEN YOU WAS SKIPPIN ALL THAT SCHOOL
YOU SHOULD HAVE STAYED IN CLASS
KNOW YOU WORTH, KNOW YOUR
BODY, KNOW YOUR TEMPLE
YOU ONLY HAVE ONE

STOP IT WITH THE EXPERMENTAL
BEAUTY AND BLOOD

LORD LET ME BE HIS TREE
AND HE BE THE WATER THAT FEEDS ME
I WILL STAND THERE LIKE A STATUE
PRODUCING NOTHING BUT GOOD THINGS
BEAUTIFUL AND FULL OF LIFE
STANDING SO TALL AND SO FIRM
BEING A SHELTHER TO THOSE AROUND ME

CHAPTER 1

I COULD NOT wait for Oz to come home from work it seemed like seconds were minutes as the clock ticked. How did this misunderstanding happen. Oz knew how furious I was the last time I had an encounter with that maniac. Shit Oz didn't have to lift one finger the lioness came out of me and when I'm mad I get straight like a beast by nature literally and there's no stopping me. I'm a female and this mutha fucka put his hands on me all because he was mad because I got married and moved on apparently because what other reason did this man have to put his hands on me. It was my birthday and I was trying to have a good time when that happened! UGH! All type of thoughts ran threw my head as I waited on Oz watching our Security Camera's closely today more than I had EVER watched them since we brought this New Home of ours. Then finally I saw the right head lights turning in the entrance of the Gate. I took a deep breathe as I checked the clock. It's 10:08 pm this mutha fuckin Oz is a whole 8 minutes late and he didn't even call to see if I wanted some Bellaire Rose or a night time snack and he knows that I love my Postachios and Mr. Pure Cranberry Juice. But wait until I snap on him for being so damn stupid! I was feeling feisty and sexy all at the same time because of my pampering however it was a long day at the Saloon and Mrs. Tessa just did not give anyone a break today about that stubborn one grey hair that after all the hair coloring just did not want to take. Mrs. Tessa is beautiful and I keep on telling her that one grey hair isn't noticeable and if it is she still looks like Angela Bassat and looks like she hasn't aged a bit, shit, I hope I look that good when I reach her age. Just as I began to fix my boobs (breast reduction looking great) and adjust my thoughts here comes Oz busting threw the door with his complaints as normal, Oz "why did them boys forget to take out the trash"? Me, Stop before you even start complaining about some Bull Shit! Why the fuck or How the fuck did Trouble get my address BRO UGH!" Oz, "Bro?" Wait and Trouble? Me, "Yea, the fuckin maintenance man!" Who did you give my number to Oz you are suppose to be on top of all of this, I can't do two things at once and If I knew that you weren't going to be able to handle having a house and taking care of our maintenance issues Oz, I would have not gotten this house. I mean damn baby you know what happened the last time and you know this mutha fucka is crazy and he already mad cause I put my finger in his ass and told his cousin about it! This shit is stupid Oz, I cant get away from the bull shit then this maniac just starts yelling to the top of his lungs! Oz, "YELLING"! wait baby what happen again because I didn't give no mutha fuckin trouble this phone number or address and you know damn well I wouldn't have done that a Guy at my job told me that he had a cheap person—Me interrupting, "Cheap! Your ass is always trying to be cheap Oz and do things your way but if you would have just listened to me baby! Oz," Yelling! What did that mutha fucka say Justice"? Me, I don't know Oz, I wouldn't let him in and he started yelling talking crazy saying things like he loves me and if he can't have me than nobody will type of shit Oz I don't know.

Oz has his way of doing things, he has been listening to all this "Raheem DeVaughn" lately so let me tell you what he did to me and how he did it. He held me close telling me that everything was going to be alright and before you knew it he was smelling my Burberry perfume then he started kissing my neck softly as he caressed my breast gently removing what little lingerie I had on. The he licked me from my neck to my inner thigh slowly spreading my legs apart. While rubbing my soles of my feet he gripped my clit with his tongue then he sucked the anger and frustration right out of me and there was no room for an argument. He ate me so good that I squirted good juices all over his face as he slurped and made sure that he made me reach my FULL THROTTLE of wetness BURSTING like a JUICY PEACH BUT like a THRUST OF WATER to where there were puddles in the bed sheets were soaked and towels were needed. Then after that he fucked the shit out of me taking any remaining juices left. We fucked from the top of the bed to the bottom of the bed in multiple positions fucking me like he was angry about something but it felt so good all I could do was take every single bit of it while I felt my insides gripping every single inch of his penis I felt every vain he had in his dick as it rubbed against my walls and I gripped my pussy muscles so tight so that he knew that I was not letting him go. After rounds of ups and downs Oz finally reached his nut and he released it assuring me that I had the best pussy and that he love me and in 1.2 seconds his ass was snoring but me nah I was up watching those security cameras for any strange movements for the next hour as I got up and washed myself up and I even washed Oz up and he didn't budge. Oz thinks that I'm done with this conversation but he has another thing coming plus he already owes me that "Hermes White Himalaya Crocodile Diamond Birkin" that he thinks I forgot about. How could he be so careless. This vibe I had got when I came face to face with this maniac sent a whole other rage in me. It was how things happened with him. I met trouble after I had my third son while I was with J-Nutt. I learned some things about trouble that down right dissqusted me into our little fling. See ladies before you lay down with a MAN make sure you NO THAT MAN. I did not know trouble from "A Can Of Paint" I didn't know him from "A Snale To A Slug" But The Whole Time I Was

Out Here "Playin with the Bugs". All I know is that I met a man who tried to charm me and maybe I was trying to charm him J-Nutt was at work most the time and I was not faithful to him, I almost had a physical encounter with a female behind him and wasn't going to back down so I was the Queen already feeling that I had a crown and as was ready to mingle until my King found me—My Prince Charming. J-Nutt wanted to live like the Hugstables he just wasn't home enough and I didn't trust him so I went with my woman intuitions and here comes this MANIAC! This man was so bad for me how did I fall for it? Yes and I put my finger in his ass so something didn't add up there but you booty hole boys want to fight woman though. I teach my boy NOT TO HIT WOMAN WE BROUGHT YOU IN THIS WORLD NO MATTER WHAT! I'm not going to judge you now to each their own if you like it I love it BUT IT'S NOT OKAY FOR MEN TO HIT WOMEN! I have much respect for J-Nutt I hit him and he DID NOT HIT ME! Something about a pedaphile and an ABUSIVE MAN that angers me. Feel free but there are consequences to actions. I love everybody just don't like everybody. I was a warm sunny day when I met trouble. Then before I knew it the night had drifted away with thoughts left unexplained.

Milton Keynes UK
Ingram Content Group UK Ltd.
UKHW042003081024
449407UK00006B/70